# 子連れ狼

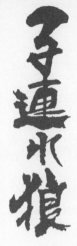

# LONE
# WOLF
## AND
# 子連れ狼 CUB

story
**KAZUO KOIKE**

art
**GOSEKI KOJIMA**

**DARK HORSE COMICS**

translation
**DANA LEWIS**

lettering & retouch
**DIGITAL CHAMELEON**

cover artwork
**FRANK MILLER** with **LYNN VARLEY**

publisher
**MIKE RICHARDSON**

editor
**MIKE HANSEN**

assistant editor
**TIM ERVIN-GORE**

consulting editor
**TOREN SMITH** for **STUDIO PROTEUS**

book design
**DARIN FABRICK**

art director
**MARK COX**

Published by Dark Horse Comics, Inc., in association
with MegaHouse and Koike Shoin Publishing Company, Ltd.

Dark Horse Comics, Inc.
10956 SE Main Street, Milwaukie, OR 97222
www.darkhorse.com

First edition: August 2001
ISBN: 1-56971-513-0

1 3 5 7 9 10 8 6 4 2

Printed in Canada

To find a comics shop in your area, call the
Comic Shop Locator Service toll-free at 1-888-266-4226

# SHATTERED STONES

子連れ狼

*By* **KAZUO KOIKE**

**& GOSEKI KOJIMA**

# VOLUME

# 12

# A NOTE TO READERS

*Lone Wolf and Cub* is famous for its carefully researched re-creation of Edo-Period Japan. To preserve the flavor of the work, we have chosen to retain many Edo-Period terms that have no direct equivalents in English. Japanese is written in a mix of Chinese ideograms and a syllabic writing system, resulting in numerous synonyms. In the glossary, you may encounter words with multiple meanings. These are words written with Chinese ideograms that are pronounced the same but carry different meanings. A Japanese reader seeing the different ideograms would know instantly which meaning it is, but these synonyms can cause confusion when Japanese is spelled out in our alphabet. *O-yurushi o* (please forgive us)!

# LONE WOLF AND CUB
## 子連れ狼

# TABLE OF CONTENTS

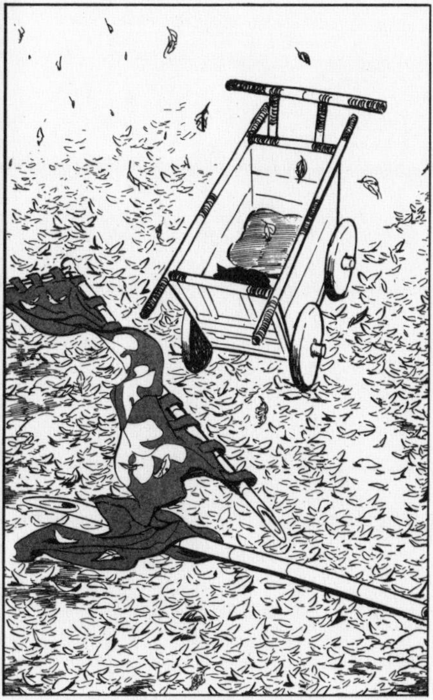

the fifty-ninth

# Nameless, Penniless, Lifeless

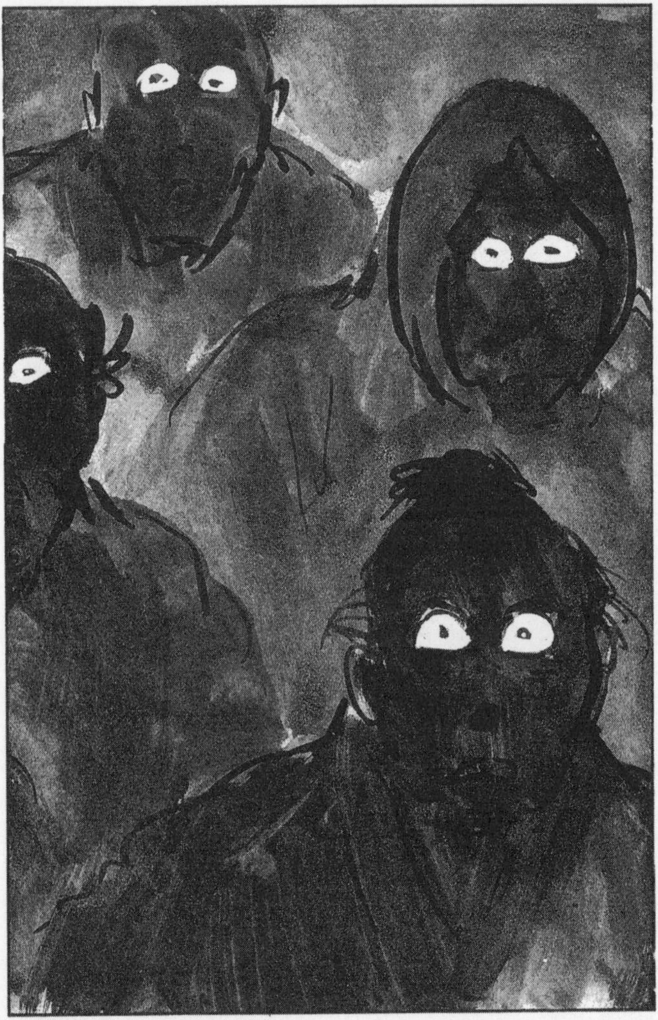

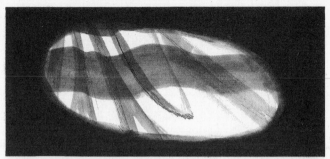

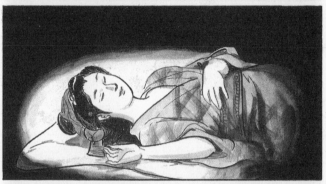

11

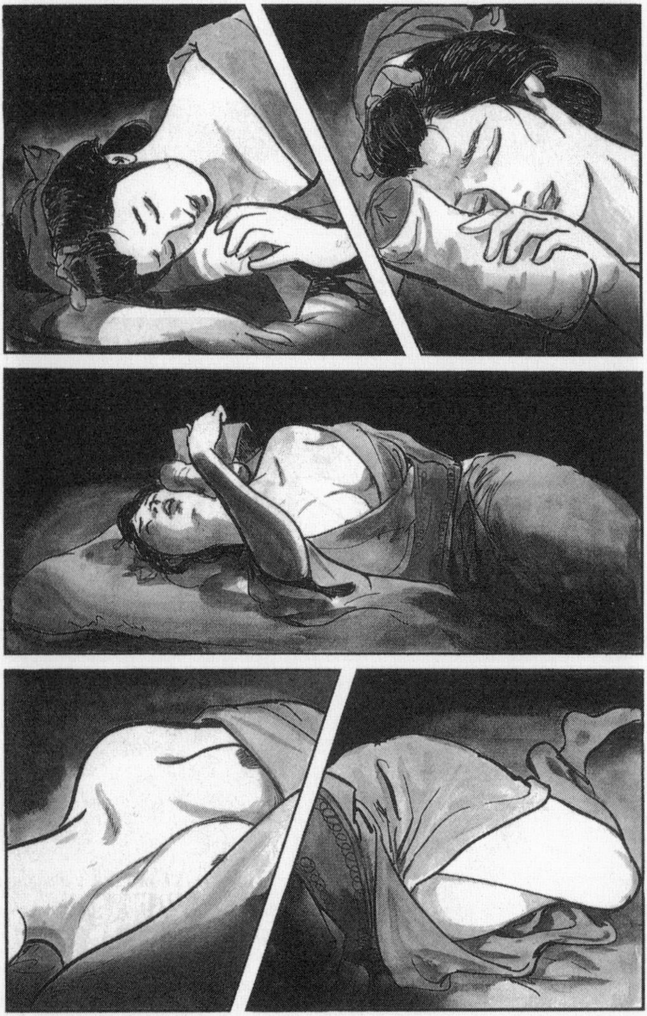

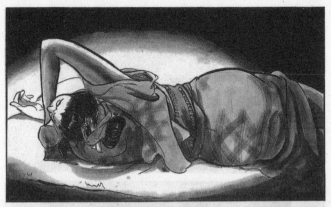

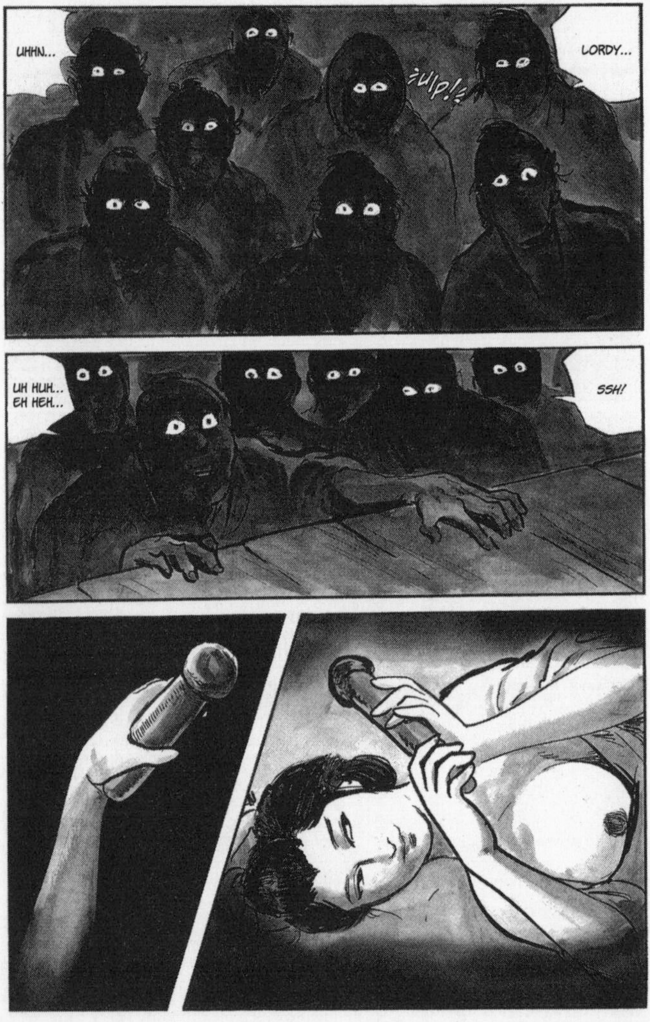
UHHN...
ULP!
LORDY...
UH HUH..
EH HEH...
SSH!

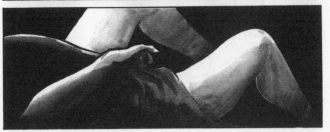

AHH!
AUGHH!
YEAH!! UMEWAKA DAYŪ!
OH, BABY!
SHUT UP!
YER RUININ' THE MOOD!
YEAH, SHADDAP!

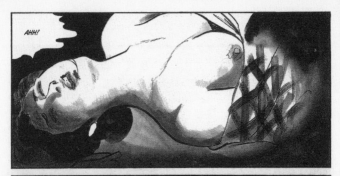

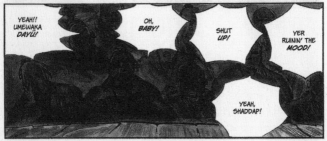

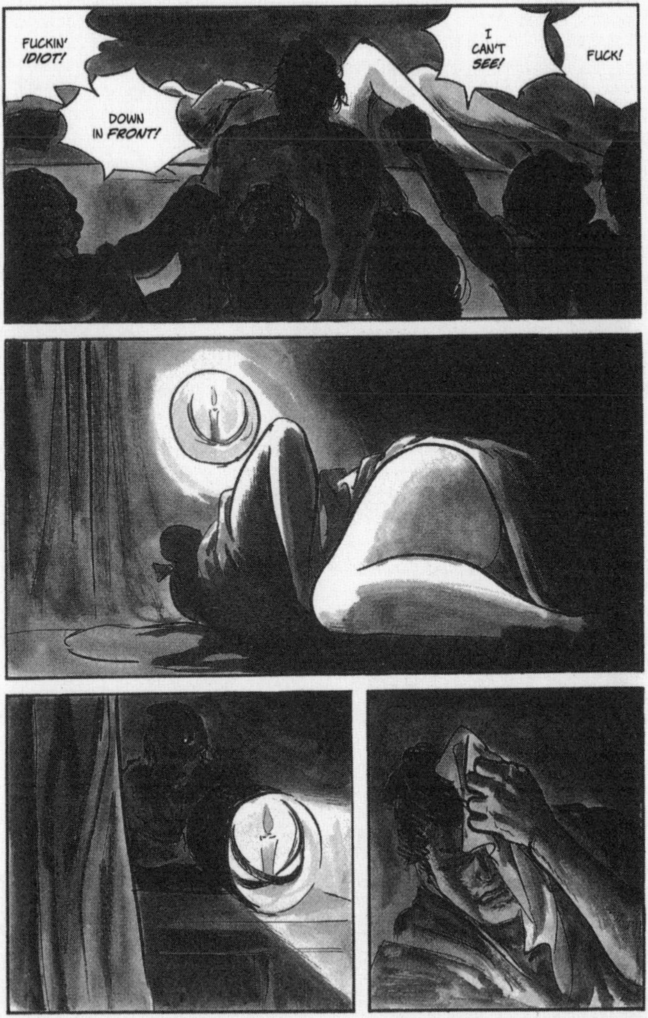
FUCKIN' *IDIOT!*
DOWN IN *FRONT!*
I CAN'T *SEE!*
FUCK!

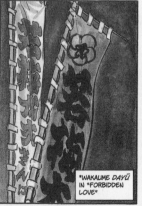

"WAKAUME DAYŪ IN "FORBIDDEN LOVE"

YO! DAYŪ!

SHOW US *MORE!*

ALL *RIGHT!*

18

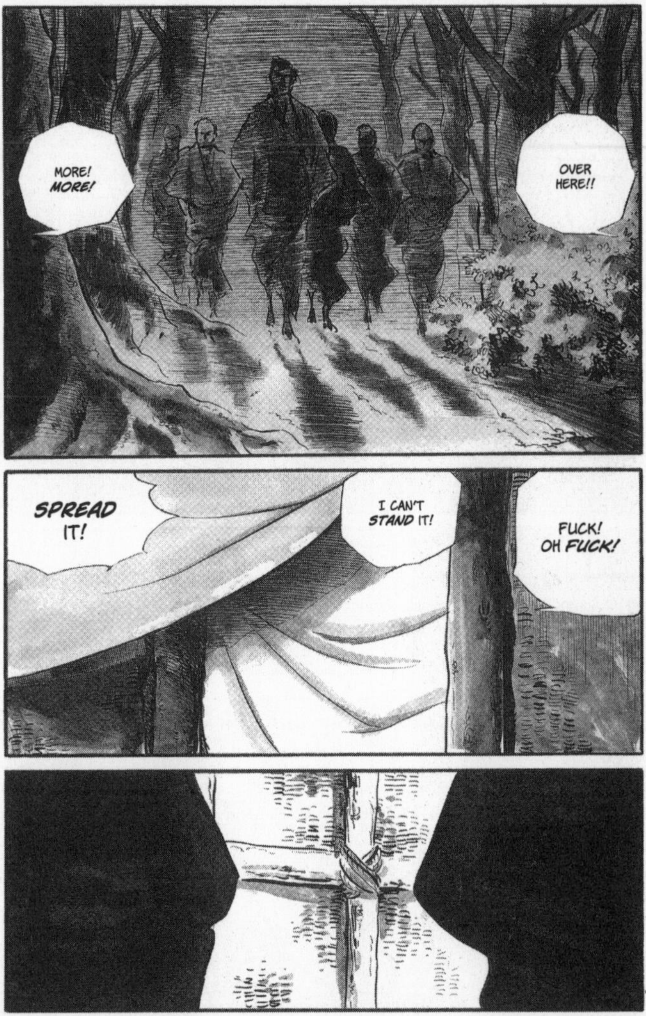
MORE! MORE!
OVER HERE!!
SPREAD IT!
I CAN'T STAND IT!
FUCK! OH FUCK!

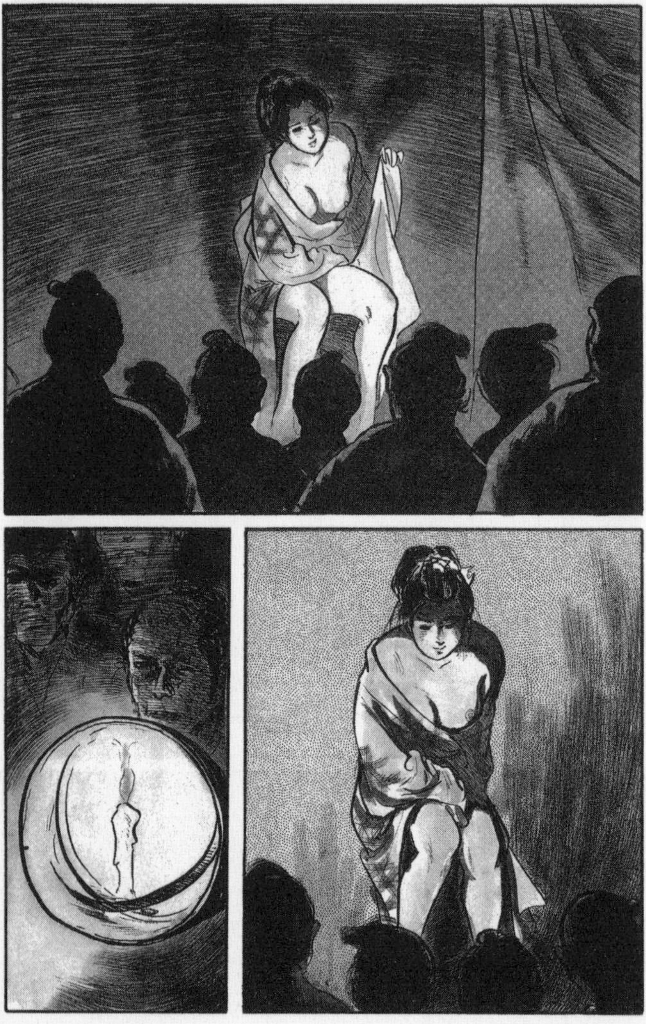

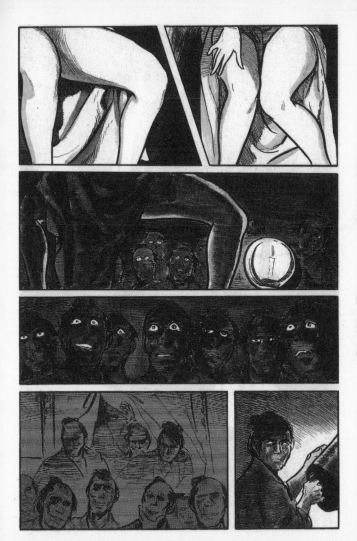

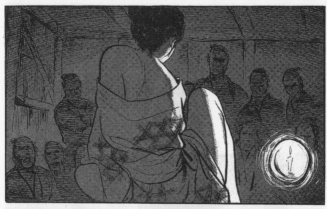

HEH HEH HEH...NOT A BAD *PIECE*, HUH?

I LIKE *WHAT'S* BETWEEN THEM *LEGS.*

HEH HEH HEH!

ALL *RIGHT!*

HEY, SHUDDUP BACK THERE!

*YEOWW!!*

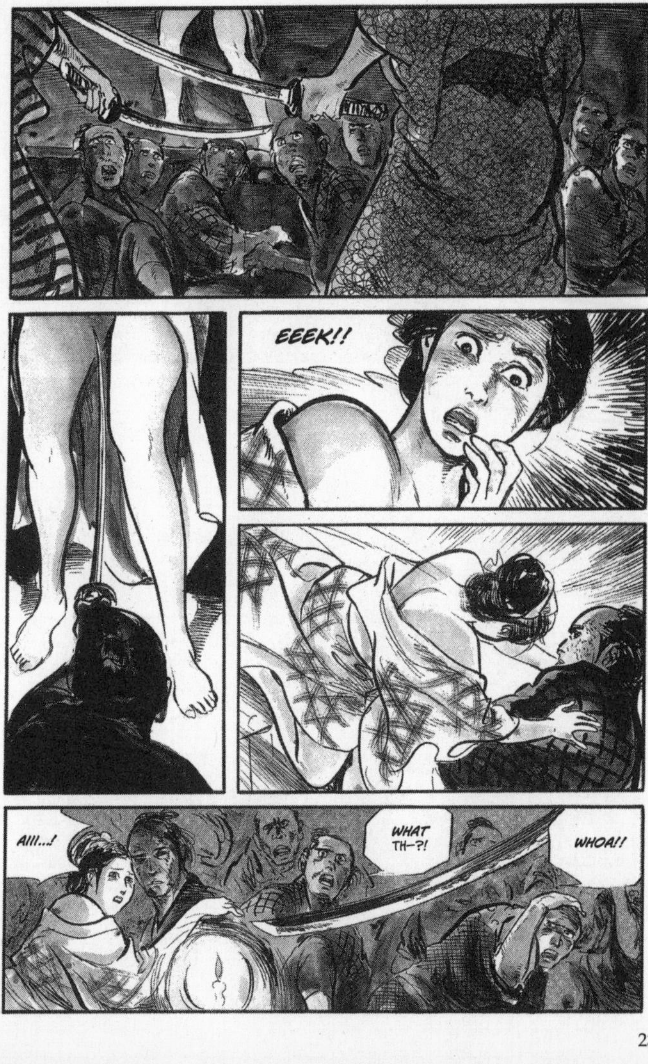
EEEK!!
AIII...!
WHAT TH-?!
WHOA!!

WE'RE THE *TENSHIN IKKA!* EVERYONE *CALM DOWN!*

IT'S *OKAY*...DON'T BE *AFRAID*...

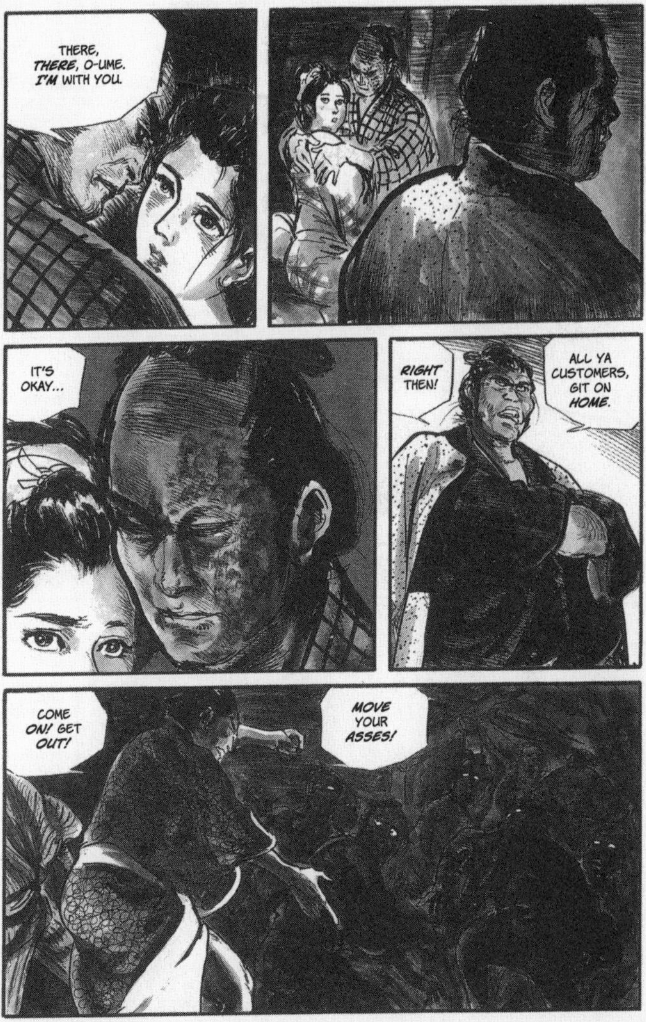
THERE, *THERE*, O-UME. *I'M* WITH YOU.
IT'S OKAY...
*RIGHT* THEN!
ALL YA CUSTOMERS, GIT ON *HOME*.
COME *ON!* GET *OUT!*
*MOVE* YOUR *ASSES!*

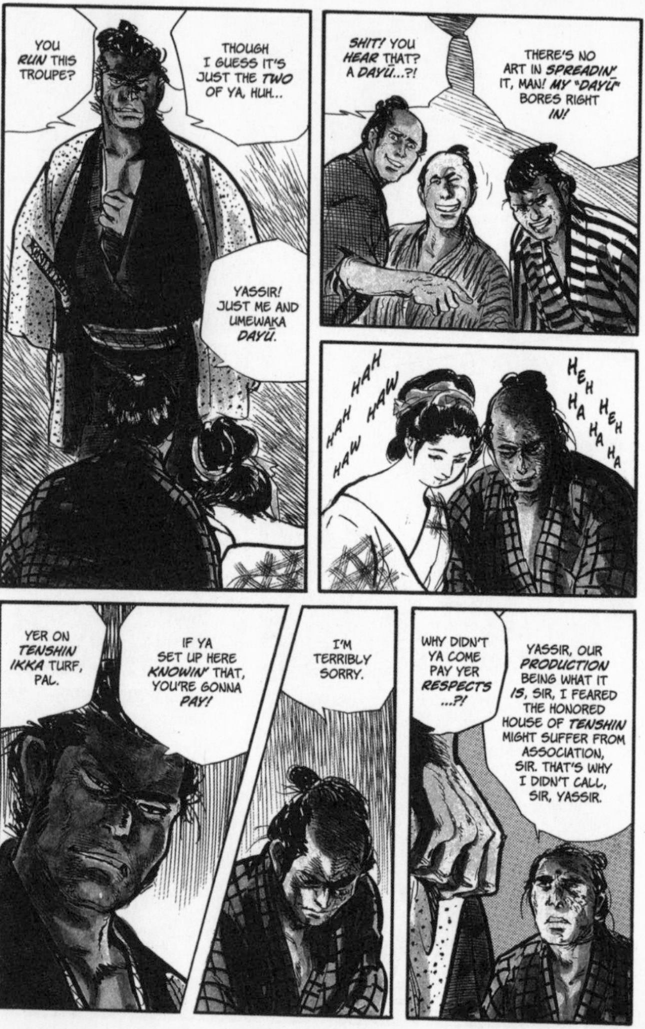
YOU RUN THIS TROUPE?
THOUGH I GUESS IT'S JUST THE TWO OF YA, HUH...
YASSIR! JUST ME AND UMEWAKA DAYŪ.
SHIT! YOU HEAR THAT? A DAYŪ...?!
THERE'S NO ART IN SPREADIN' IT, MAN! MY "DAYŪ" BORES RIGHT IN!
HAH HAH HAH HAW HAW HAW
HEH HEH HA HA HA HA HA
YER ON TENSHIN IKKA TURF, PAL.
IF YA SET UP HERE KNOWIN' THAT, YOU'RE GONNA PAY!
I'M TERRIBLY SORRY.
WHY DIDN'T YA COME PAY YER RESPECTS ...?!
YASSIR, OUR PRODUCTION BEING WHAT IT IS, SIR, I FEARED THE HONORED HOUSE OF TENSHIN MIGHT SUFFER FROM ASSOCIATION, SIR. THAT'S WHY I DIDN'T CALL, SIR, YASSIR.

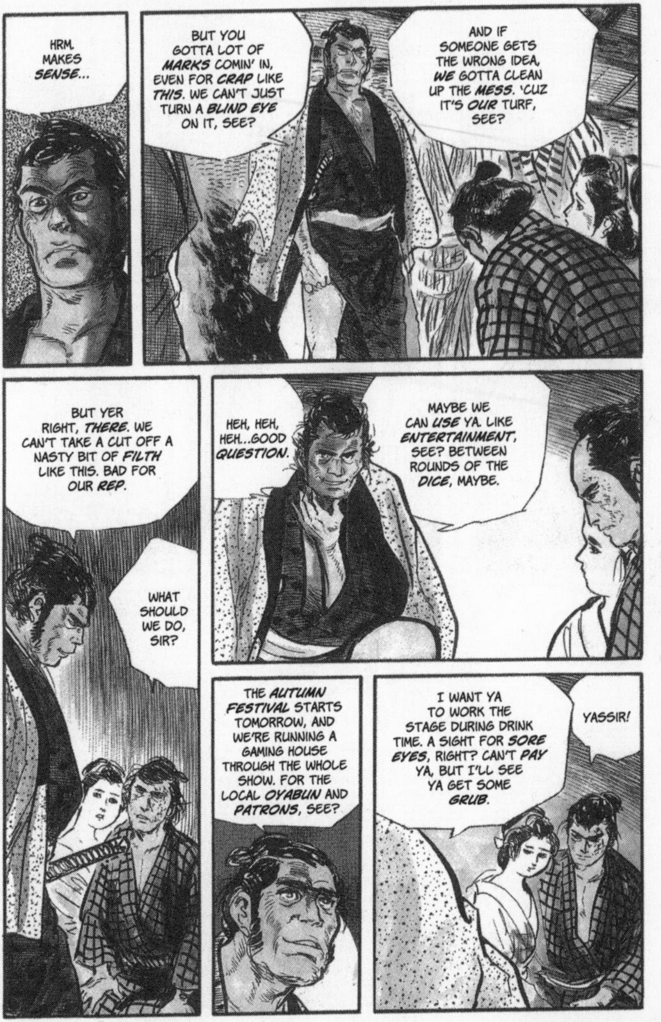
HRM. MAKES *SENSE*...
BUT YOU GOTTA LOT OF *MARKS* COMIN' IN, EVEN FOR *CRAP* LIKE *THIS*. WE CAN'T JUST TURN A *BLIND EYE* ON IT, SEE?
AND IF SOMEONE GETS THE WRONG IDEA, *WE* GOTTA CLEAN UP THE *MESS*. 'CUZ IT'S *OUR* TURF, SEE?
BUT YER RIGHT, *THERE*. WE CAN'T TAKE A CUT OFF A NASTY BIT OF *FILTH* LIKE THIS. BAD FOR OUR *REP*.
WHAT SHOULD WE DO, SIR?
HEH, HEH, HEH...GOOD *QUESTION*.
MAYBE WE CAN *USE* YA. LIKE *ENTERTAINMENT*, SEE? BETWEEN ROUNDS OF THE *DICE*, MAYBE.
THE *AUTUMN FESTIVAL* STARTS TOMORROW, AND WE'RE RUNNING A GAMING HOUSE THROUGH THE WHOLE SHOW. FOR THE LOCAL *OYABUN* AND *PATRONS*, SEE?
I WANT YA TO WORK THE STAGE DURING DRINK TIME. A SIGHT FOR *SORE EYES*, RIGHT? CAN'T *PAY* YA, BUT I'LL SEE YA GET SOME *GRUB*.
YASSIR!

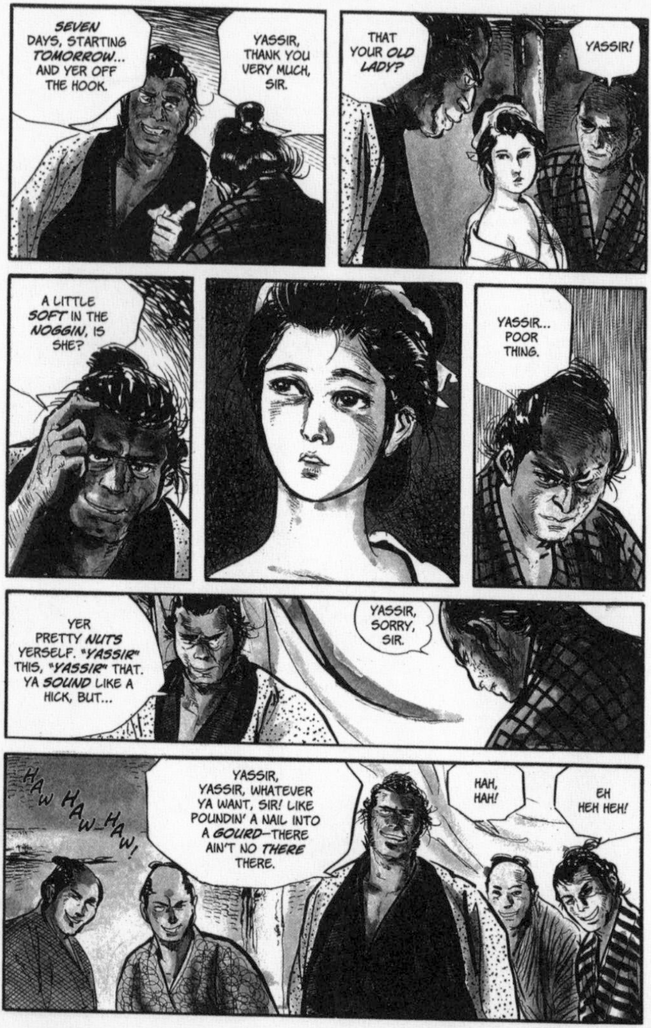
SEVEN DAYS, STARTING TOMORROW... AND YER OFF THE HOOK.
YASSIR, THANK YOU VERY MUCH, SIR.
THAT YOUR OLD LADY?
YASSIR!
A LITTLE SOFT IN THE NOGGIN, IS SHE?
YASSIR... POOR THING.
YER PRETTY NUTS YERSELF. "YASSIR" THIS, "YASSIR" THAT. YA SOUND LIKE A HICK, BUT...
YASSIR, SORRY, SIR.
HAW HAW HAW HAW!
YASSIR, YASSIR, WHATEVER YA WANT, SIR! LIKE POUNDIN' A NAIL INTO A GOURD—THERE AIN'T NO THERE THERE.
HAH, HAH!
EH HEH HEH!

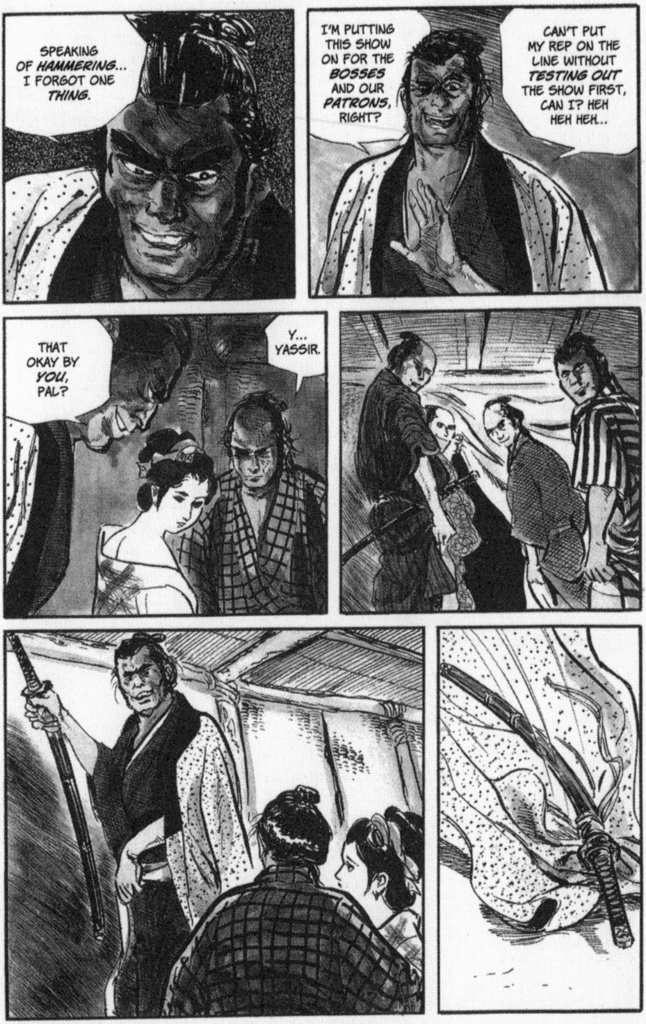
SPEAKING OF *HAMMERING*... I FORGOT ONE *THING*.
I'M PUTTING THIS SHOW ON FOR THE *BOSSES* AND OUR *PATRONS*, RIGHT?
CAN'T PUT MY REP ON THE LINE WITHOUT *TESTING OUT* THE SHOW FIRST, CAN I? HEH HEH HEH...
THAT OKAY BY *YOU*, PAL?
Y... YASSIR.

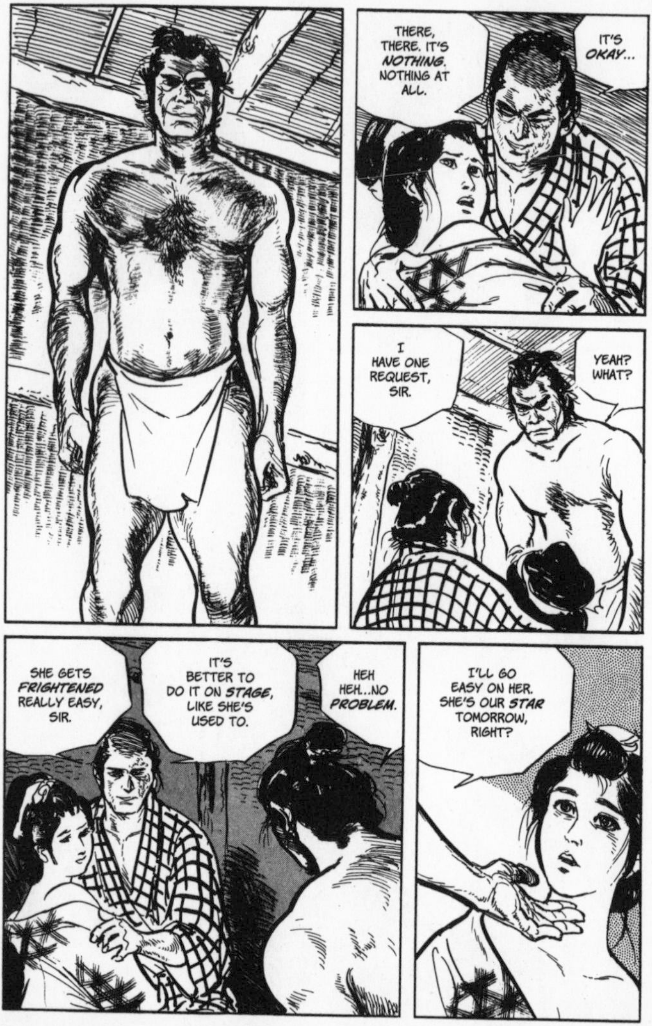
THERE, THERE. IT'S NOTHING. NOTHING AT ALL.
IT'S OKAY...
I HAVE ONE REQUEST, SIR.
YEAH? WHAT?
SHE GETS FRIGHTENED REALLY EASY, SIR.
IT'S BETTER TO DO IT ON STAGE, LIKE SHE'S USED TO.
HEH HEH...NO PROBLEM.
I'LL GO EASY ON HER. SHE'S OUR STAR TOMORROW, RIGHT?

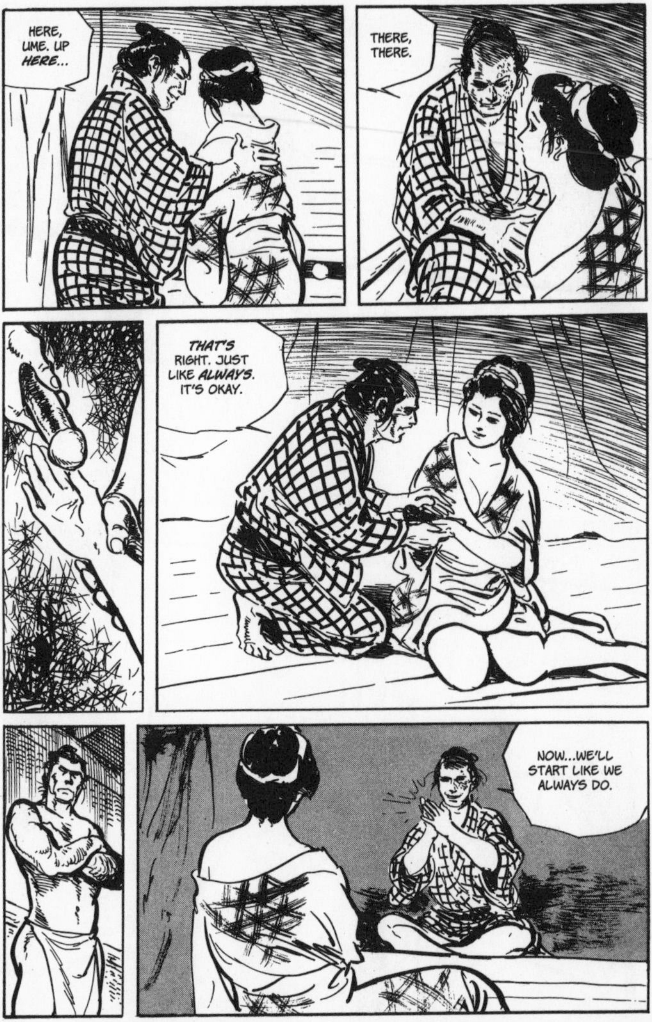
HERE, UME. UP *HERE*...
THERE, THERE.
*THAT'S* RIGHT. JUST LIKE *ALWAYS*. IT'S OKAY.
NOW...WE'LL START LIKE WE ALWAYS DO.

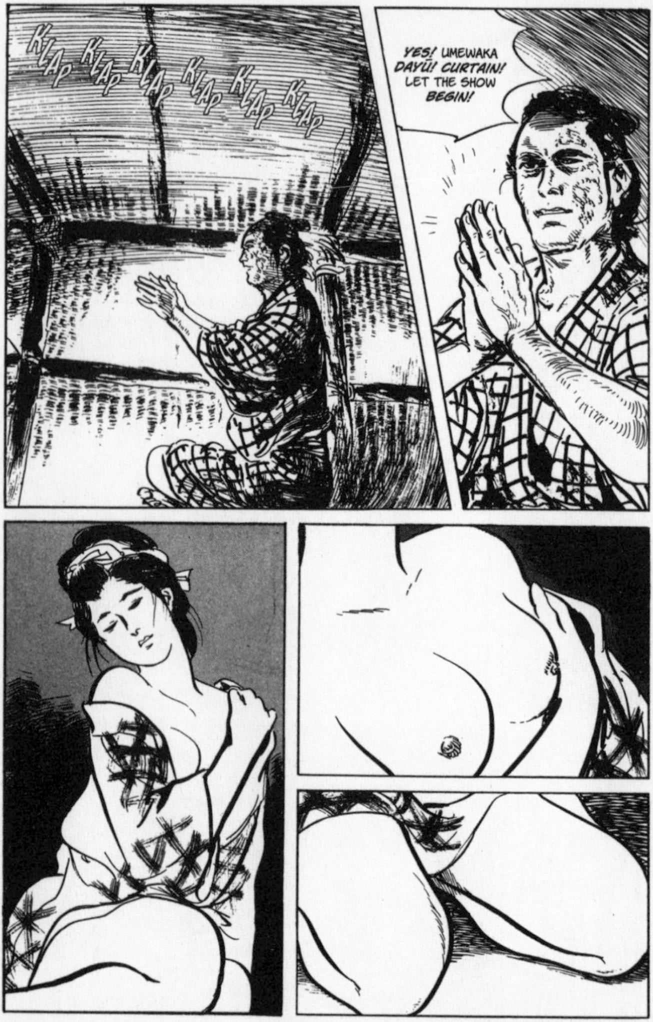
KLAP KLAP KLAP KLAP KLAP KLAP
YES! UMEWAKA DAYŪ! CURTAIN! LET THE SHOW BEGIN!

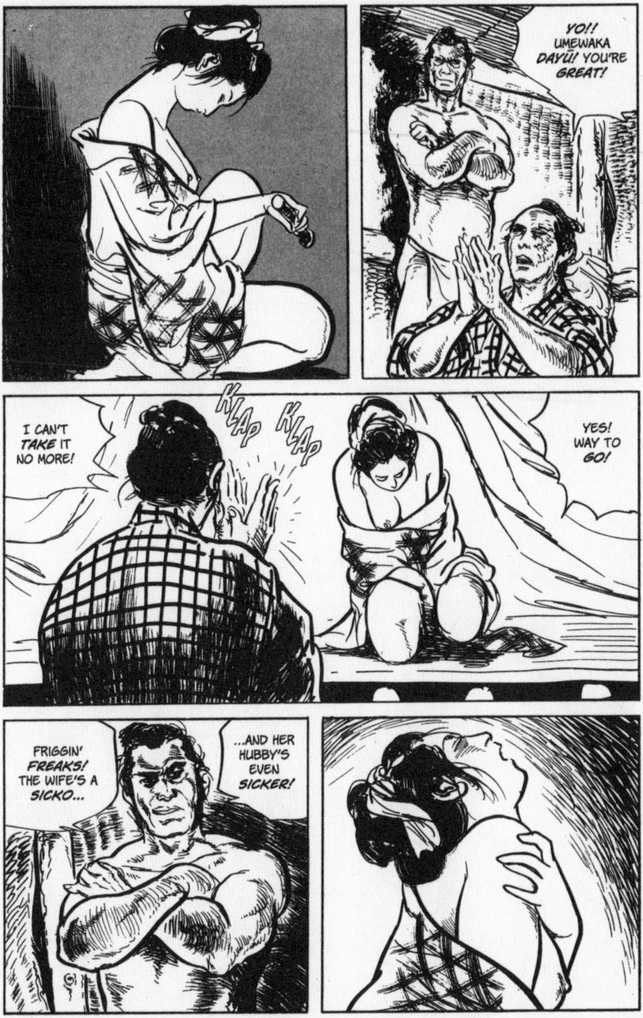
YO!! UMEWAKA DAYŪ! YOU'RE GREAT!
I CAN'T TAKE IT NO MORE!
KLAP KLAP
YES! WAY TO GO!
FRIGGIN' FREAKS! THE WIFE'S A SICKO...
...AND HER HUBBY'S EVEN SICKER!

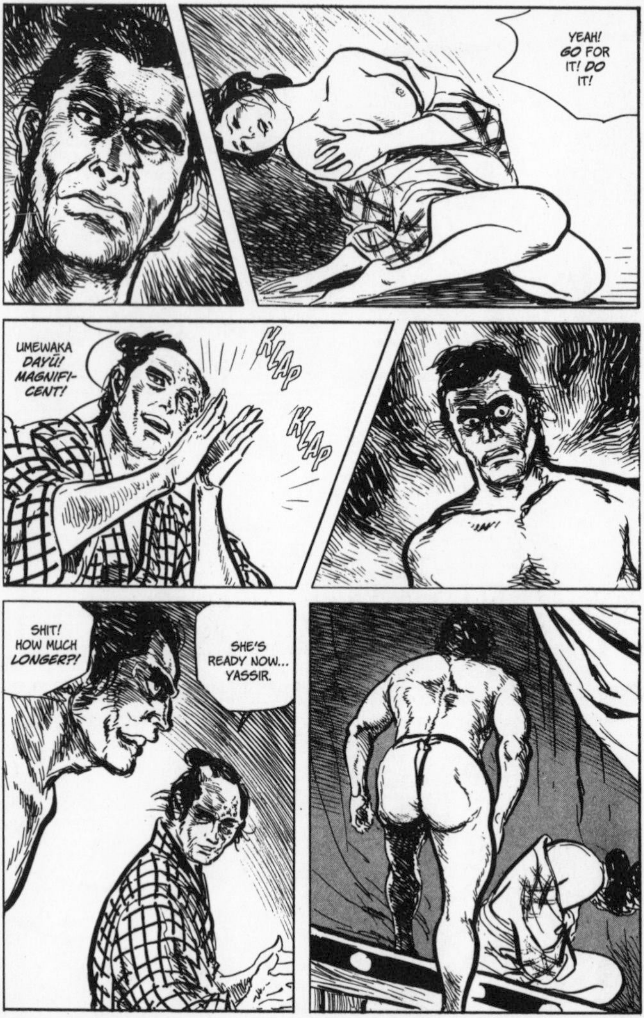
YEAH! GO FOR IT! DO IT!
UMEWAKA DAYŪ! MAGNIFI-CENT!
KLAP
KLAP
SHIT! HOW MUCH LONGER?!
SHE'S READY NOW... YASSIR.

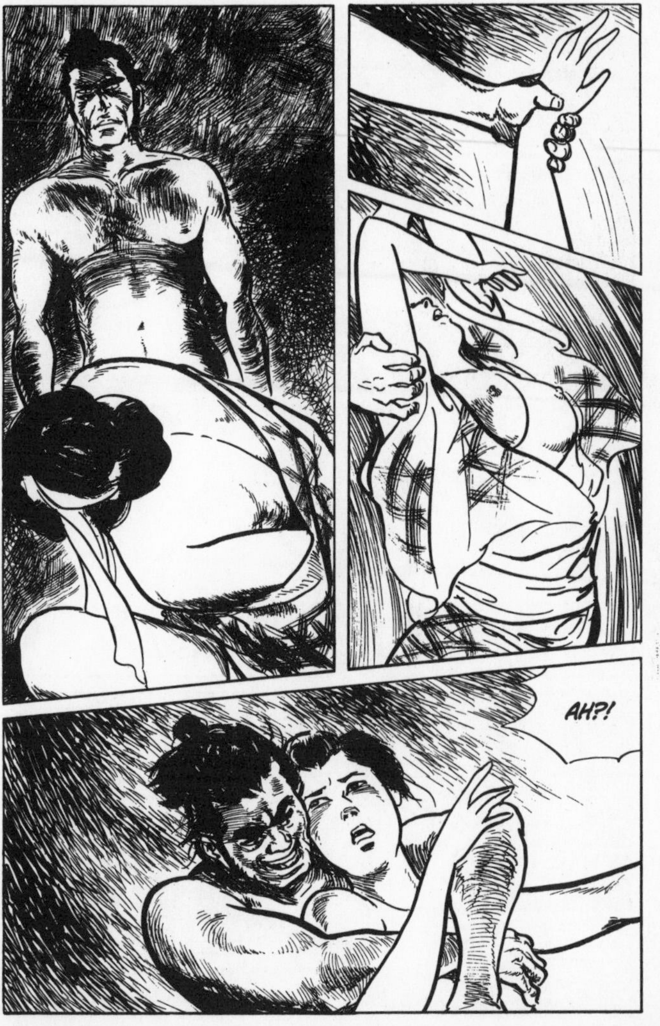
AH?!

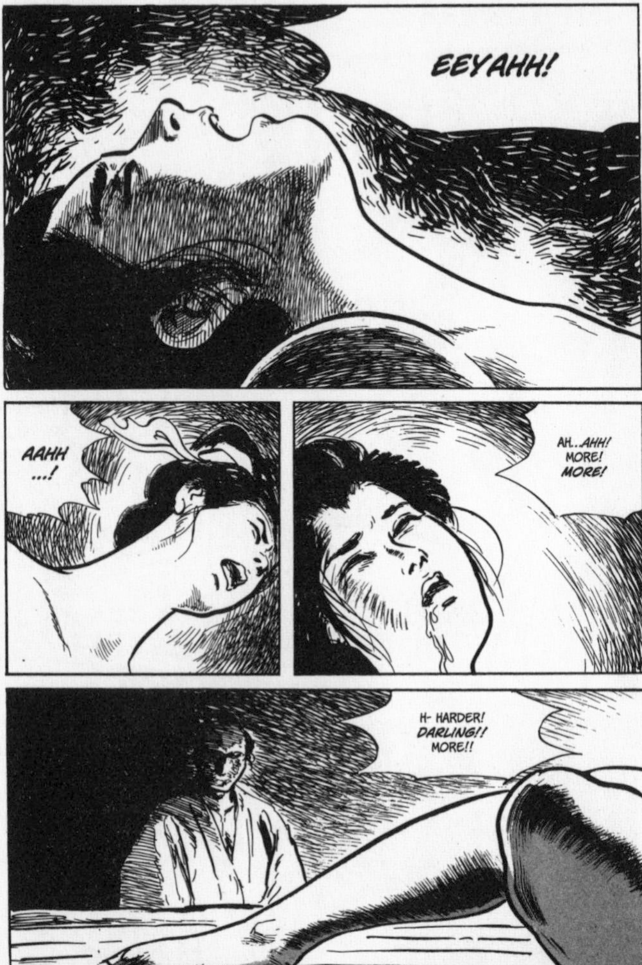
EEYAHH!
AAHH ...!
AH..AHH! MORE! MORE!
H- HARDER! DARLING!! MORE!!

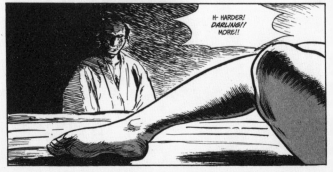

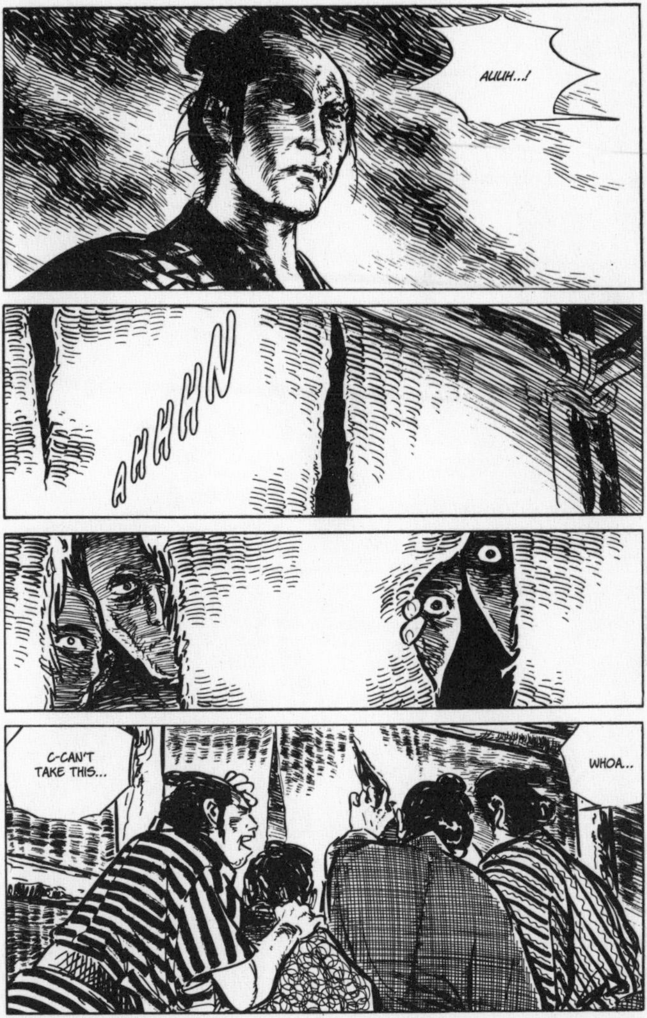
AUUH...!
AHHHN
C-CAN'T TAKE THIS...
WHOA...

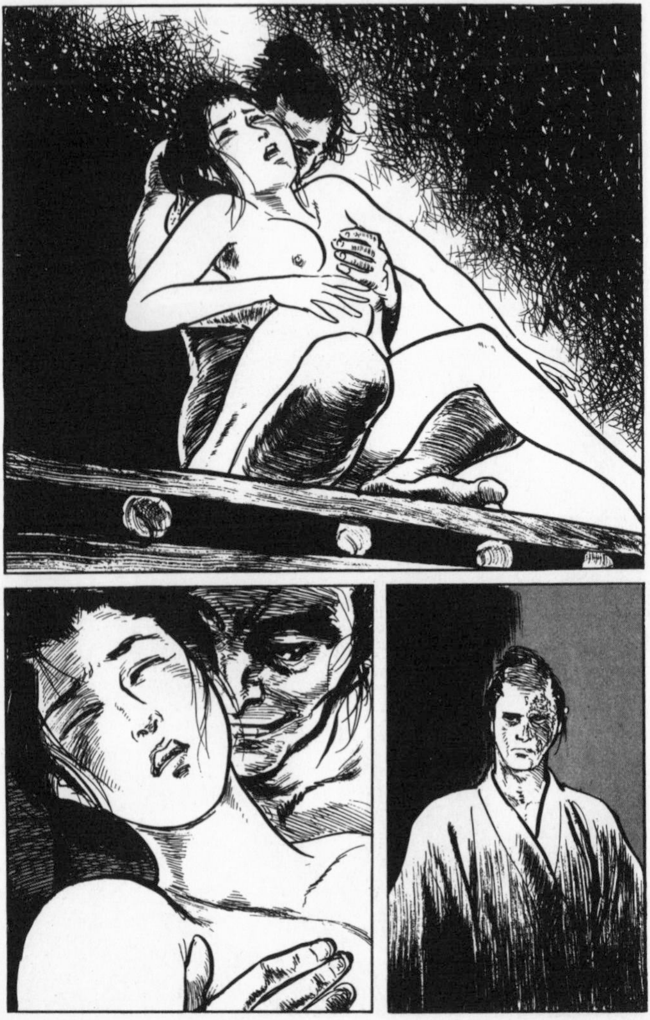

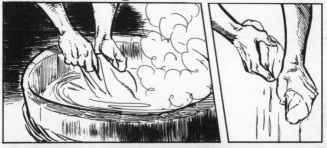

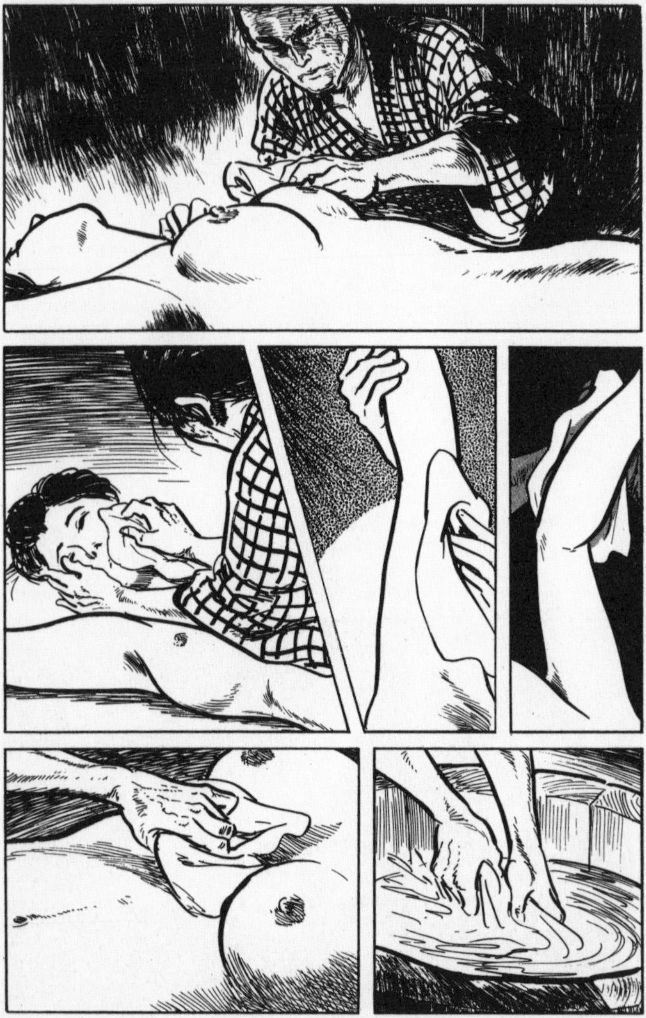

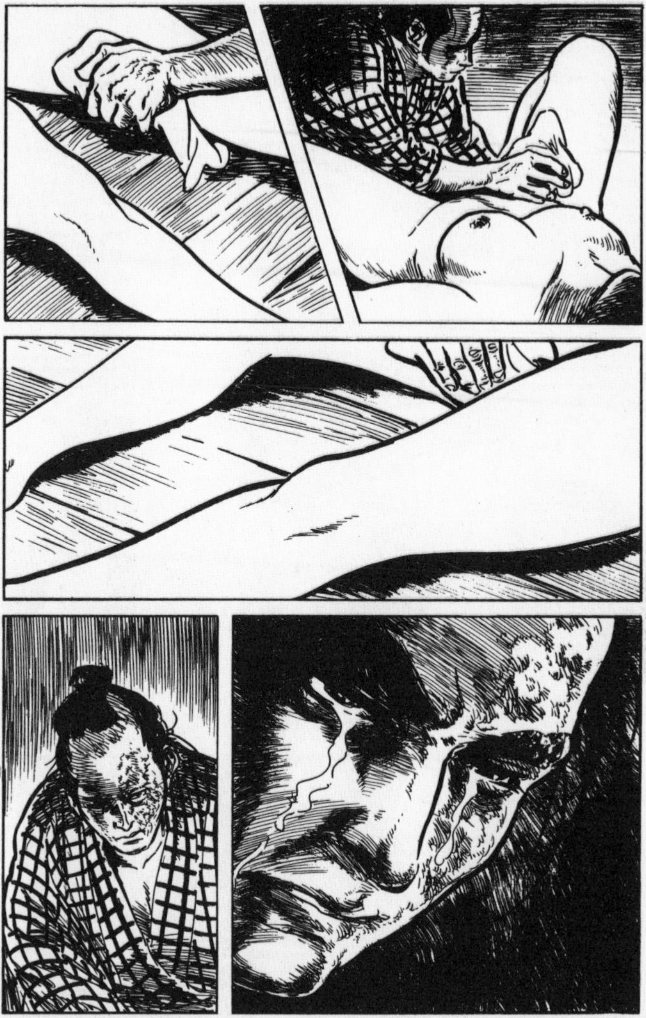

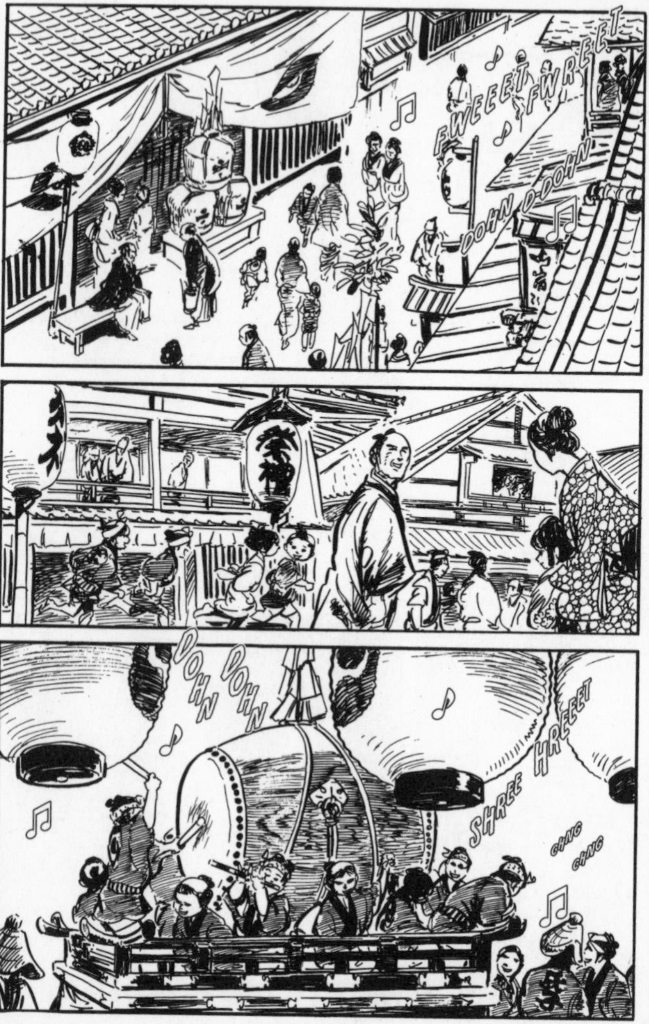
FWEEEET FWREEET
DOHN D-DOHN
DOHN
DOHN
SHREE HREEET
CHNG
CHNG

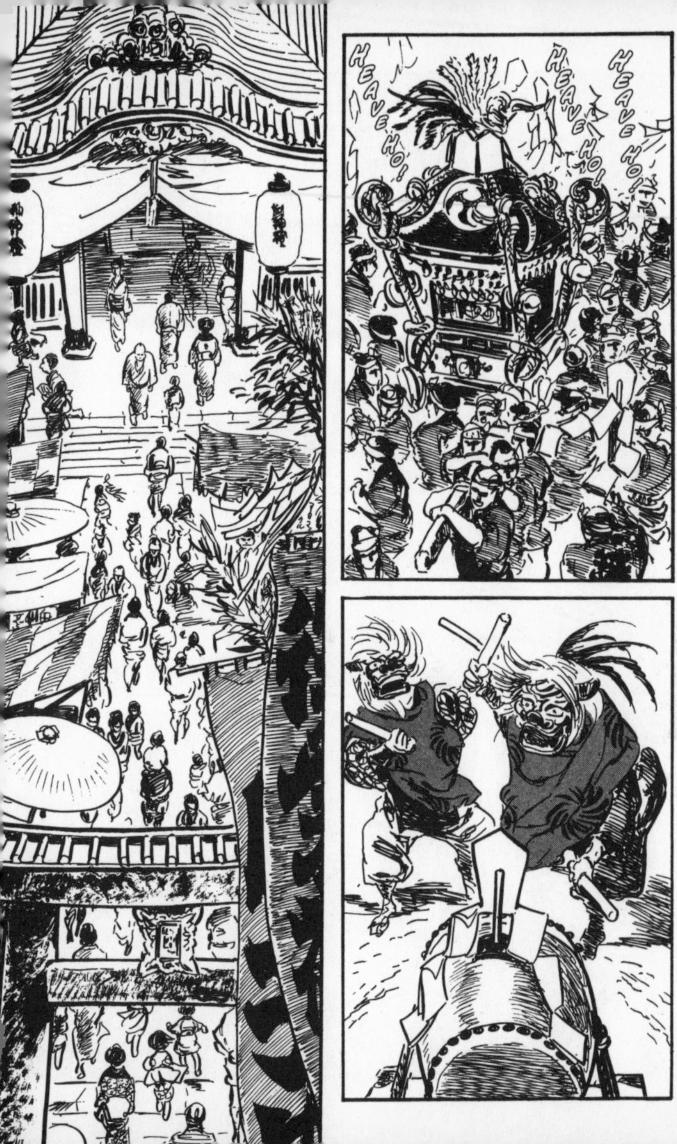
HEAVE HO!
HEAVE HO!
HEAVE HO!

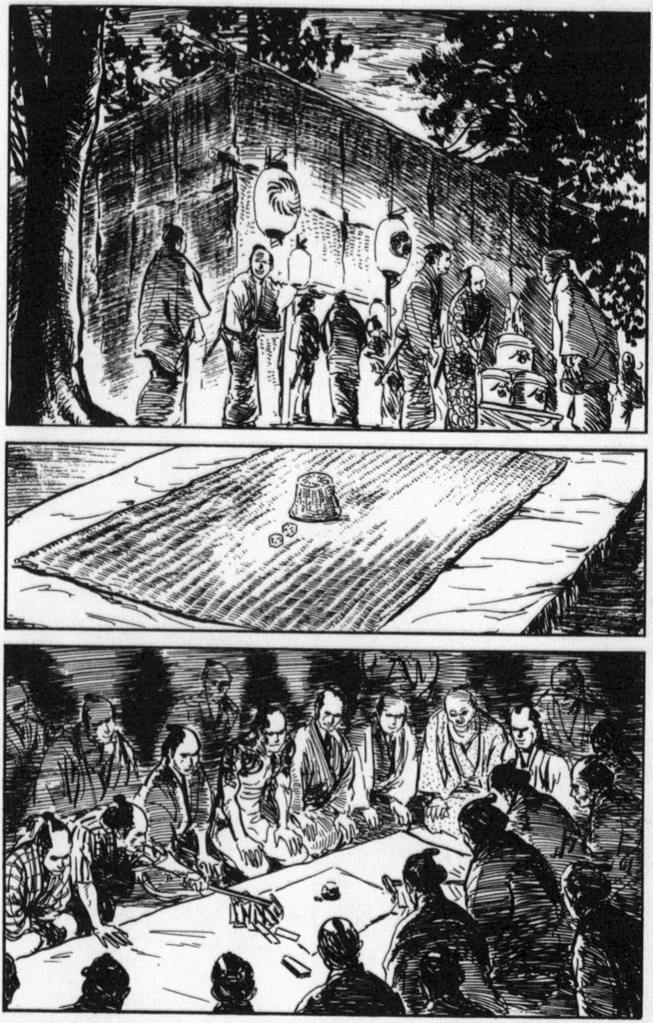

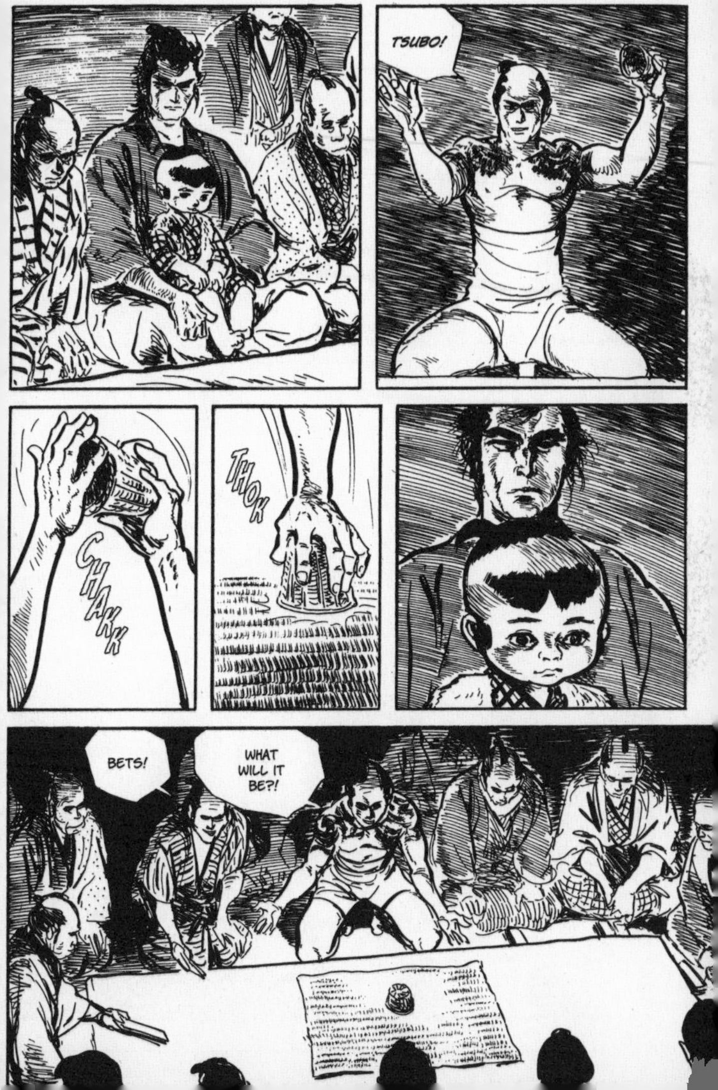
TSUBO!
CHAKK
THOK
BETS!
WHAT WILL IT BE?!

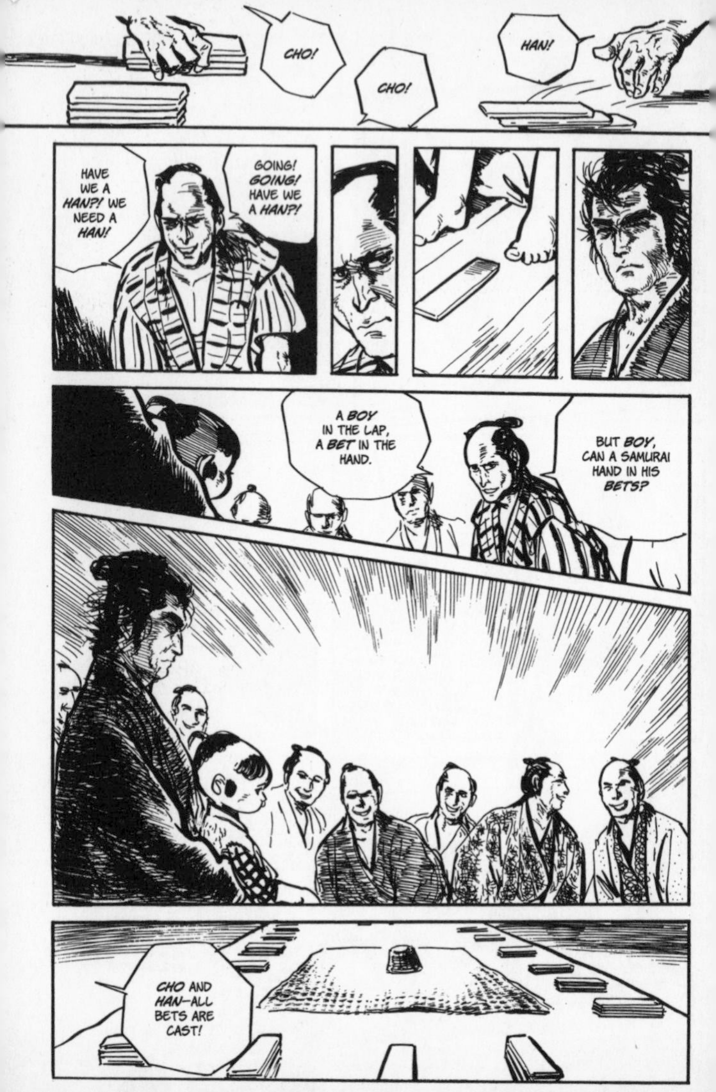
CHO!
CHO!
HAN!
HAVE WE A HAN?! WE NEED A HAN!
GOING! GOING! HAVE WE A HAN?!
A BOY IN THE LAP, A BET IN THE HAND.
BUT BOY, CAN A SAMURAI HAND IN HIS BETS?
CHO AND HAN—ALL BETS ARE CAST!

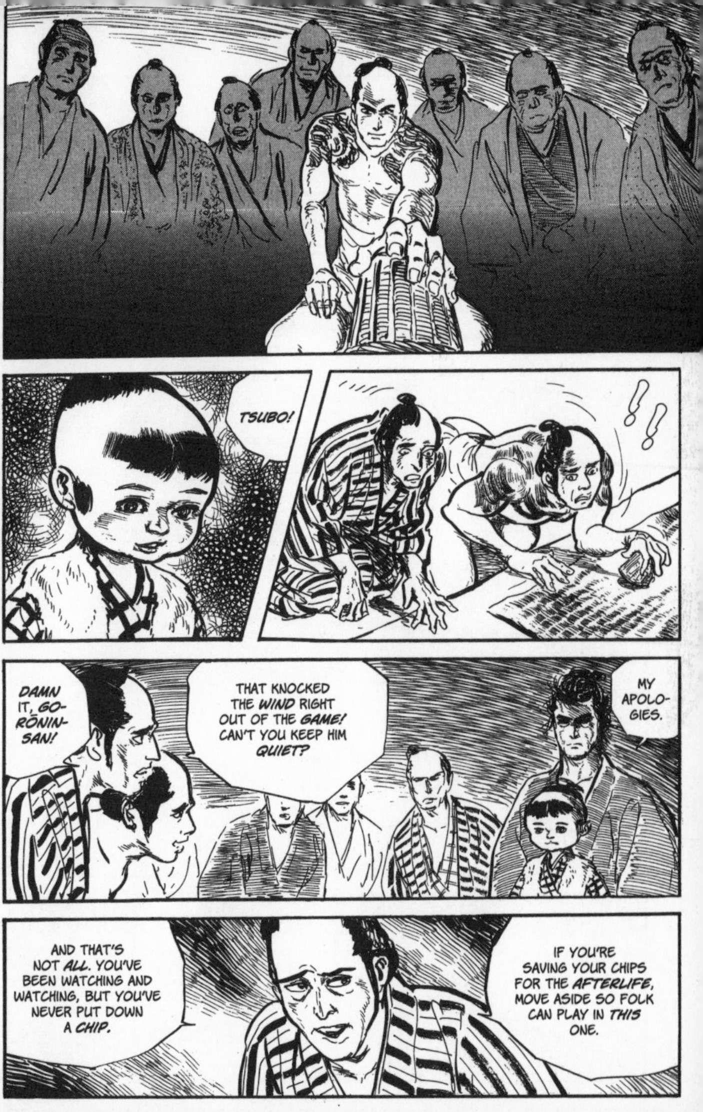
TSUBO!
DAMN IT, GO-RŌNIN-SAN!
THAT KNOCKED THE WIND RIGHT OUT OF THE GAME! CAN'T YOU KEEP HIM QUIET?
MY APOLOGIES.
AND THAT'S NOT ALL. YOU'VE BEEN WATCHING AND WATCHING, BUT YOU'VE NEVER PUT DOWN A CHIP.
IF YOU'RE SAVING YOUR CHIPS FOR THE AFTERLIFE, MOVE ASIDE SO FOLK CAN PLAY IN THIS ONE.

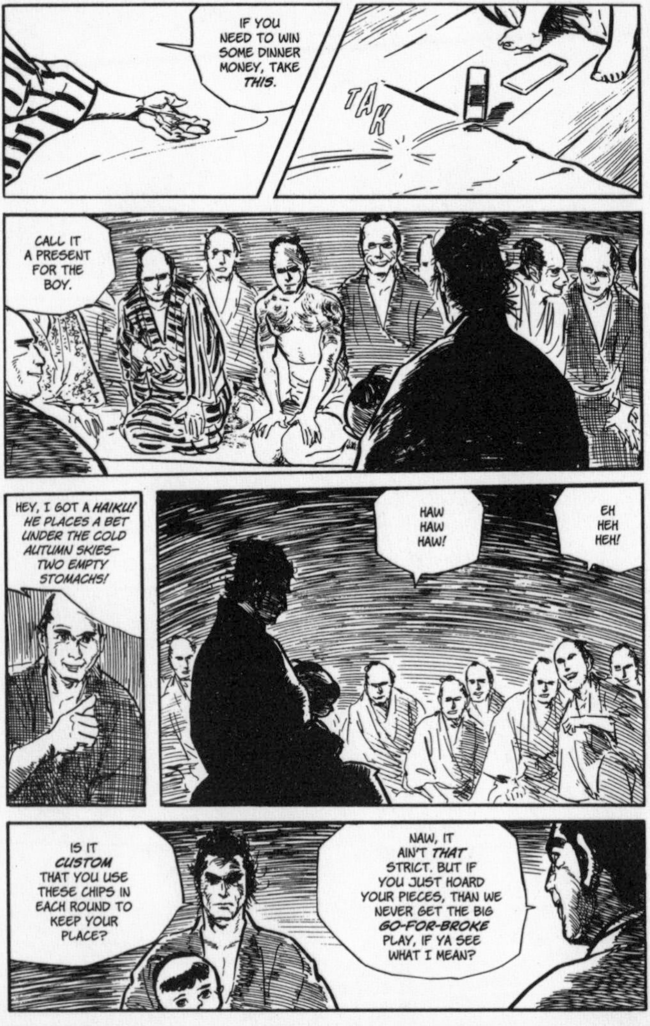
IF YOU NEED TO WIN SOME DINNER MONEY, TAKE *THIS*.
TAK
CALL IT A PRESENT FOR THE BOY.
HEY, I GOT A *HAIKU!* HE PLACES A BET UNDER THE COLD AUTUMN SKIES— TWO EMPTY STOMACHS!
HAW HAW HAW!
EH HEH HEH!
IS IT *CUSTOM* THAT YOU USE THESE CHIPS IN EACH ROUND TO KEEP YOUR PLACE?
NAW, IT AIN'T *THAT* STRICT. BUT IF YOU JUST HOARD YOUR PIECES, THAN WE NEVER GET THE BIG *GO-FOR-BROKE* PLAY, IF YA SEE WHAT I MEAN?

FWDD

SHAKK

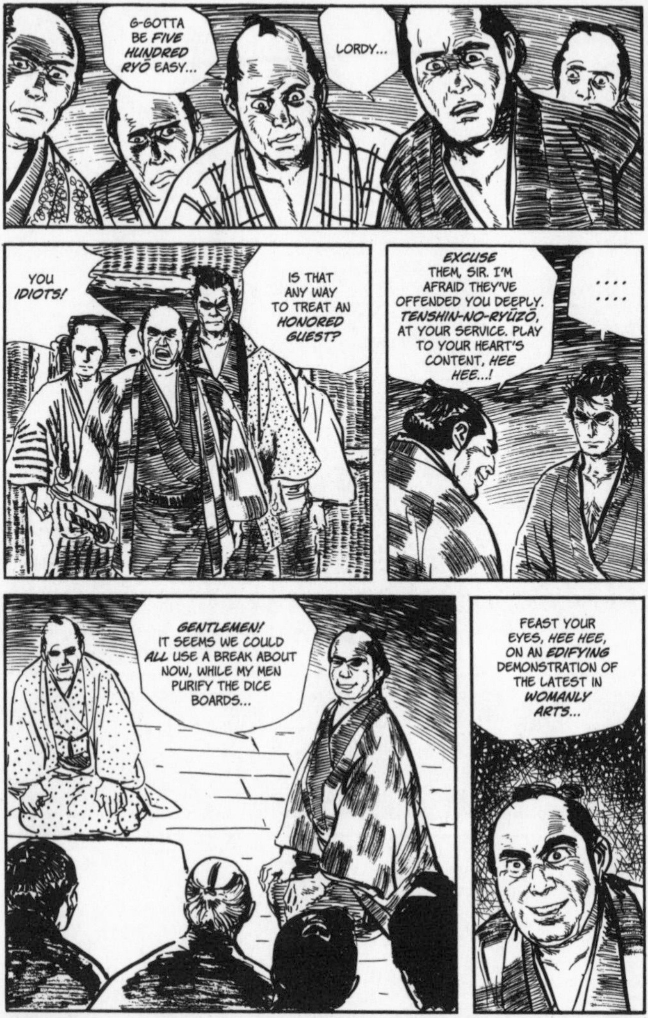
G-GOTTA BE FIVE HUNDRED RYŌ EASY...
LORDY...
YOU IDIOTS!
IS THAT ANY WAY TO TREAT AN HONORED GUEST?
EXCUSE THEM, SIR. I'M AFRAID THEY'VE OFFENDED YOU DEEPLY. TENSHIN-NO-RYŪZŌ, AT YOUR SERVICE. PLAY TO YOUR HEART'S CONTENT, HEE HEE...!
....
....
GENTLEMEN! IT SEEMS WE COULD ALL USE A BREAK ABOUT NOW, WHILE MY MEN PURIFY THE DICE BOARDS...
FEAST YOUR EYES, HEE HEE, ON AN EDIFYING DEMONSTRATION OF THE LATEST IN WOMANLY ARTS...

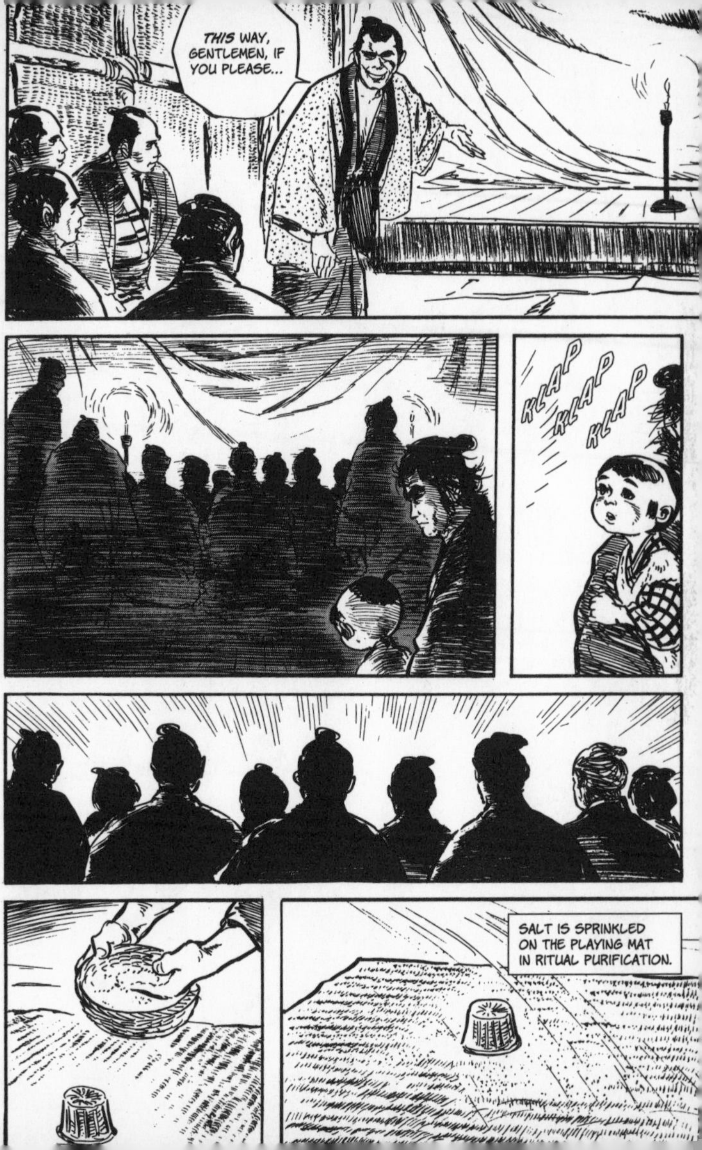
THIS WAY, GENTLEMEN, IF YOU PLEASE...
KLAP KLAP KLAP
SALT IS SPRINKLED ON THE PLAYING MAT IN RITUAL PURIFICATION.

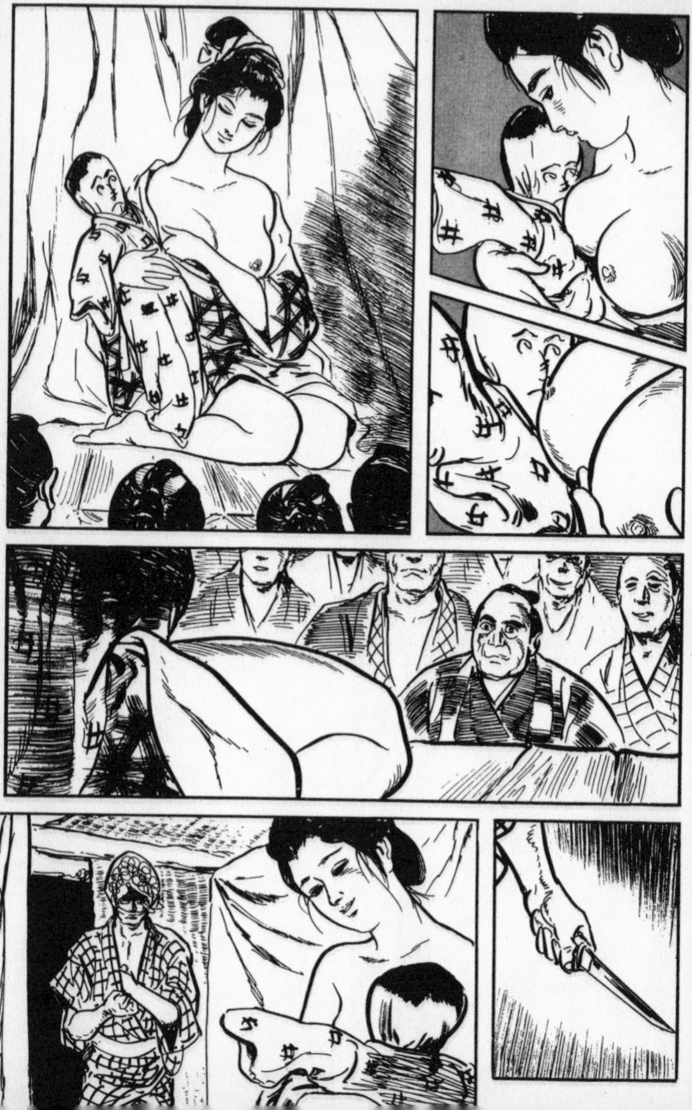

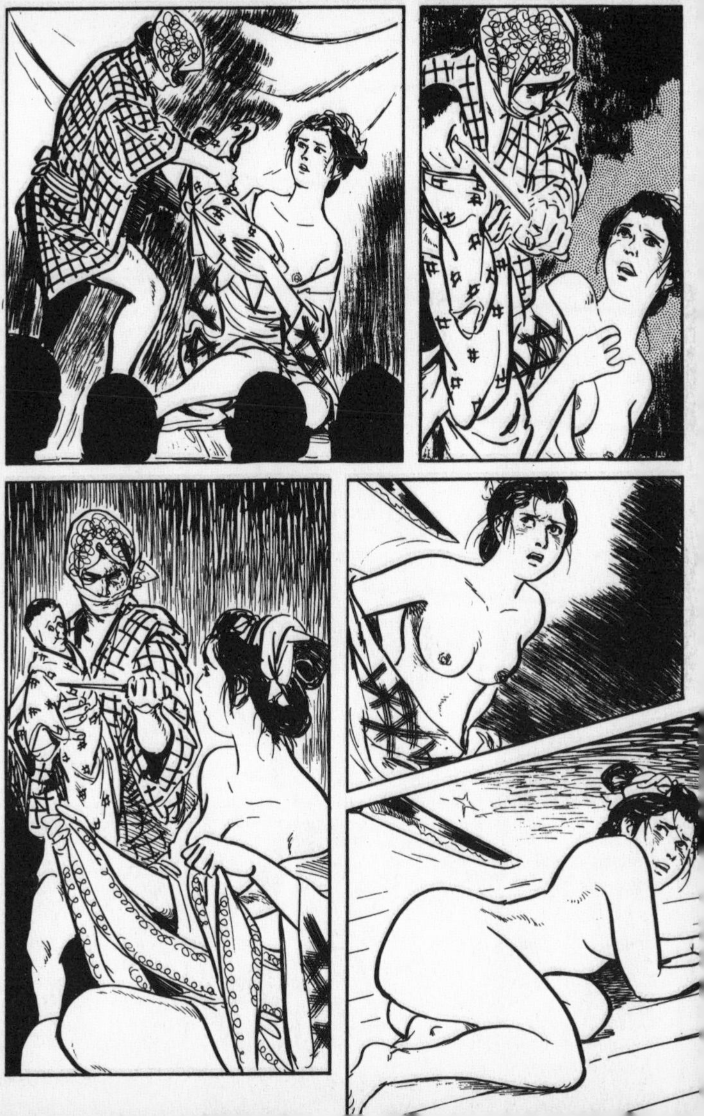

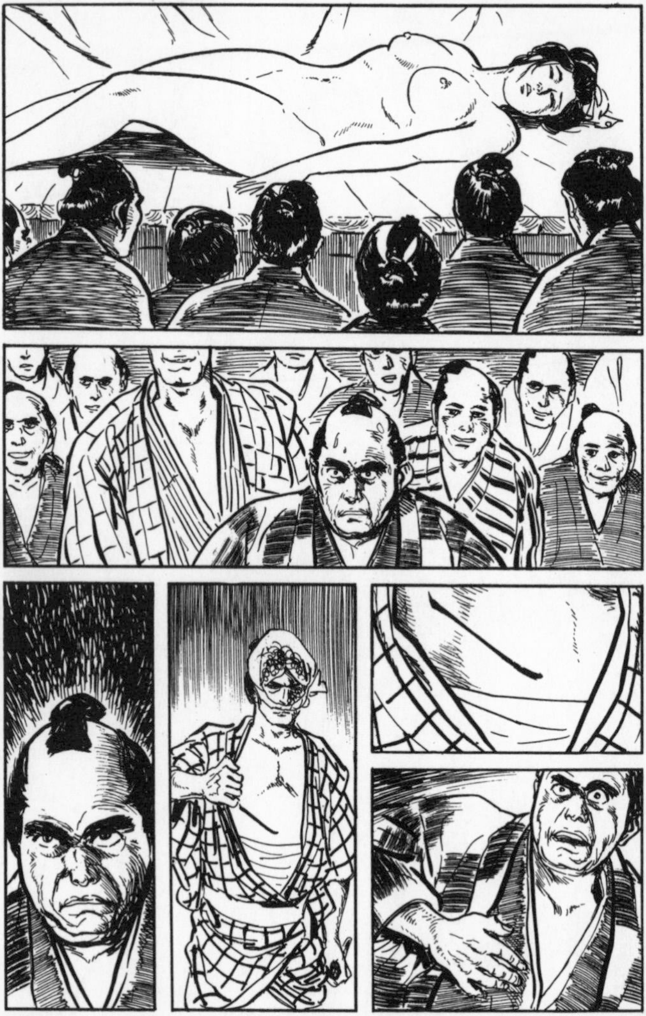

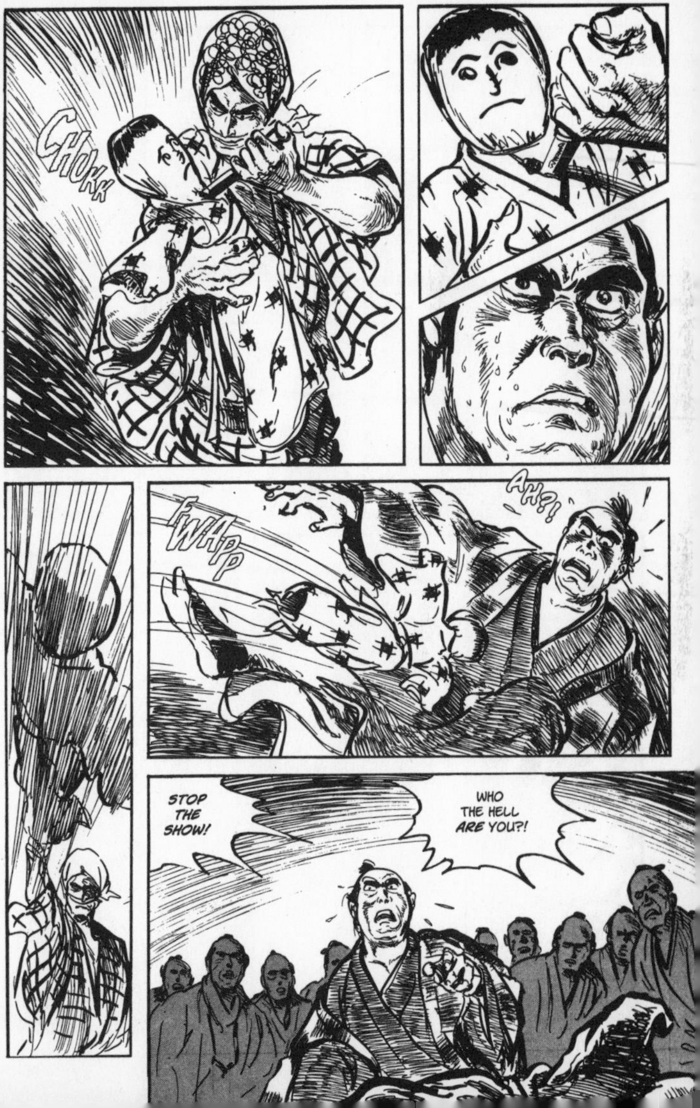
CHOKK
FWAPP
AH?!
STOP THE SHOW!
WHO THE HELL ARE YOU?!

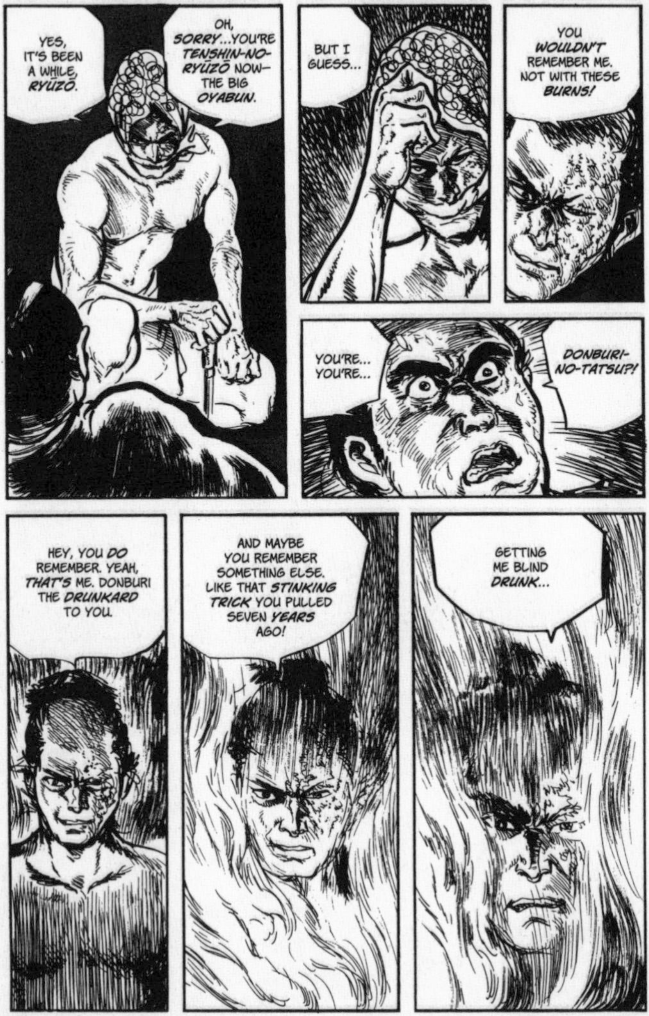
YES, IT'S BEEN A WHILE, RYŪZŌ.
OH, SORRY...YOU'RE TENSHIN-NO-RYŪZŌ NOW—THE BIG OYABUN.
BUT I GUESS...
YOU WOULDN'T REMEMBER ME. NOT WITH THESE BURNS!
YOU'RE... YOU'RE...
DONBURI-NO-TATSU?!
HEY, YOU DO REMEMBER. YEAH, THAT'S ME. DONBURI THE DRUNKARD TO YOU.
AND MAYBE YOU REMEMBER SOMETHING ELSE. LIKE THAT STINKING TRICK YOU PULLED SEVEN YEARS AGO!
GETTING ME BLIND DRUNK...

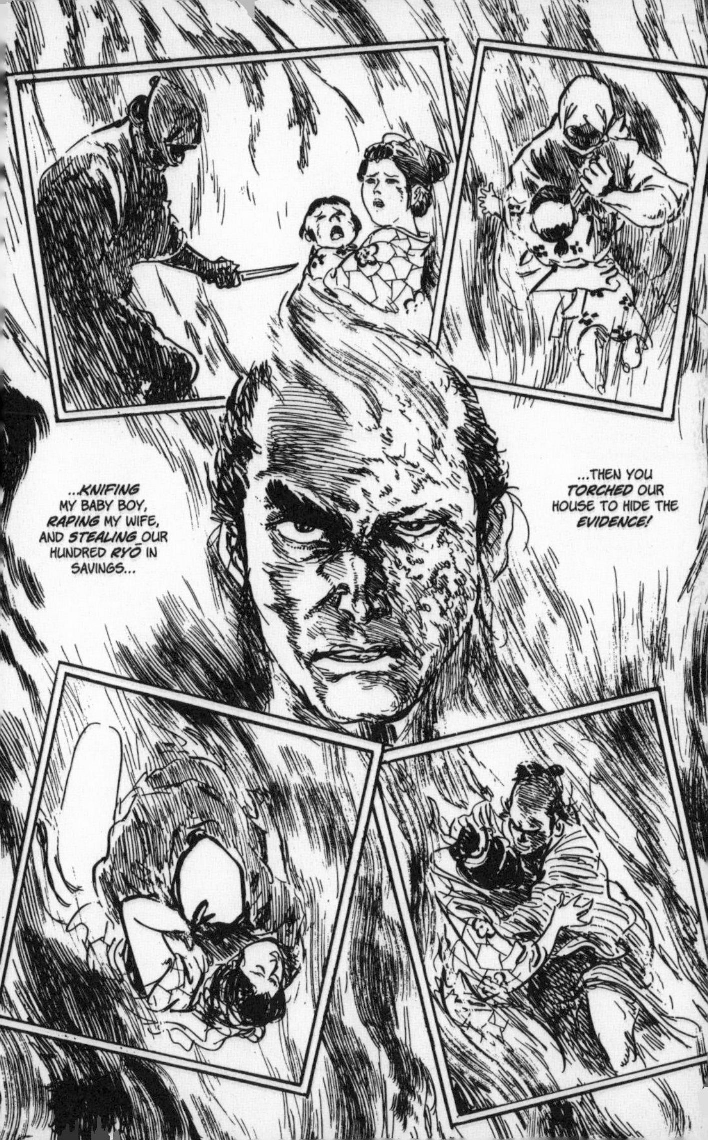
...KNIFING MY BABY BOY, RAPING MY WIFE, AND STEALING OUR HUNDRED RYŌ IN SAVINGS...
...THEN YOU TORCHED OUR HOUSE TO HIDE THE EVIDENCE!

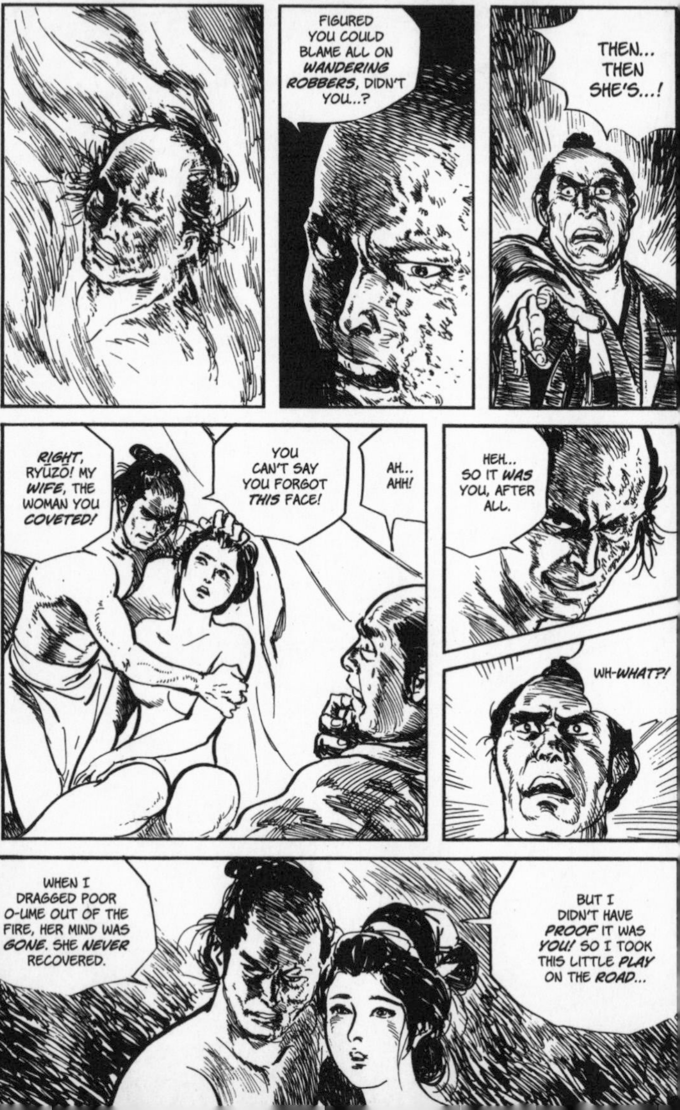
FIGURED YOU COULD BLAME ALL ON WANDERING ROBBERS, DIDN'T YOU...?
THEN... THEN SHE'S...!
RIGHT, RYŪZŌ! MY WIFE, THE WOMAN YOU COVETED!
YOU CAN'T SAY YOU FORGOT THIS FACE!
AH... AHH!
HEH... SO IT WAS YOU, AFTER ALL.
WH-WHAT?!
WHEN I DRAGGED POOR O-UME OUT OF THE FIRE, HER MIND WAS GONE. SHE NEVER RECOVERED.
BUT I DIDN'T HAVE PROOF IT WAS YOU! SO I TOOK THIS LITTLE PLAY ON THE ROAD...

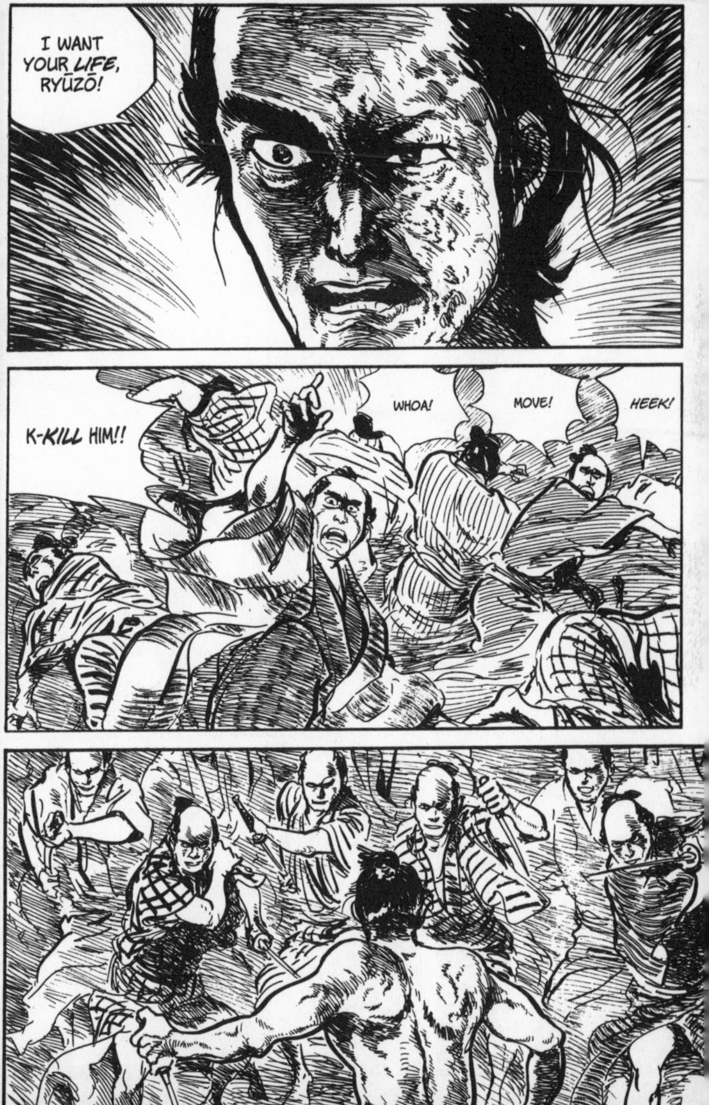
I WANT YOUR LIFE, RYŪZŌ!
K-KILL HIM!!
WHOA!
MOVE!
HEEK!

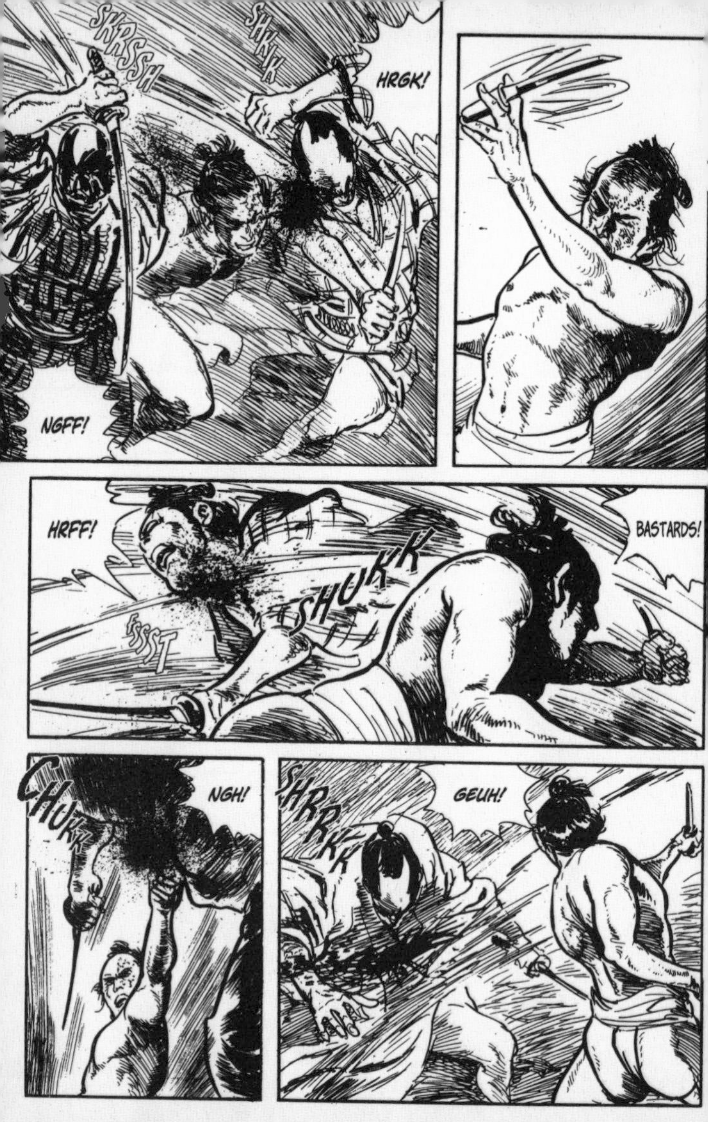
SKRSSH
SHKKK
HRGK!
NGFF!
HRFF!
SHUKK
FSSST
BASTARDS!
CHUKK
NGH!
SHRRKKK
GEUH!

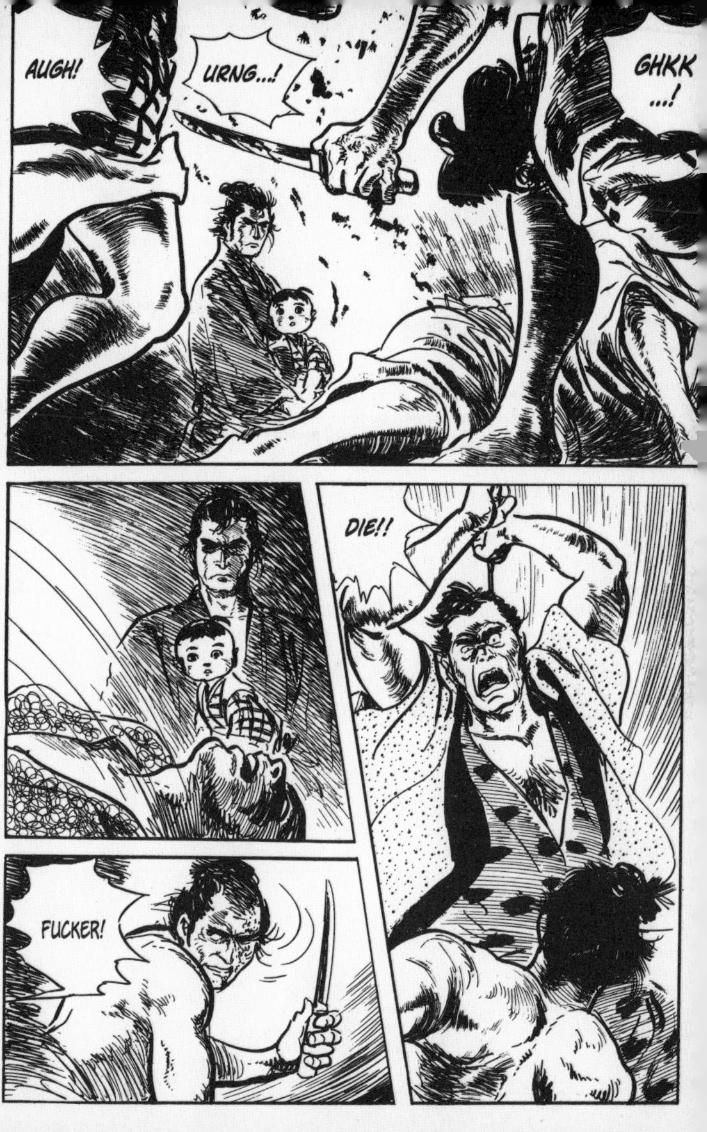
AUGH!
URNG...!
GHKK ...!
FUCKER!
DIE!!

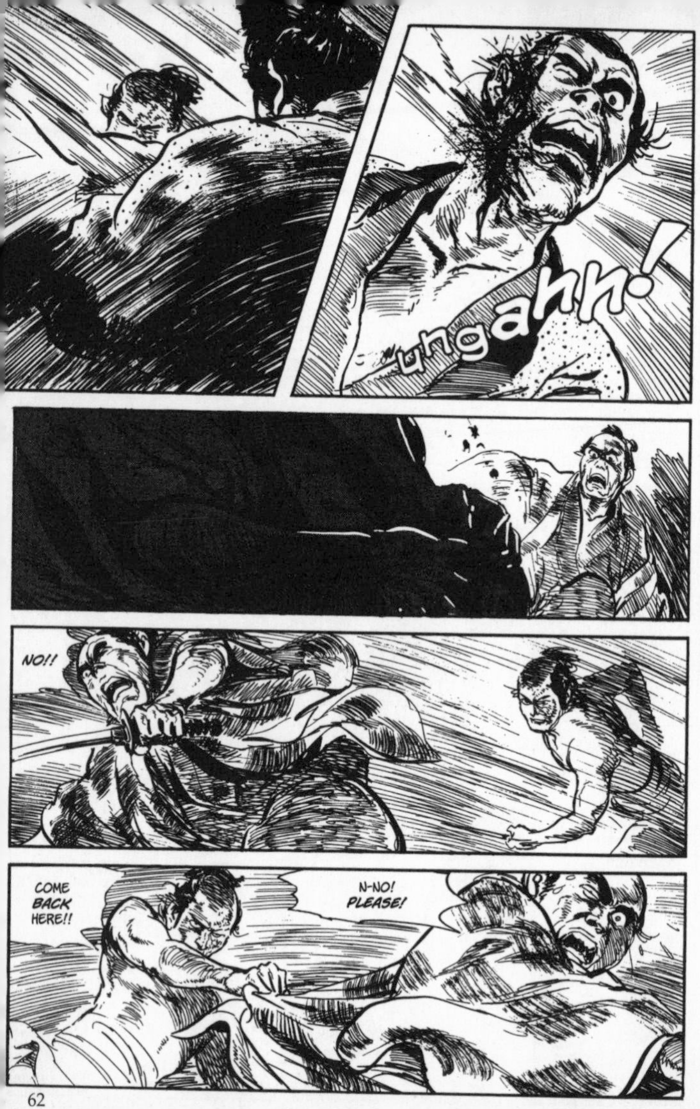
UNGAHH!
NO!!
COME BACK HERE!!
N-NO! PLEASE!

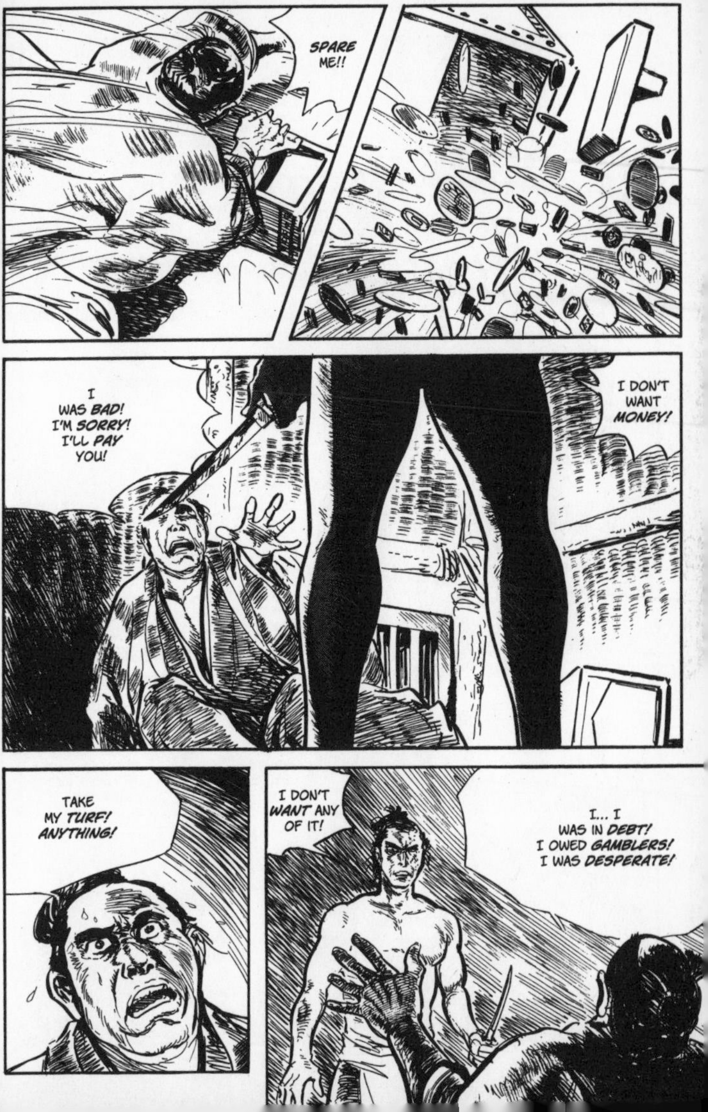
SPARE ME!!
I WAS BAD! I'M SORRY! I'LL PAY YOU!
I DON'T WANT MONEY!
TAKE MY TURF! ANYTHING!
I DON'T WANT ANY OF IT!
I... I WAS IN DEBT! I OWED GAMBLERS! I WAS DESPERATE!

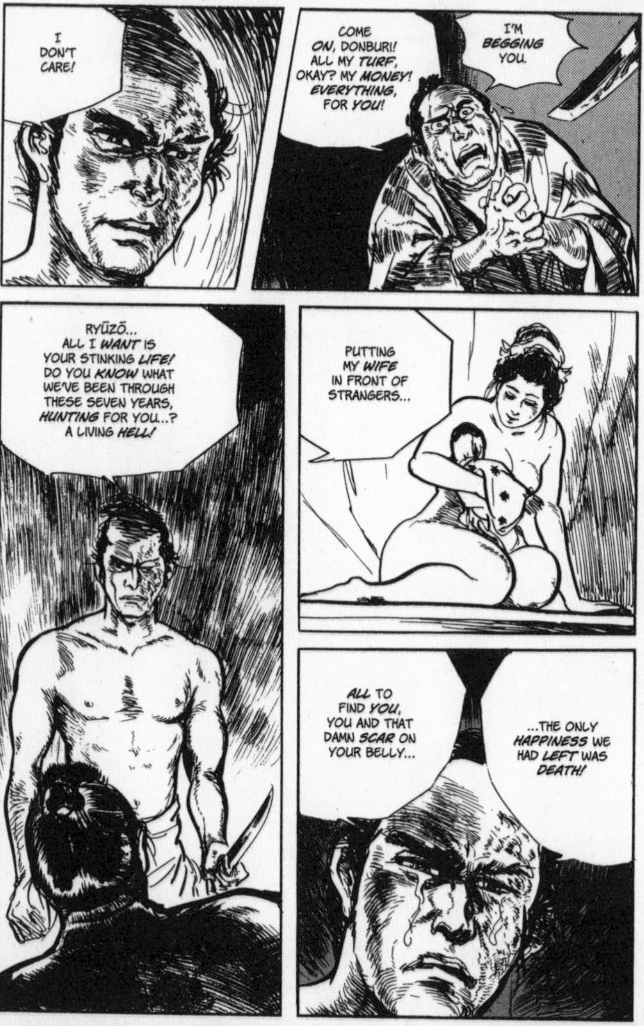
I DON'T CARE!
COME ON, DONBURI! ALL MY TURF, OKAY? MY MONEY! EVERYTHING, FOR YOU!
I'M BEGGING YOU.
RYŪZŌ... ALL I WANT IS YOUR STINKING LIFE! DO YOU KNOW WHAT WE'VE BEEN THROUGH THESE SEVEN YEARS, HUNTING FOR YOU..? A LIVING HELL!
PUTTING MY WIFE IN FRONT OF STRANGERS...
ALL TO FIND YOU, YOU AND THAT DAMN SCAR ON YOUR BELLY...
...THE ONLY HAPPINESS WE HAD LEFT WAS DEATH!

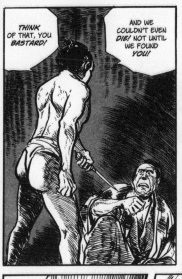

THINK OF THAT, YOU *BASTARD!*

AND WE COULDN'T EVEN *DIE!* NOT UNTIL WE FOUND *YOU!*

IT'S FUCKING *HARD* TO LIVE, RYŪZŌ...

...WHEN ALL YOU'VE GOT IS *HATE.*

NO... NO...

HY-AHH!!

SHUNK

ASSHK!

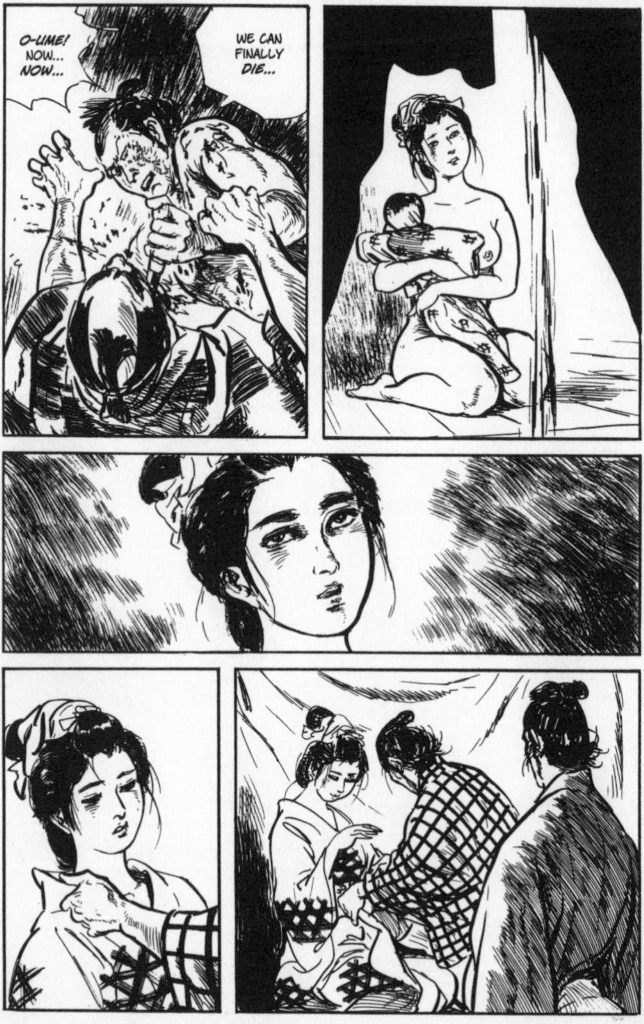
O-UME! NOW... NOW...
WE CAN FINALLY DIE...

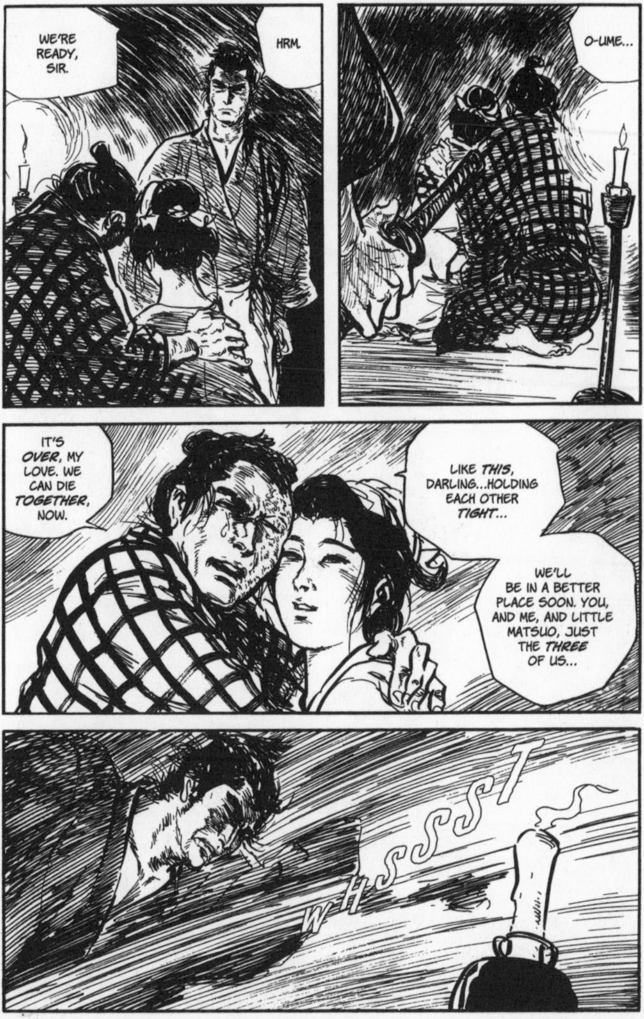
WE'RE READY, SIR.
HRM.
O-UME...
IT'S *OVER*, MY LOVE. WE CAN DIE *TOGETHER*, NOW.
LIKE *THIS*, DARLING...HOLDING EACH OTHER *TIGHT*...
WE'LL BE IN A BETTER PLACE SOON. YOU, AND ME, AND LITTLE MATSUO, JUST THE *THREE* OF US...
WHSSSST

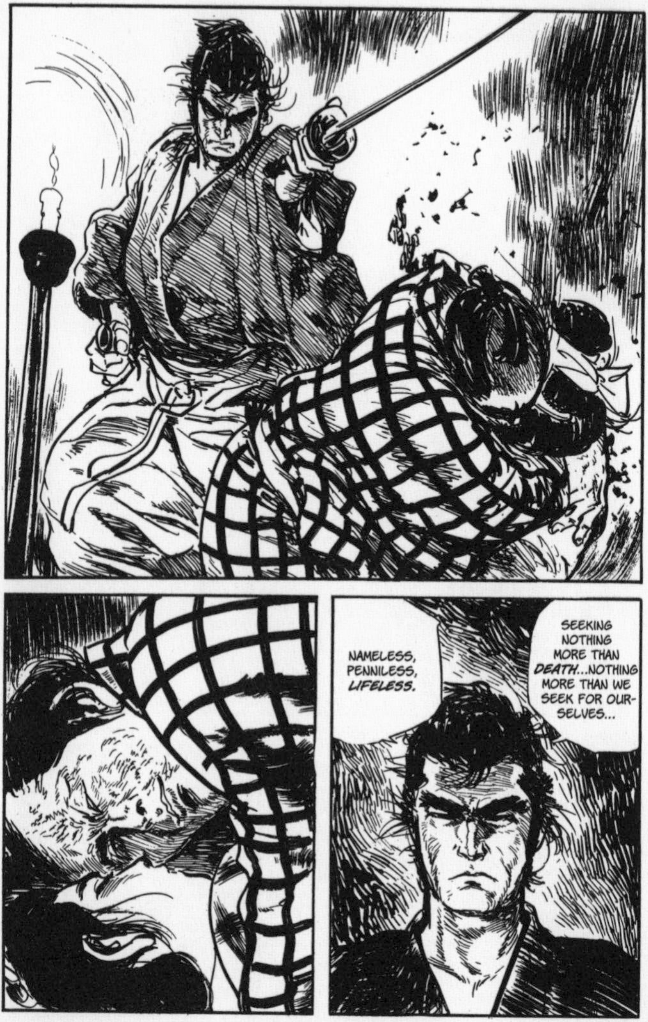
NAMELESS, PENNILESS, *LIFELESS.*
SEEKING NOTHING MORE THAN *DEATH*...NOTHING MORE THAN WE SEEK FOR OURSELVES...

# the sixtieth

# Body Check

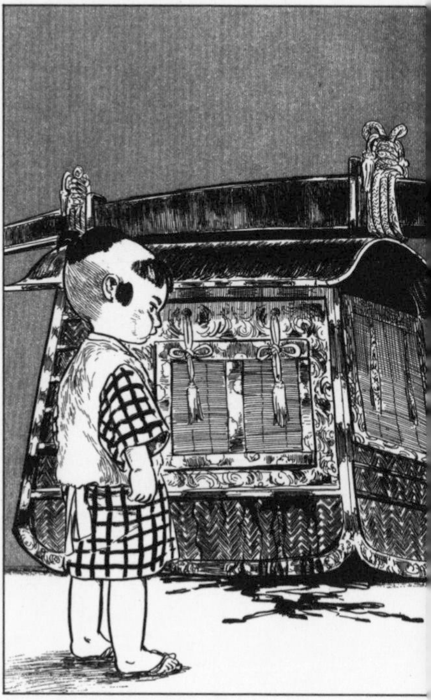

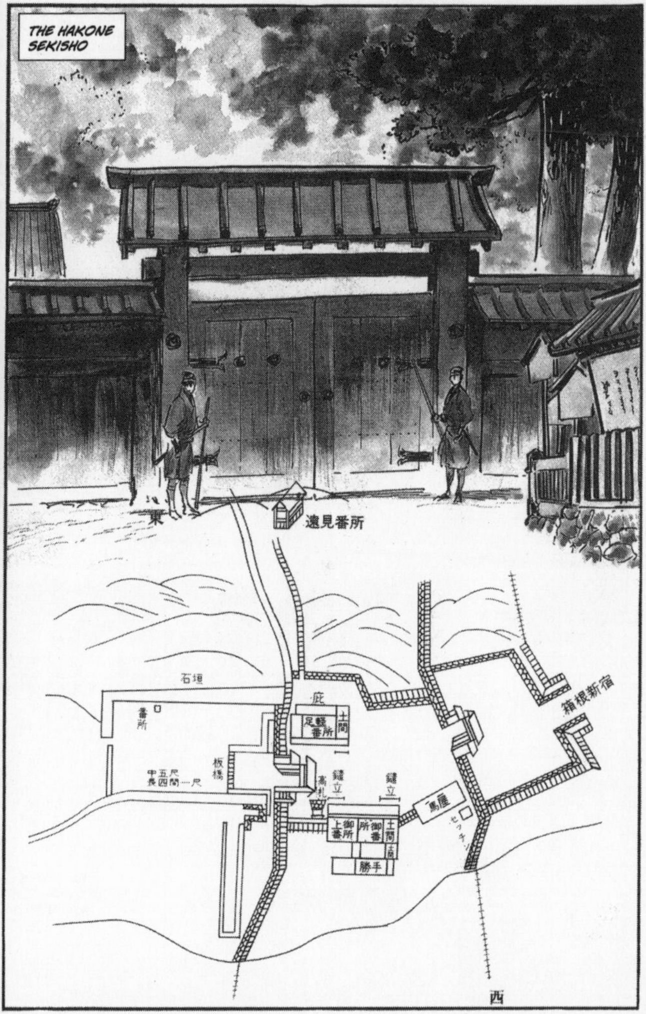
THE HAKONE SEKISHO
東
遠見番所
石垣
番所
庇
足軽番所
土間
板橋
中五尺
長四間一尺
高札
鑓立
鑓立
馬屋
上御番所
御番所
土間
土間
勝手
セッチン
箱根新宿
西

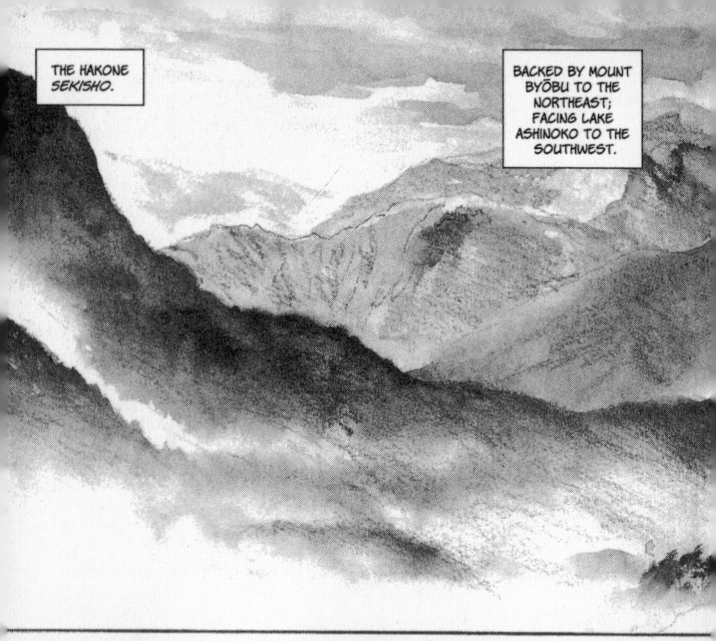
THE HAKONE SEKISHO.
BACKED BY MOUNT BYŌBU TO THE NORTHEAST; FACING LAKE ASHINOKO TO THE SOUTHWEST.
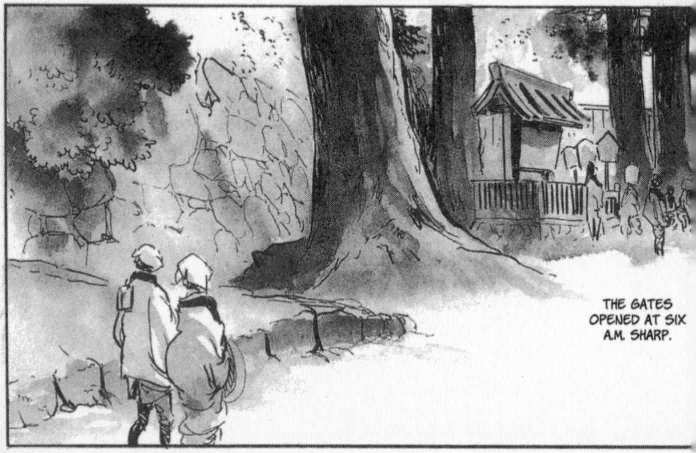
THE GATES OPENED AT SIX A.M. SHARP.

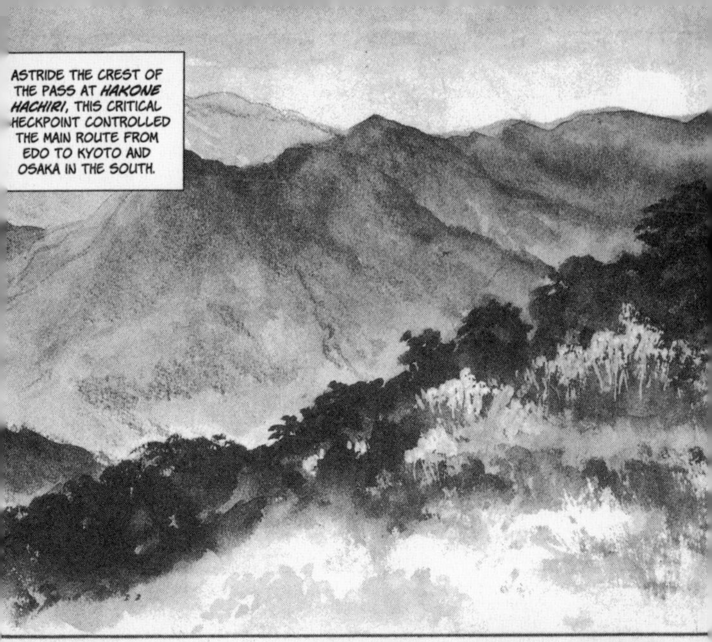
ASTRIDE THE CREST OF THE PASS AT *HAKONE HACHIRI*, THIS CRITICAL HECKPOINT CONTROLLED THE MAIN ROUTE FROM EDO TO KYOTO AND OSAKA IN THE SOUTH.
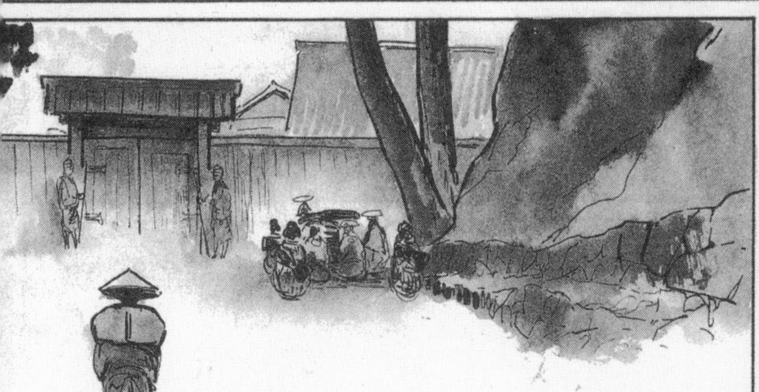

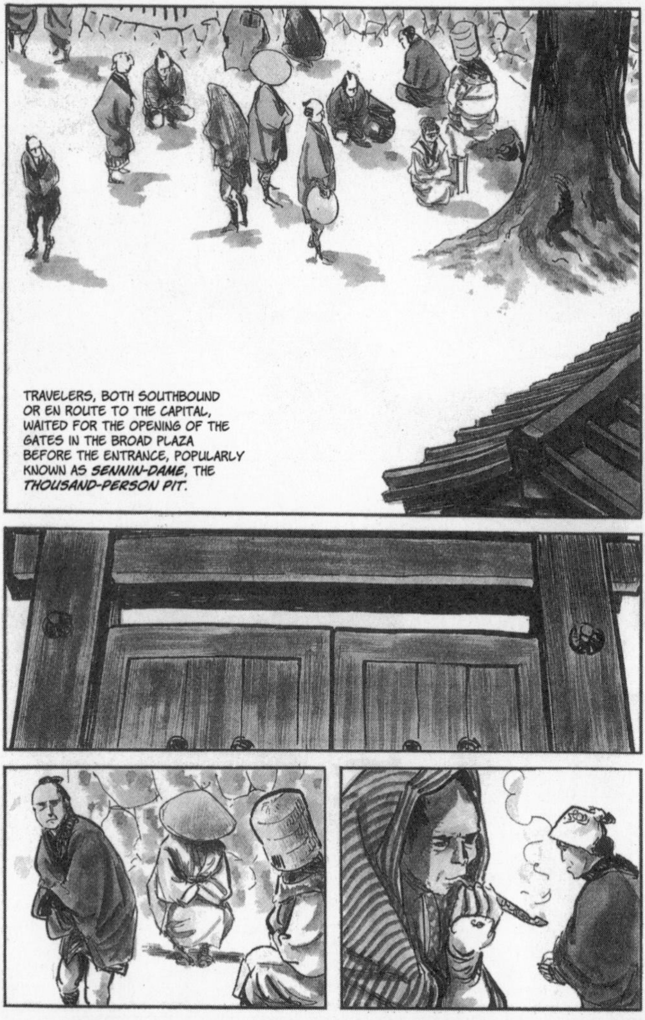
TRAVELERS, BOTH SOUTHBOUND OR EN ROUTE TO THE CAPITAL, WAITED FOR THE OPENING OF THE GATES IN THE BROAD PLAZA BEFORE THE ENTRANCE, POPULARLY KNOWN AS *SENNIN-DAME*, THE *THOUSAND-PERSON PIT*.

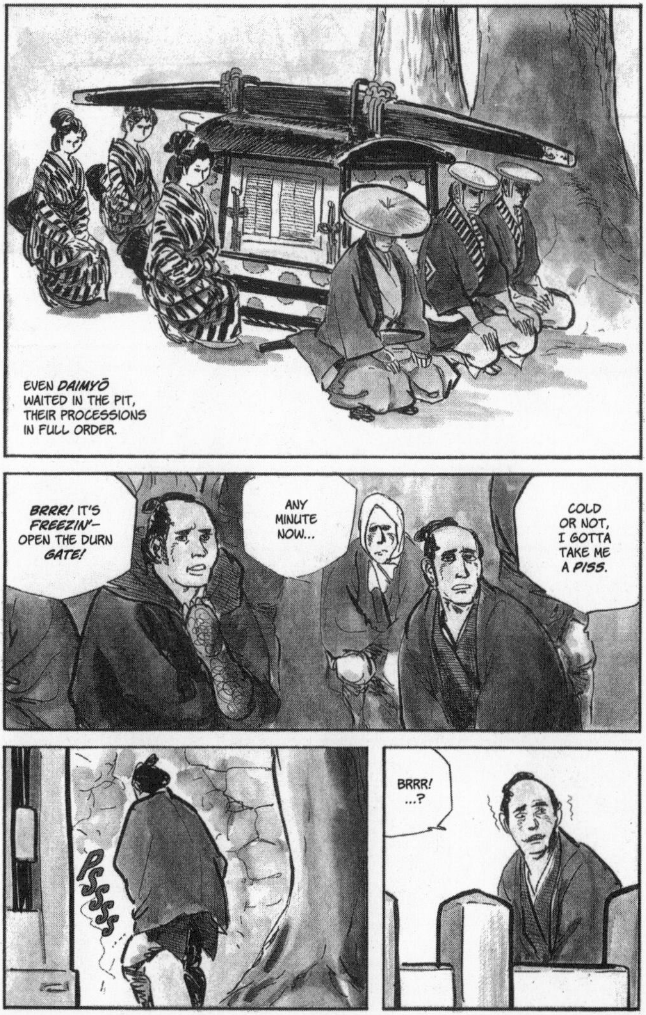
EVEN *DAIMYŌ* WAITED IN THE PIT, THEIR PROCESSIONS IN FULL ORDER.
*BRRR!* IT'S *FREEZIN'*– OPEN THE DURN *GATE!*
ANY MINUTE NOW...
COLD OR NOT, I GOTTA TAKE ME A *PISS.*
PSSSS
BRRR! ...?

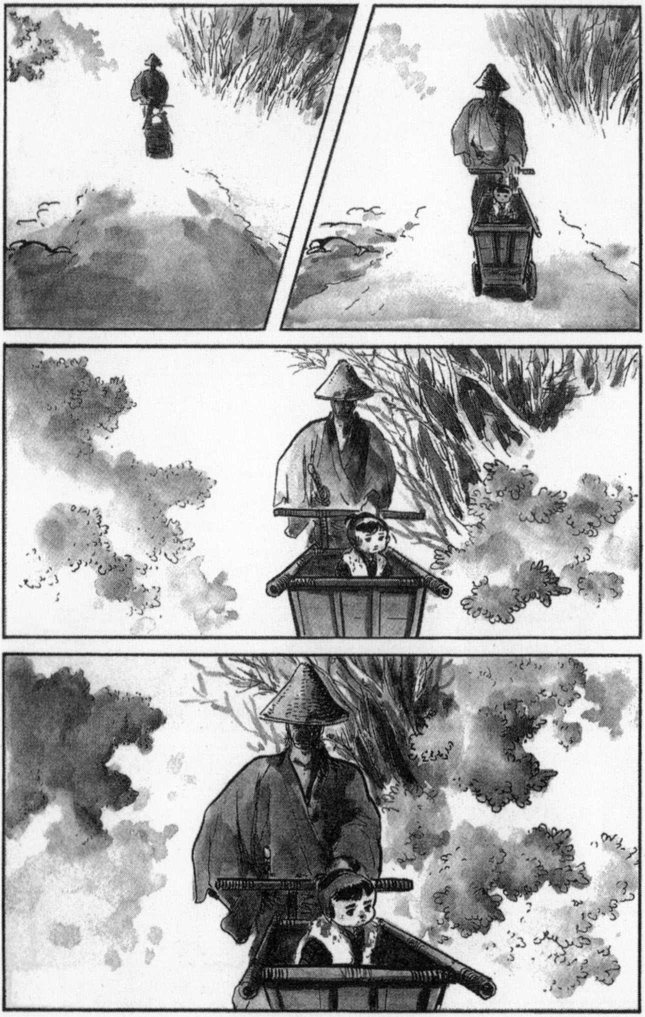

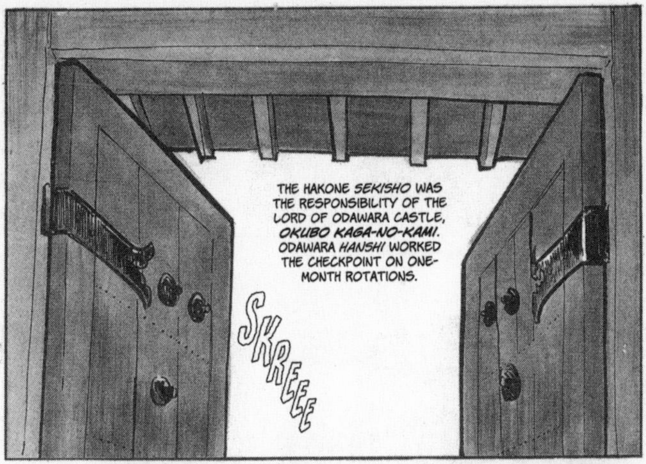
THE HAKONE *SEKISHO* WAS THE RESPONSIBILITY OF THE LORD OF ODAWARA CASTLE, ***OKUBO KAGA-NO-KAMI.*** ODAWARA *HANSHI* WORKED THE CHECKPOINT ON ONE-MONTH ROTATIONS.
SKREEE
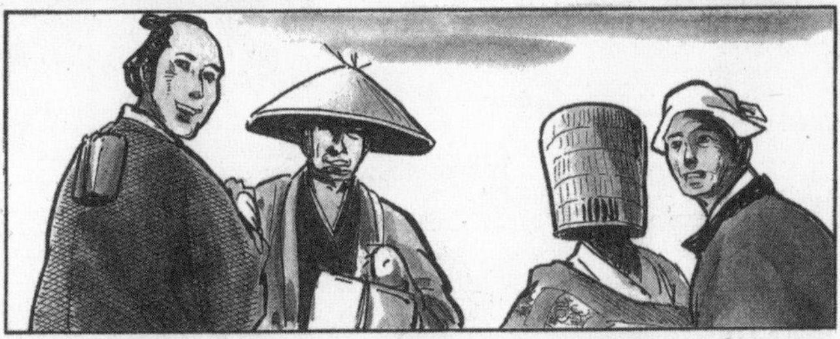
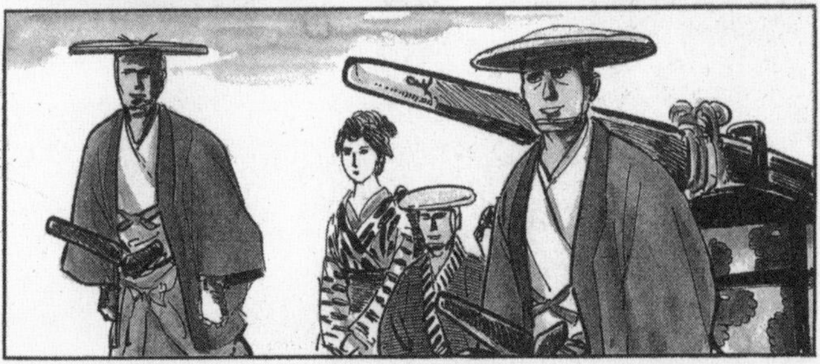

78

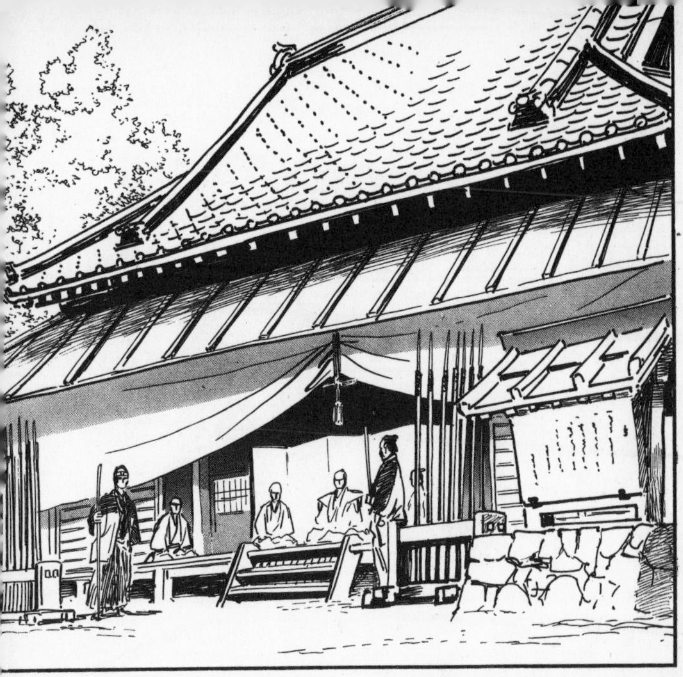

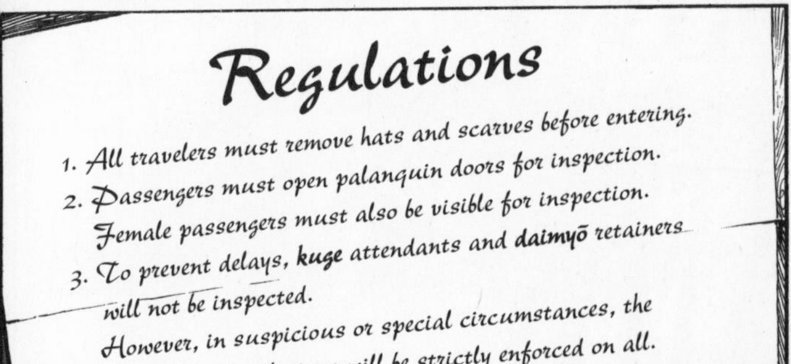
Regulations
1. All travelers must remove hats and scarves before entering.
2. Passengers must open palanquin doors for inspection.
Female passengers must also be visible for inspection.
3. To prevent delays, kuge attendants and daimyō retainers will not be inspected.
However, in suspicious or special circumstances, the aforelisted regulations will be strictly enforced on all.
Sekisho Magistrate, Odawara han

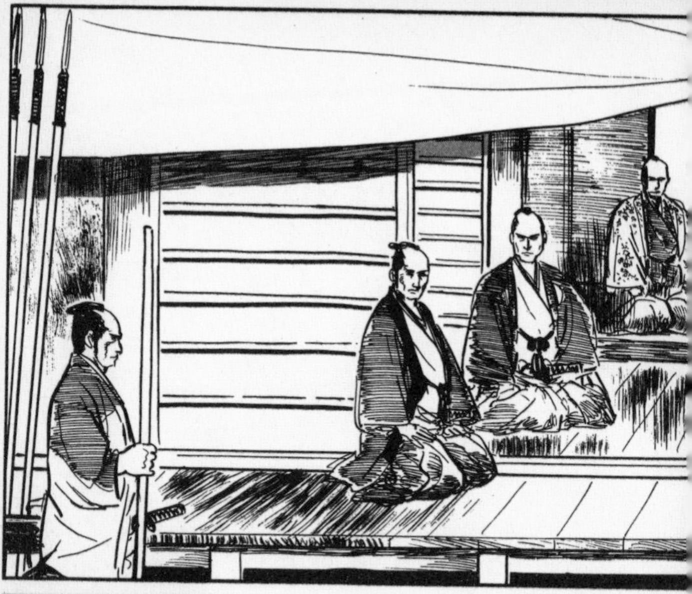

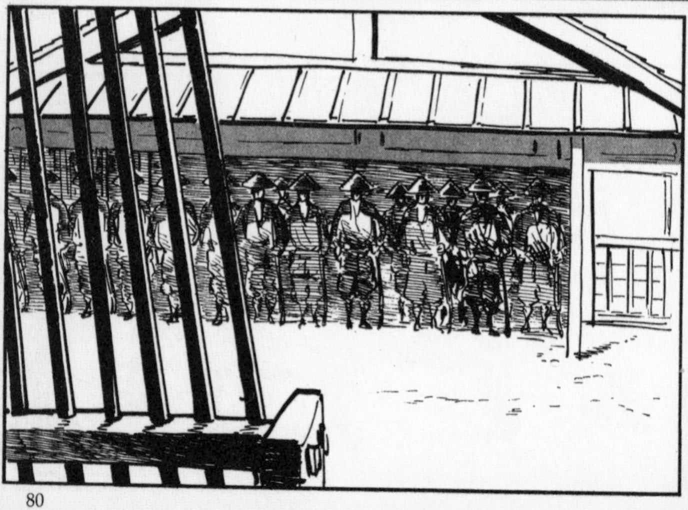

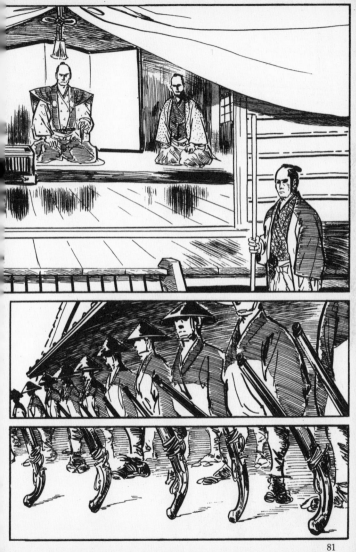

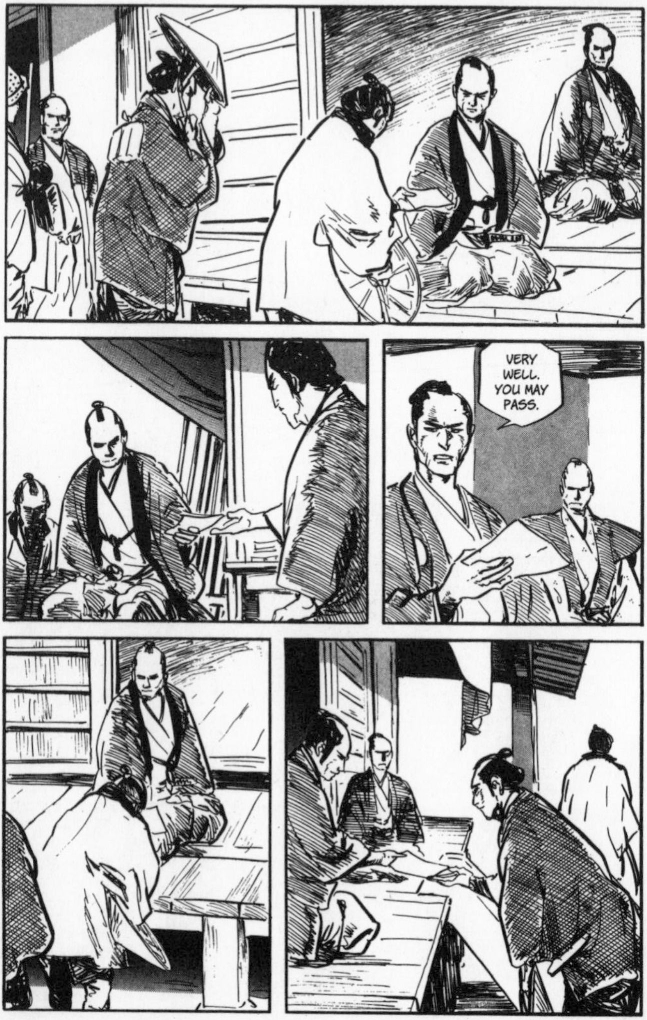
VERY WELL. YOU MAY PASS.

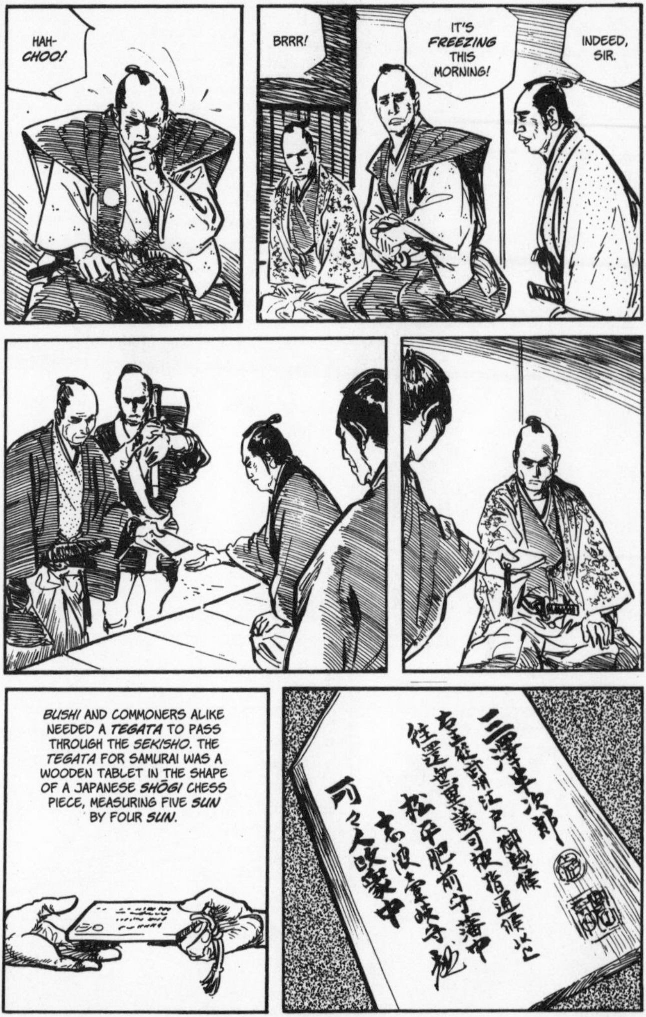
HAH-CHOO!
BRRR!
IT'S FREEZING THIS MORNING!
INDEED, SIR.
BUSHI AND COMMONERS ALIKE NEEDED A TEGATA TO PASS THROUGH THE SEKISHO. THE TEGATA FOR SAMURAI WAS A WOODEN TABLET IN THE SHAPE OF A JAPANESE SHŌGI CHESS PIECE, MEASURING FIVE SUN BY FOUR SUN.

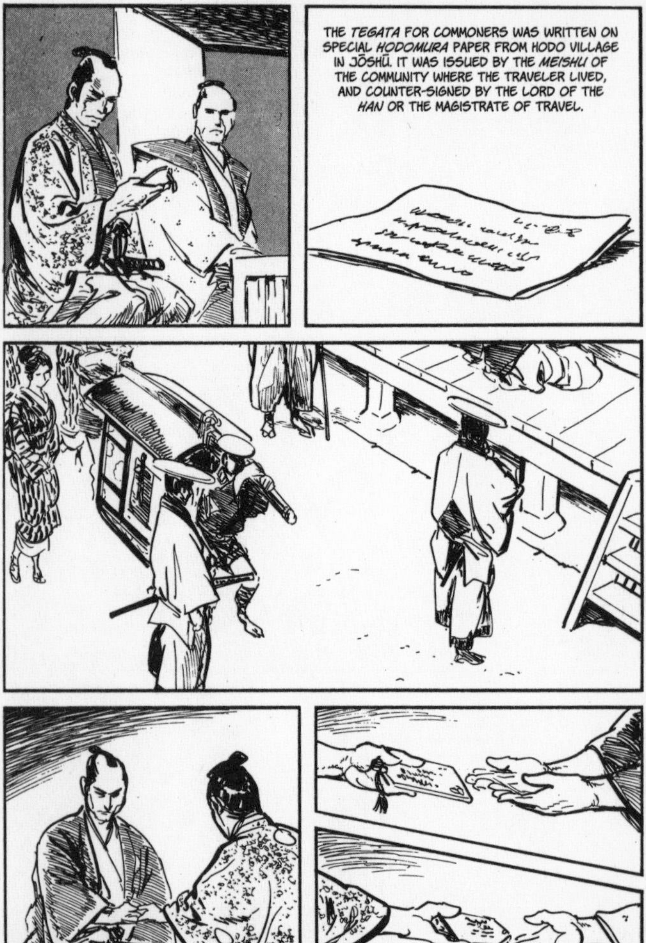
THE *TEGATA* FOR COMMONERS WAS WRITTEN ON SPECIAL *HODOMURA* PAPER FROM HODO VILLAGE IN JŌSHŪ. IT WAS ISSUED BY THE *MEISHU* OF THE COMMUNITY WHERE THE TRAVELER LIVED, AND COUNTER-SIGNED BY THE LORD OF THE *HAN* OR THE MAGISTRATE OF TRAVEL.

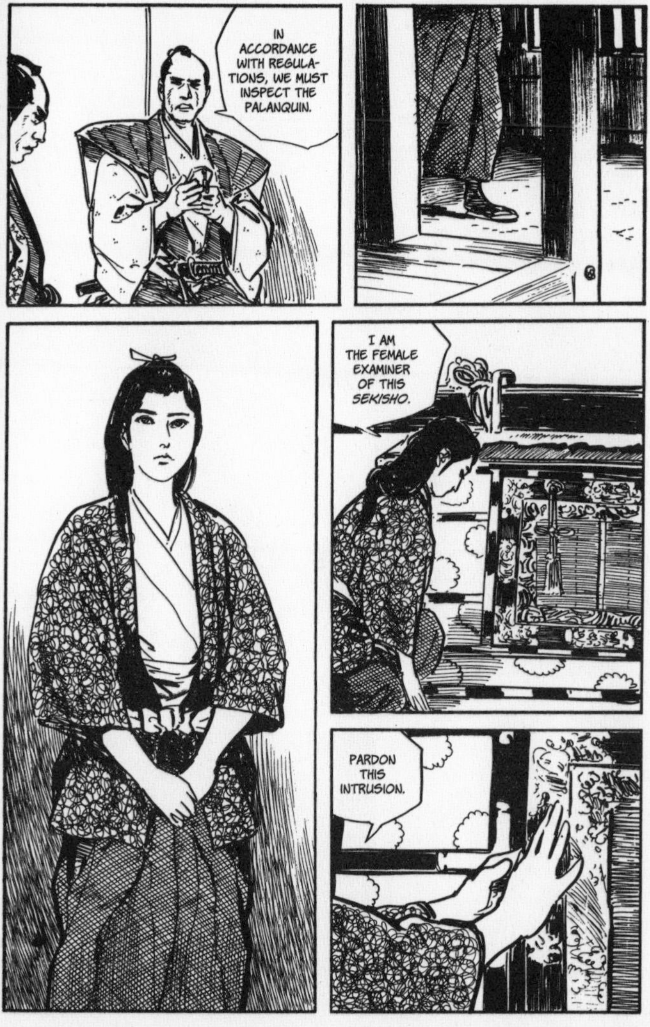
IN ACCORDANCE WITH REGULATIONS, WE MUST INSPECT THE PALANQUIN.
I AM THE FEMALE EXAMINER OF THIS SEKISHO.
PARDON THIS INTRUSION.

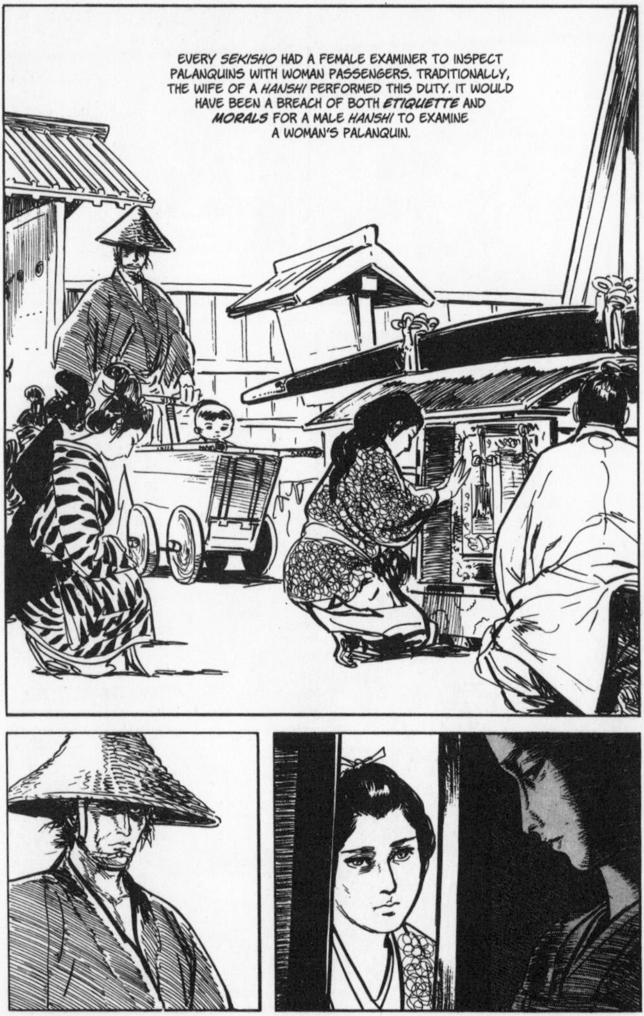
EVERY *SEKISHO* HAD A FEMALE EXAMINER TO INSPECT PALANQUINS WITH WOMAN PASSENGERS. TRADITIONALLY, THE WIFE OF A *HANSHI* PERFORMED THIS DUTY. IT WOULD HAVE BEEN A BREACH OF BOTH ***ETIQUETTE*** AND ***MORALS*** FOR A MALE *HANSHI* TO EXAMINE A WOMAN'S PALANQUIN.

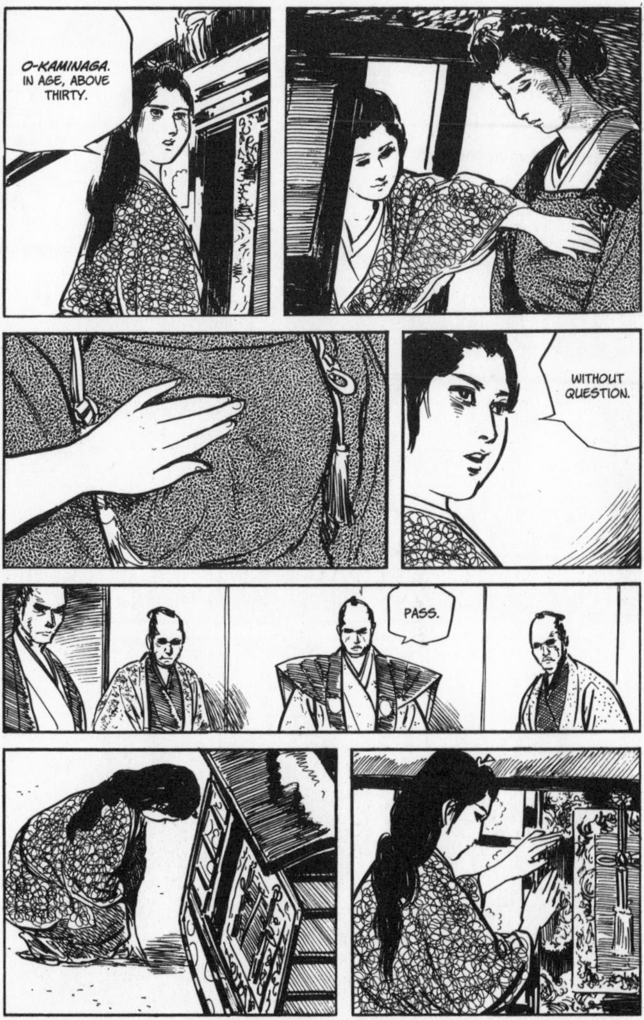
O-KAMINAGA. IN AGE, ABOVE THIRTY.
WITHOUT QUESTION.
PASS.

GARA
GARA

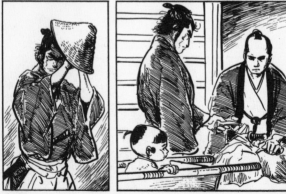

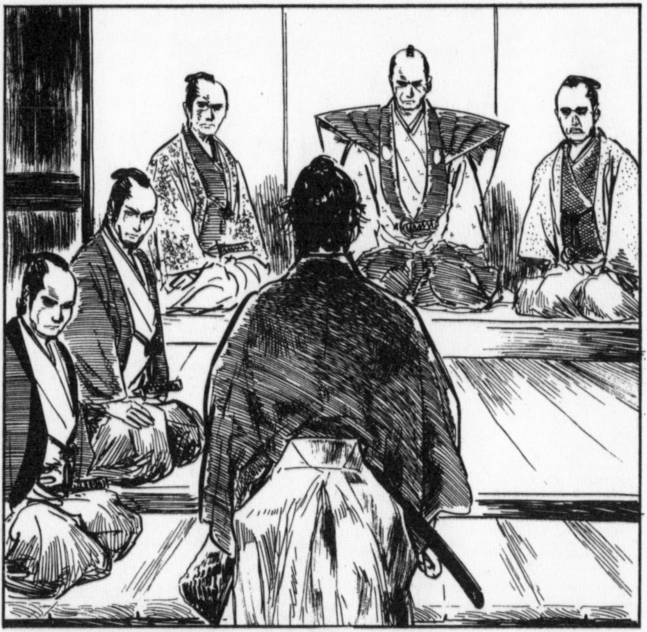
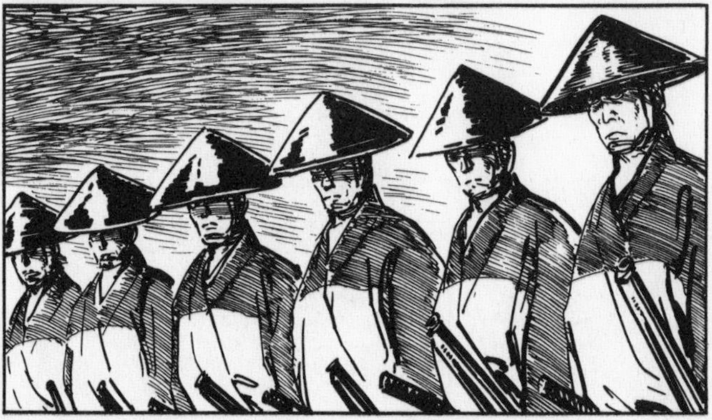

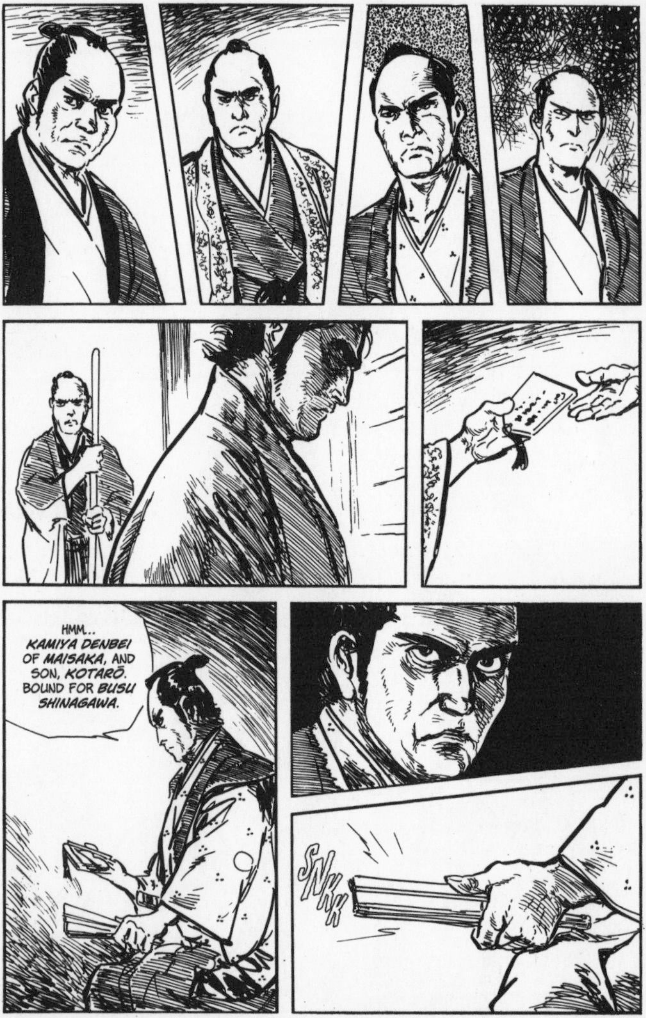
HMM... *KAMIYA DENBEI* OF *MAISAKA*, AND SON, *KOTARŌ*. BOUND FOR *BUSU SHINAGAWA*.
SNKK

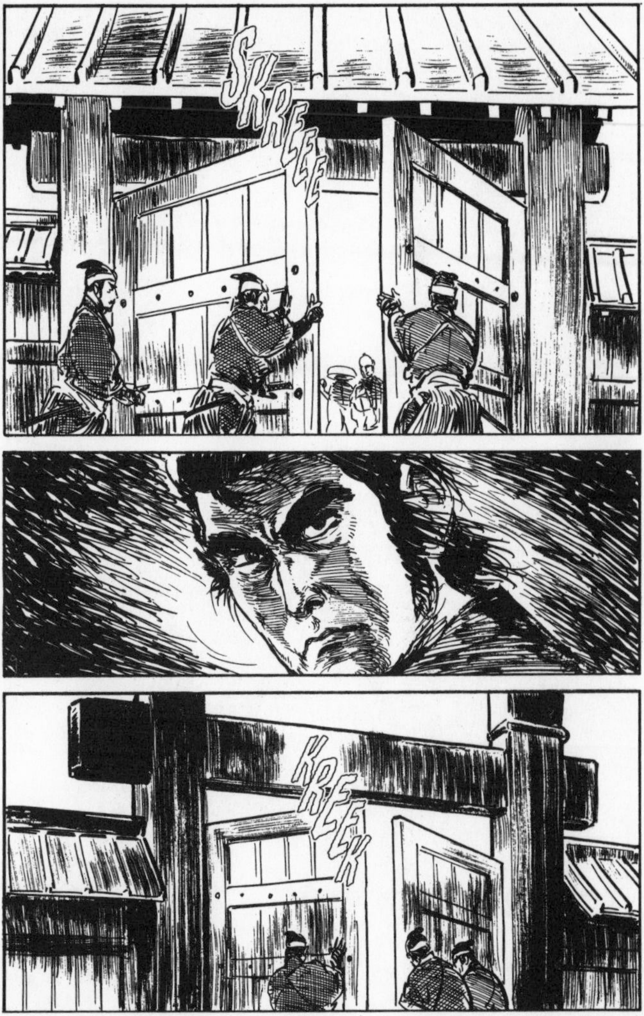
SKREEEE
KREEK

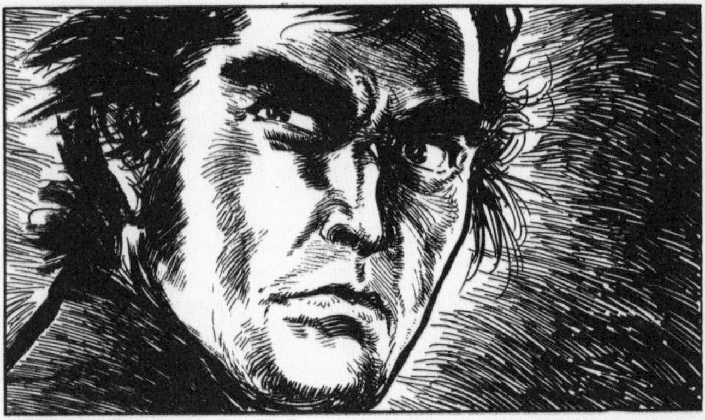

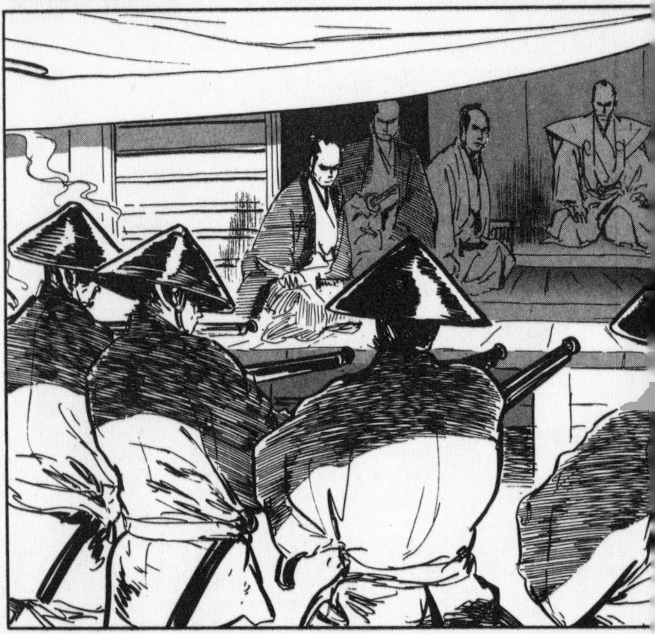

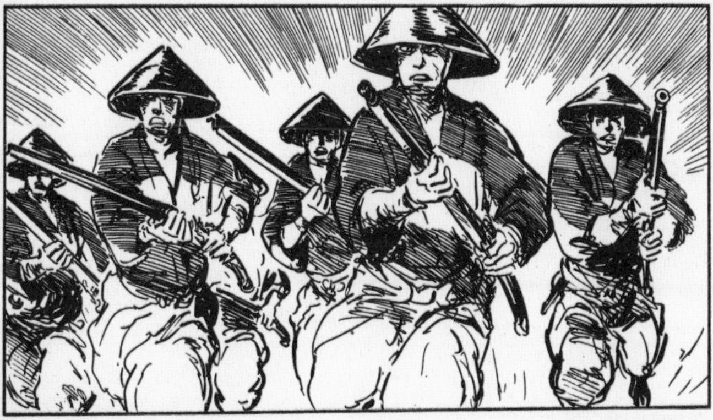

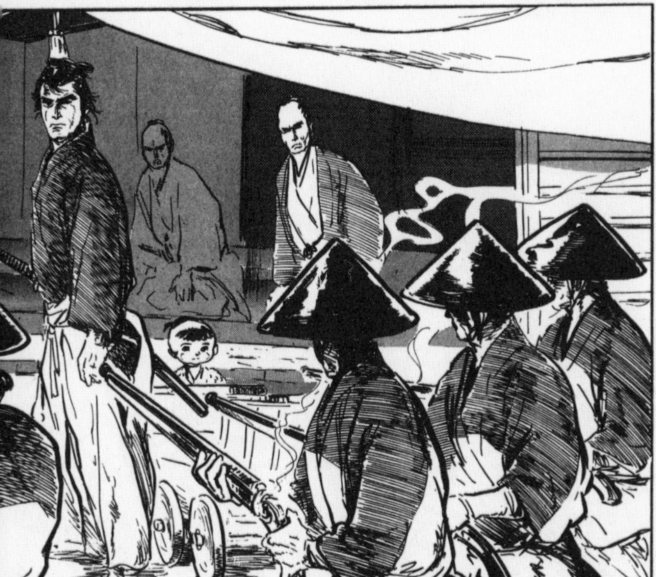

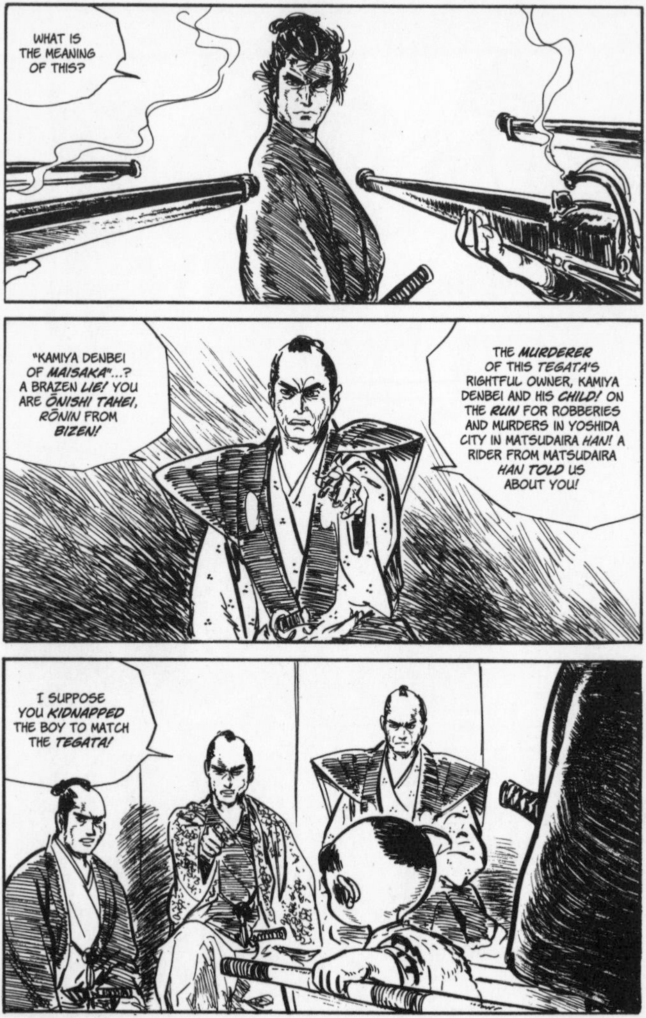
WHAT IS THE MEANING OF THIS?
"KAMIYA DENBEI OF *MAISAKA*"...? A BRAZEN *LIE!* YOU ARE *ŌNISHI TAHEI, RŌNIN* FROM *BIZEN!*
THE *MURDERER* OF THIS *TEGATA'S* RIGHTFUL OWNER, KAMIYA DENBEI AND HIS *CHILD!* ON THE *RUN* FOR ROBBERIES AND MURDERS IN YOSHIDA CITY IN MATSUDAIRA *HAN!* A RIDER FROM MATSUDAIRA *HAN TOLD* US ABOUT YOU!
I SUPPOSE YOU *KIDNAPPED* THE BOY TO MATCH THE *TEGATA!*

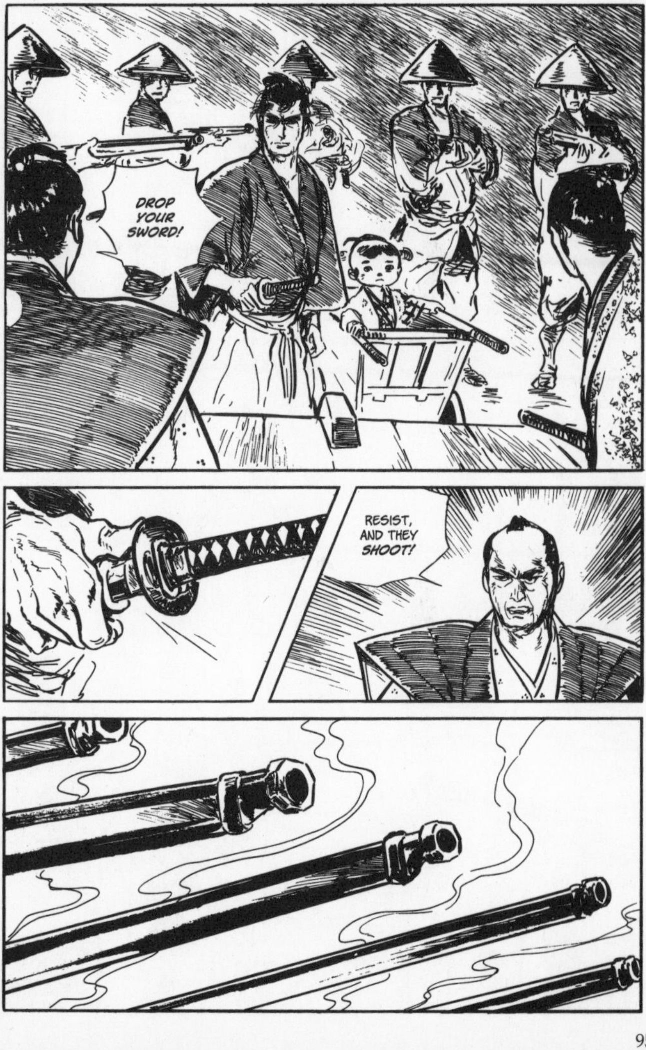
DROP YOUR SWORD!
RESIST, AND THEY SHOOT!

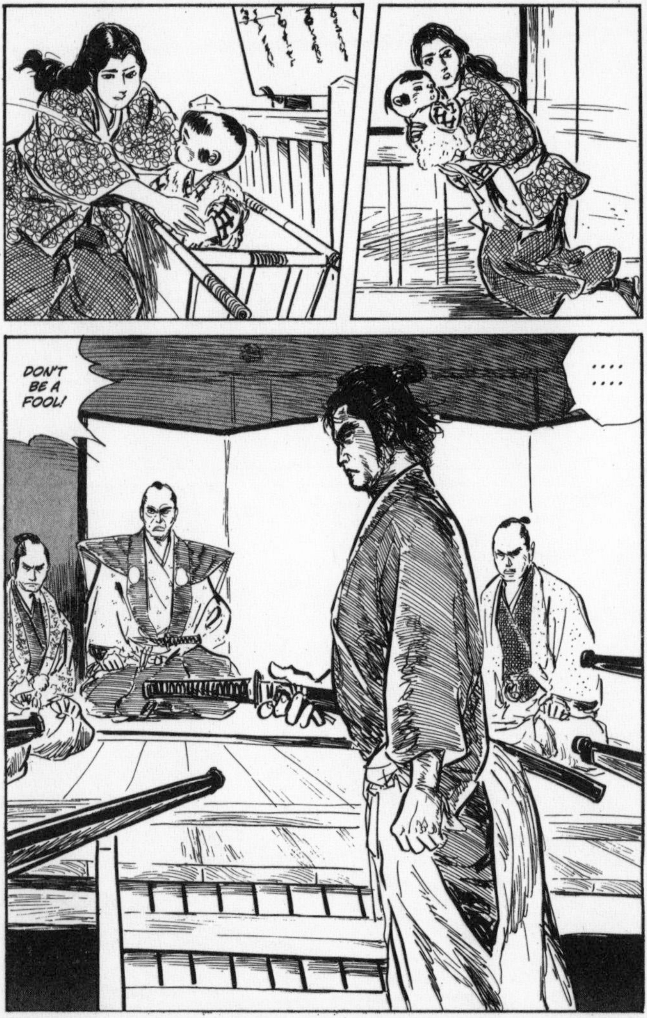
DON'T BE A FOOL!
....
....

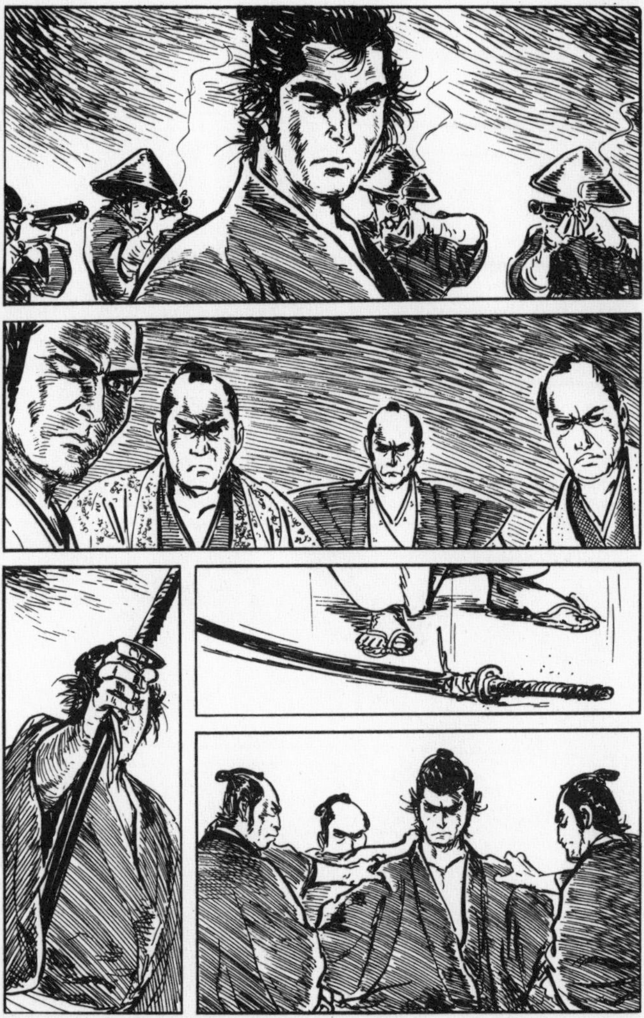

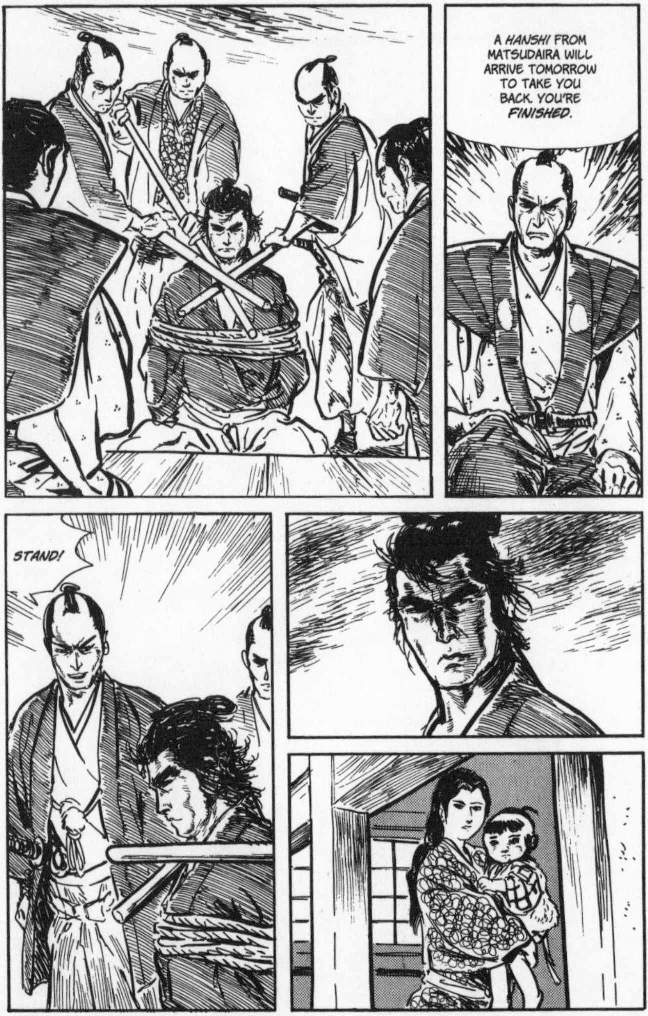
A *HANSHI* FROM MATSUDAIRA WILL ARRIVE TOMORROW TO TAKE YOU BACK. YOU'RE *FINISHED*.
*STAND!*

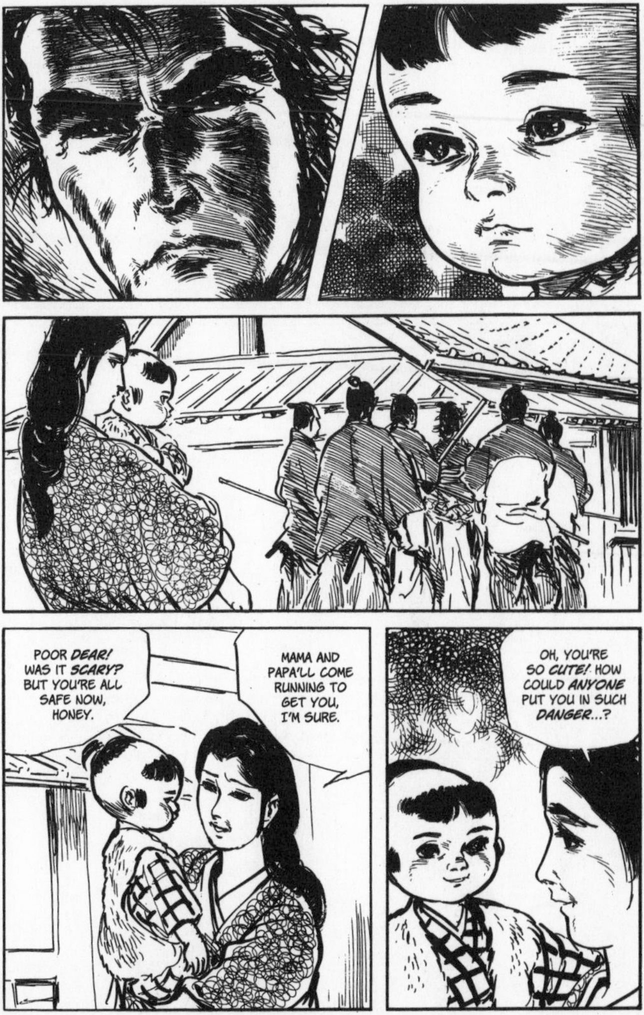
POOR DEAR! WAS IT SCARY? BUT YOU'RE ALL SAFE NOW, HONEY.
MAMA AND PAPA'LL COME RUNNING TO GET YOU, I'M SURE.
OH, YOU'RE SO CUTE! HOW COULD ANYONE PUT YOU IN SUCH DANGER...?

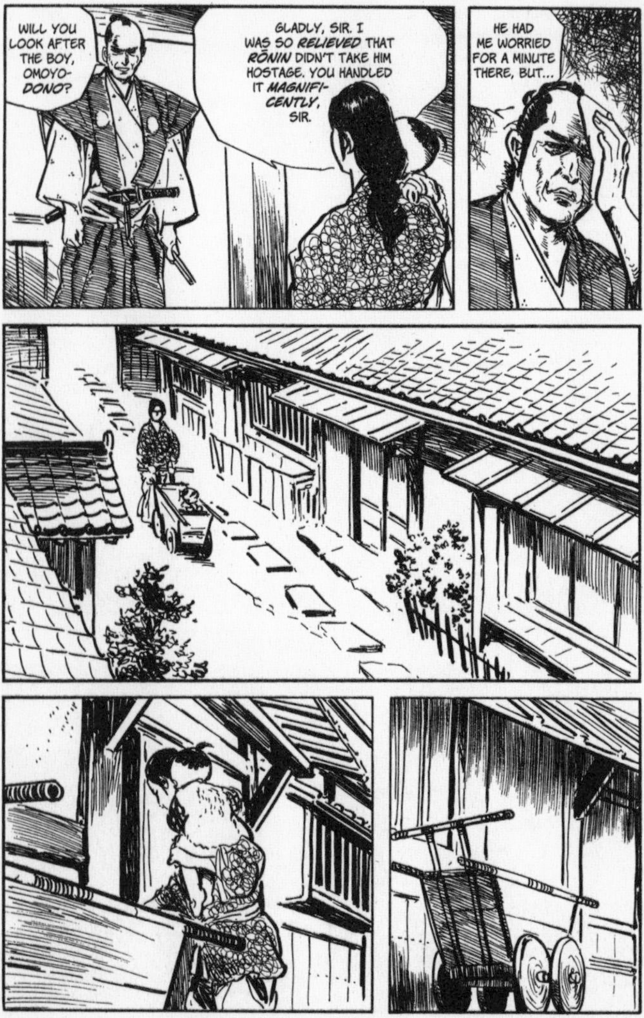
WILL YOU LOOK AFTER THE BOY, OMOYO-DONO?
GLADLY, SIR. I WAS SO RELIEVED THAT RŌNIN DIDN'T TAKE HIM HOSTAGE. YOU HANDLED IT MAGNIFICENTLY, SIR.
HE HAD ME WORRIED FOR A MINUTE THERE, BUT...

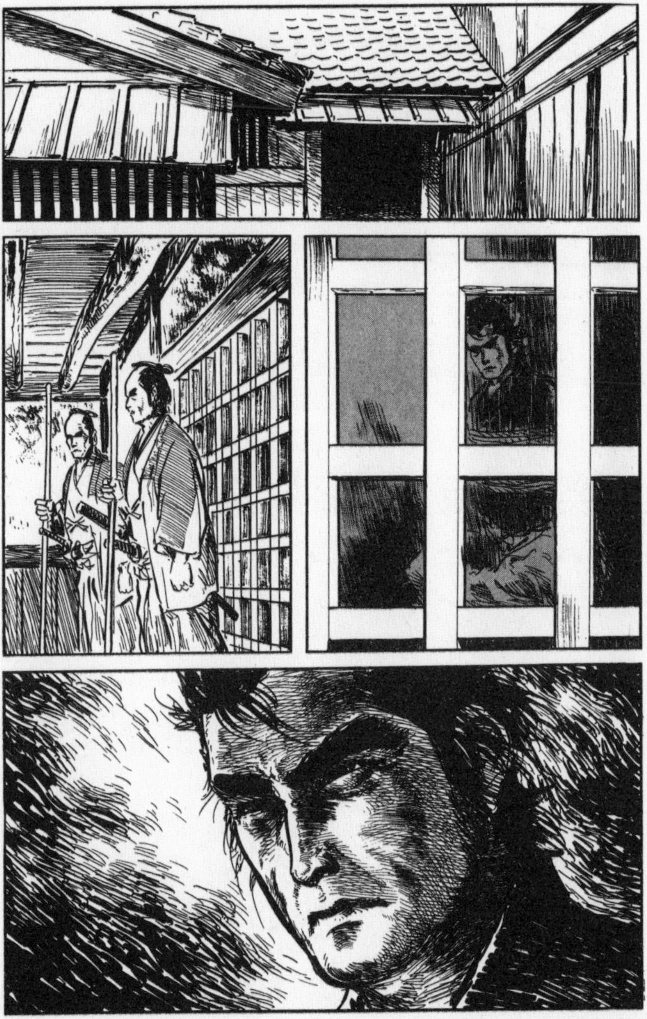

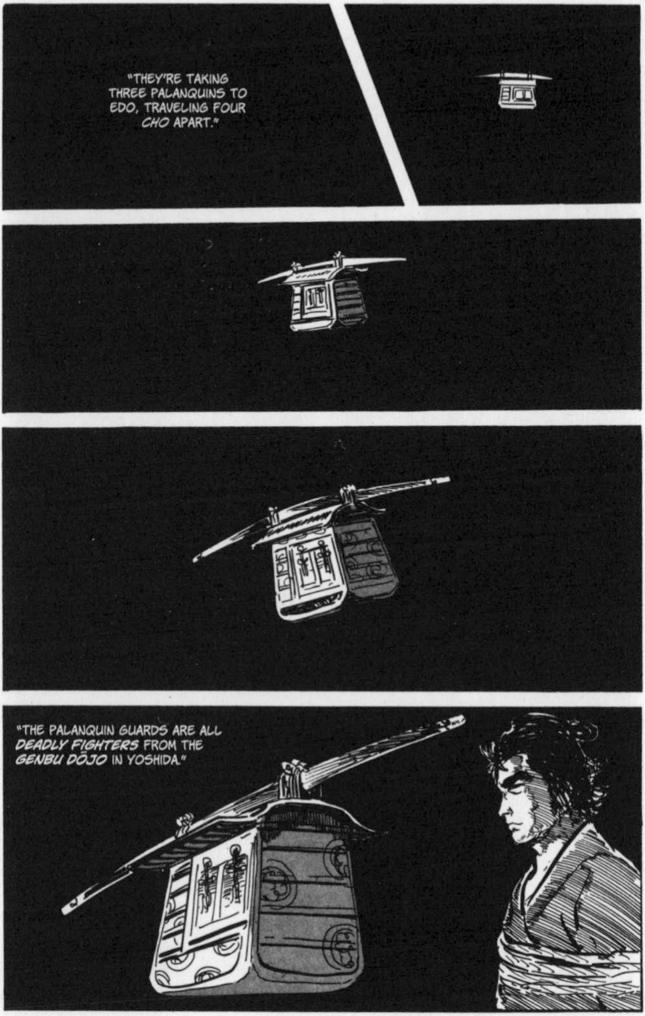
"THEY'RE TAKING THREE PALANQUINS TO EDO, TRAVELING FOUR *CHO* APART."
"THE PALANQUIN GUARDS ARE ALL *DEADLY FIGHTERS* FROM THE *GENBU DŌJO* IN YOSHIDA."

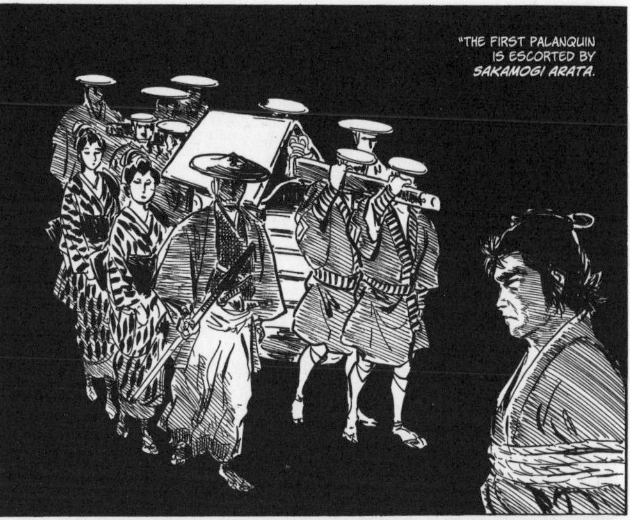
"THE FIRST PALANQUIN IS ESCORTED BY *SAKAMOGI ARATA*.

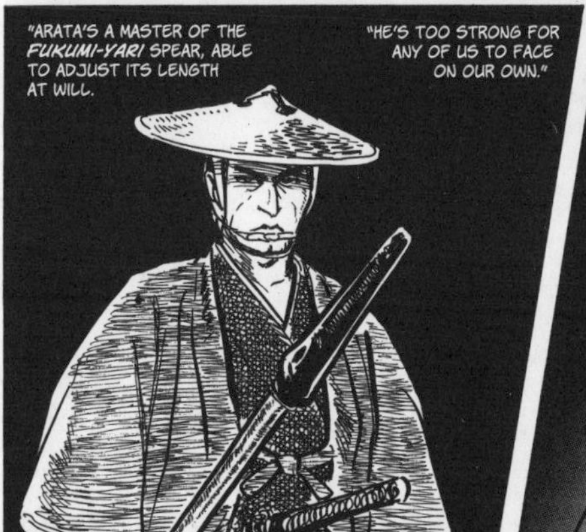
"ARATA'S A MASTER OF THE *FUKUMI-YARI* SPEAR, ABLE TO ADJUST ITS LENGTH AT WILL.
"HE'S TOO STRONG FOR ANY OF US TO FACE ON OUR OWN."

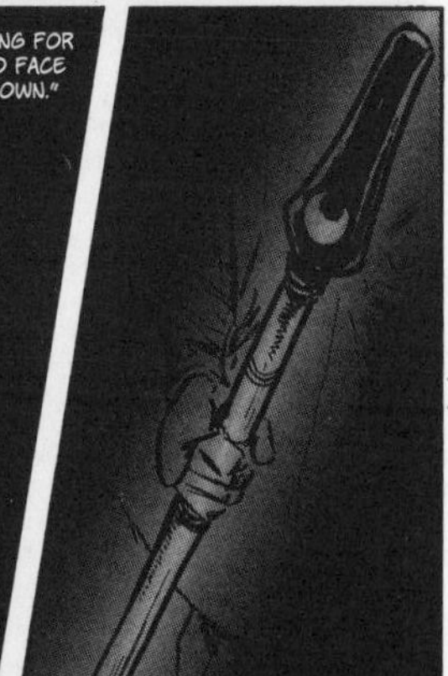

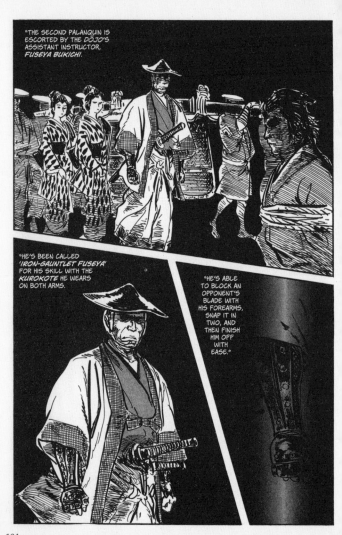

"THE SECOND PALANQUIN IS ESCORTED BY THE DOJO'S ASSISTANT INSTRUCTOR, *FUSEYA BUKICHI.*

"HE'S BEEN CALLED *'IRON-GAUNTLET FUSEYA'* FOR HIS SKILL WITH THE *KUROKOTE* HE WEARS ON BOTH ARMS.

"HE'S ABLE TO BLOCK AN OPPONENT'S BLADE WITH HIS FOREARMS, SNAP IT IN TWO, AND THEN FINISH HIM OFF WITH EASE."

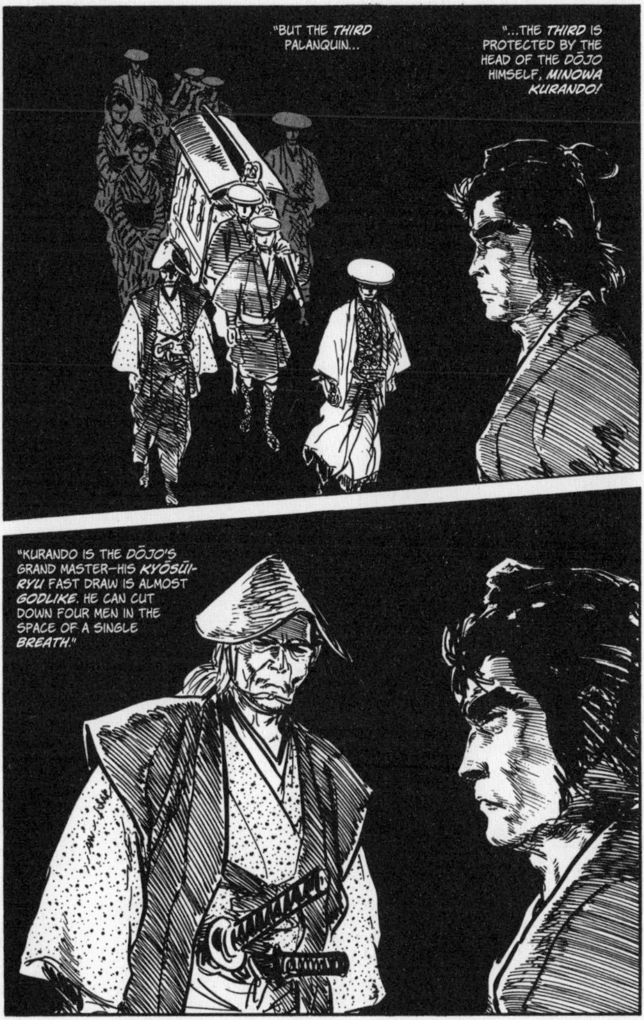
"BUT THE THIRD PALANQUIN...
"...THE THIRD IS PROTECTED BY THE HEAD OF THE DŌJO HIMSELF, MINOWA KURANDO!
"KURANDO IS THE DŌJO'S GRAND MASTER—HIS KYŌSŪI-RYU FAST DRAW IS ALMOST GODLIKE. HE CAN CUT DOWN FOUR MEN IN THE SPACE OF A SINGLE BREATH."

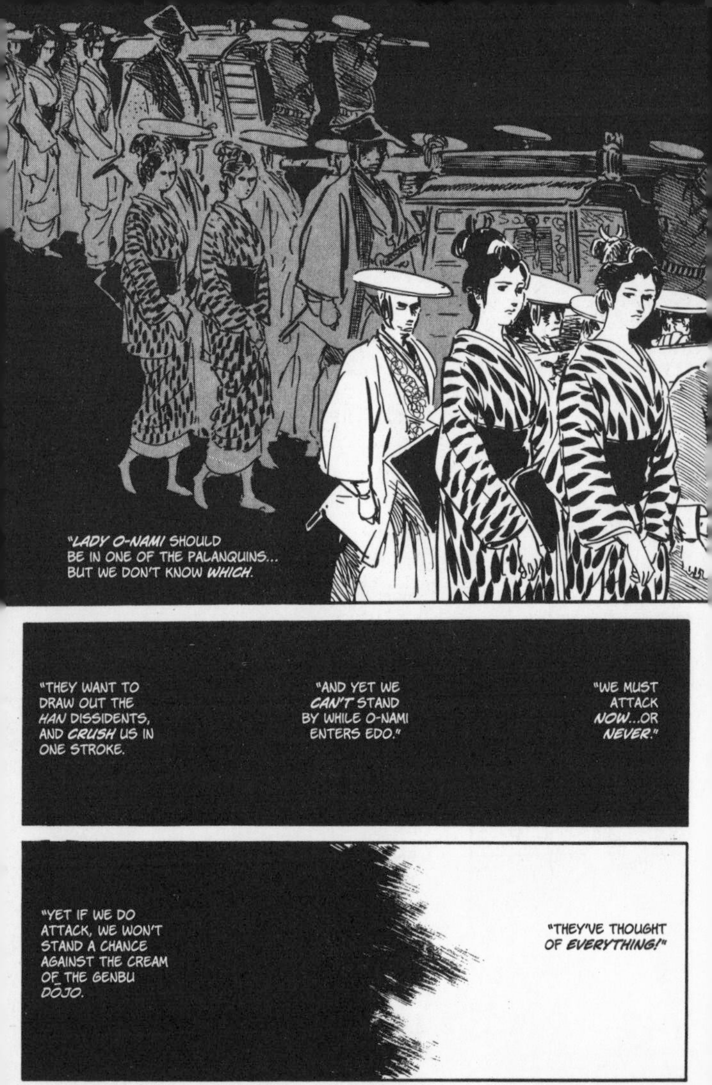
"*LADY O-NAMI* SHOULD BE IN ONE OF THE PALANQUINS... BUT WE DON'T KNOW *WHICH*.
"THEY WANT TO DRAW OUT THE *HAN* DISSIDENTS, AND *CRUSH* US IN ONE STROKE.
"AND YET WE *CAN'T* STAND BY WHILE O-NAMI ENTERS EDO."
"WE MUST ATTACK *NOW*...OR *NEVER*."
"YET IF WE DO ATTACK, WE WON'T STAND A CHANCE AGAINST THE CREAM OF THE GENBU *DŌJO*.
"THEY'VE THOUGHT OF *EVERYTHING!*"

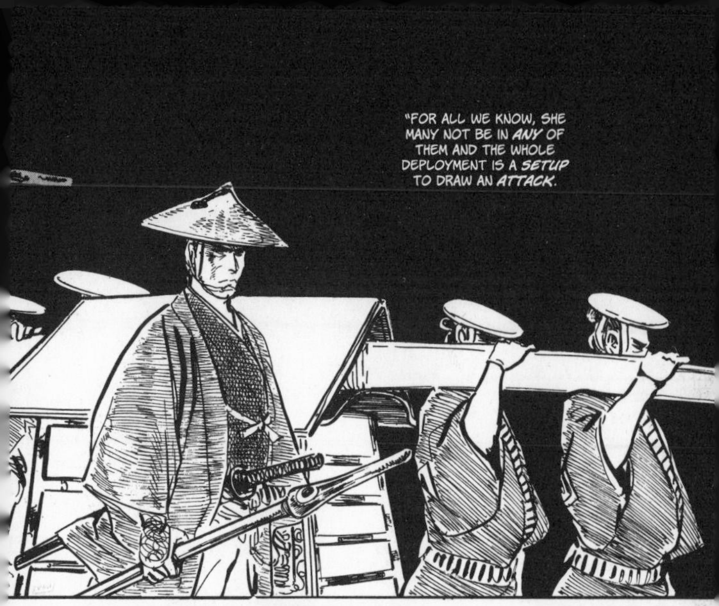
"FOR ALL WE KNOW, SHE MANY NOT BE IN ANY OF THEM AND THE WHOLE DEPLOYMENT IS A SETUP TO DRAW AN ATTACK.

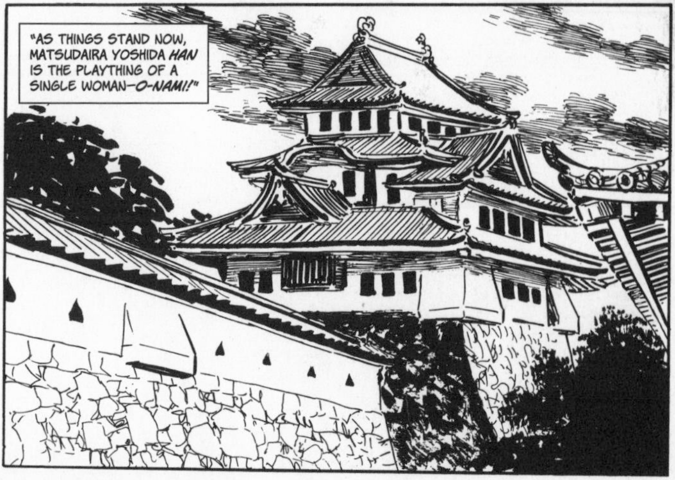
"AS THINGS STAND NOW, MATSUDAIRA YOSHIDA HAN IS THE PLAYTHING OF A SINGLE WOMAN—O-NAMI!"

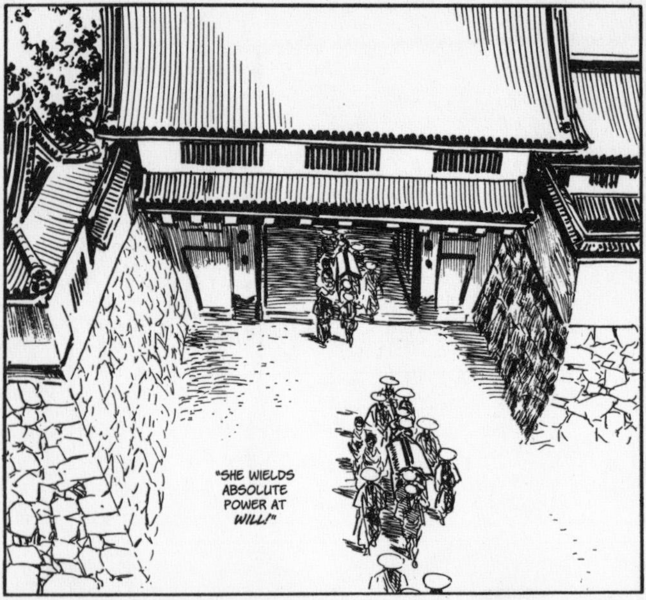
"SHE WIELDS ABSOLUTE POWER AT *WILL!*"

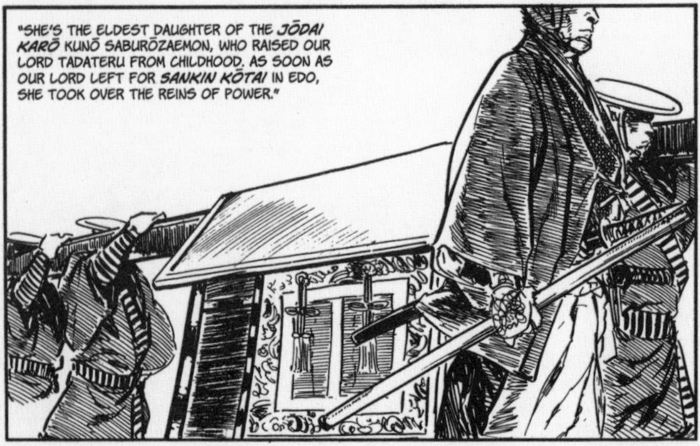
"SHE'S THE ELDEST DAUGHTER OF THE *JŌDAI KARŌ* KUNŌ SABURŌZAEMON, WHO RAISED OUR LORD TADATERU FROM CHILDHOOD. AS SOON AS OUR LORD LEFT FOR *SANKIN KŌTAI* IN EDO, SHE TOOK OVER THE REINS OF POWER."

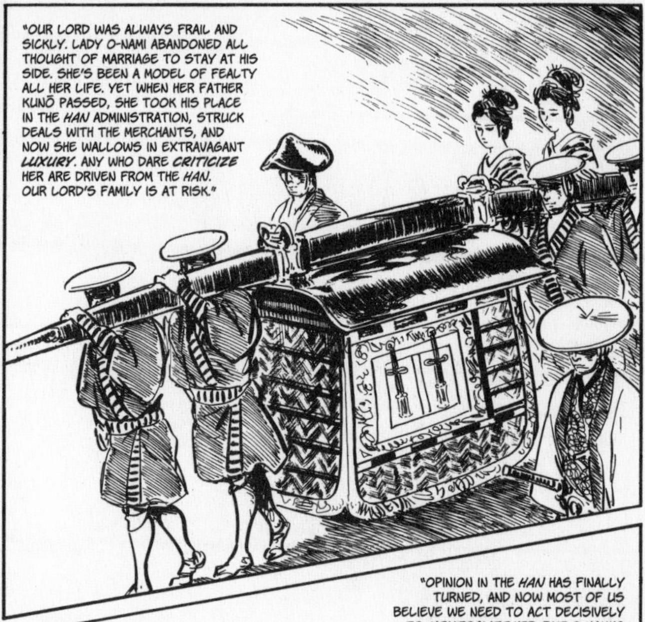
"OUR LORD WAS ALWAYS FRAIL AND SICKLY. LADY O-NAMI ABANDONED ALL THOUGHT OF MARRIAGE TO STAY AT HIS SIDE. SHE'S BEEN A MODEL OF FEALTY ALL HER LIFE. YET WHEN HER FATHER KUNŌ PASSED, SHE TOOK HIS PLACE IN THE *HAN* ADMINISTRATION, STRUCK DEALS WITH THE MERCHANTS, AND NOW SHE WALLOWS IN EXTRAVAGANT ***LUXURY***. ANY WHO DARE ***CRITICIZE*** HER ARE DRIVEN FROM THE *HAN*. OUR LORD'S FAMILY IS AT RISK."

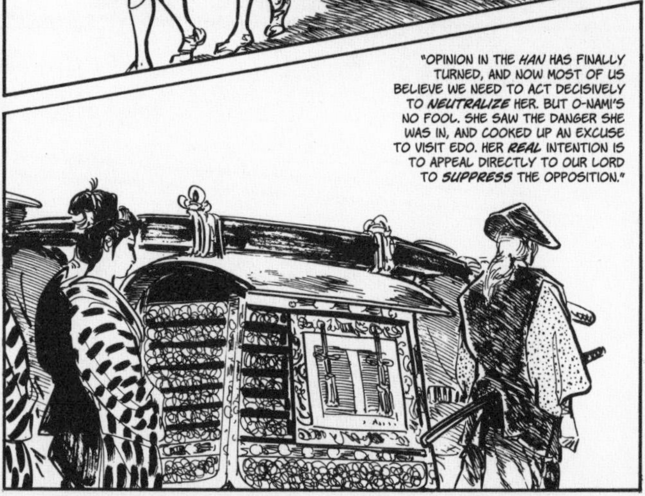
"OPINION IN THE *HAN* HAS FINALLY TURNED, AND NOW MOST OF US BELIEVE WE NEED TO ACT DECISIVELY TO ***NEUTRALIZE*** HER. BUT O-NAMI'S NO FOOL. SHE SAW THE DANGER SHE WAS IN, AND COOKED UP AN EXCUSE TO VISIT EDO. HER ***REAL*** INTENTION IS TO APPEAL DIRECTLY TO OUR LORD TO ***SUPPRESS*** THE OPPOSITION."

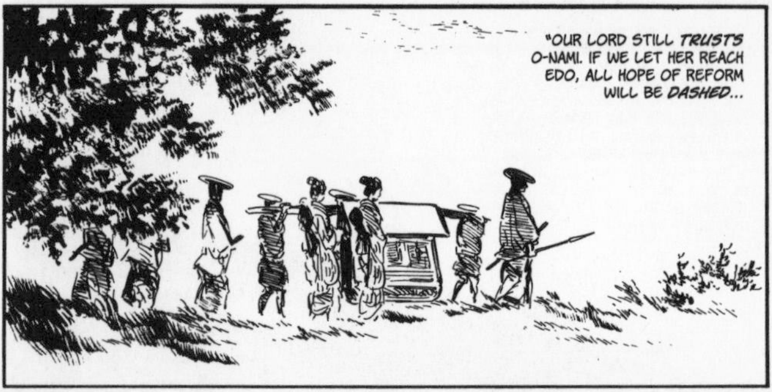
"OUR LORD STILL TRUSTS O-NAMI. IF WE LET HER REACH EDO, ALL HOPE OF REFORM WILL BE DASHED...

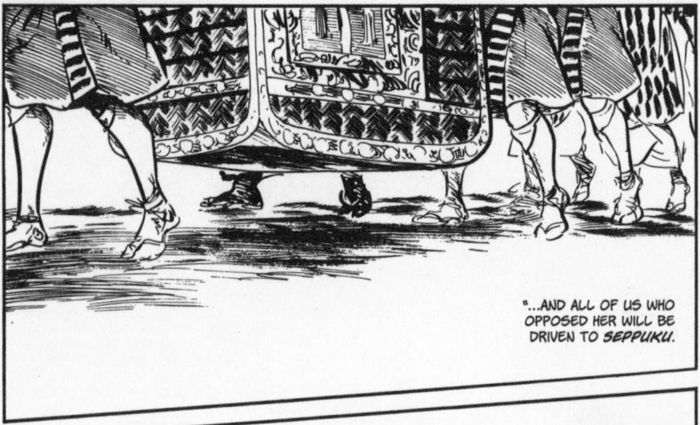
"...AND ALL OF US WHO OPPOSED HER WILL BE DRIVEN TO SEPPUKU.

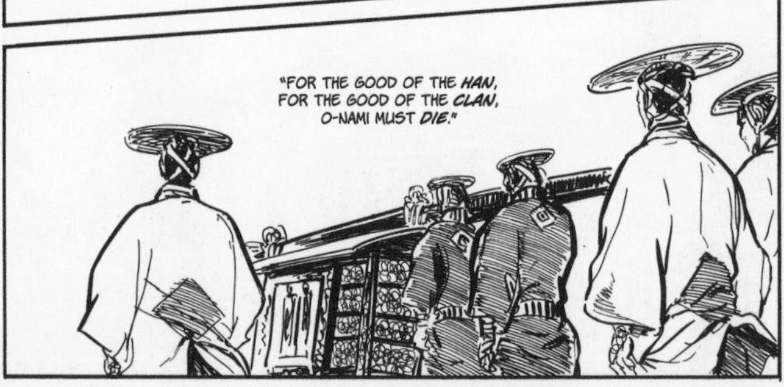
"FOR THE GOOD OF THE HAN, FOR THE GOOD OF THE CLAN, O-NAMI MUST DIE."

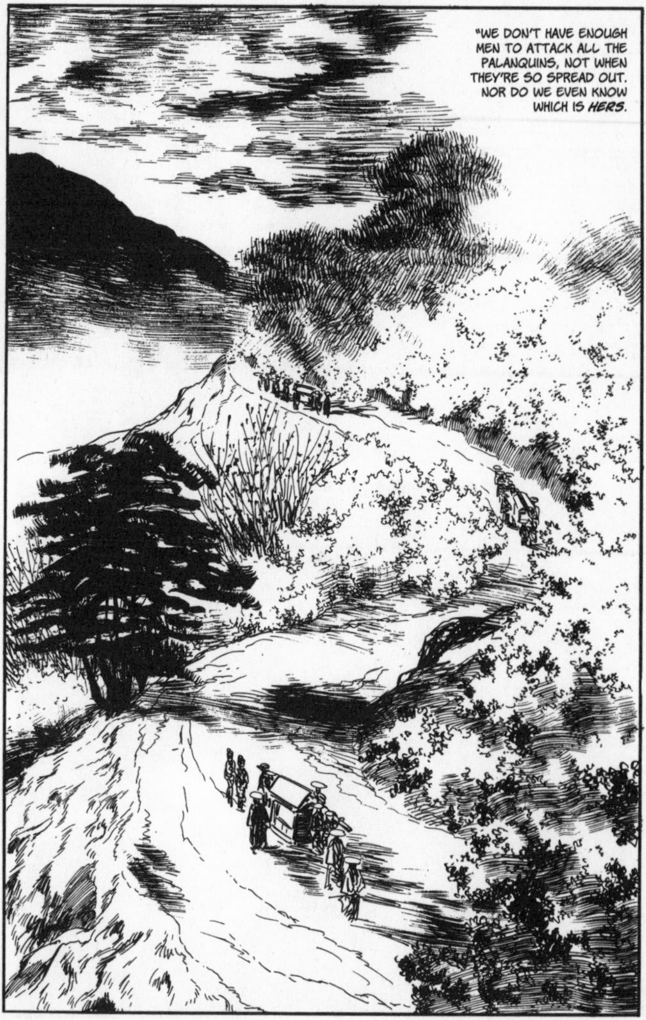
"WE DON'T HAVE ENOUGH MEN TO ATTACK ALL THE PALANQUINS, NOT WHEN THEY'RE SO SPREAD OUT. NOR DO WE EVEN KNOW WHICH IS *HERS*.

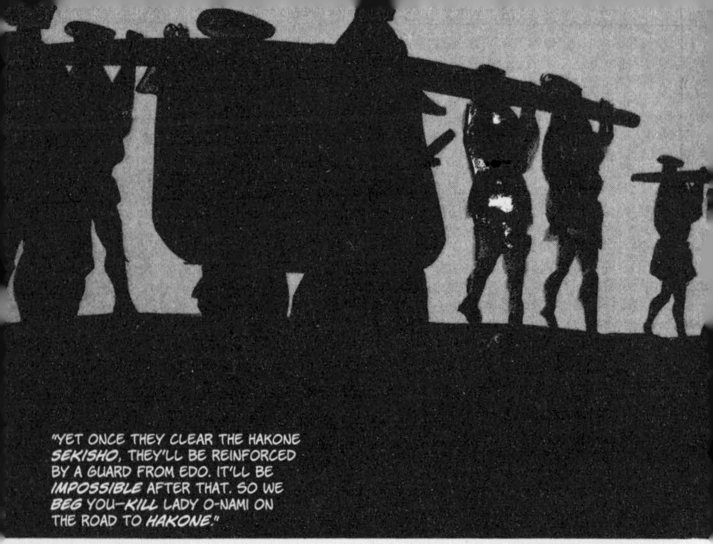
"YET ONCE THEY CLEAR THE HAKONE SEKISHO, THEY'LL BE REINFORCED BY A GUARD FROM EDO. IT'LL BE IMPOSSIBLE AFTER THAT. SO WE BEG YOU—KILL LADY O-NAMI ON THE ROAD TO HAKONE."

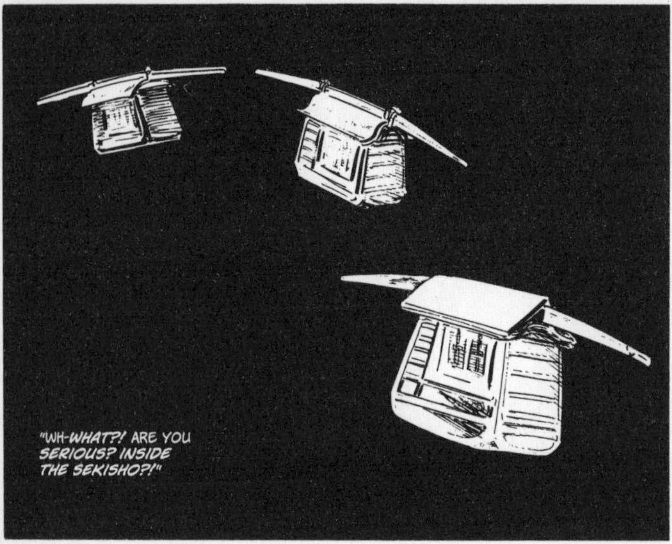
"WH-WHAT?! ARE YOU SERIOUS? INSIDE THE SEKISHO?!"

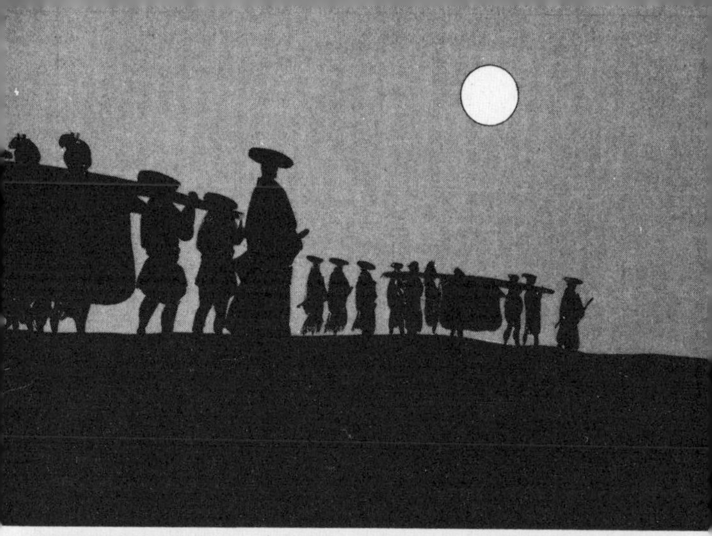

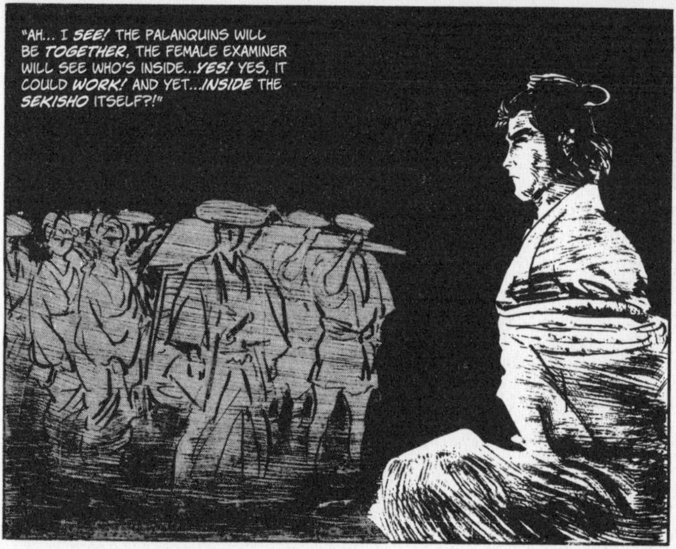
"AH... I SEE! THE PALANQUINS WILL BE TOGETHER, THE FEMALE EXAMINER WILL SEE WHO'S INSIDE...YES! YES, IT COULD WORK! AND YET...INSIDE THE SEKISHO ITSELF?!"

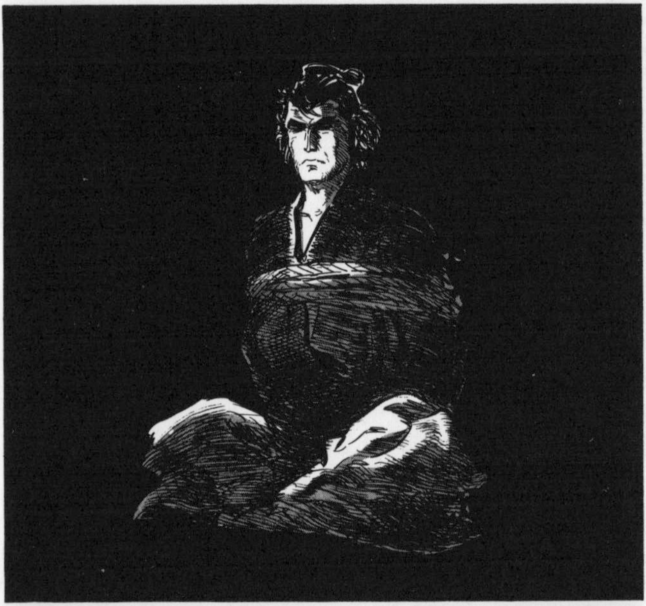

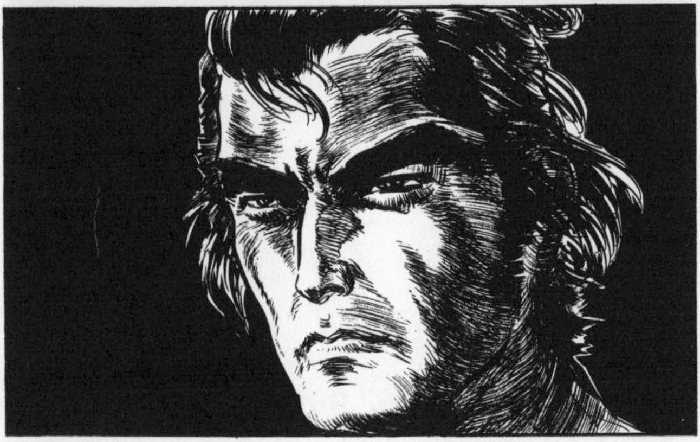

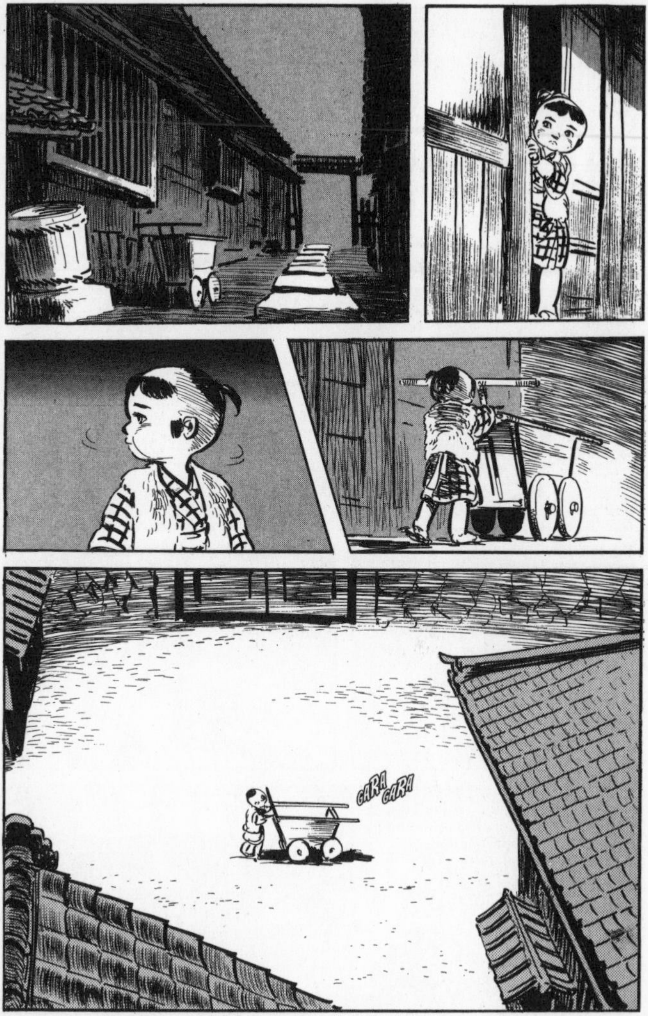
GARA
GARA

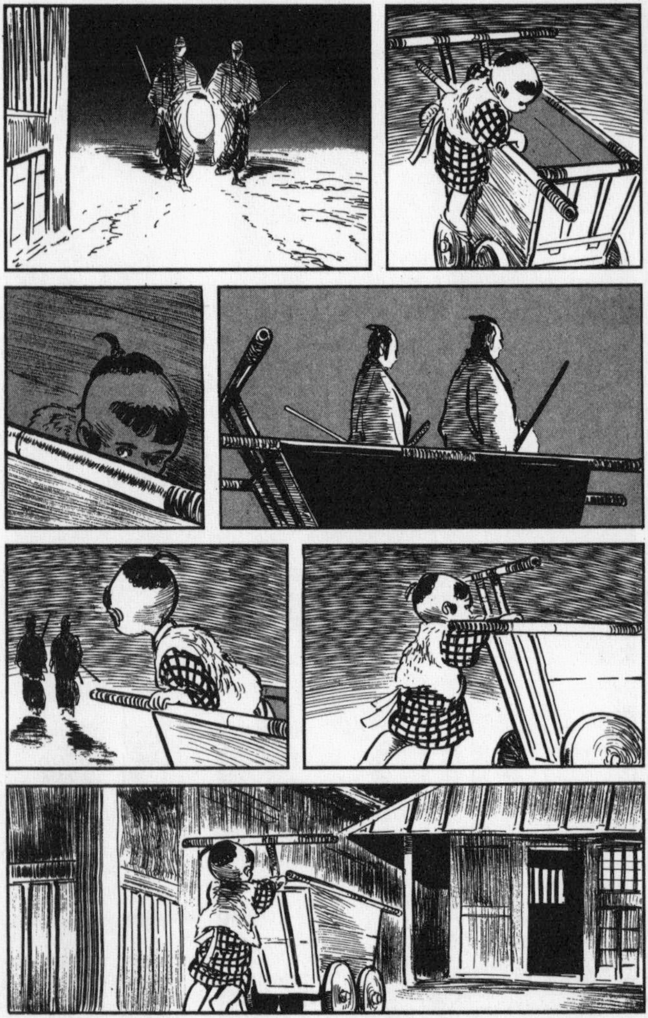

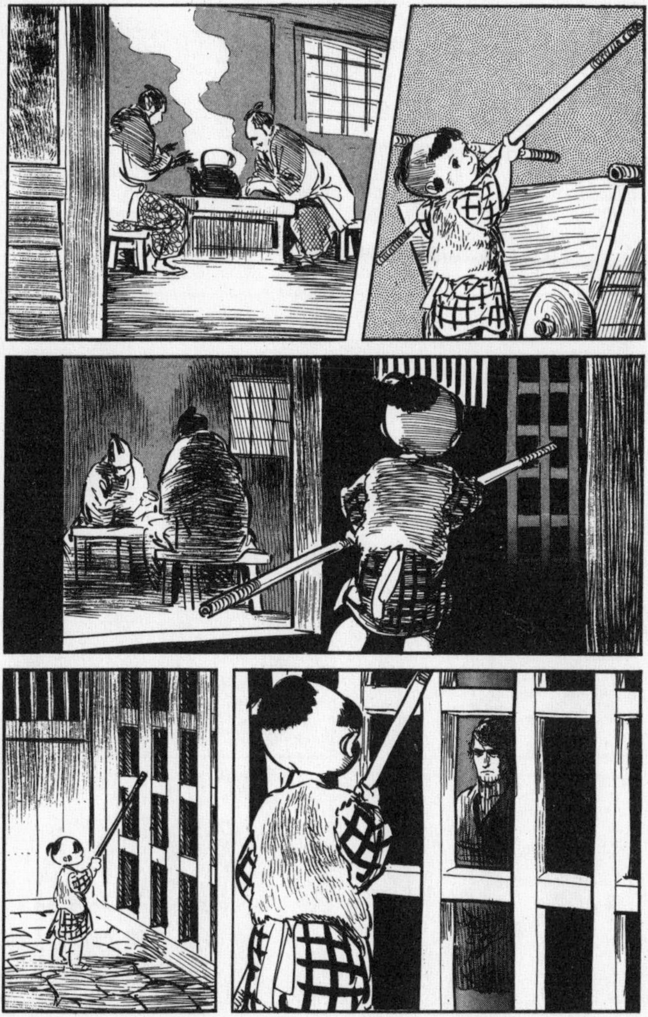

SHINNG

118

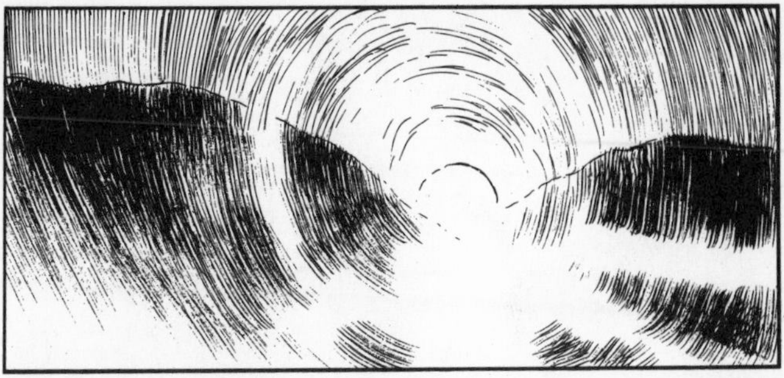
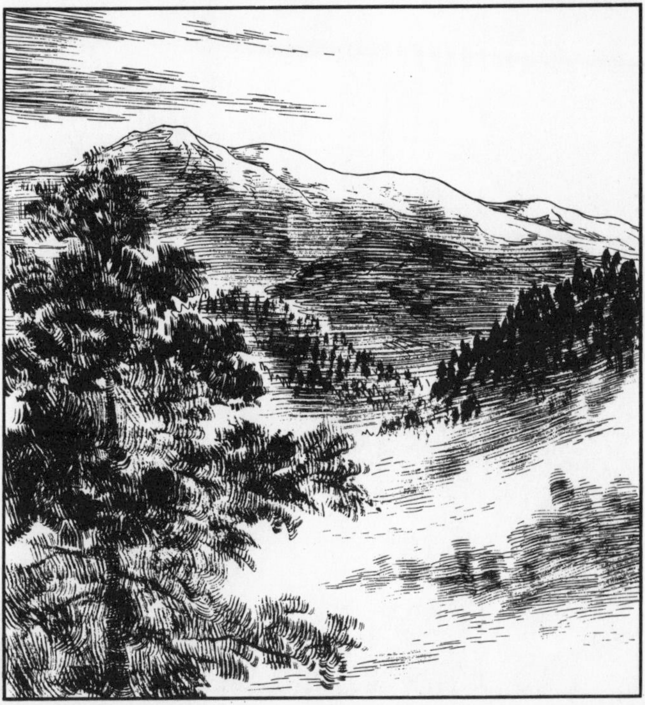

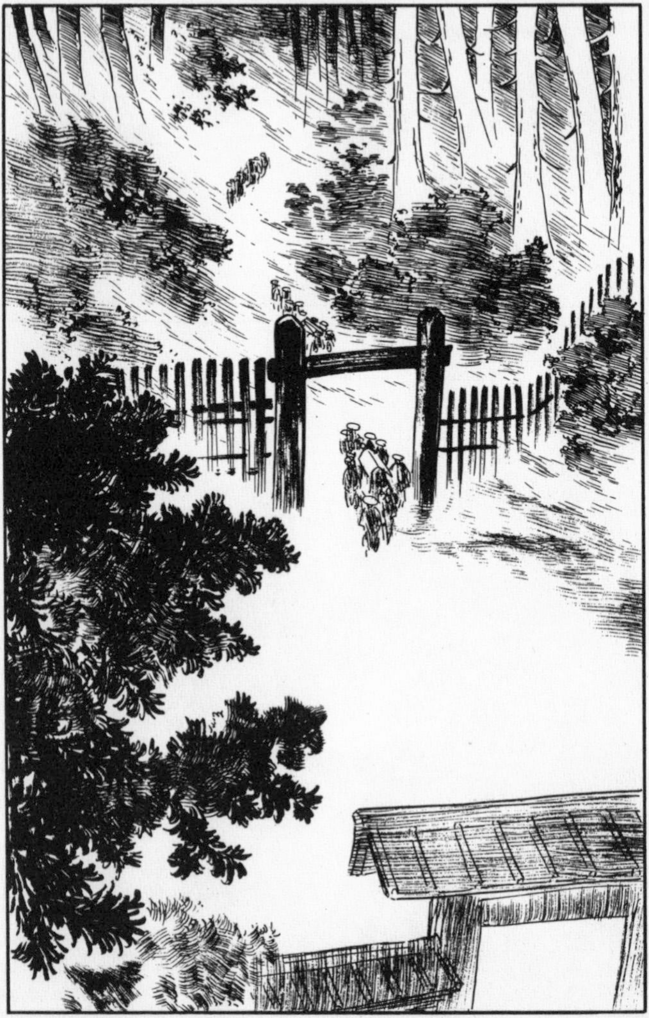

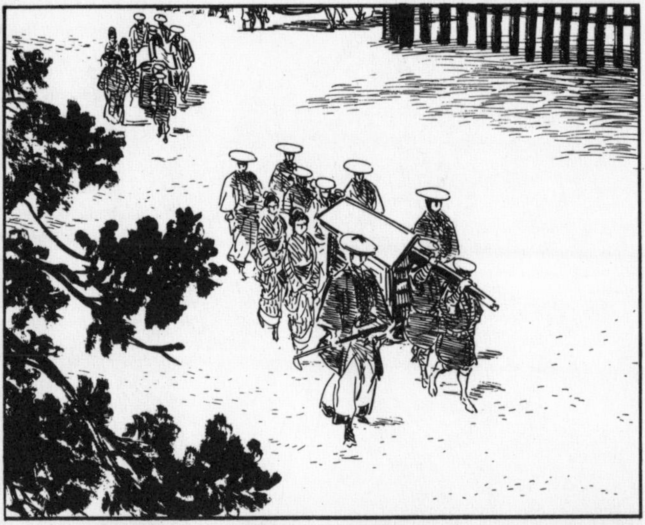
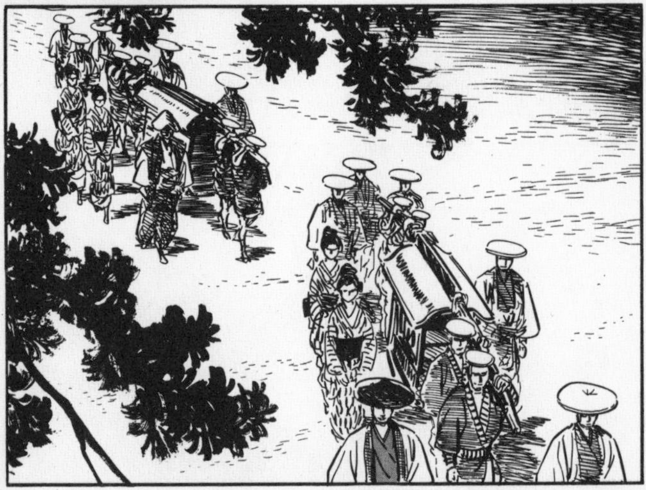

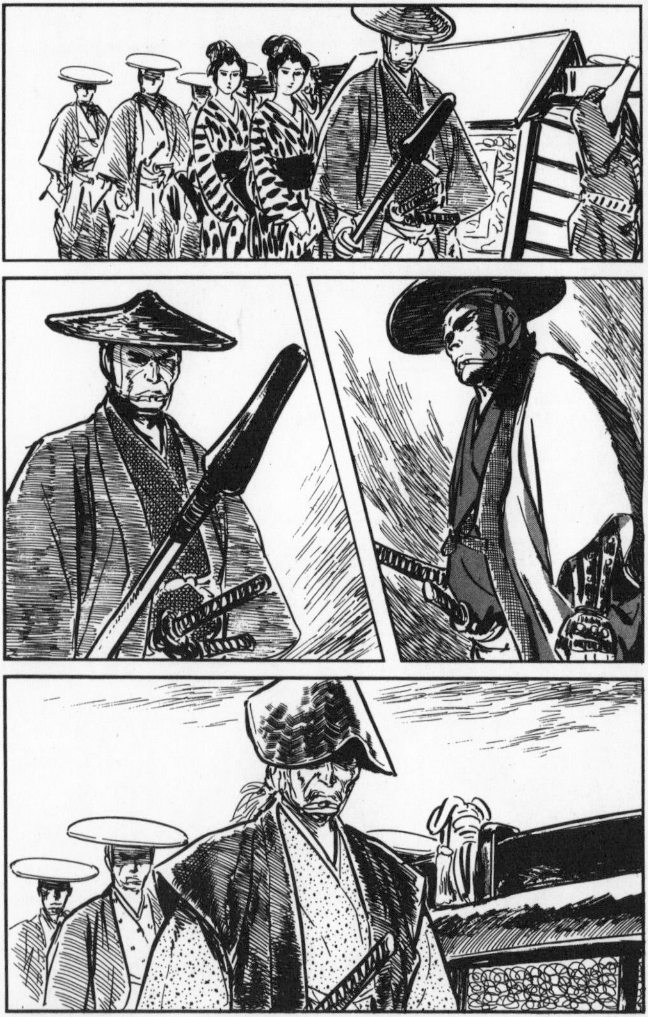

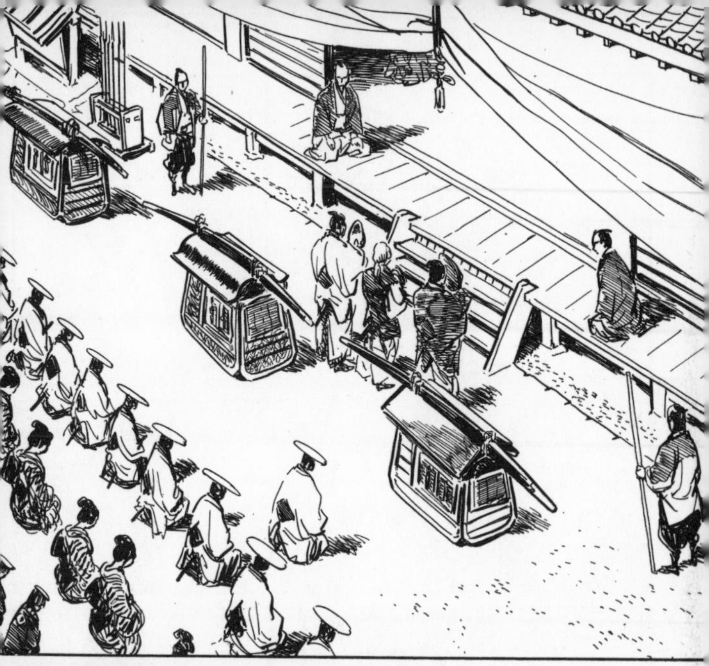
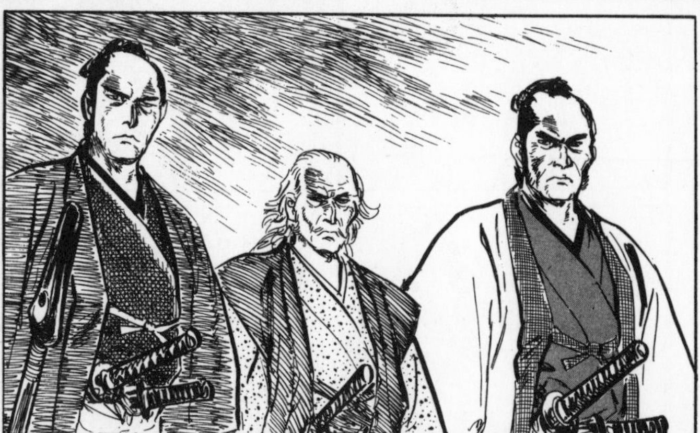

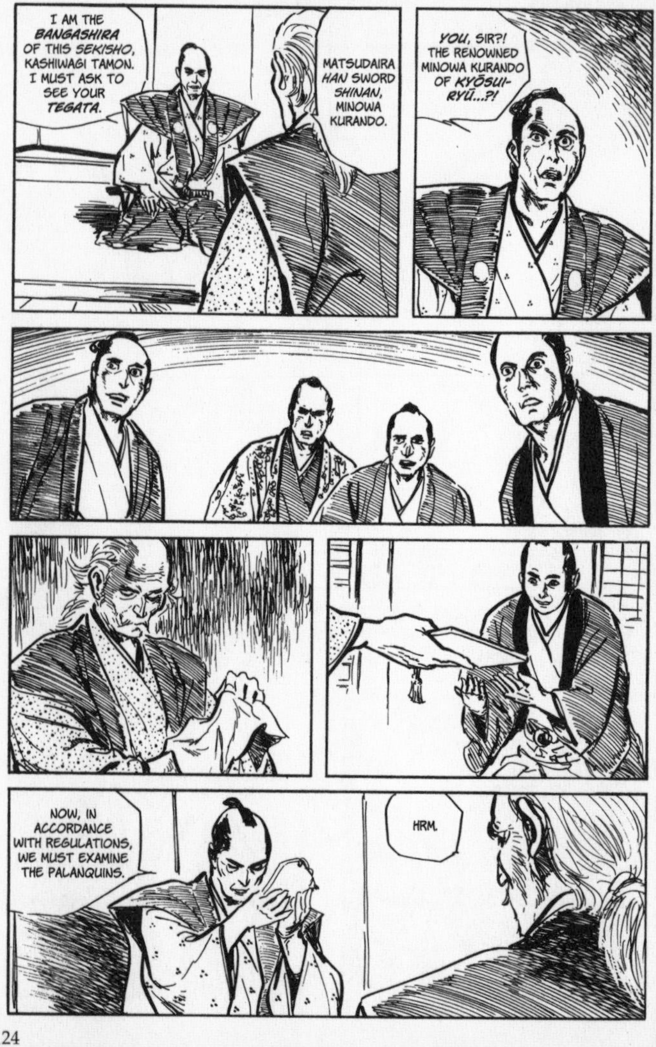
I AM THE *BANGASHIRA* OF THIS *SEKISHO*, KASHIWAGI TAMON. I MUST ASK TO SEE YOUR *TEGATA*.
MATSUDAIRA *HAN* SWORD *SHINAN*, MINOWA KURANDO.
*YOU*, SIR?! THE RENOWNED MINOWA KURANDO OF *KYŌSUI-RYŪ*...?!
NOW, IN ACCORDANCE WITH REGULATIONS, WE MUST EXAMINE THE PALANQUINS.
HRM.

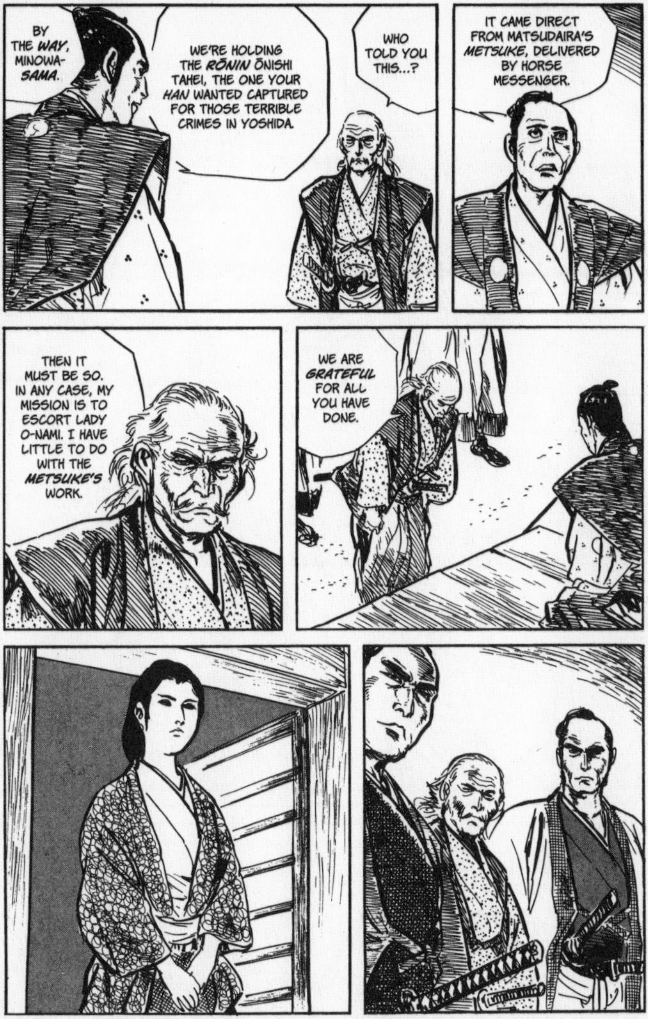
BY THE *WAY*, MINOWA-*SAMA*.
WE'RE HOLDING THE *RŌNIN* ŌNISHI TAHEI, THE ONE YOUR *HAN* WANTED CAPTURED FOR THOSE TERRIBLE CRIMES IN YOSHIDA.
WHO TOLD YOU THIS...?
IT CAME DIRECT FROM MATSUDAIRA'S *METSUKE*, DELIVERED BY HORSE MESSENGER.
THEN IT MUST BE SO. IN ANY CASE, MY MISSION IS TO ESCORT LADY O-NAMI. I HAVE LITTLE TO DO WITH THE *METSUKE'S* WORK.
WE ARE *GRATEFUL* FOR ALL YOU HAVE DONE.

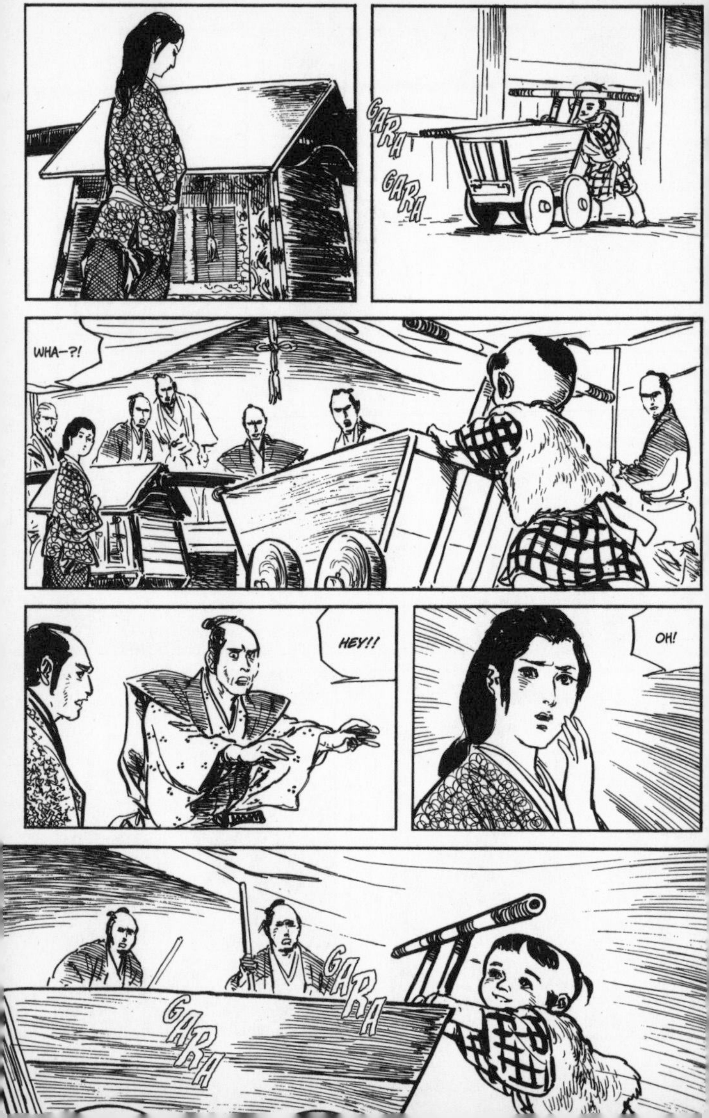
GARA
GARA
WHA–?!
HEY!!
OH!
GARA
GARA

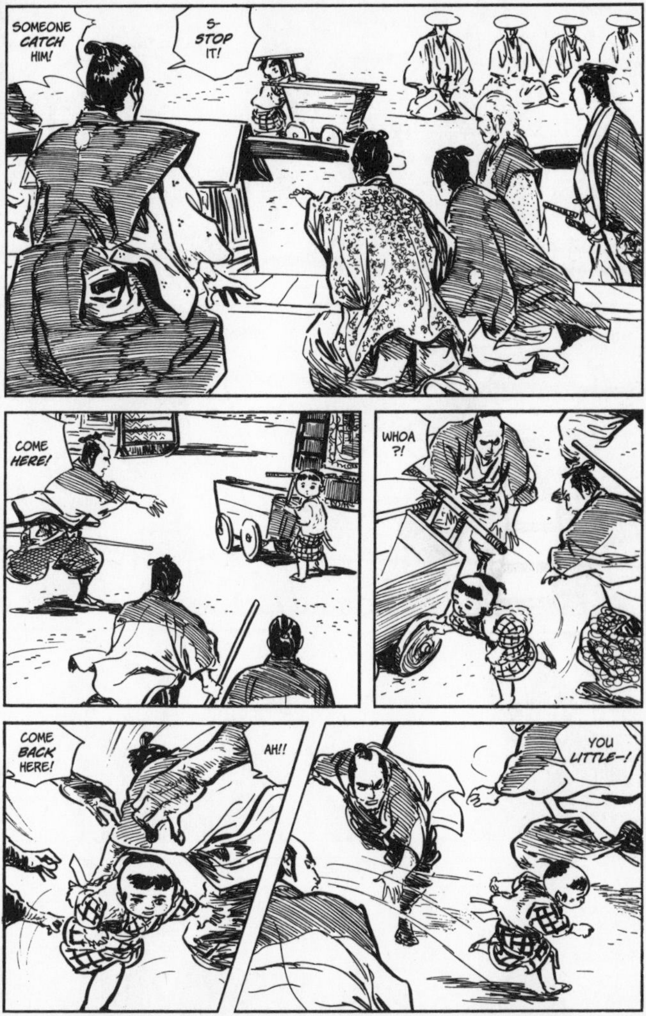
SOMEONE CATCH HIM!
S-STOP IT!
COME HERE!
WHOA?!
COME BACK HERE!
AH!!
YOU LITTLE-!

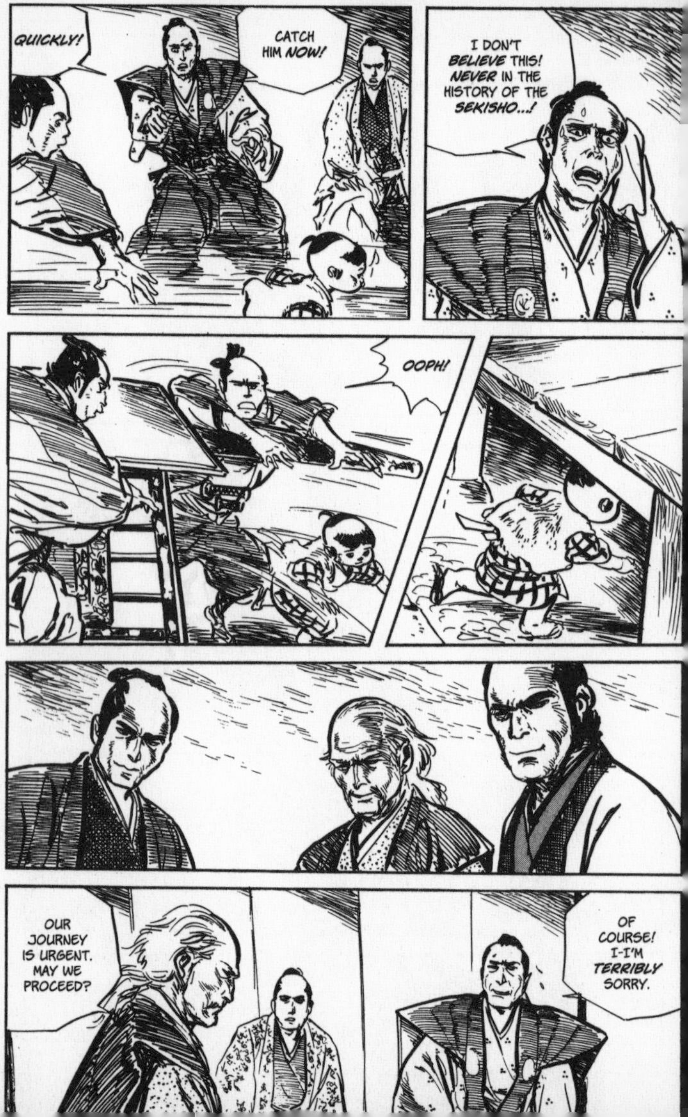
QUICKLY!
CATCH HIM NOW!
I DON'T BELIEVE THIS! NEVER IN THE HISTORY OF THE SEKISHO...!
OOPH!
OUR JOURNEY IS URGENT. MAY WE PROCEED?
OF COURSE! I-I'M TERRIBLY SORRY.

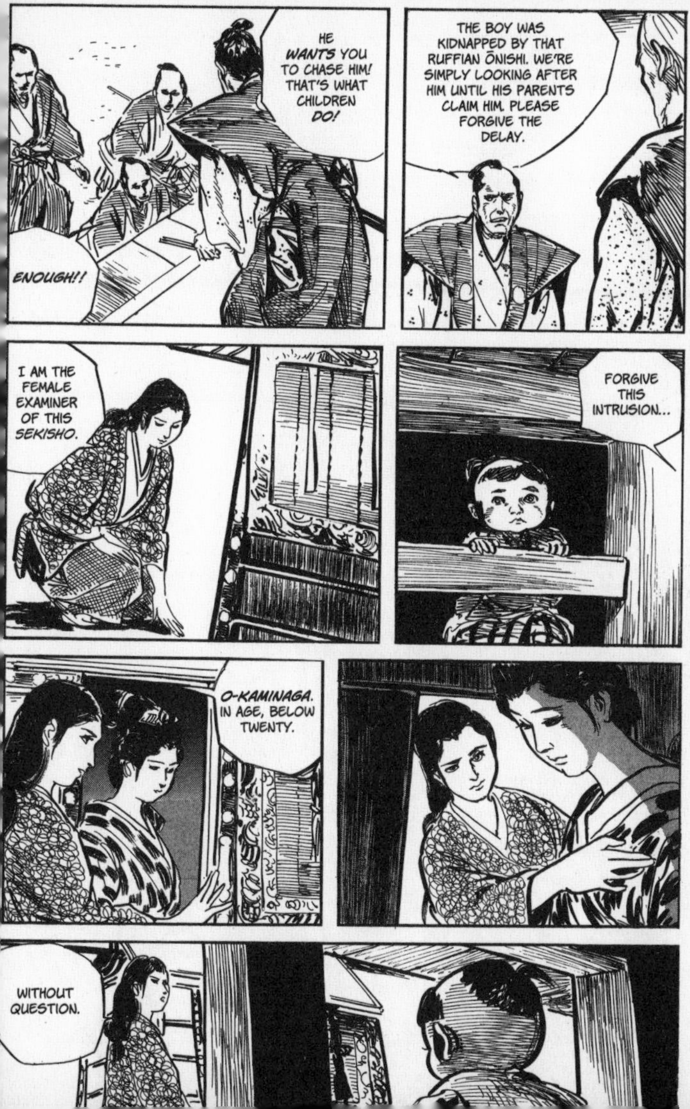
HE *WANTS* YOU TO CHASE HIM! THAT'S WHAT CHILDREN *DO!*
*ENOUGH!!*
THE BOY WAS KIDNAPPED BY THAT RUFFIAN ŌNISHI. WE'RE SIMPLY LOOKING AFTER HIM UNTIL HIS PARENTS CLAIM HIM. PLEASE FORGIVE THE DELAY.
I AM THE FEMALE EXAMINER OF THIS *SEKISHO*.
FORGIVE THIS INTRUSION...
O-KAMINAGA. IN AGE, BELOW TWENTY.
WITHOUT QUESTION.

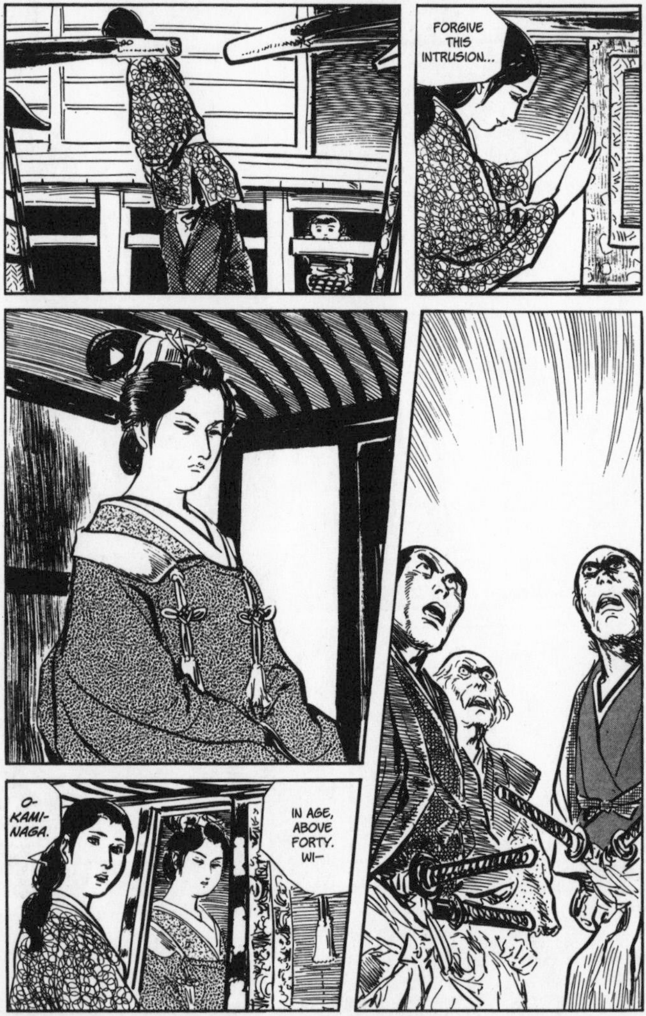
FORGIVE THIS INTRUSION...
O-KAMI-NAGA.
IN AGE, ABOVE FORTY. WI—

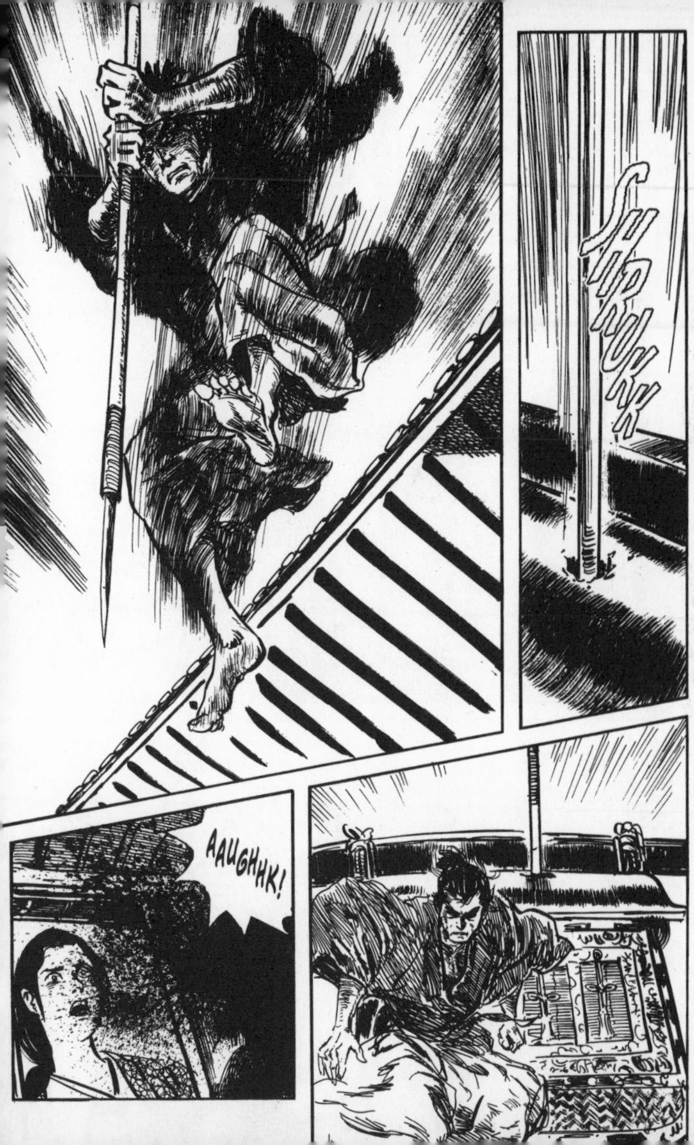
CHRUKK
AAUGHHK!

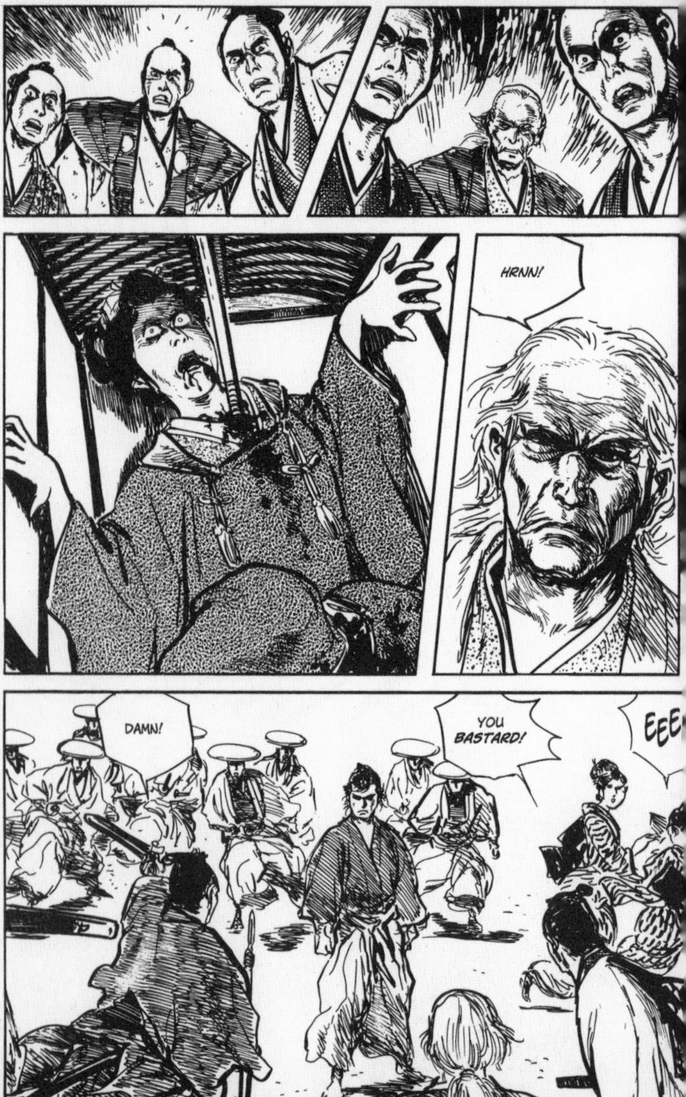
HRNN!
DAMN!
YOU BASTARD!
EEE

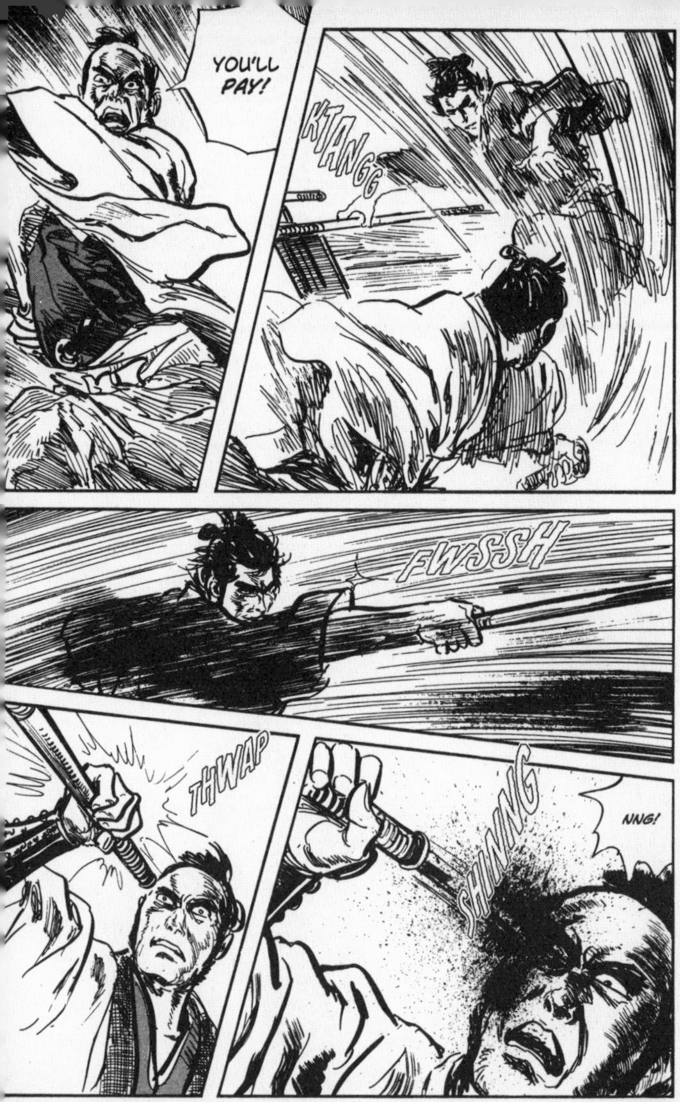
YOU'LL PAY!
KTANGG
FWSSH
THWAP
SHING
NNG!

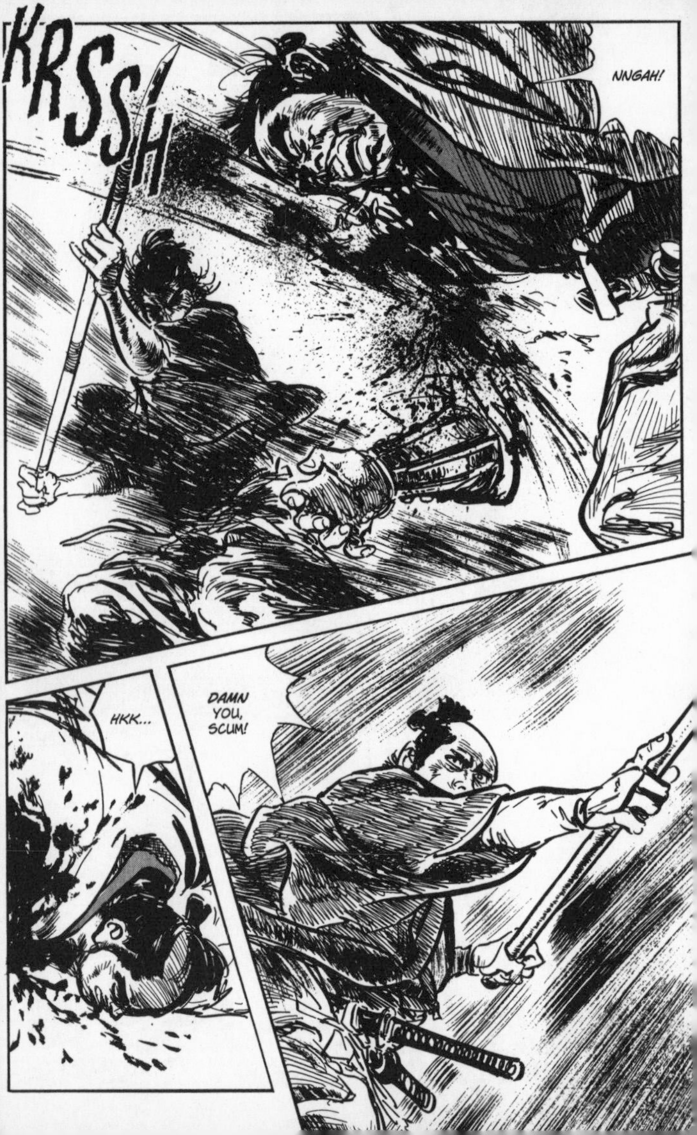
KRSSH
NNGAH!
HKK...
DAMN YOU, SCUM!

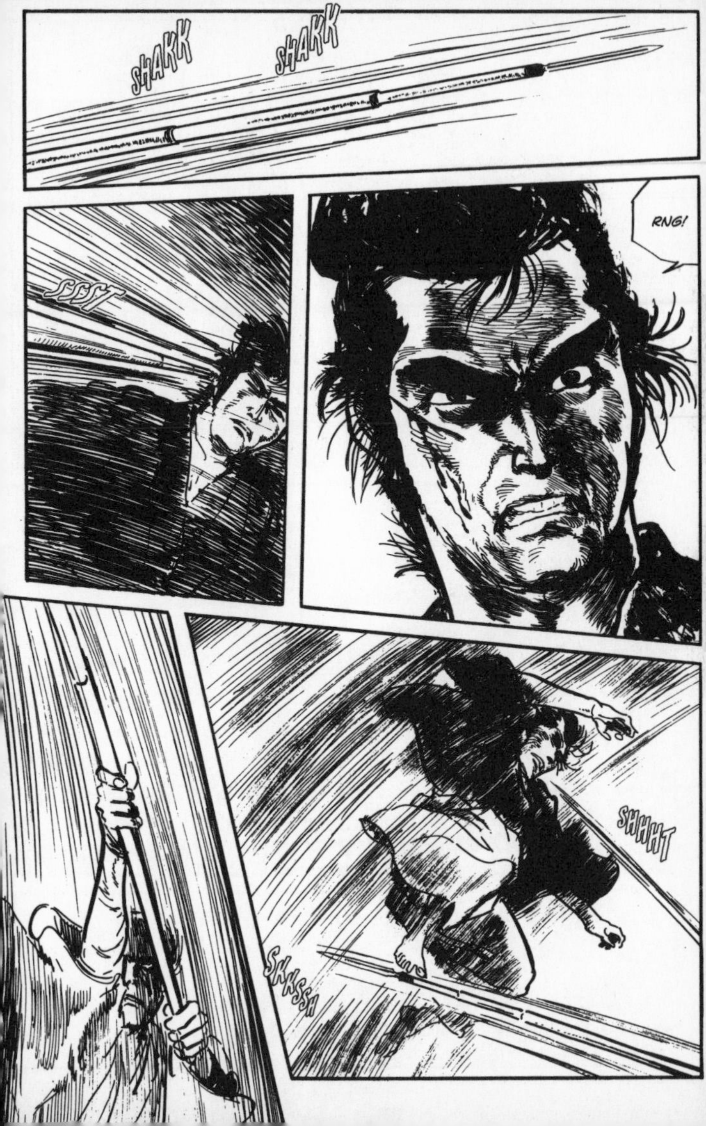
SHAKK
SHAKK
SSST
RNG!
SHHHT
SKKSSH

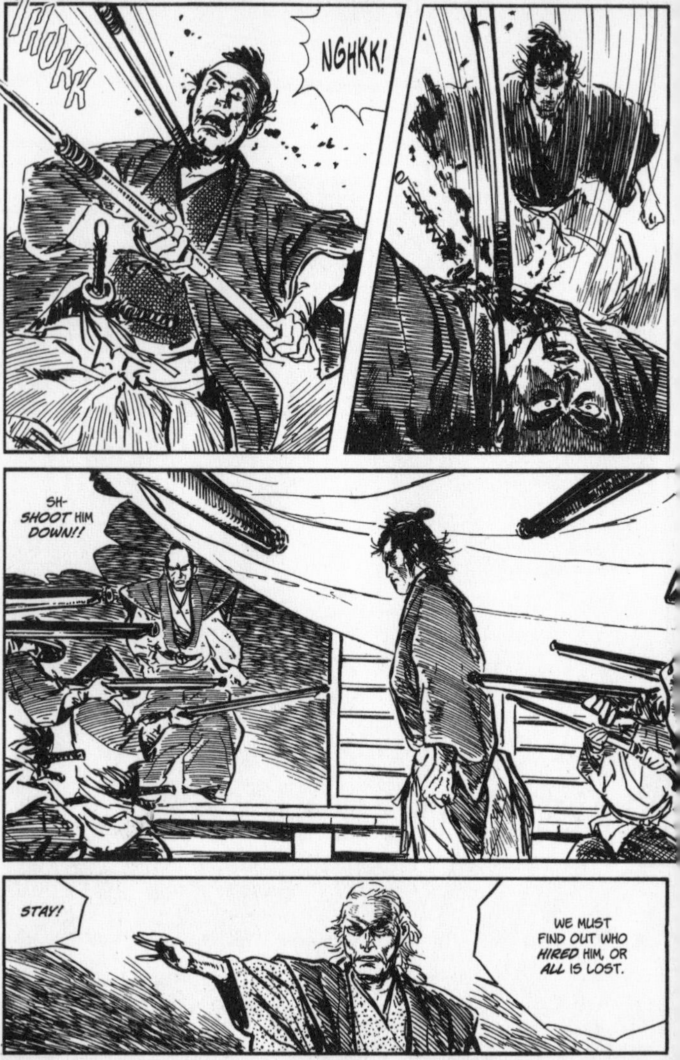

THUKK
NGHKK!
SH-SHOOT HIM DOWN!!
STAY!
WE MUST FIND OUT WHO HIRED HIM, OR ALL IS LOST.

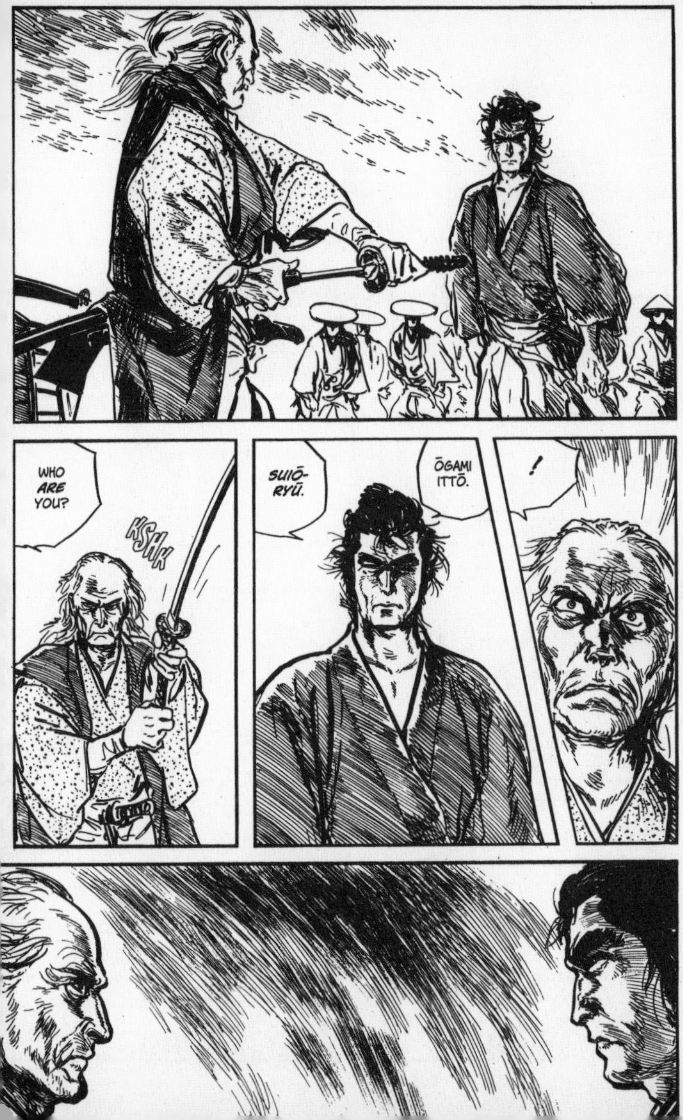
WHO ARE YOU?
KSHK
SUIŌ-RYŪ.
ŌGAMI ITTŌ.
!

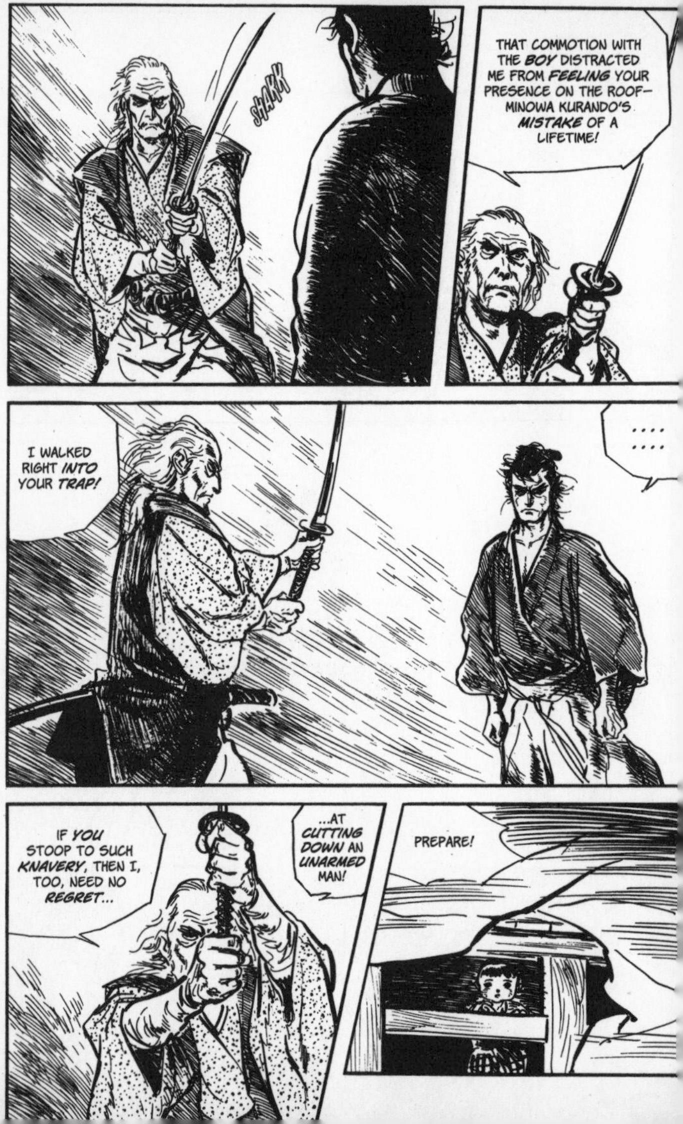
SHAKK
THAT COMMOTION WITH THE *BOY* DISTRACTED ME FROM *FEELING* YOUR PRESENCE ON THE ROOF— MINOWA KURANDO'S *MISTAKE* OF A LIFETIME!
I WALKED RIGHT *INTO* YOUR *TRAP!*
....
....
IF *YOU* STOOP TO SUCH *KNAVERY*, THEN I, TOO, NEED NO *REGRET*...
...AT *CUTTING DOWN* AN *UNARMED* MAN!
PREPARE!

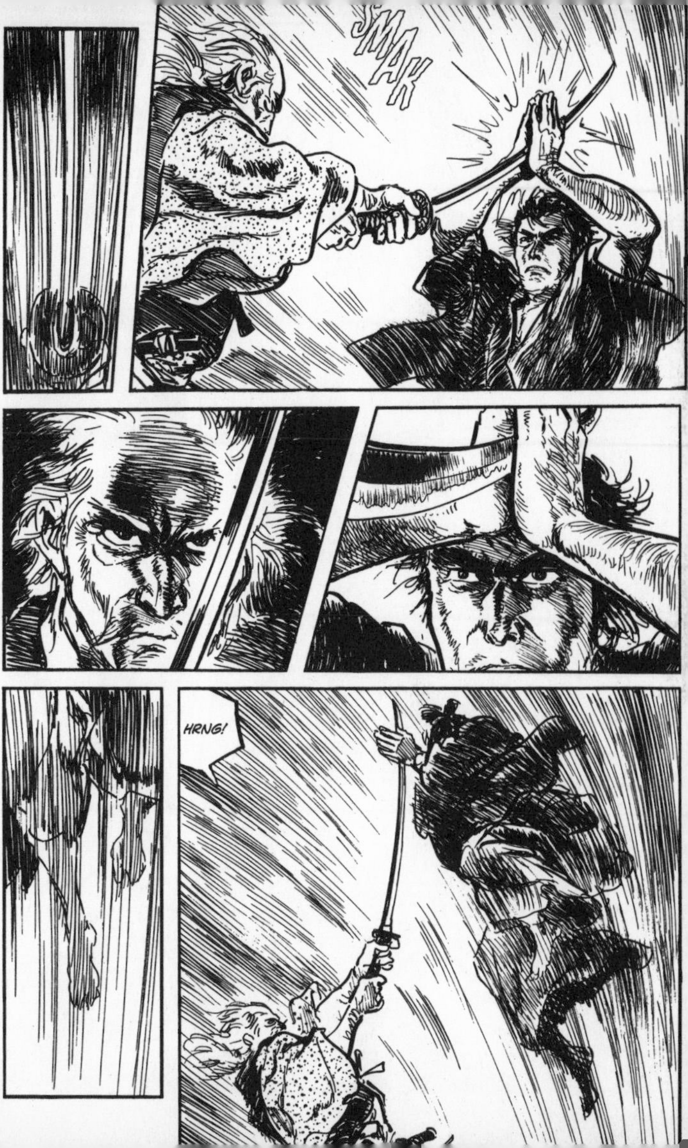
SMAK
HRNG!

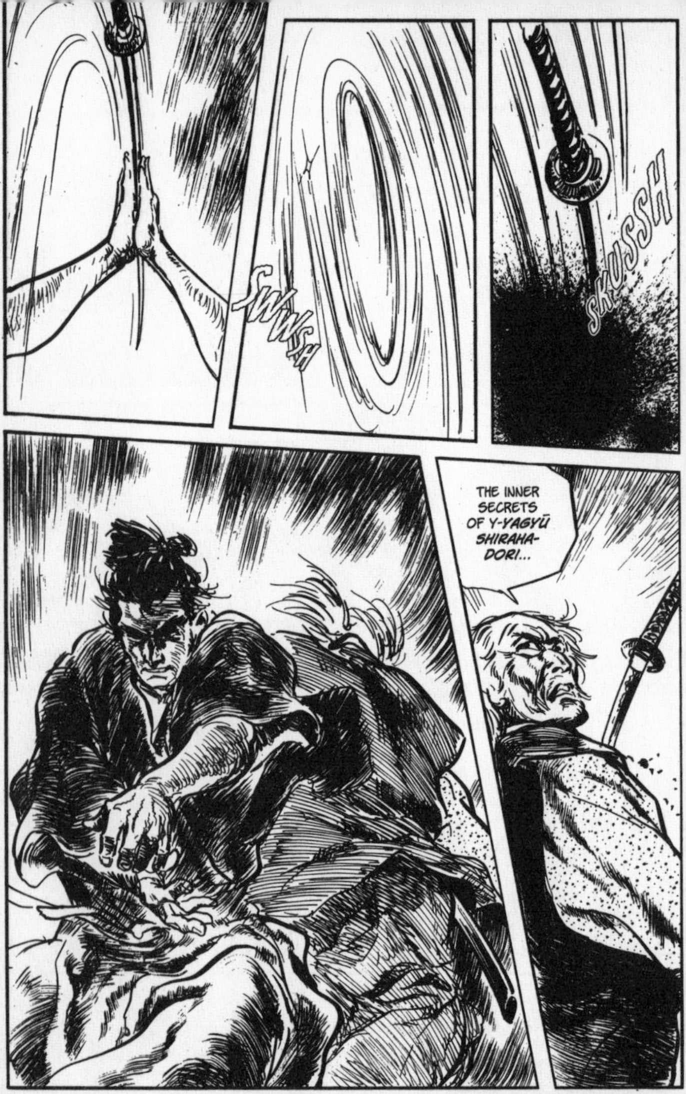
SWISH
SKUSSH
THE INNER SECRETS OF Y-YAGYŪ SHIRAHA-DORI...

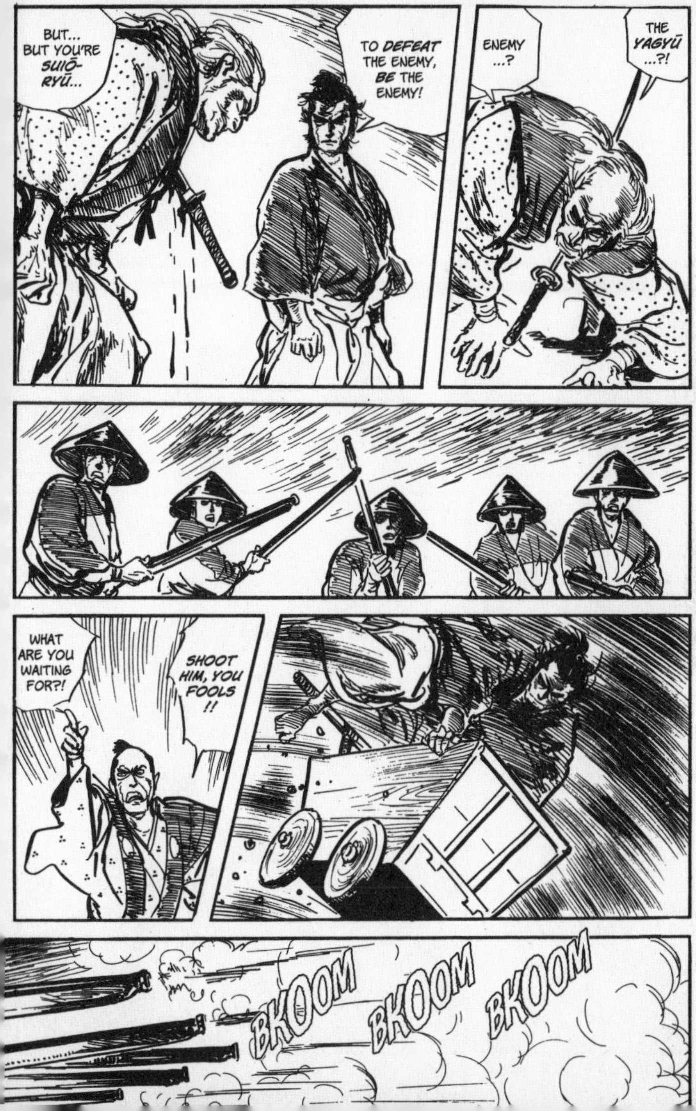
BUT...
BUT YOU'RE SUIŌ-RYŪ...
TO DEFEAT THE ENEMY, BE THE ENEMY!
ENEMY ...?
THE YAGYŪ ...?!
WHAT ARE YOU WAITING FOR?!
SHOOT HIM, YOU FOOLS !!
BKOOM
BKOOM
BKOOM

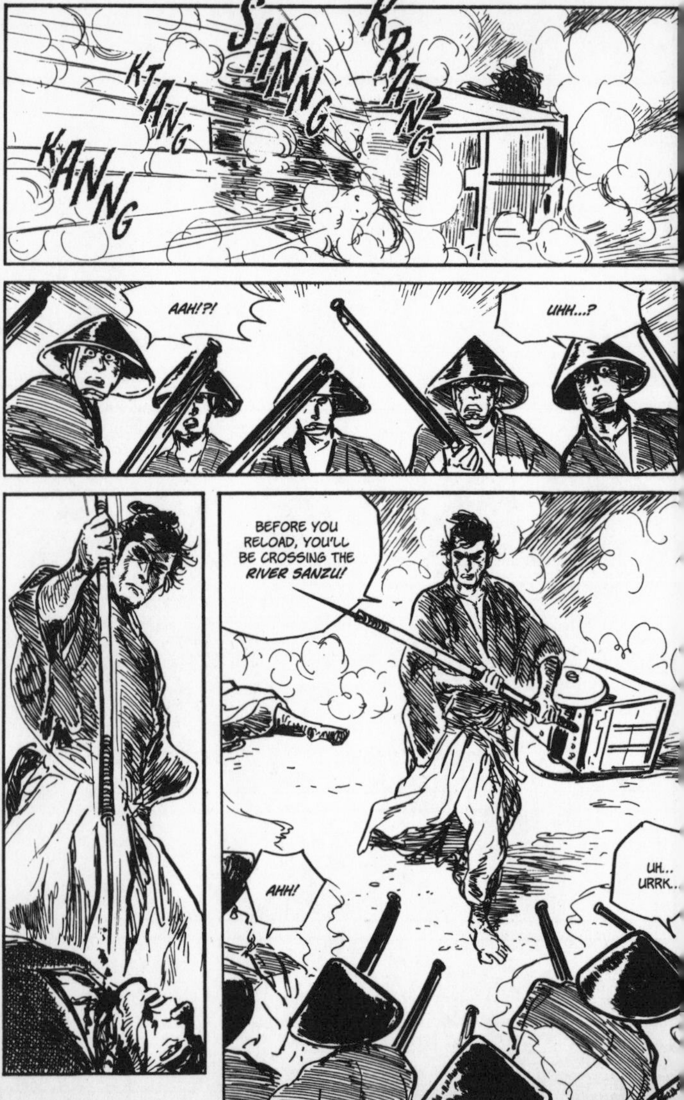
KANNG
KTANG
SHNNG
KRANG
AAH!?!
UHH...?
BEFORE YOU RELOAD, YOU'LL BE CROSSING THE RIVER SANZU!
AHH!
UH... URRK...

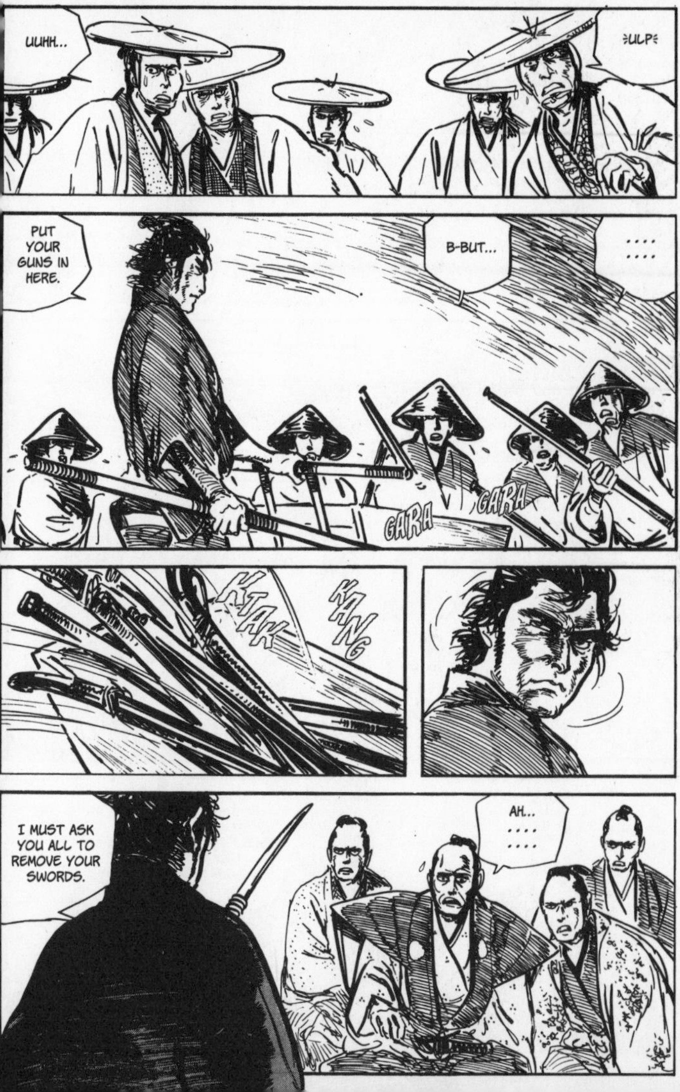
UUHH...
ULP
PUT YOUR GUNS IN HERE.
B-BUT...
....
....
GARA
GARA
KTAK
KANG
I MUST ASK YOU ALL TO REMOVE YOUR SWORDS.
AH...
....
....

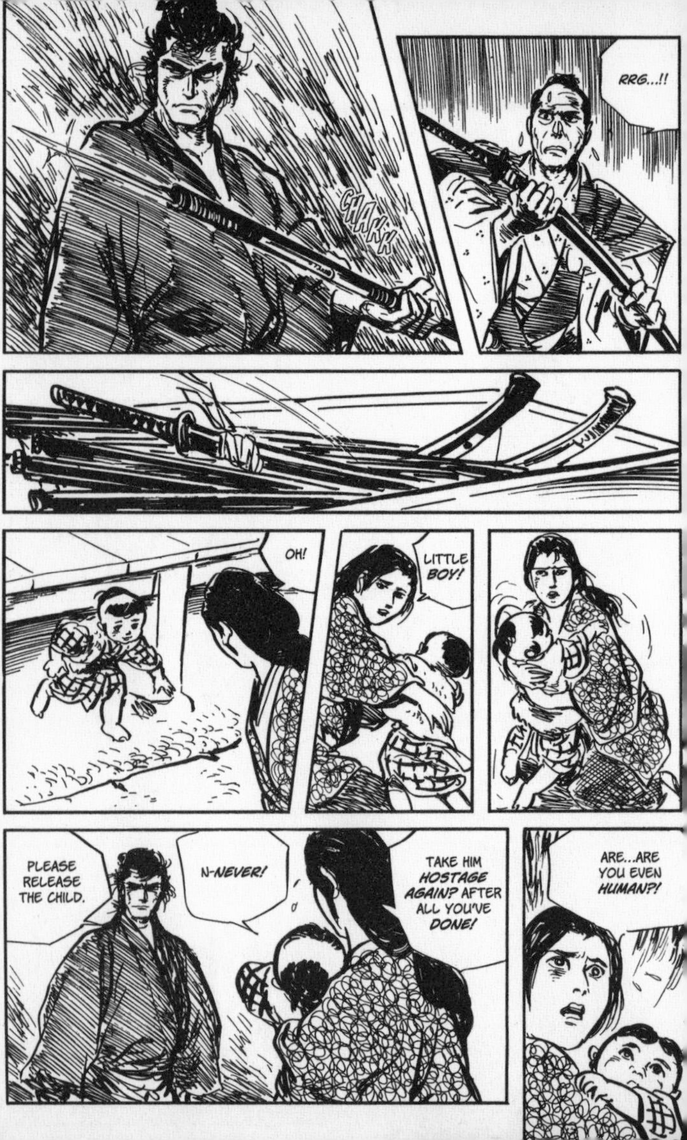
CHAKKK
RRG...!!
OH!
LITTLE BOY!
PLEASE RELEASE THE CHILD.
N-NEVER!
TAKE HIM HOSTAGE AGAIN? AFTER ALL YOU'VE DONE!
ARE...ARE YOU EVEN HUMAN?!

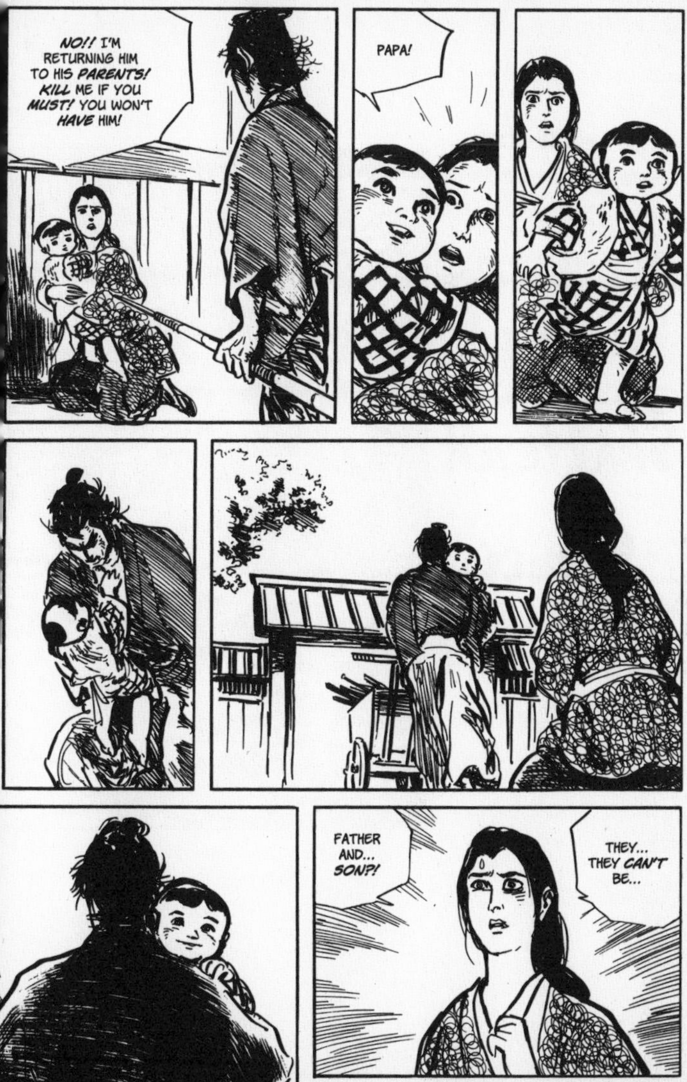
NO!! I'M RETURNING HIM TO HIS PARENTS! KILL ME IF YOU MUST! YOU WON'T HAVE HIM!
PAPA!
FATHER AND... SON?!
THEY... THEY CAN'T BE...

the sixty-first

# Shattered Stones

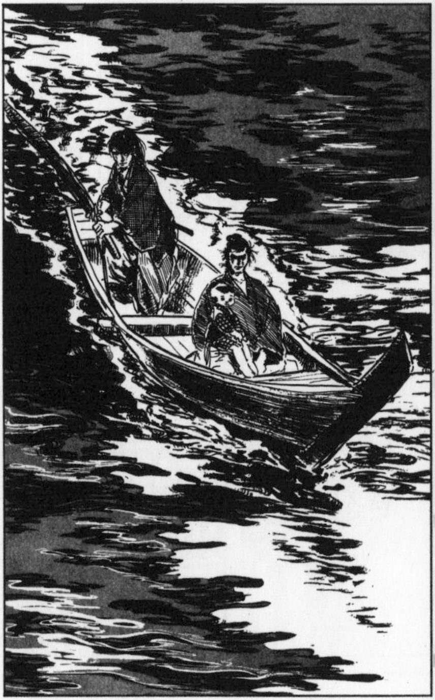

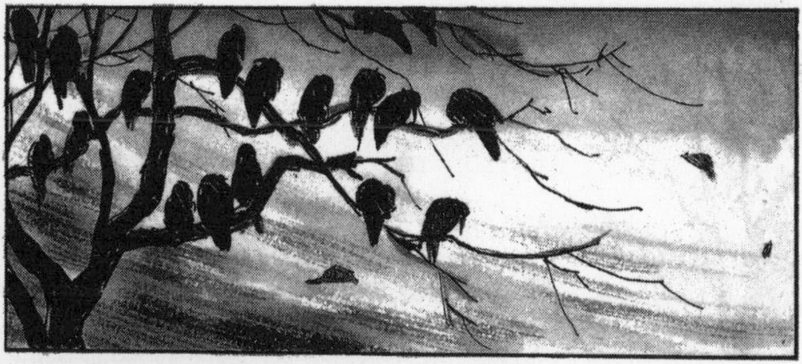

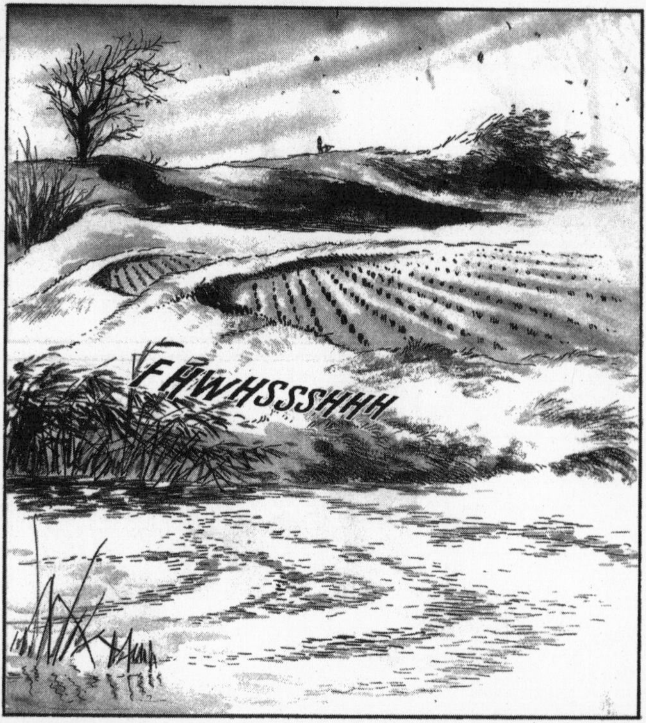
FHWHSSSHHH

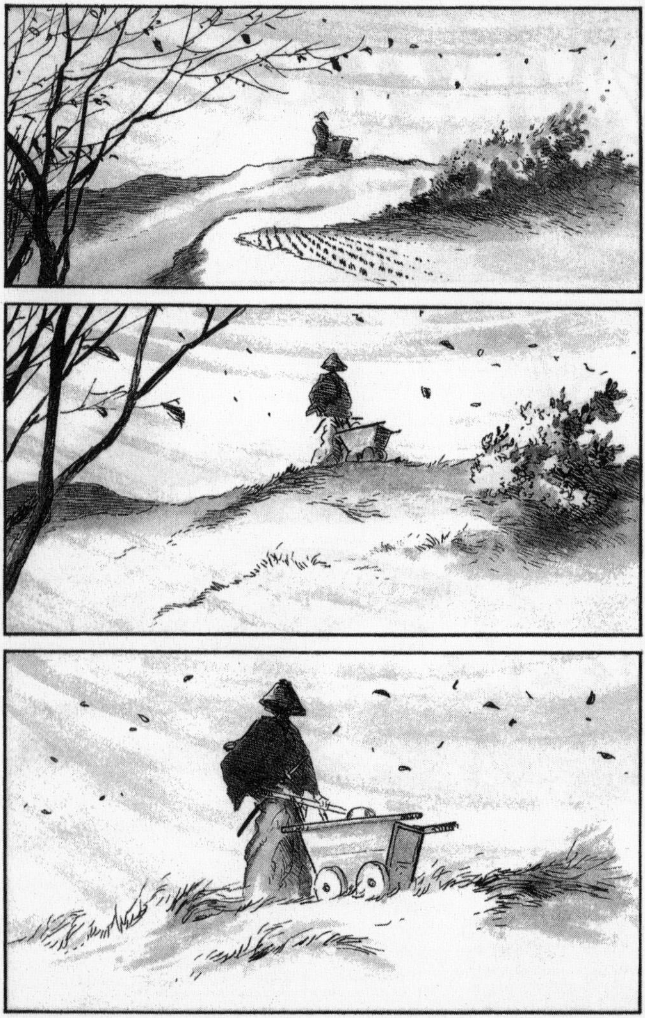

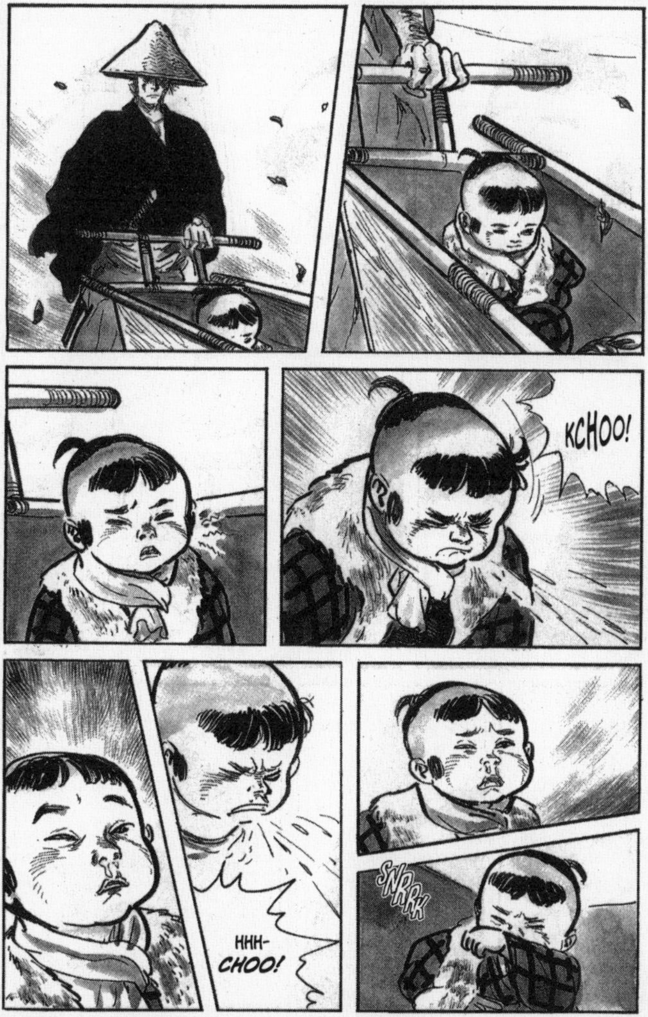
KCHOO!
HHH-
CHOO!
SNRRK

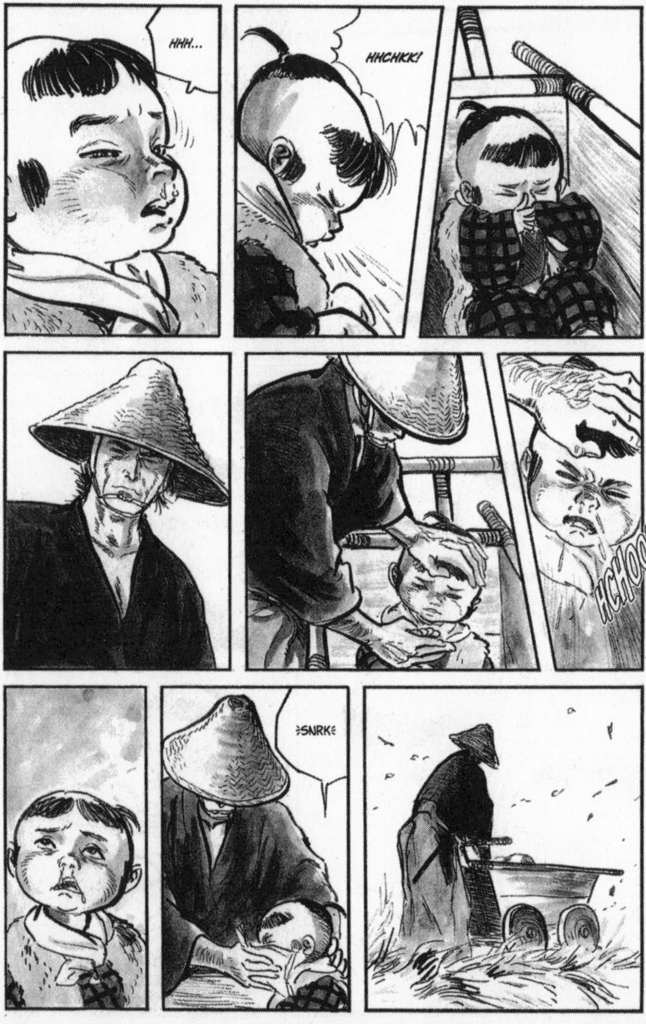
HHH...
HHCHKK!
HCHOO!
SNRK

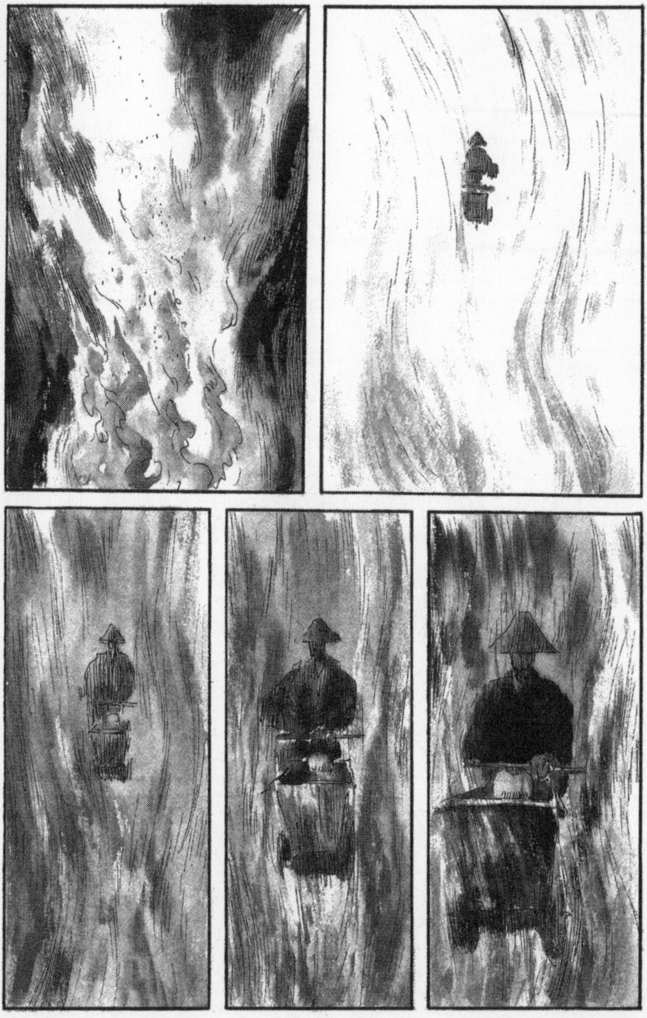

おんじゃく ミ文

*HOT ROCKS
THREE MON

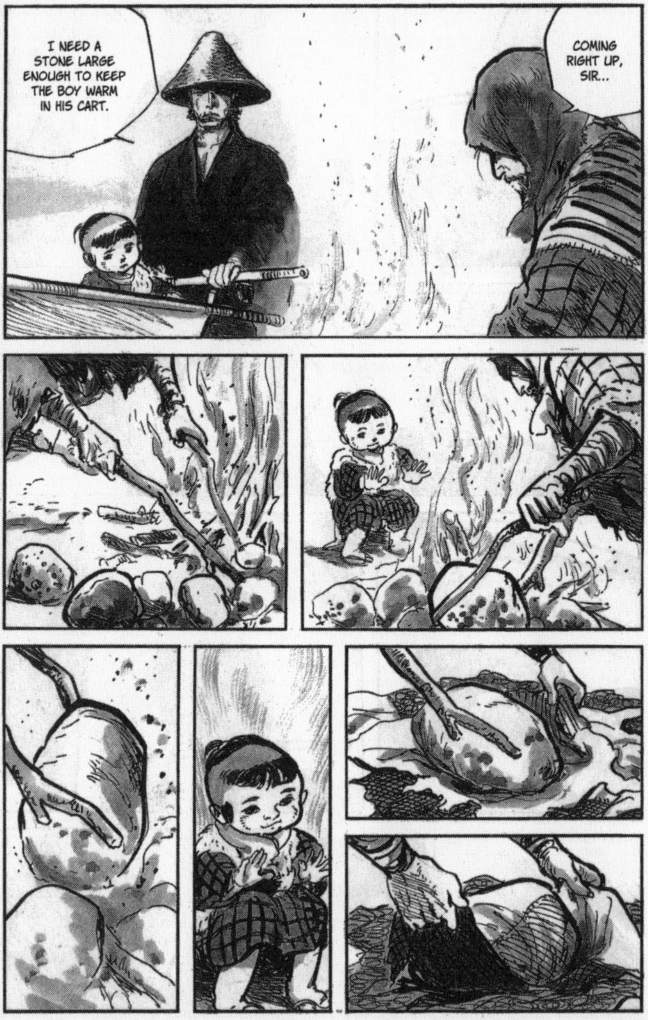
I NEED A STONE LARGE ENOUGH TO KEEP THE BOY WARM IN HIS CART.
COMING RIGHT UP, SIR...

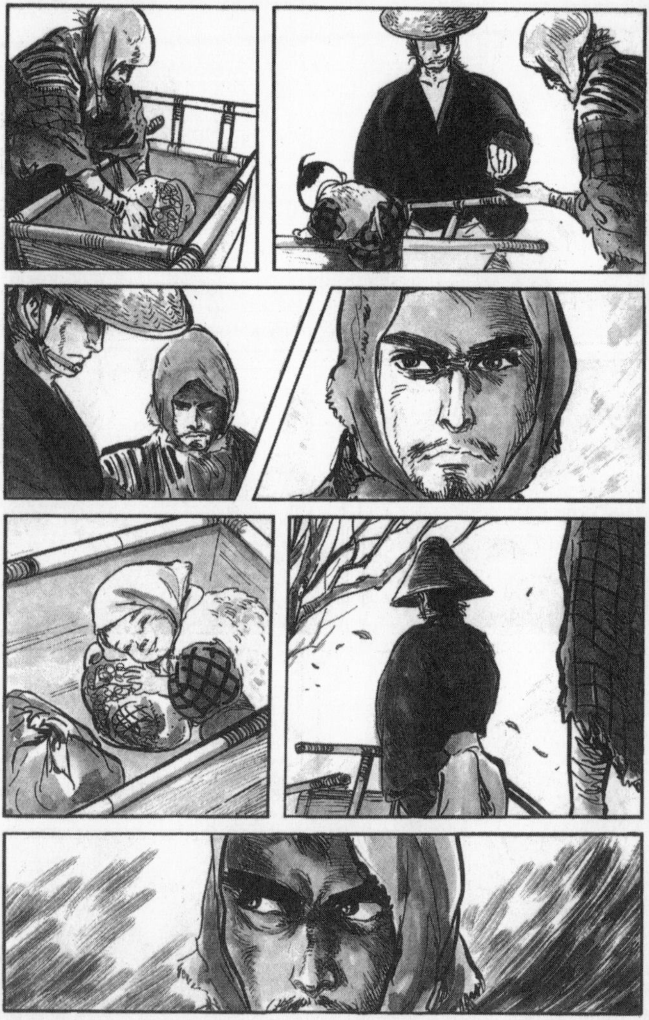

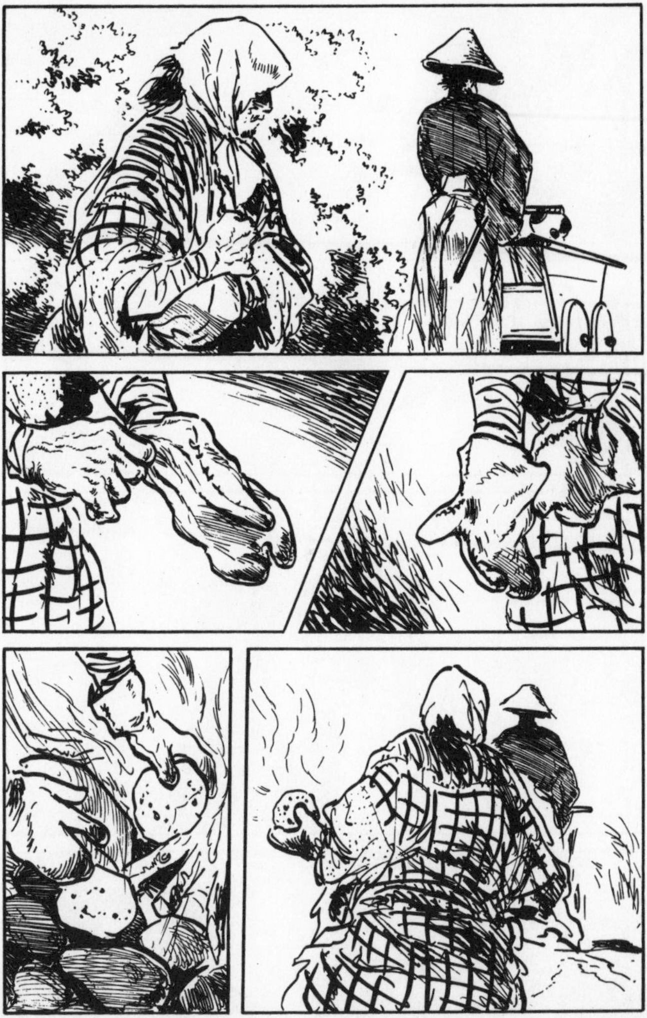

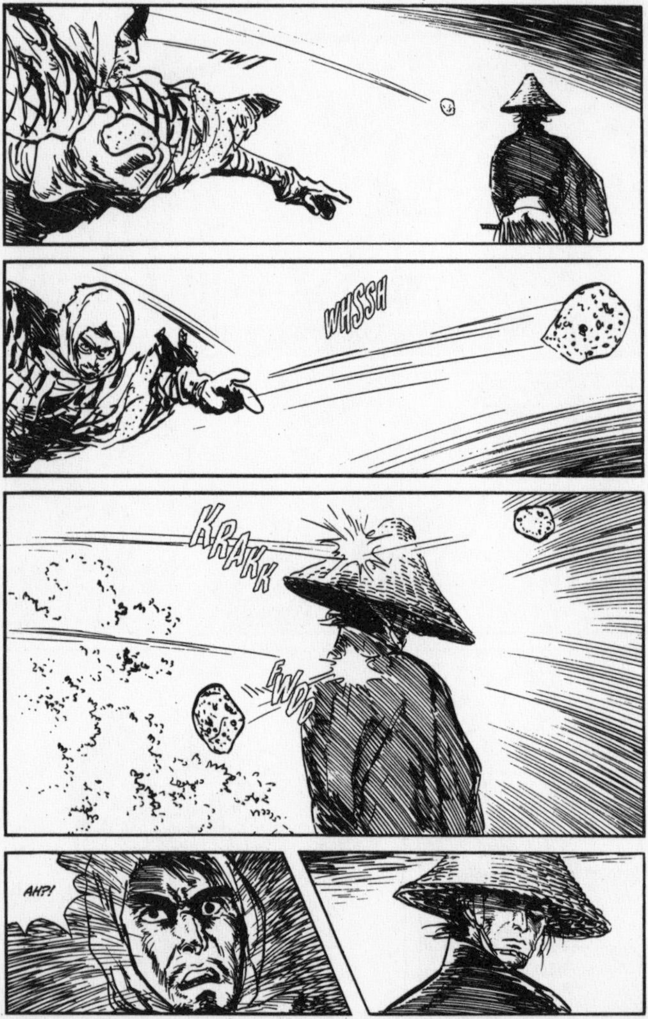
FWT
WHSSH
KRAKK
FWOO
AH?!

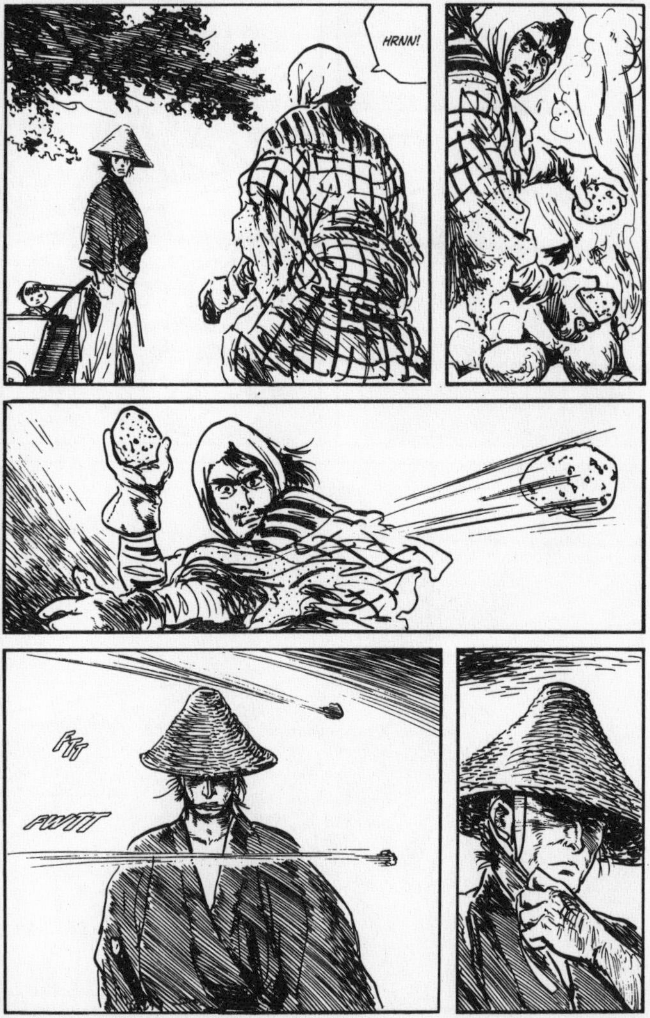
HRNN!
FTT
FWITT

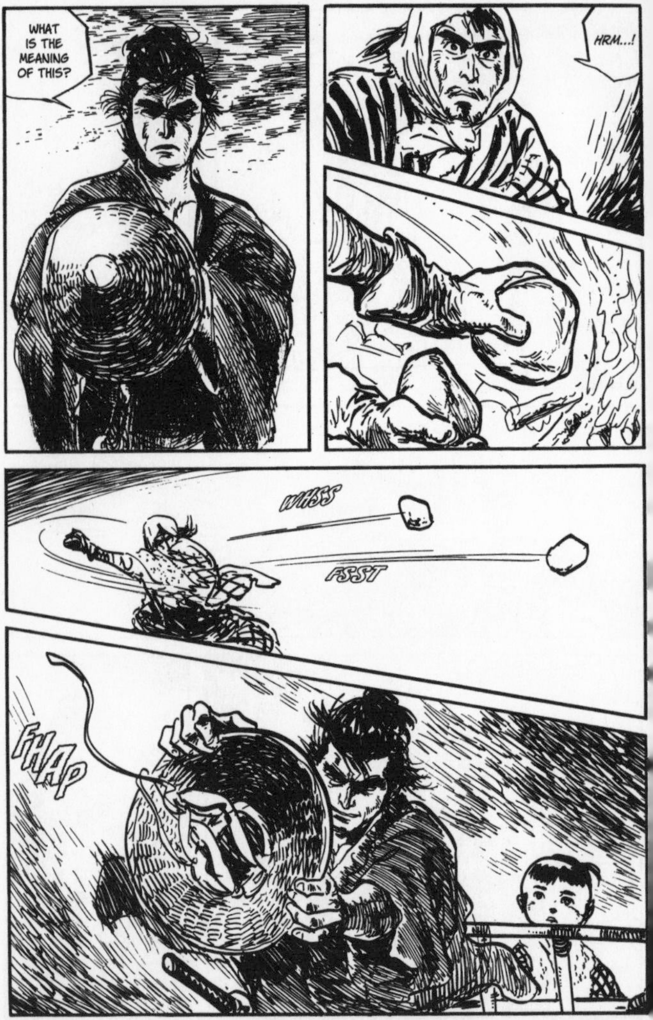
WHAT IS THE MEANING OF THIS?
HRM...!
WHSS
FSST
FHAP

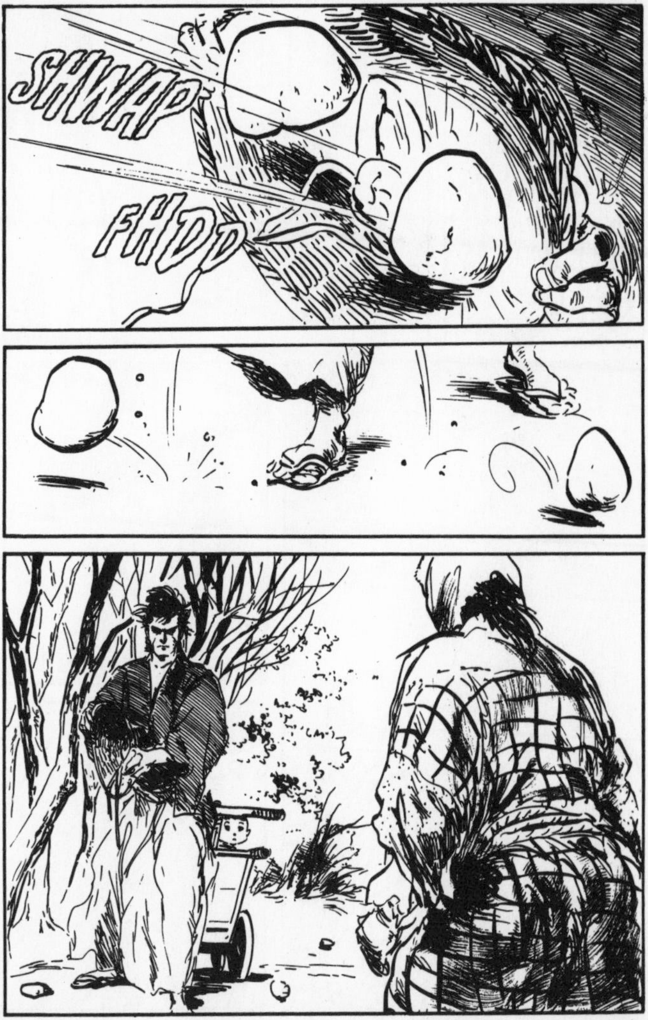
SHWAP
FHDD

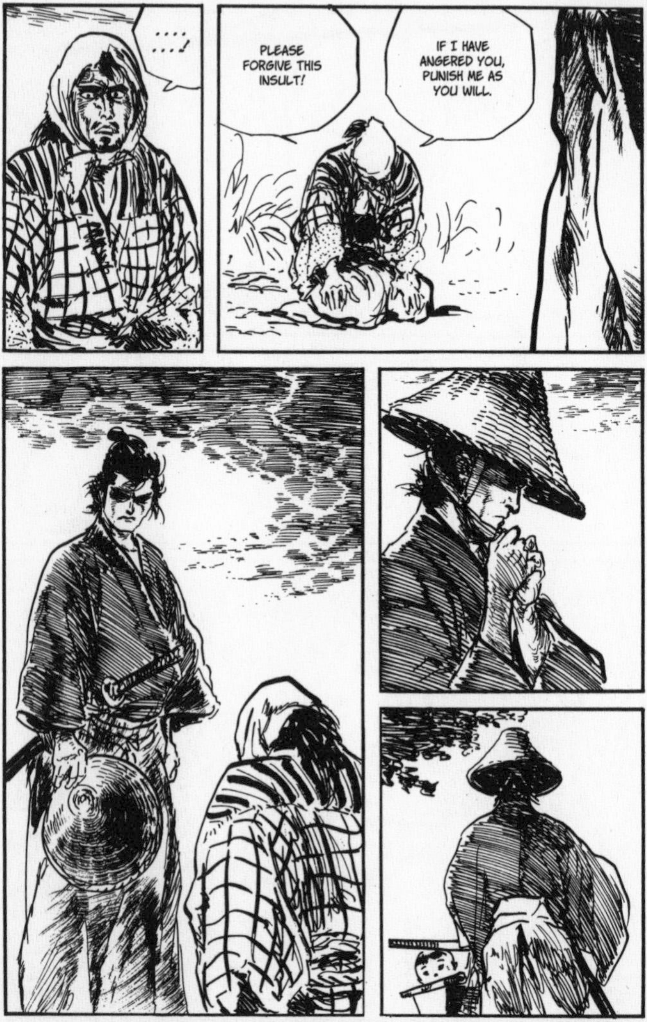
....
....!
PLEASE FORGIVE THIS INSULT!
IF I HAVE ANGERED YOU, PUNISH ME AS YOU WILL.

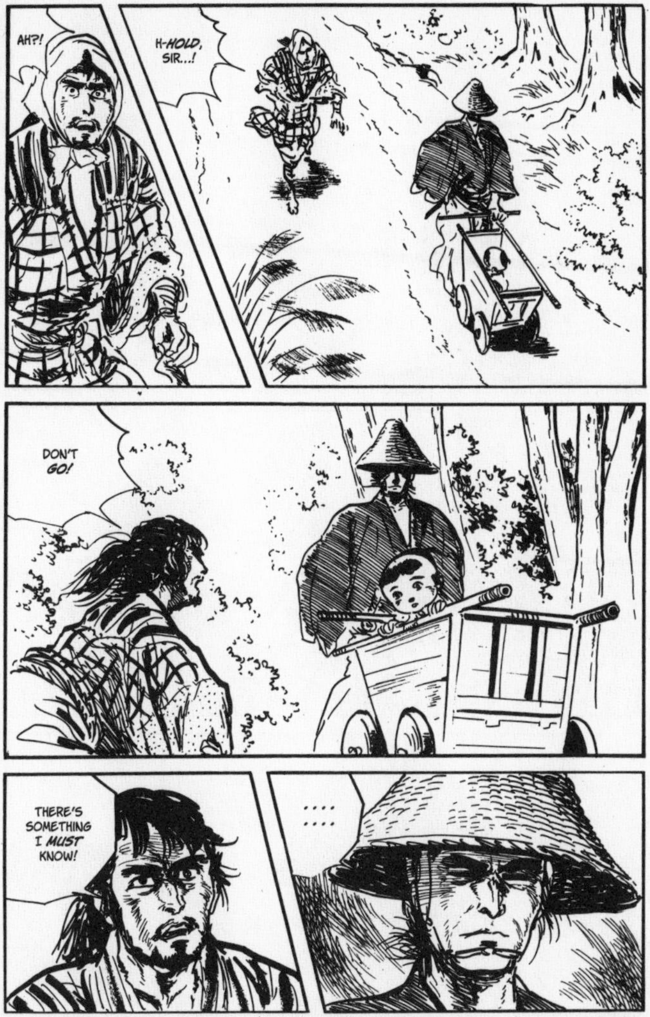
AH?!
H-HOLD, SIR...!
DON'T GO!
THERE'S SOMETHING I MUST KNOW!
....
....

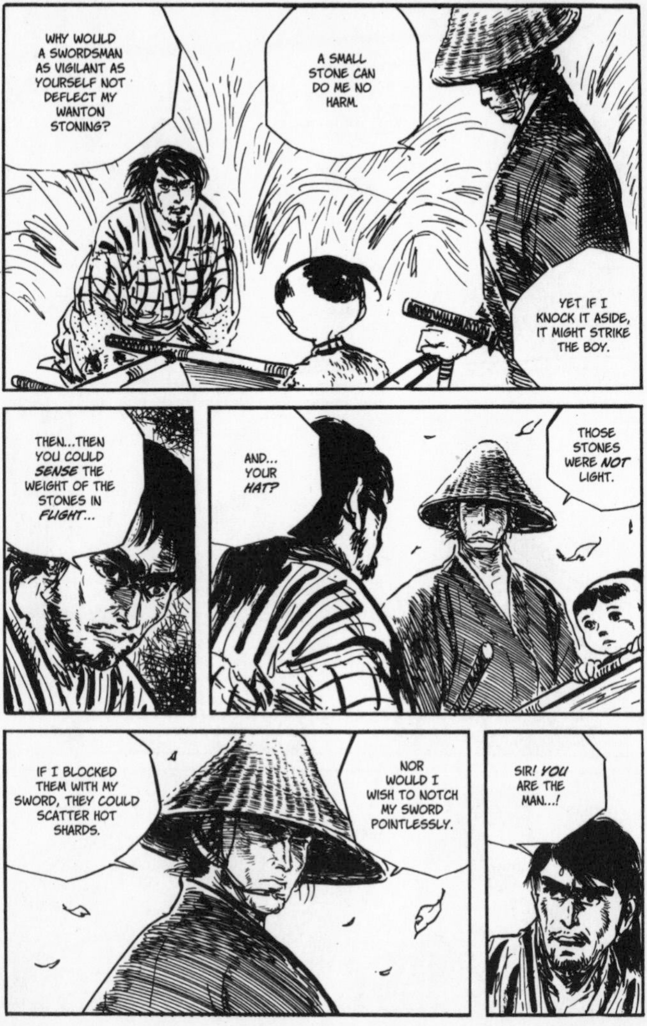
WHY WOULD A SWORDSMAN AS VIGILANT AS YOURSELF NOT DEFLECT MY WANTON STONING?
A SMALL STONE CAN DO ME NO HARM.
YET IF I KNOCK IT ASIDE, IT MIGHT STRIKE THE BOY.
THEN...THEN YOU COULD *SENSE* THE WEIGHT OF THE STONES IN *FLIGHT*...
AND... YOUR *HAT?*
THOSE STONES WERE *NOT* LIGHT.
IF I BLOCKED THEM WITH MY SWORD, THEY COULD SCATTER HOT SHARDS.
NOR WOULD I WISH TO NOTCH MY SWORD POINTLESSLY.
SIR! *YOU* ARE THE MAN...!

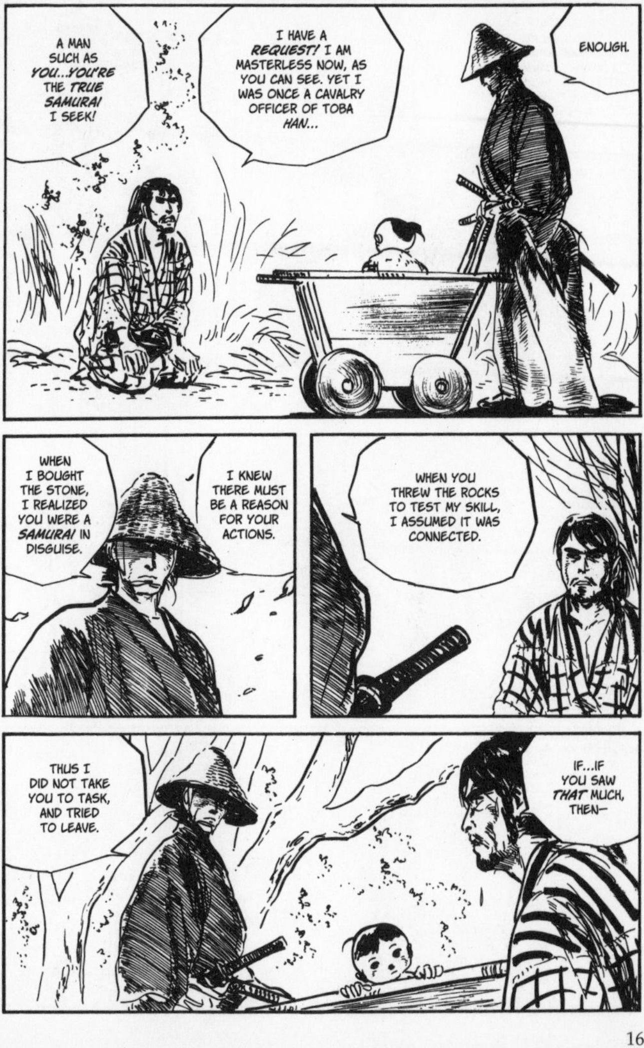

A MAN SUCH AS *YOU...YOU'RE* THE *TRUE SAMURAI* I SEEK!
I HAVE A *REQUEST!* I AM MASTERLESS NOW, AS YOU CAN SEE. YET I WAS ONCE A CAVALRY OFFICER OF TOBA *HAN...*
ENOUGH.
WHEN I BOUGHT THE STONE, I REALIZED YOU WERE A *SAMURAI* IN DISGUISE.
I KNEW THERE MUST BE A REASON FOR YOUR ACTIONS.
WHEN YOU THREW THE ROCKS TO TEST MY SKILL, I ASSUMED IT WAS CONNECTED.
THUS I DID NOT TAKE YOU TO TASK, AND TRIED TO LEAVE.
IF...IF YOU SAW *THAT* MUCH, THEN—

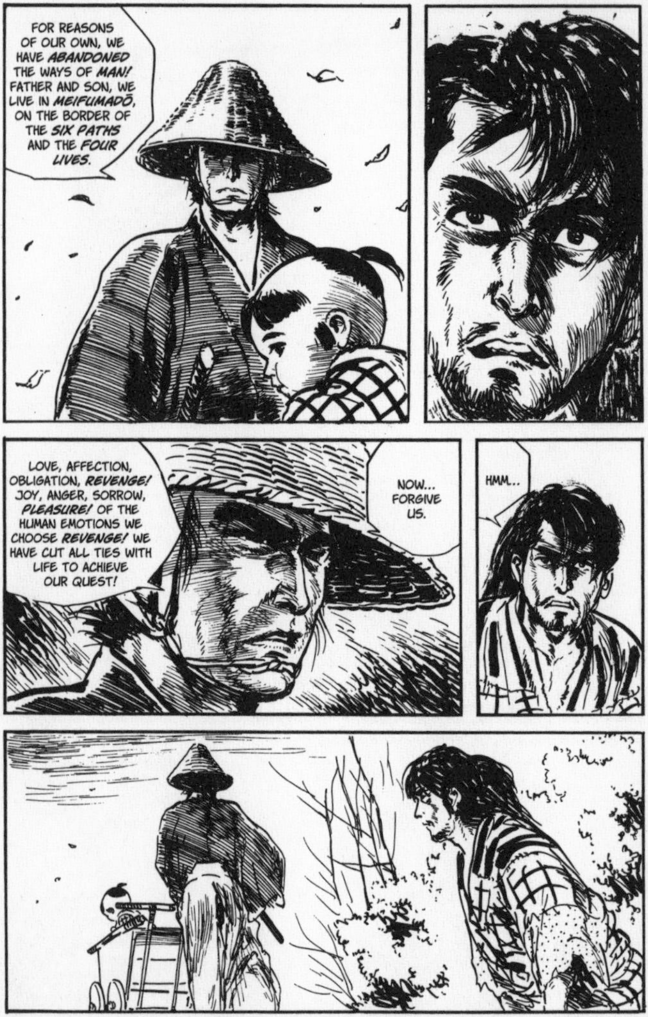
FOR REASONS OF OUR OWN, WE HAVE *ABANDONED* THE WAYS OF *MAN!* FATHER AND SON, WE LIVE IN *MEIFUMADŌ*, ON THE BORDER OF THE *SIX PATHS* AND THE *FOUR LIVES*.
LOVE, AFFECTION, OBLIGATION, *REVENGE!* JOY, ANGER, SORROW, *PLEASURE!* OF THE HUMAN EMOTIONS WE CHOOSE *REVENGE!* WE HAVE CUT ALL TIES WITH LIFE TO ACHIEVE OUR QUEST!
NOW... FORGIVE US.
HMM...

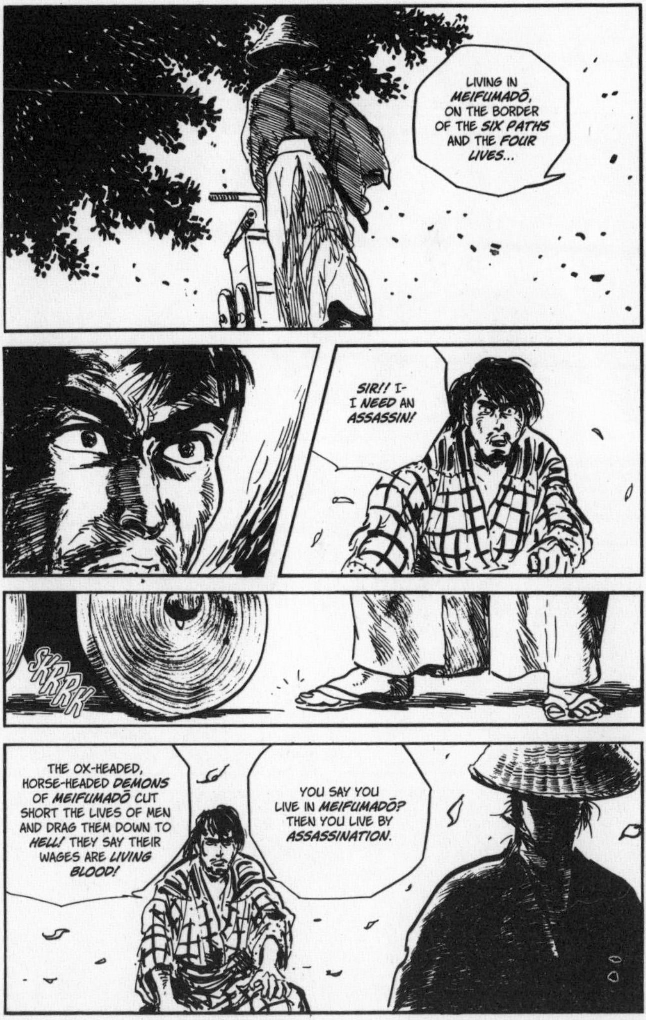
LIVING IN MEIFUMADŌ, ON THE BORDER OF THE SIX PATHS AND THE FOUR LIVES...
SIR!! I- I NEED AN ASSASSIN!
SKRRRK
THE OX-HEADED, HORSE-HEADED DEMONS OF MEIFUMADŌ CUT SHORT THE LIVES OF MEN AND DRAG THEM DOWN TO HELL! THEY SAY THEIR WAGES ARE LIVING BLOOD!
YOU SAY YOU LIVE IN MEIFUMADŌ? THEN YOU LIVE BY ASSASSINATION.

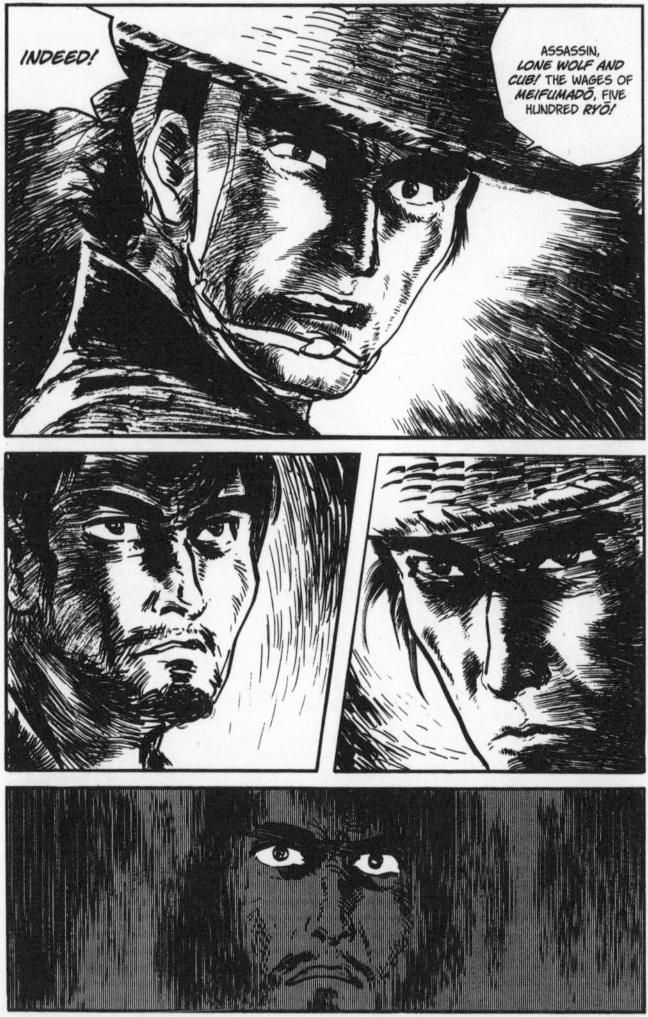
INDEED!
ASSASSIN, LONE WOLF AND CUB! THE WAGES OF MEIFUMADŌ, FIVE HUNDRED RYŌ!

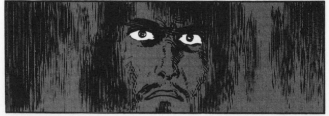

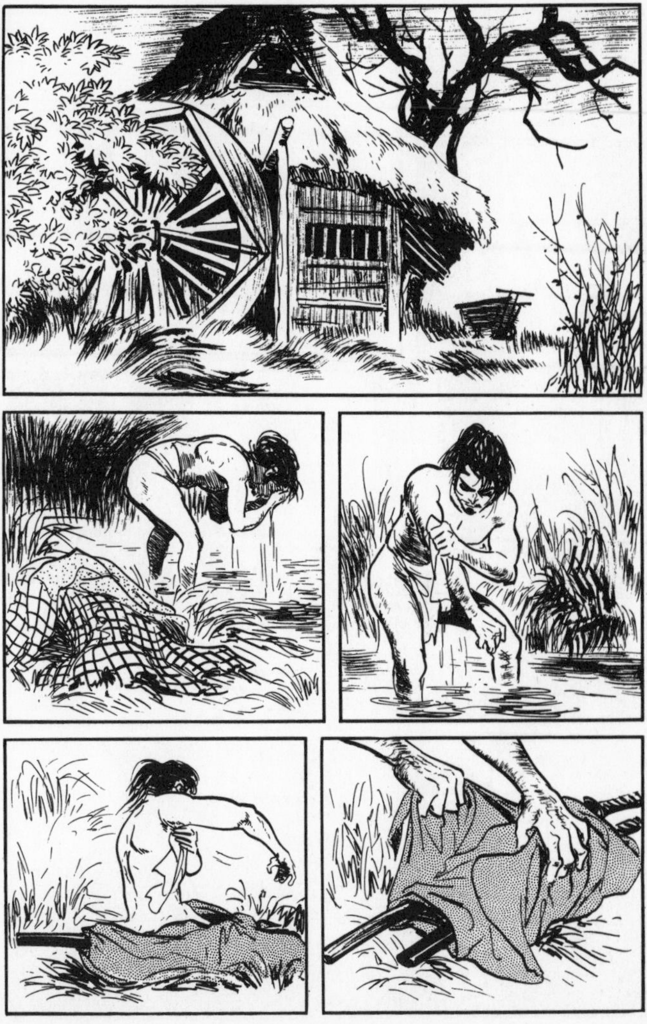

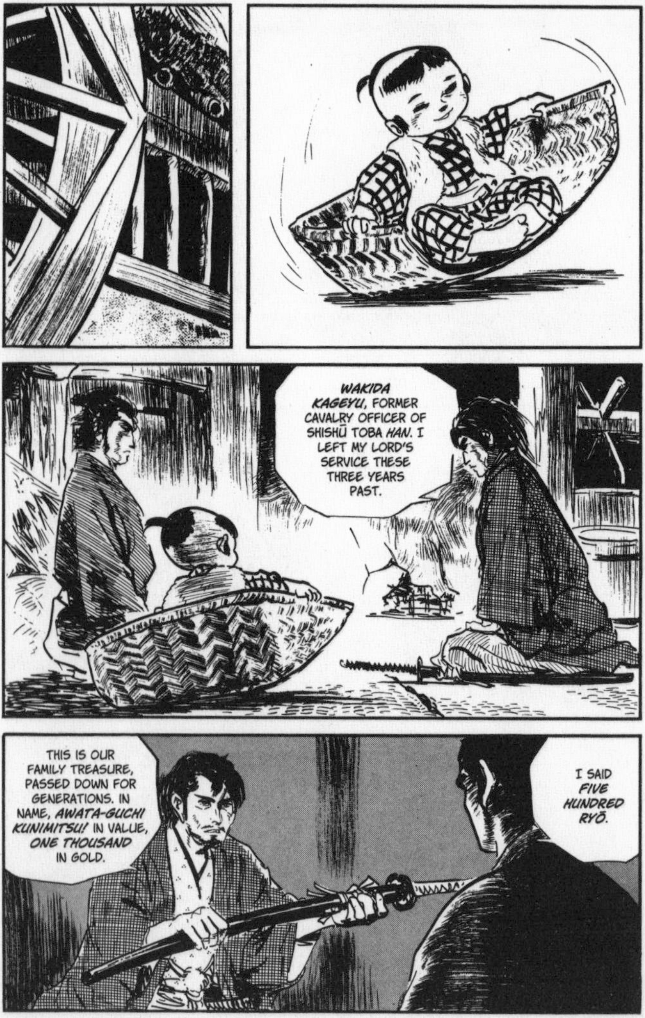
WAKIDA KAGEYU, FORMER CAVALRY OFFICER OF SHISHŪ TOBA HAN. I LEFT MY LORD'S SERVICE THESE THREE YEARS PAST.
THIS IS OUR FAMILY TREASURE, PASSED DOWN FOR GENERATIONS. IN NAME, AWATA-GUCHI KUNIMITSU! IN VALUE, ONE THOUSAND IN GOLD.
I SAID FIVE HUNDRED RYŌ.

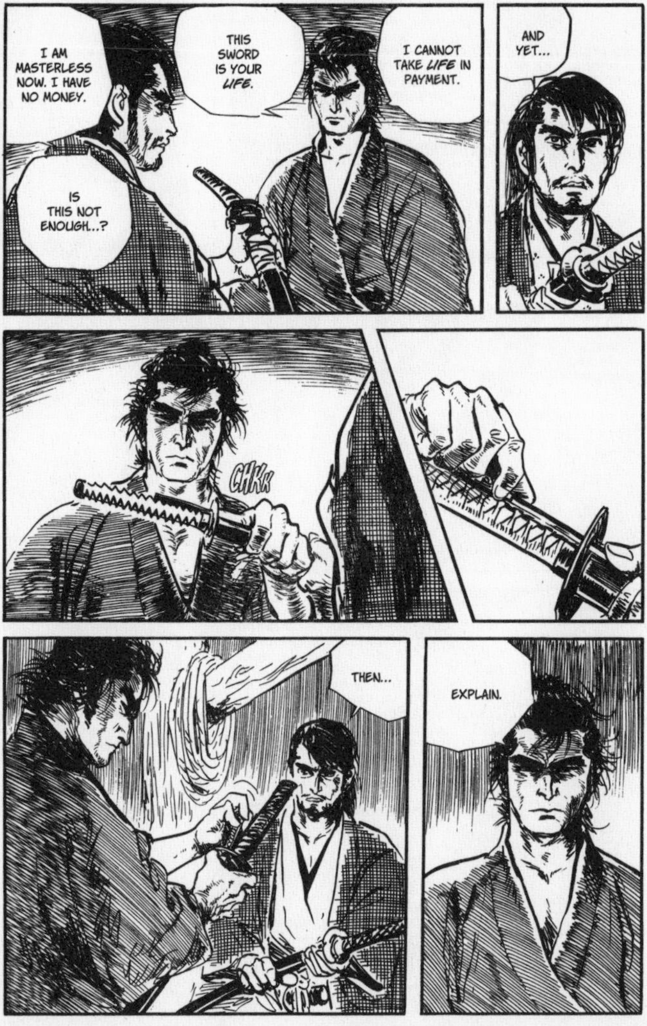
I AM MASTERLESS NOW. I HAVE NO MONEY.
THIS SWORD IS YOUR *LIFE*.
I CANNOT TAKE *LIFE* IN PAYMENT.
IS THIS NOT ENOUGH...?
AND YET...
CHKK
THEN...
EXPLAIN.

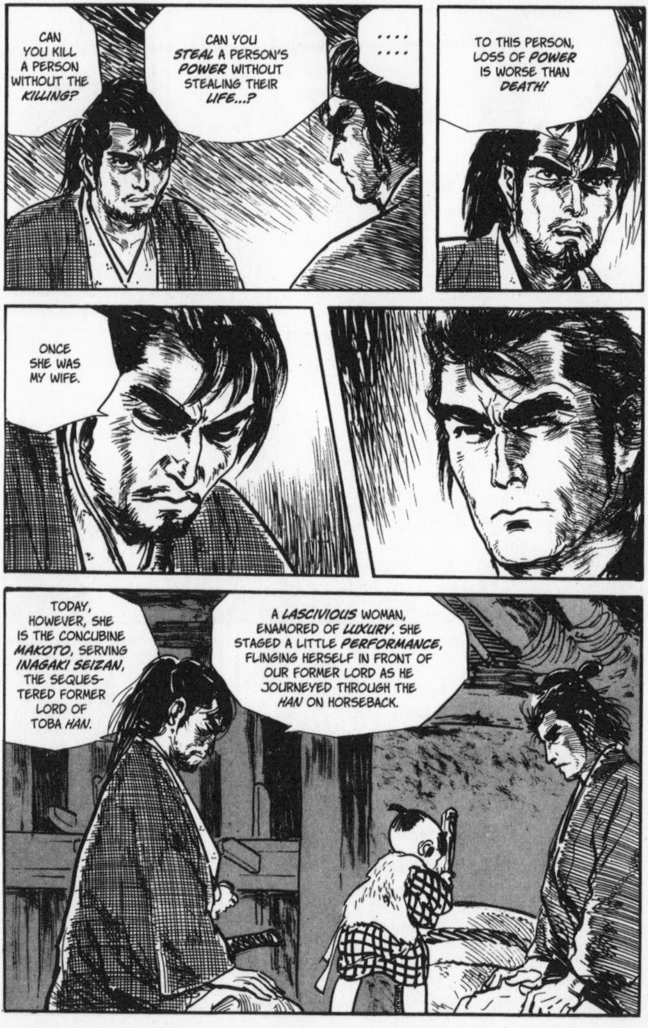
CAN YOU KILL A PERSON WITHOUT THE KILLING?
CAN YOU STEAL A PERSON'S POWER WITHOUT STEALING THEIR LIFE...?
....
....
TO THIS PERSON, LOSS OF POWER IS WORSE THAN DEATH!
ONCE SHE WAS MY WIFE.
TODAY, HOWEVER, SHE IS THE CONCUBINE MAKOTO, SERVING INAGAKI SEIZAN, THE SEQUESTERED FORMER LORD OF TOBA HAN.
A LASCIVIOUS WOMAN, ENAMORED OF LUXURY. SHE STAGED A LITTLE PERFORMANCE, FLINGING HERSELF IN FRONT OF OUR FORMER LORD AS HE JOURNEYED THROUGH THE HAN ON HORSEBACK.

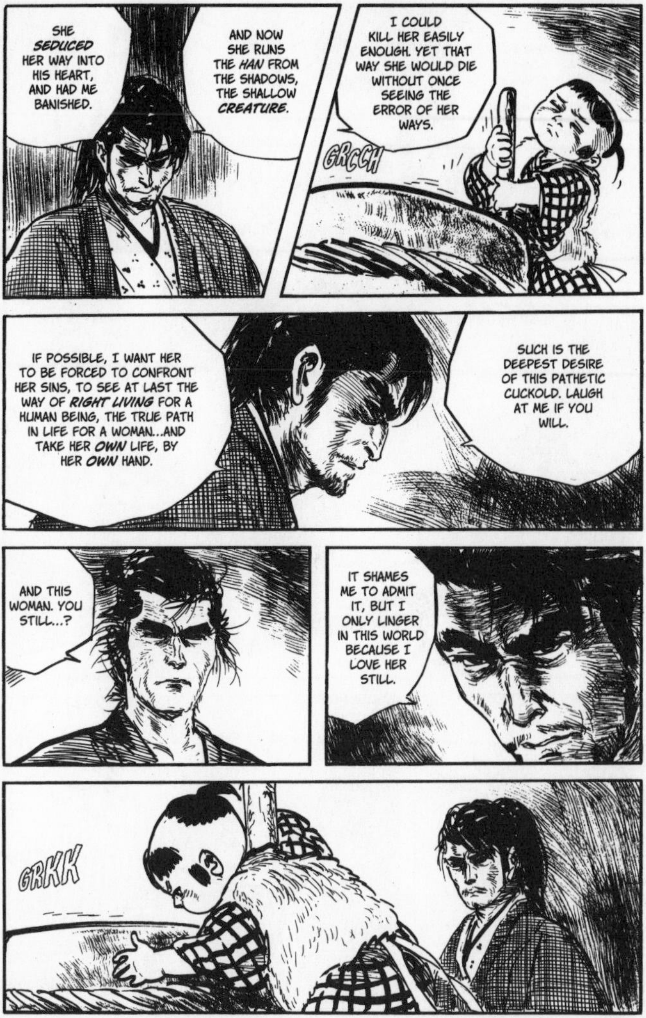
SHE SEDUCED HER WAY INTO HIS HEART, AND HAD ME BANISHED.
AND NOW SHE RUNS THE HAN FROM THE SHADOWS, THE SHALLOW CREATURE.
I COULD KILL HER EASILY ENOUGH. YET THAT WAY SHE WOULD DIE WITHOUT ONCE SEEING THE ERROR OF HER WAYS.
GRCCH
IF POSSIBLE, I WANT HER TO BE FORCED TO CONFRONT HER SINS, TO SEE AT LAST THE WAY OF RIGHT LIVING FOR A HUMAN BEING, THE TRUE PATH IN LIFE FOR A WOMAN...AND TAKE HER OWN LIFE, BY HER OWN HAND.
SUCH IS THE DEEPEST DESIRE OF THIS PATHETIC CUCKOLD. LAUGH AT ME IF YOU WILL.
AND THIS WOMAN. YOU STILL...?
IT SHAMES ME TO ADMIT IT, BUT I ONLY LINGER IN THIS WORLD BECAUSE I LOVE HER STILL.
GRKK

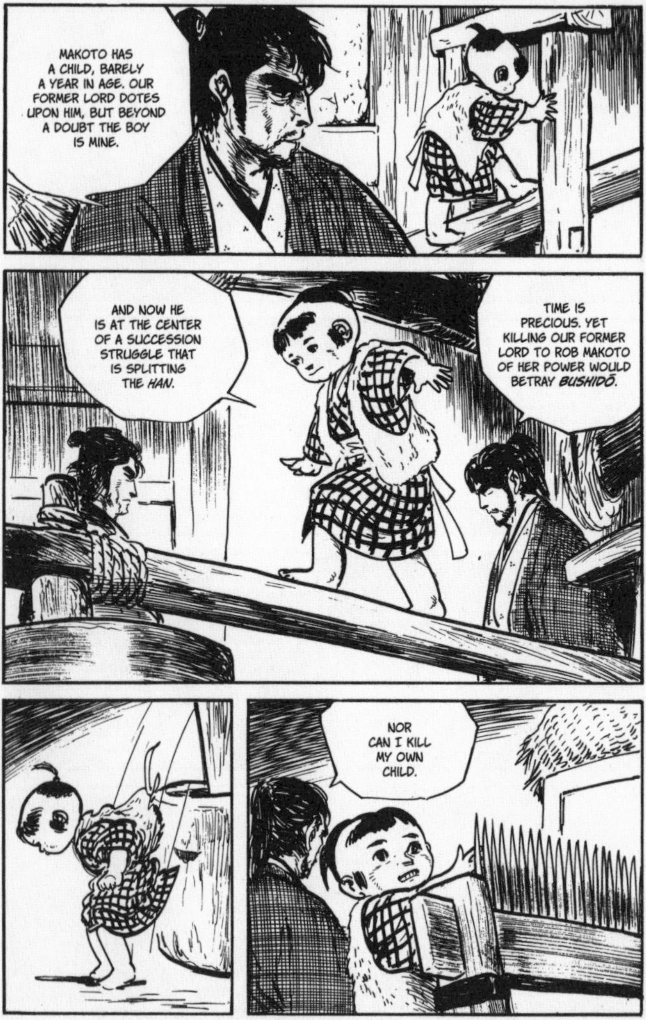
MAKOTO HAS A CHILD, BARELY A YEAR IN AGE. OUR FORMER LORD DOTES UPON HIM, BUT BEYOND A DOUBT THE BOY IS MINE.
AND NOW HE IS AT THE CENTER OF A SUCCESSION STRUGGLE THAT IS SPLITTING THE *HAN*.
TIME IS PRECIOUS. YET KILLING OUR FORMER LORD TO ROB MAKOTO OF HER POWER WOULD BETRAY *BUSHIDŌ*.
NOR CAN I KILL MY OWN CHILD.

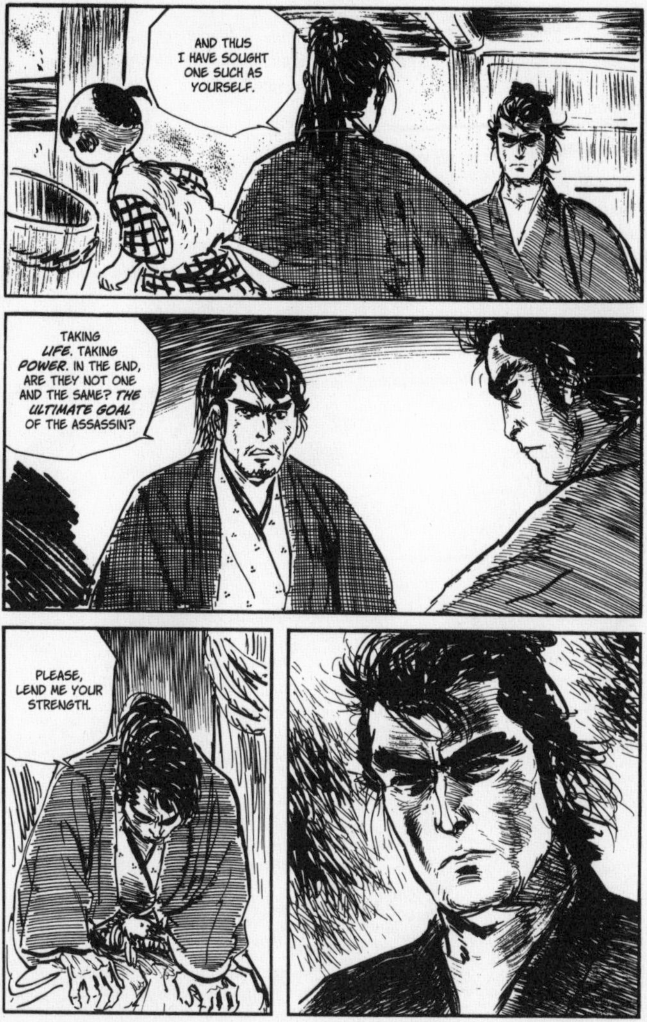
AND THUS I HAVE SOUGHT ONE SUCH AS YOURSELF.
TAKING *LIFE*. TAKING *POWER*. IN THE END, ARE THEY NOT ONE AND THE SAME? *THE ULTIMATE GOAL* OF THE ASSASSIN?
PLEASE, LEND ME YOUR STRENGTH.

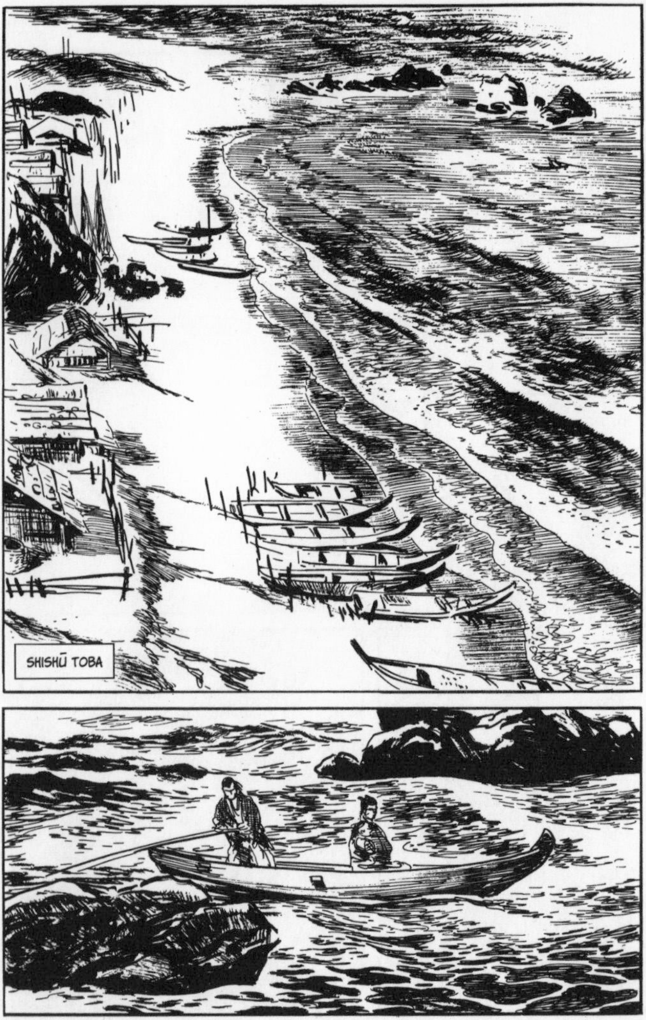
SHISHŪ TOBA

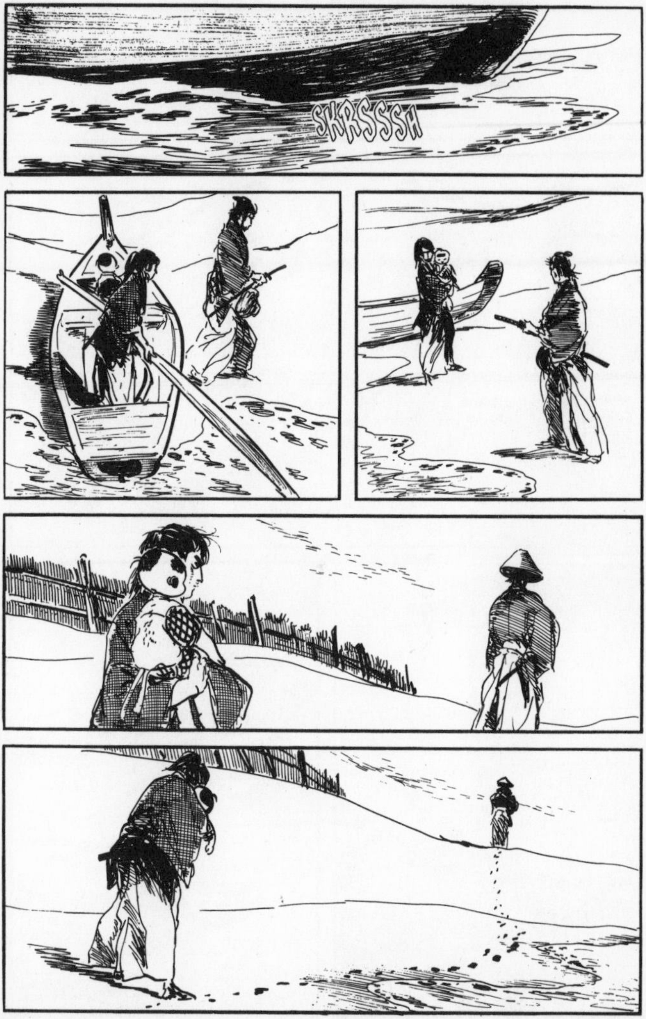
SKRSSSH

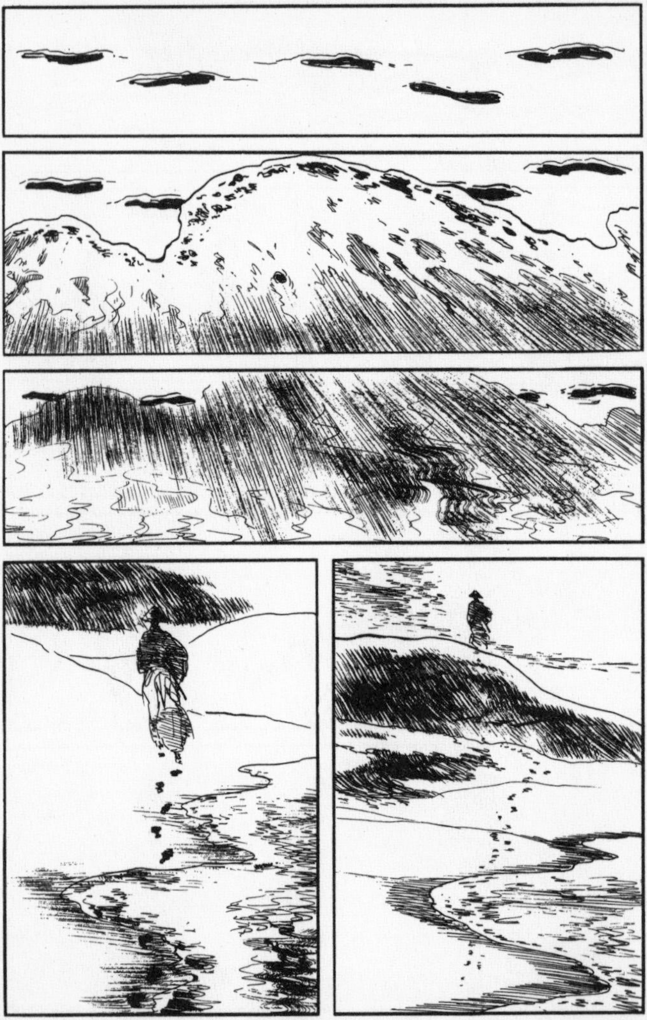

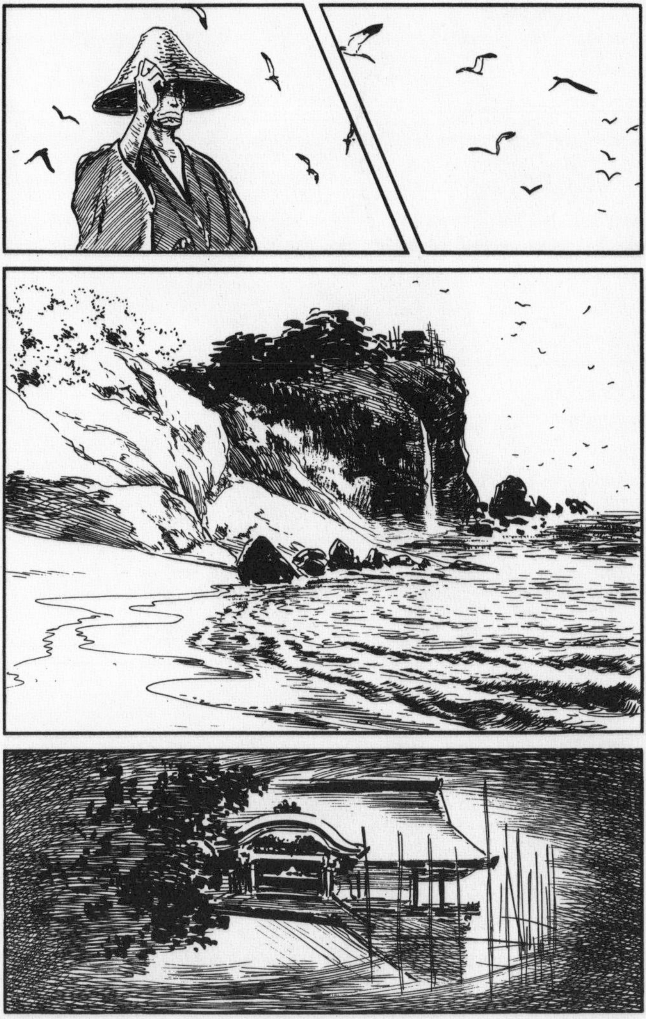

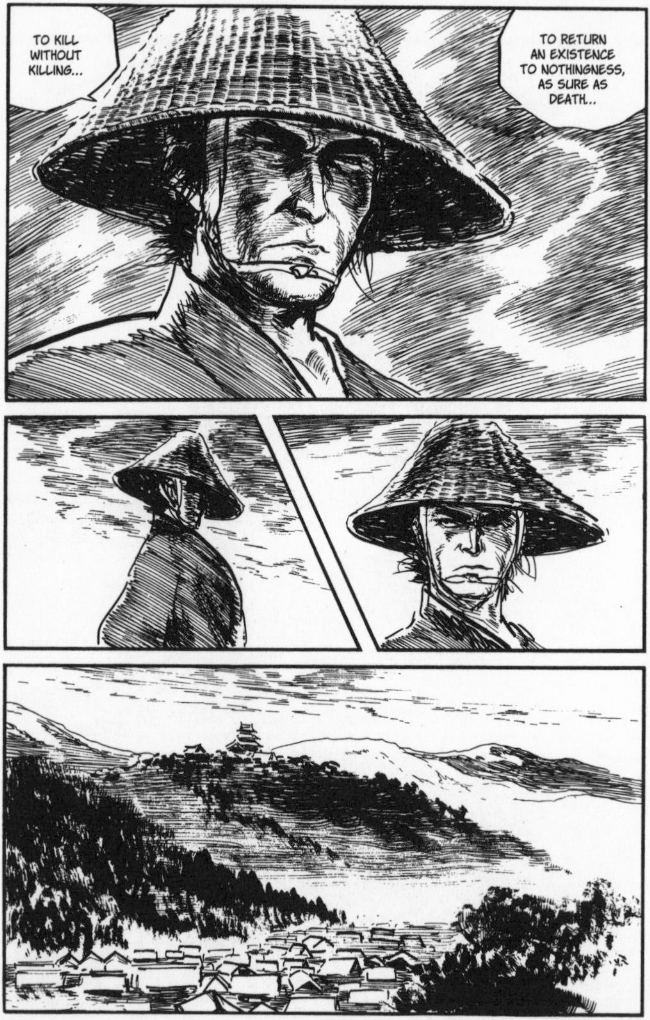
TO KILL WITHOUT KILLING...
TO RETURN AN EXISTENCE TO NOTHINGNESS, AS SURE AS DEATH...

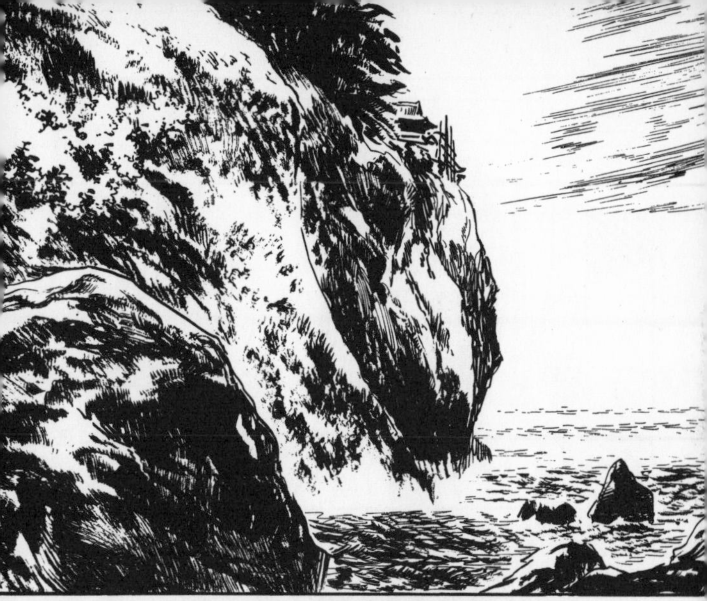
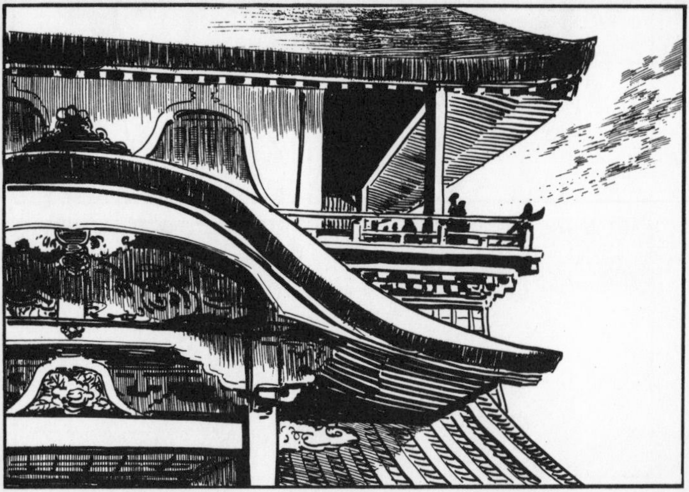

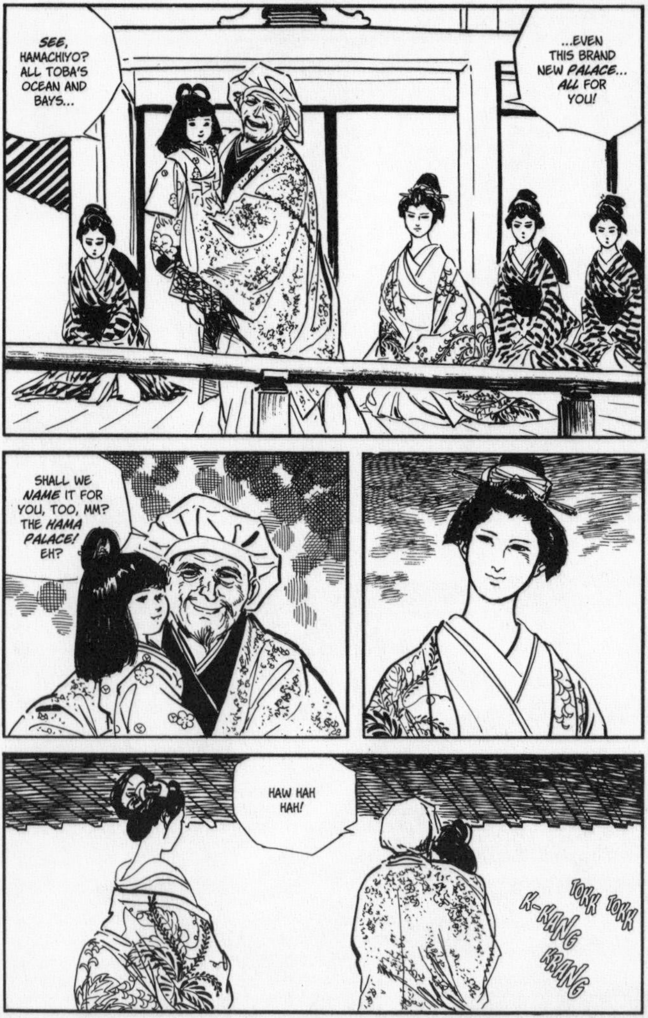

SEE, HAMACHIYO? ALL TOBA'S OCEAN AND BAYS...
...EVEN THIS BRAND NEW PALACE... ALL FOR YOU!
SHALL WE NAME IT FOR YOU, TOO, MM? THE HAMA PALACE! EH?
HAW HAH HAH!
TOKK TOKK
K-KANG KRANG

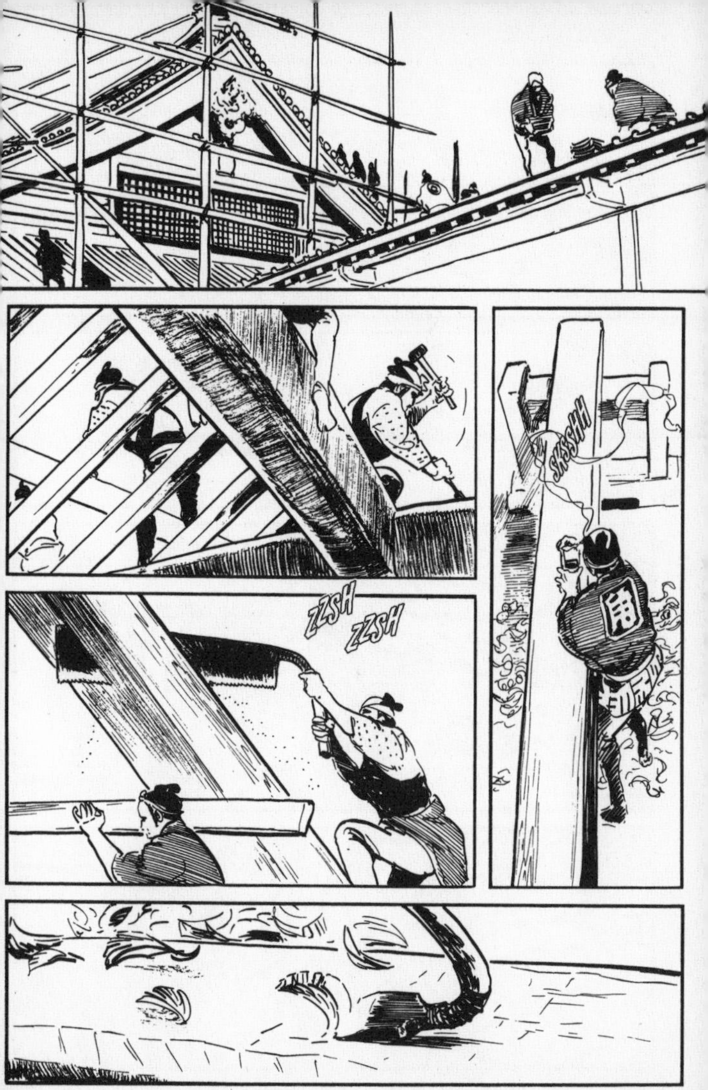
ZZSH
ZZSH
SKSSHH

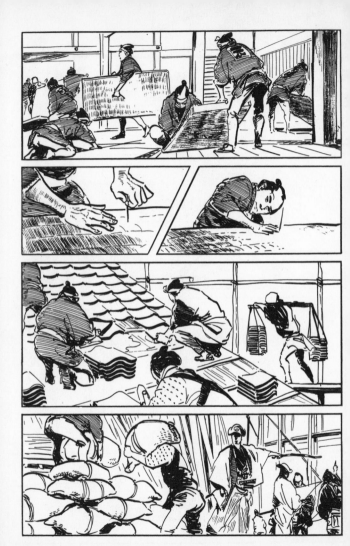

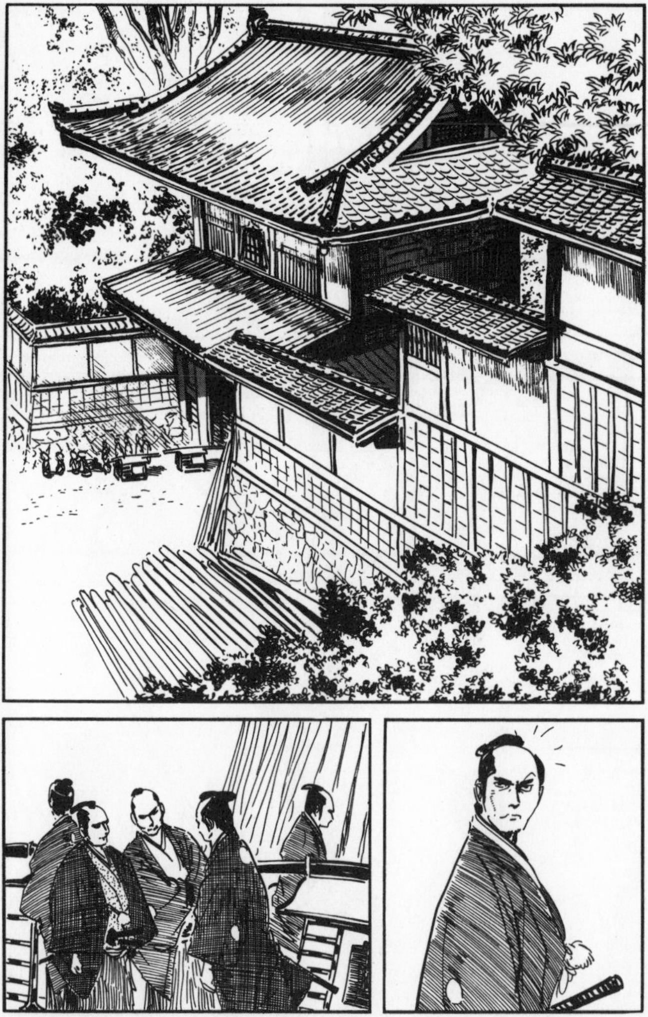

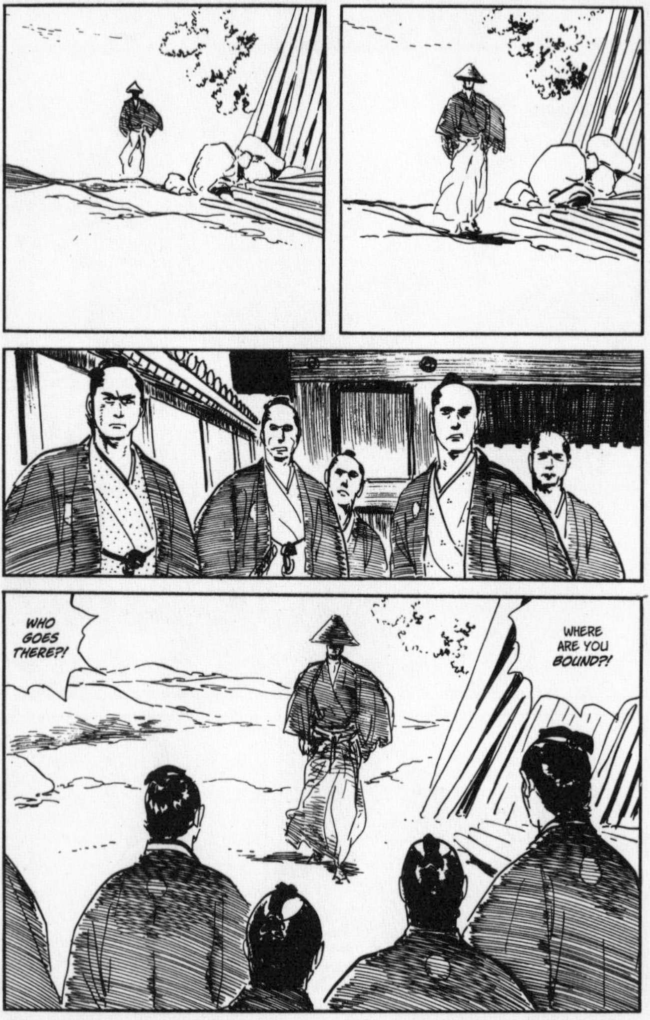
WHO GOES THERE?!
WHERE ARE YOU BOUND?!

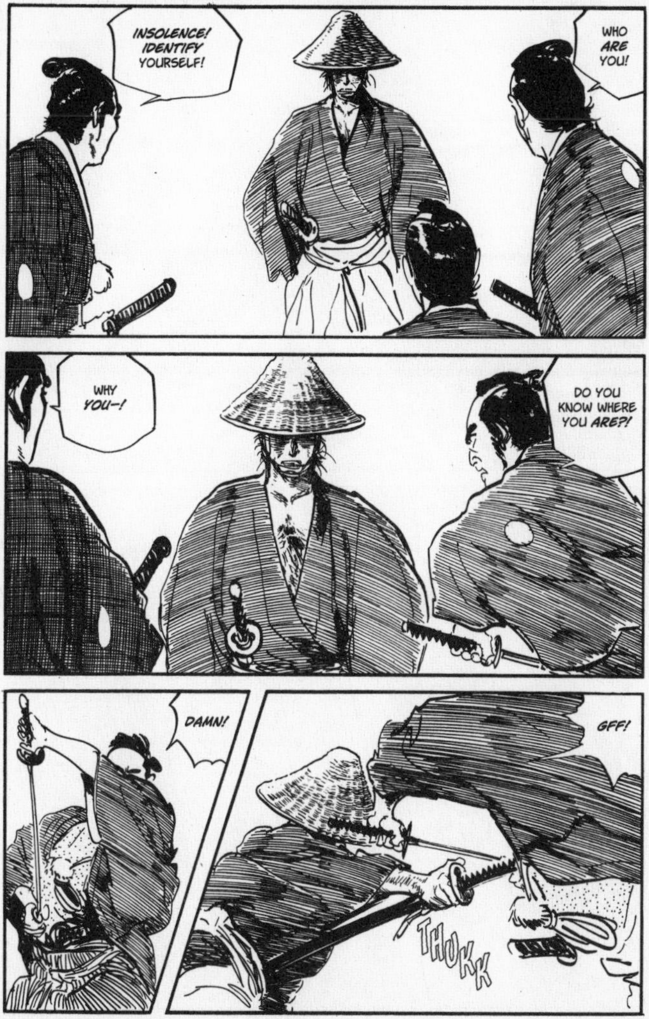
INSOLENCE! IDENTIFY YOURSELF!
WHO ARE YOU!
WHY YOU--!
DO YOU KNOW WHERE YOU ARE?!
DAMN!
GFF!
THUKK

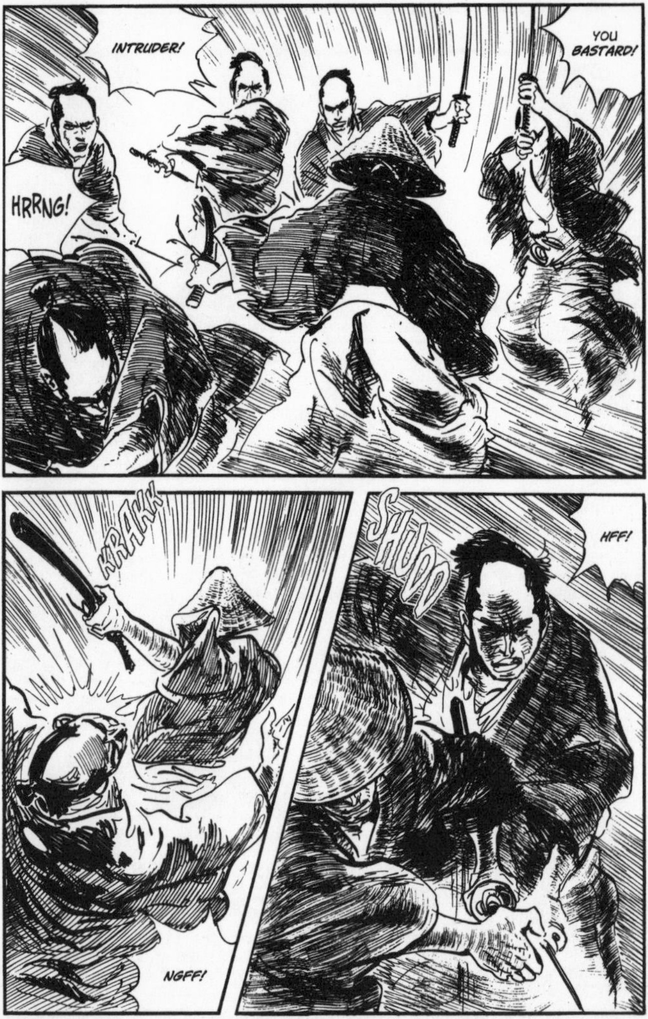
INTRUDER!
YOU BASTARD!
HRRNG!
KRAKK
NGFF!
SHUNN
HFF!

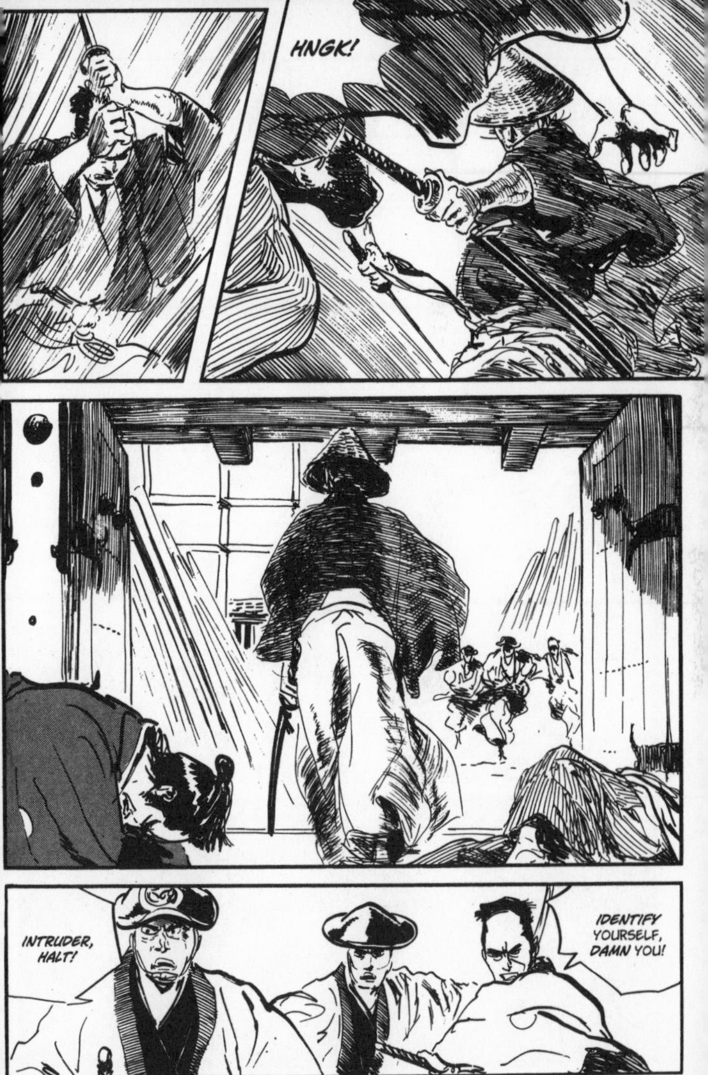
HNGK!
INTRUDER, HALT!
IDENTIFY YOURSELF, DAMN YOU!

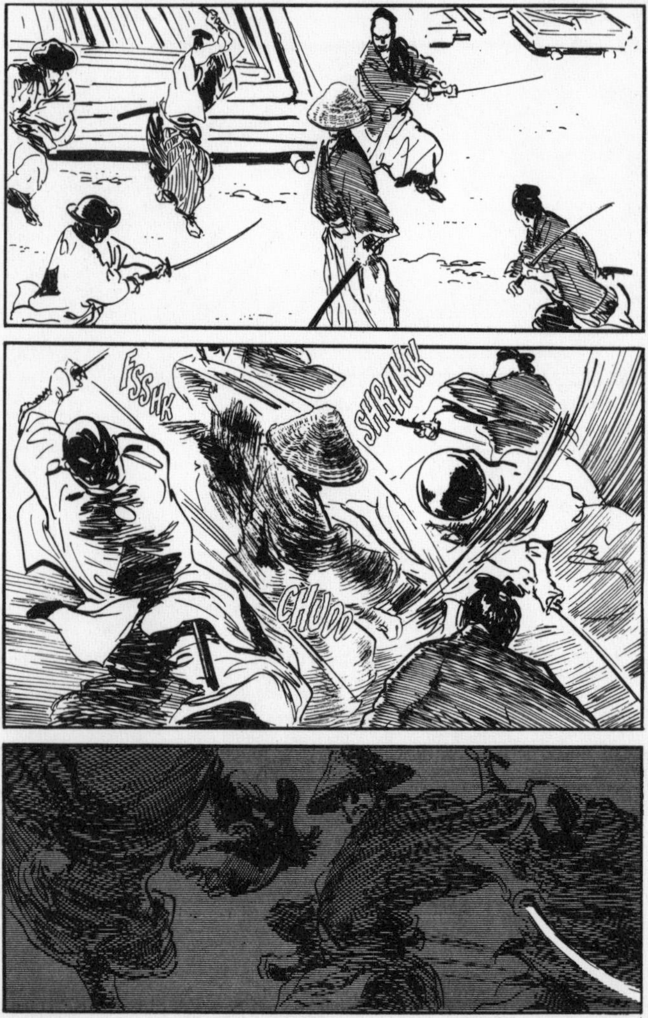
FSSHK
SHRAKK
CHUDD

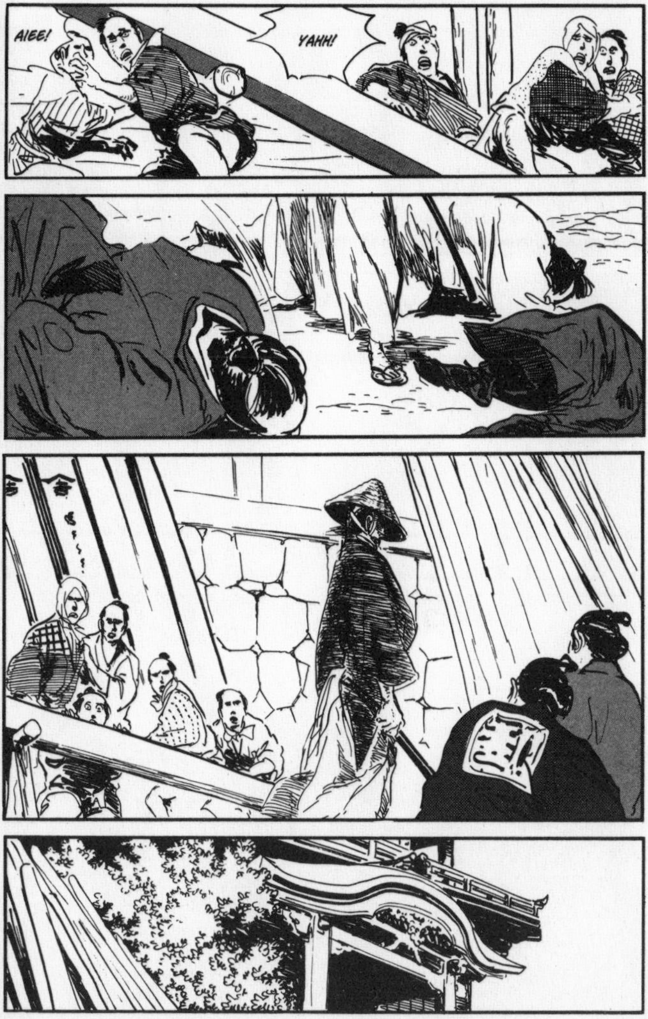
AIEE!
YAHH!

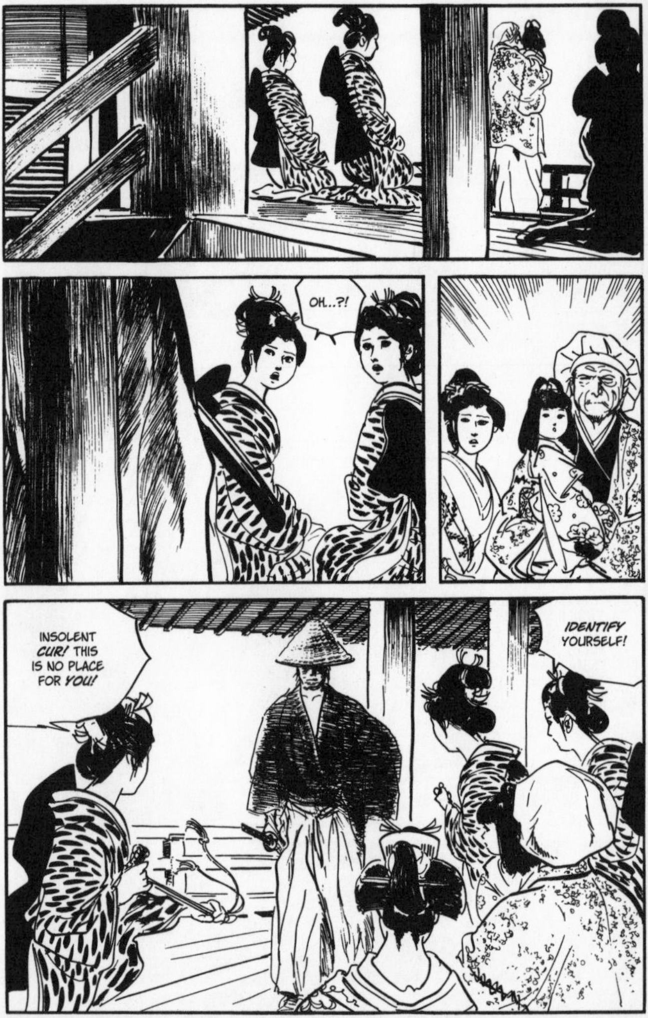
OH...?!
INSOLENT CUR! THIS IS NO PLACE FOR YOU!
IDENTIFY YOURSELF!

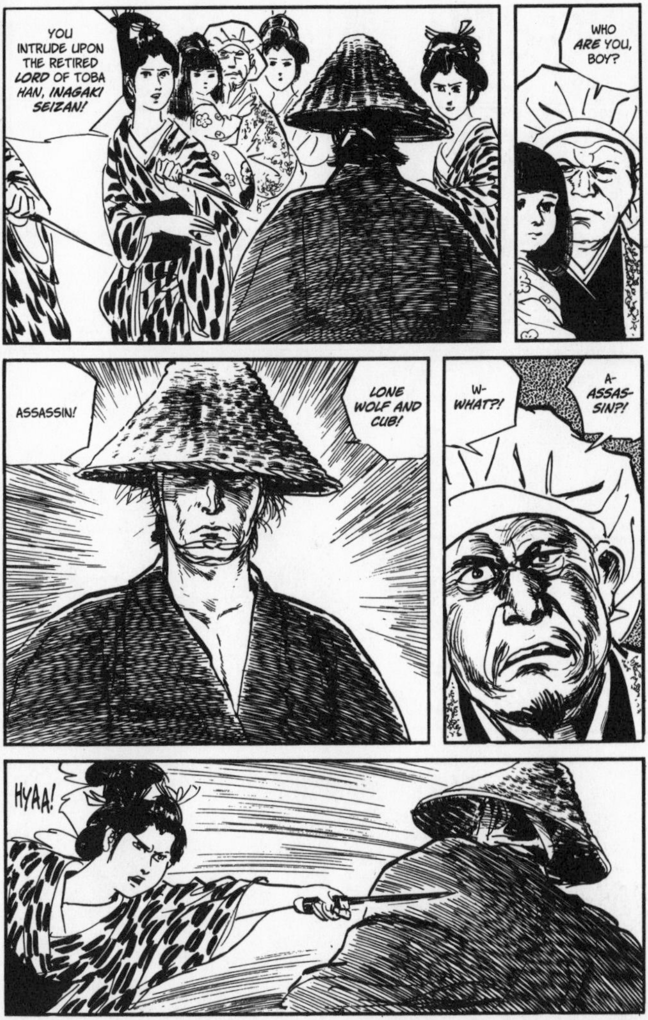
YOU INTRUDE UPON THE RETIRED LORD OF TOBA HAN, INAGAKI SEIZAN!
WHO ARE YOU, BOY?
ASSASSIN!
LONE WOLF AND CUB!
W-WHAT?!
A-ASSAS-SIN?!
HYAA!

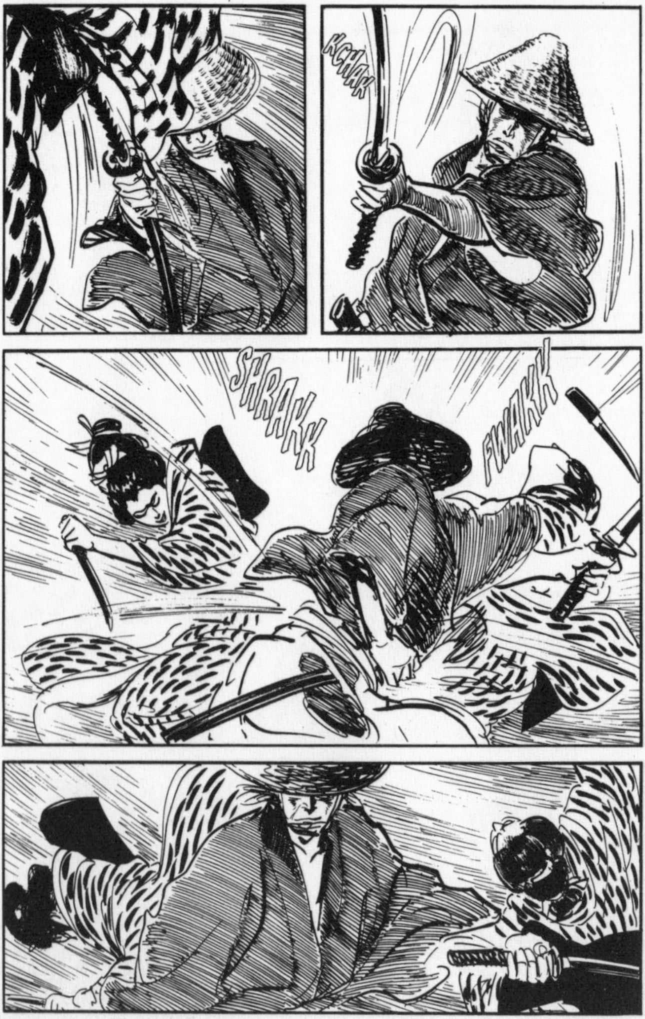
KCHAK
SHRAKK
FWAKK

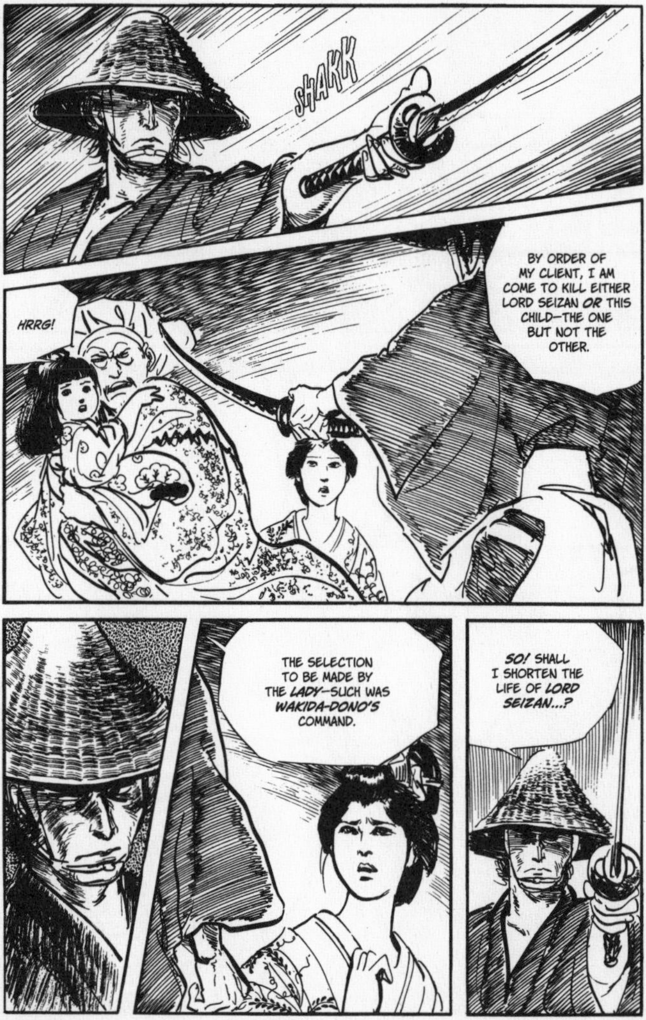
SHAKK
HRRG!
BY ORDER OF MY CLIENT, I AM COME TO KILL EITHER LORD SEIZAN OR THIS CHILD—THE ONE BUT NOT THE OTHER.
THE SELECTION TO BE MADE BY THE LADY—SUCH WAS WAKIDA-DONO'S COMMAND.
SO! SHALL I SHORTEN THE LIFE OF LORD SEIZAN...?

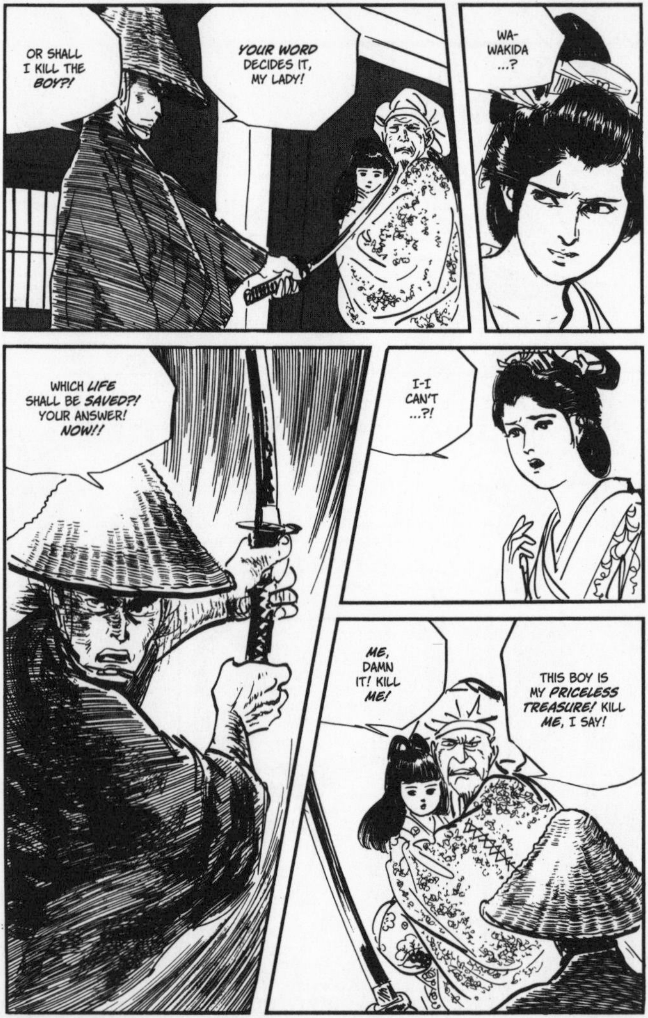
OR SHALL I KILL THE BOY?!
YOUR WORD DECIDES IT, MY LADY!
WA-WAKIDA ...?
WHICH LIFE SHALL BE SAVED?! YOUR ANSWER! NOW!!
I-I CAN'T ...?!
ME, DAMN IT! KILL ME!
THIS BOY IS MY PRICELESS TREASURE! KILL ME, I SAY!

I SEEK AN ANSWER FROM YOUR LADY!

WHICH ...?!

AHH...! I...

IF I RECEIVE NO *ANSWER*, I SHALL TAKE *BOTH* THEIR HONORED LIVES!

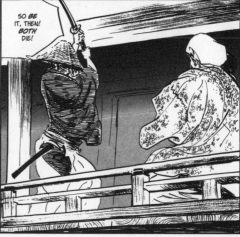

SO *BE* IT, THEN! *BOTH* DIE!

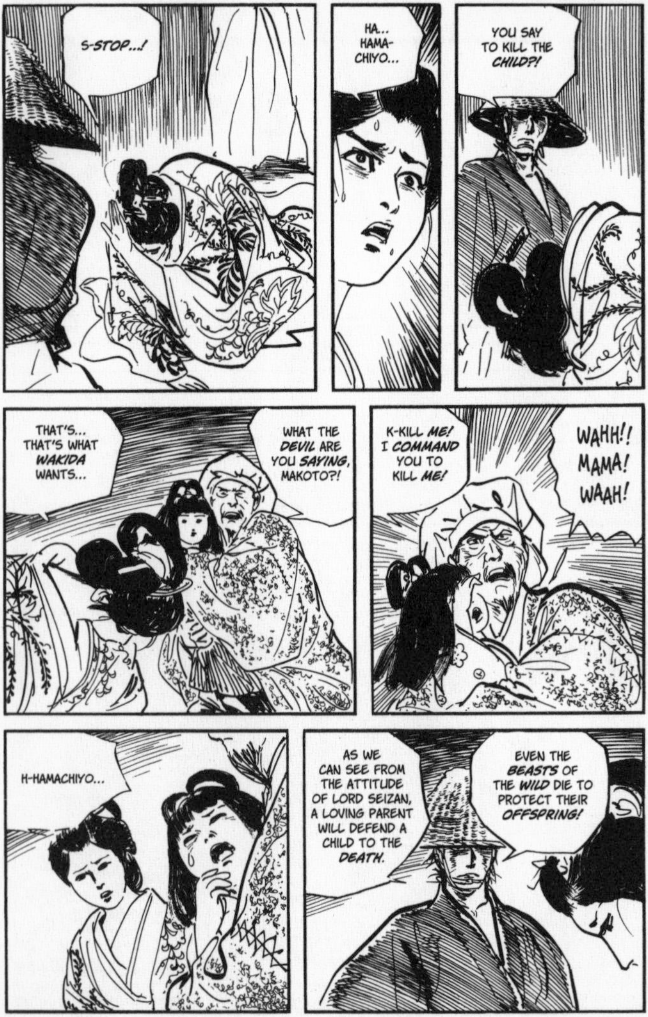
S-STOP...!
HA... HAMA-CHIYO...
YOU SAY TO KILL THE CHILD?!
THAT'S... THAT'S WHAT WAKIDA WANTS...
WHAT THE DEVIL ARE YOU SAYING, MAKOTO?!
K-KILL ME! I COMMAND YOU TO KILL ME!
WAHH!! MAMA! WAAH!
H-HAMACHIYO...
AS WE CAN SEE FROM THE ATTITUDE OF LORD SEIZAN, A LOVING PARENT WILL DEFEND A CHILD TO THE DEATH.
EVEN THE BEASTS OF THE WILD DIE TO PROTECT THEIR OFFSPRING!

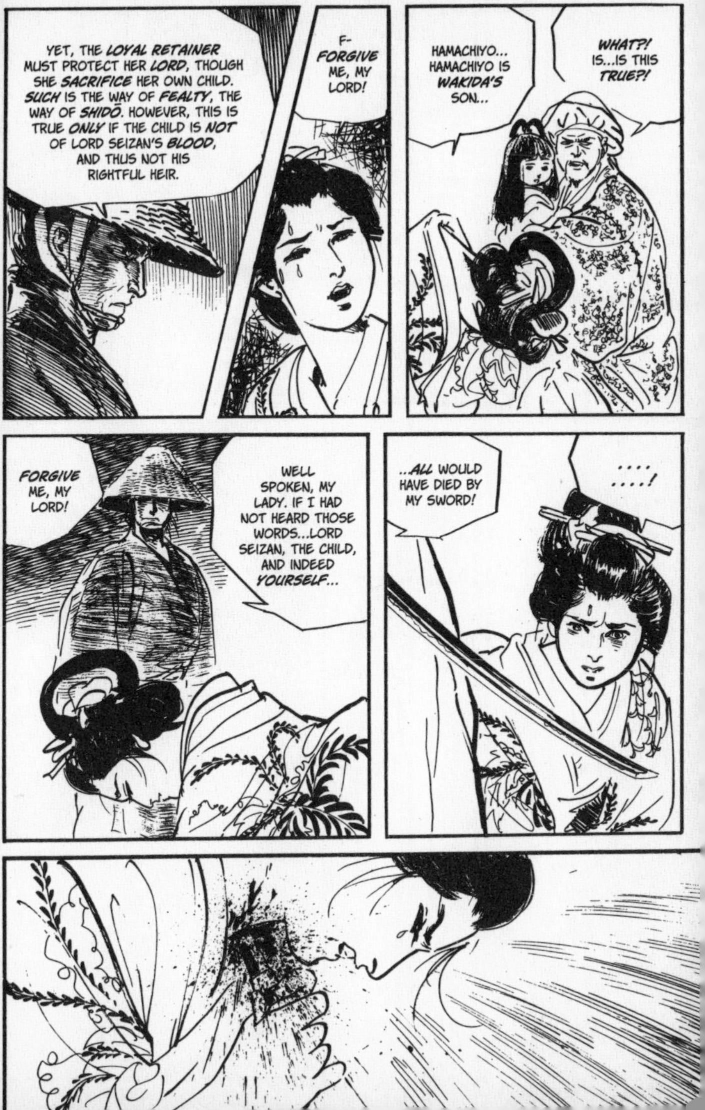
YET, THE LOYAL RETAINER MUST PROTECT HER LORD, THOUGH SHE SACRIFICE HER OWN CHILD. SUCH IS THE WAY OF FEALTY, THE WAY OF SHIDŌ. HOWEVER, THIS IS TRUE ONLY IF THE CHILD IS NOT OF LORD SEIZAN'S BLOOD, AND THUS NOT HIS RIGHTFUL HEIR.
F- FORGIVE ME, MY LORD!
HAMACHIYO... HAMACHIYO IS WAKIDA'S SON...
WHAT?! IS...IS THIS TRUE?!
FORGIVE ME, MY LORD!
WELL SPOKEN, MY LADY. IF I HAD NOT HEARD THOSE WORDS...LORD SEIZAN, THE CHILD, AND INDEED YOURSELF...
...ALL WOULD HAVE DIED BY MY SWORD!
....
....!

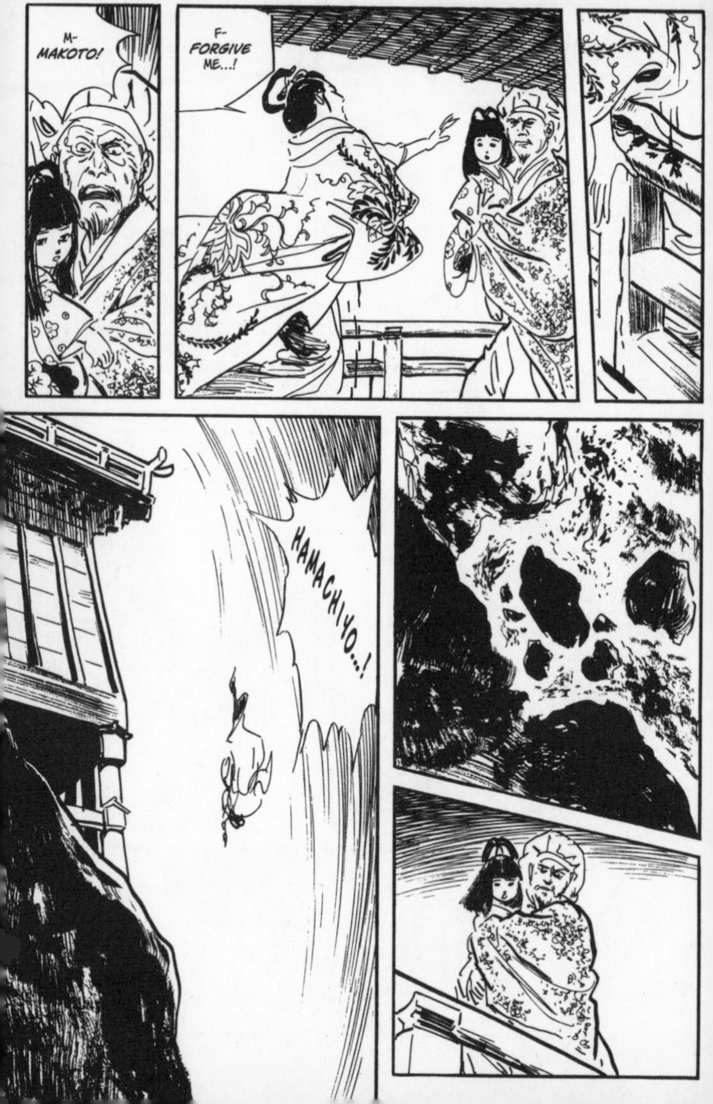
M-
MAKOTO!
F-
FORGIVE
ME...!
HAMACHIYO...!

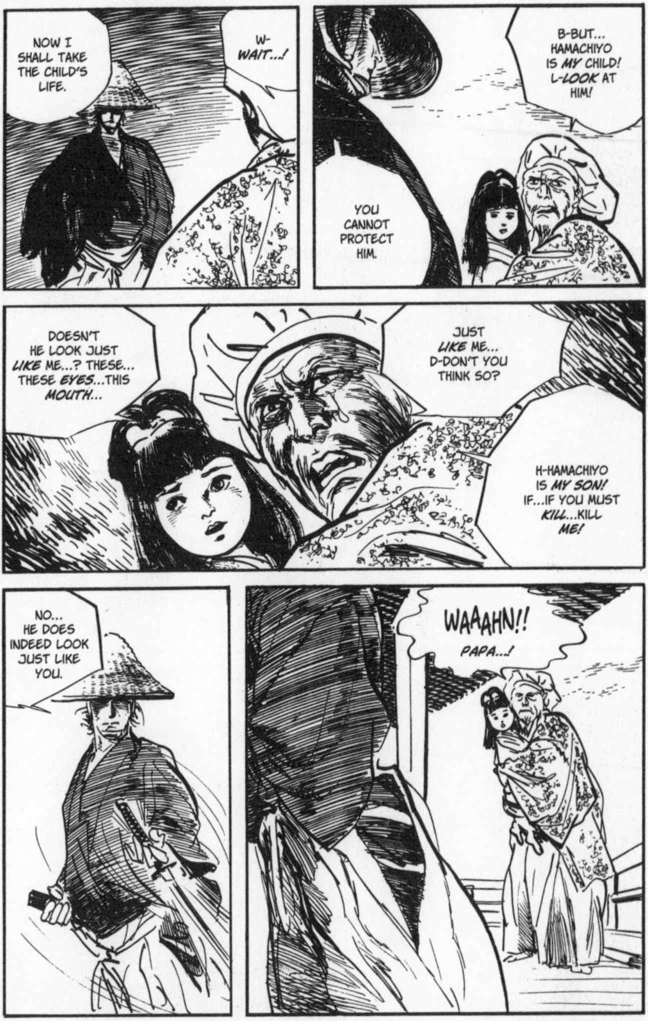
NOW I SHALL TAKE THE CHILD'S LIFE.
W- WAIT...!
B-BUT... HAMACHIYO IS MY CHILD! L-LOOK AT HIM!
YOU CANNOT PROTECT HIM.
DOESN'T HE LOOK JUST LIKE ME...? THESE... THESE EYES...THIS MOUTH...
JUST LIKE ME... D-DON'T YOU THINK SO?
H-HAMACHIYO IS MY SON! IF...IF YOU MUST KILL...KILL ME!
NO... HE DOES INDEED LOOK JUST LIKE YOU.
WAAAHN!!
PAPA...!

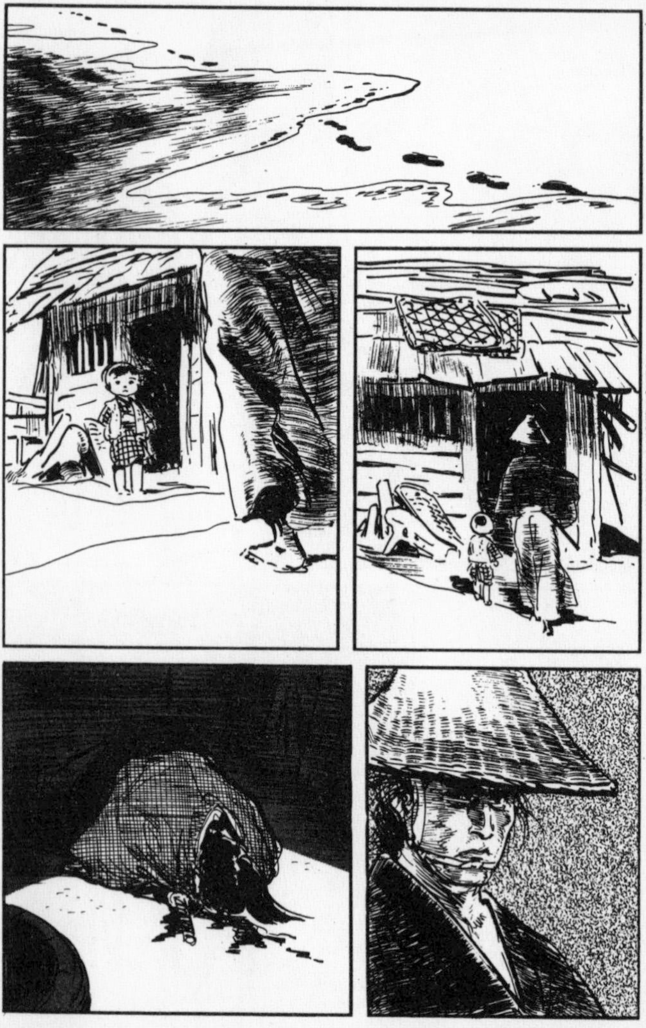

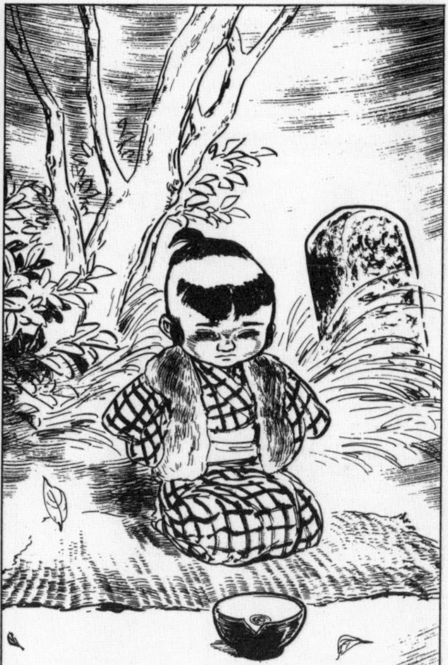

the sixty-second

# A Promise of Potatoes

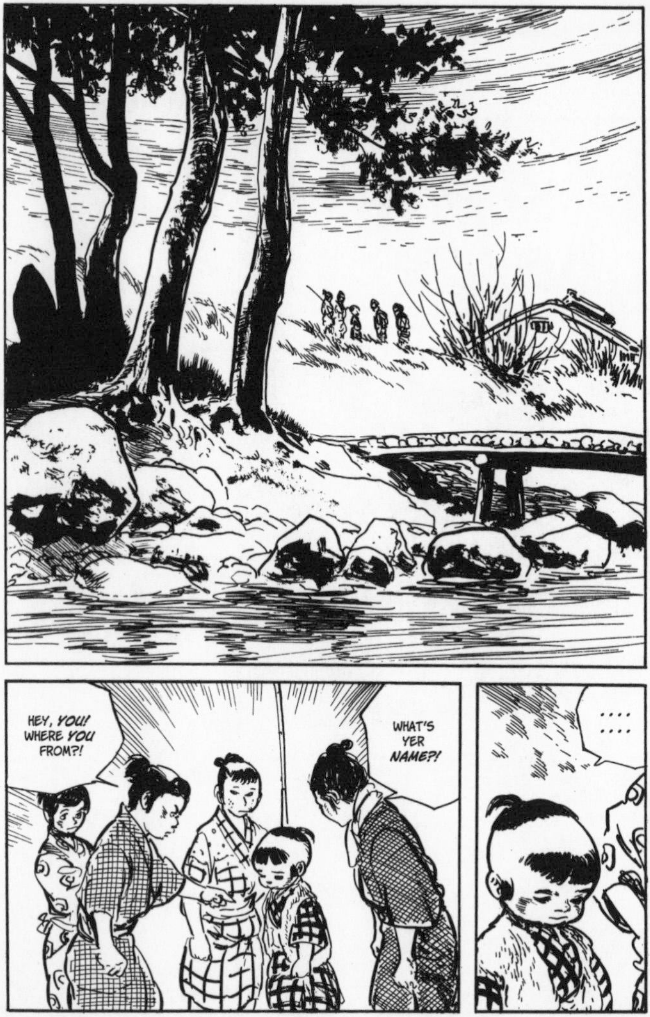
HEY, YOU! WHERE YOU FROM?!
WHAT'S YER NAME?!
....
....

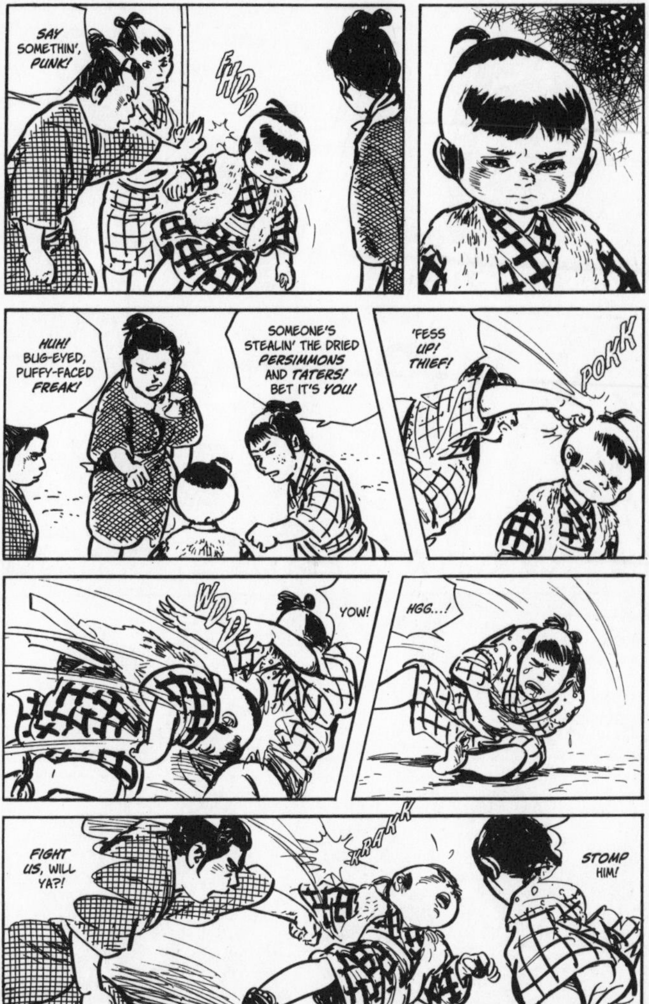
SAY SOMETHIN', PUNK!
FHDD
HUH! BUG-EYED, PUFFY-FACED FREAK!
SOMEONE'S STEALIN' THE DRIED PERSIMMONS AND TATERS! BET IT'S YOU!
'FESS UP! THIEF!
POKK
WDD
YOW!
HGG...!
FIGHT US, WILL YA?!
KRAKK
STOMP HIM!

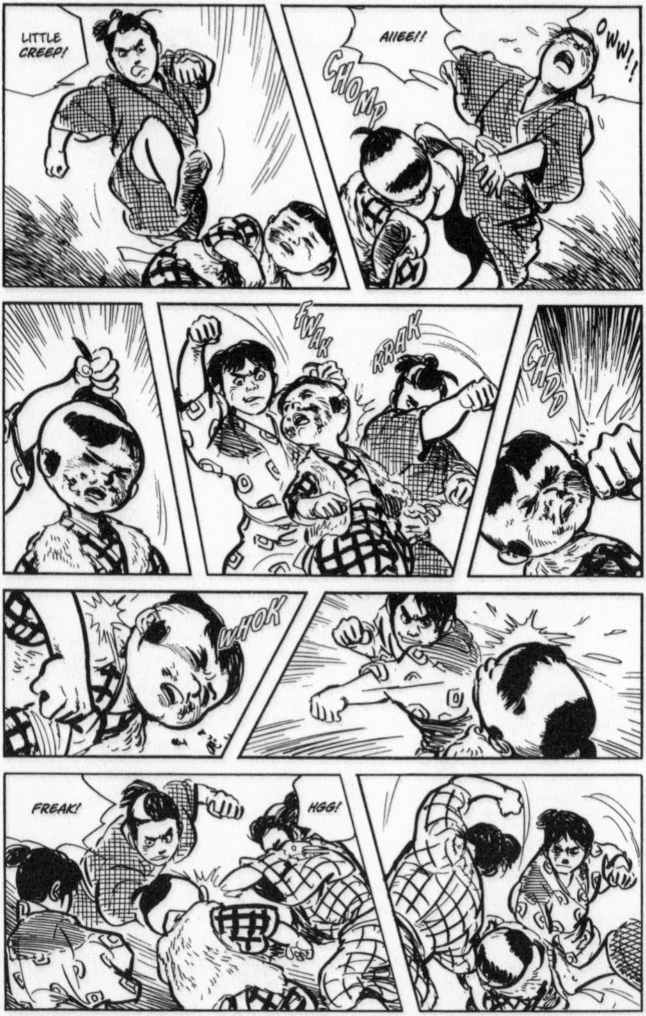
LITTLE CREEP!
AIIEE!!
OWW!!
CHOMP
FWAK
KRAK
CHDD
WHOK
FREAK!
HGG!

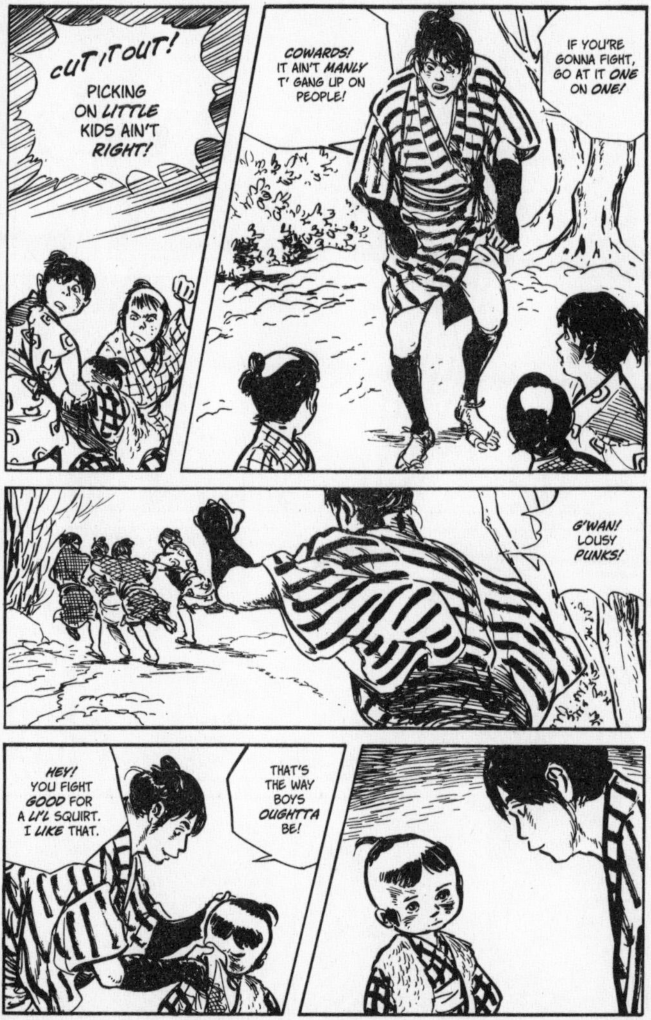
CUT IT OUT!
PICKING ON LITTLE KIDS AIN'T RIGHT!
COWARDS! IT AIN'T MANLY T' GANG UP ON PEOPLE!
IF YOU'RE GONNA FIGHT, GO AT IT ONE ON ONE!
G'WAN! LOUSY PUNKS!
HEY! YOU FIGHT GOOD FOR A LI'L SQUIRT. I LIKE THAT.
THAT'S THE WAY BOYS OUGHTTA BE!

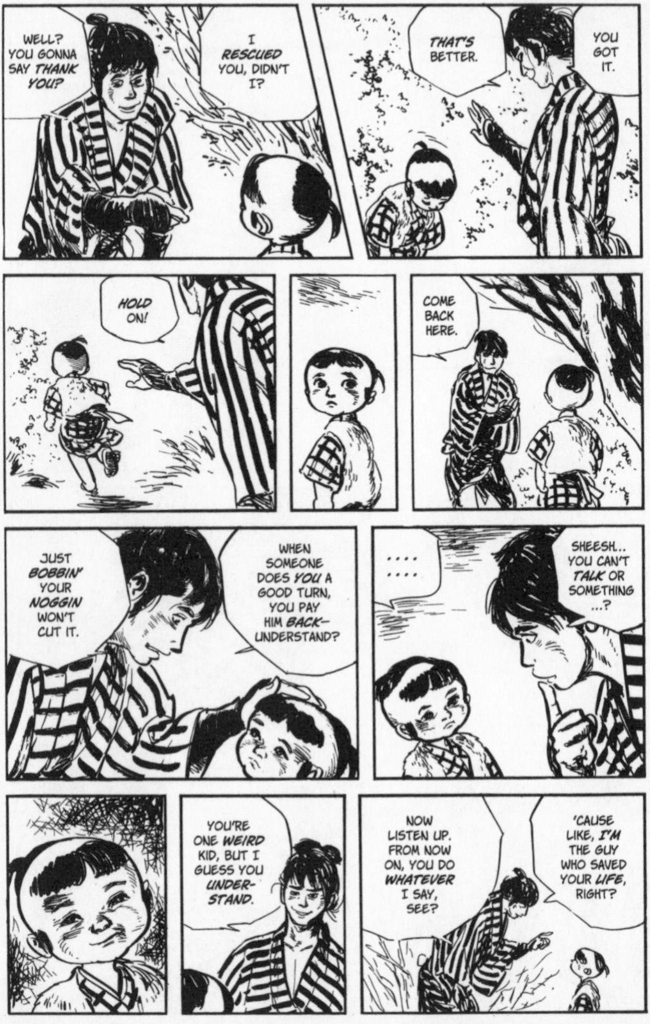
WELL? YOU GONNA SAY THANK YOU?
I RESCUED YOU, DIDN'T I?
THAT'S BETTER.
YOU GOT IT.
HOLD ON!
COME BACK HERE.
JUST BOBBIN' YOUR NOGGIN WON'T CUT IT.
WHEN SOMEONE DOES YOU A GOOD TURN, YOU PAY HIM BACK–UNDERSTAND?
....
....
SHEESH... YOU CAN'T TALK OR SOMETHING ...?
YOU'RE ONE WEIRD KID, BUT I GUESS YOU UNDERSTAND.
NOW LISTEN UP. FROM NOW ON, YOU DO WHATEVER I SAY, SEE?
'CAUSE LIKE, I'M THE GUY WHO SAVED YOUR LIFE, RIGHT?

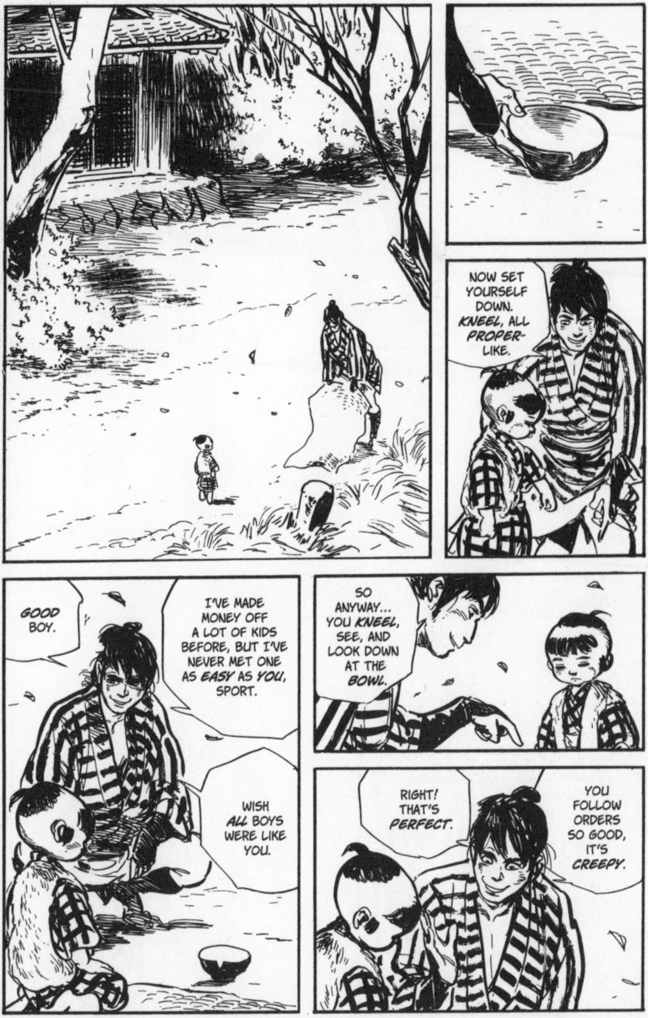
NOW SET YOURSELF DOWN. KNEEL, ALL PROPER-LIKE.
GOOD BOY.
I'VE MADE MONEY OFF A LOT OF KIDS BEFORE, BUT I'VE NEVER MET ONE AS EASY AS YOU, SPORT.
WISH ALL BOYS WERE LIKE YOU.
SO ANYWAY... YOU KNEEL, SEE, AND LOOK DOWN AT THE BOWL.
RIGHT! THAT'S PERFECT.
YOU FOLLOW ORDERS SO GOOD, IT'S CREEPY.

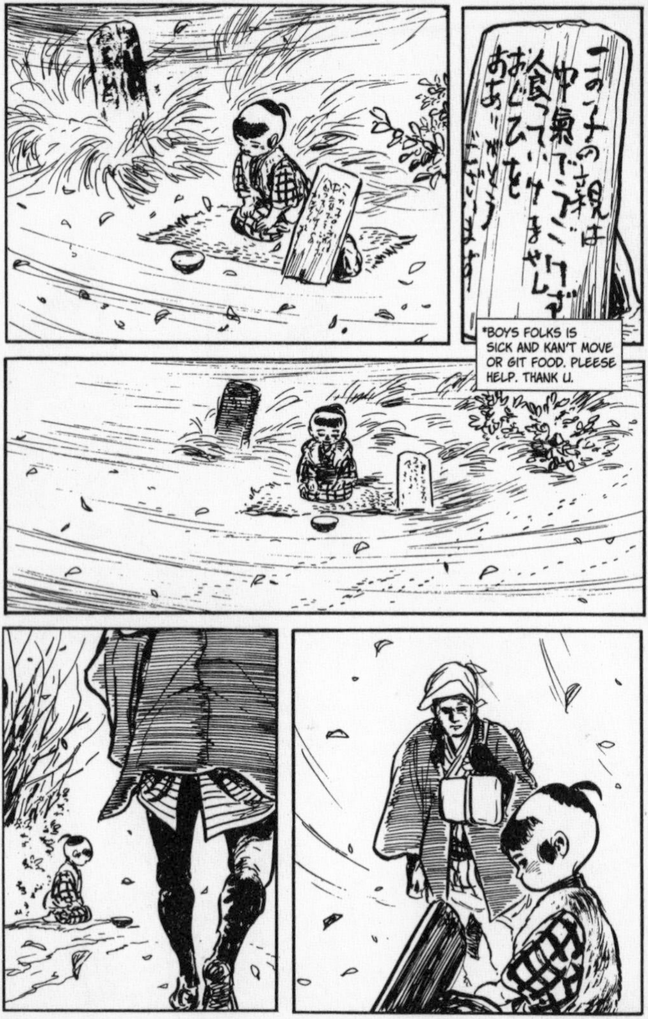
この子の親は
中氣でうごけず
食っていけません
ありがとうございます
*BOYS FOLKS IS SICK AND KAN'T MOVE OR GIT FOOD. PLEESE HELP. THANK U.

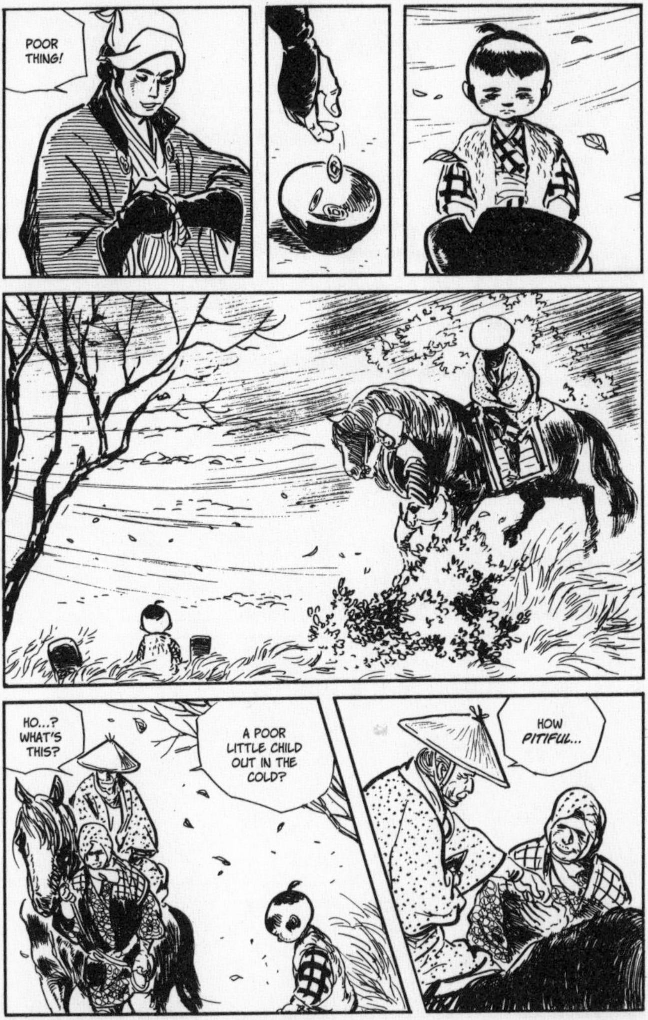
POOR THING!
HO...? WHAT'S THIS?
A POOR LITTLE CHILD OUT IN THE COLD?
HOW *PITIFUL*...

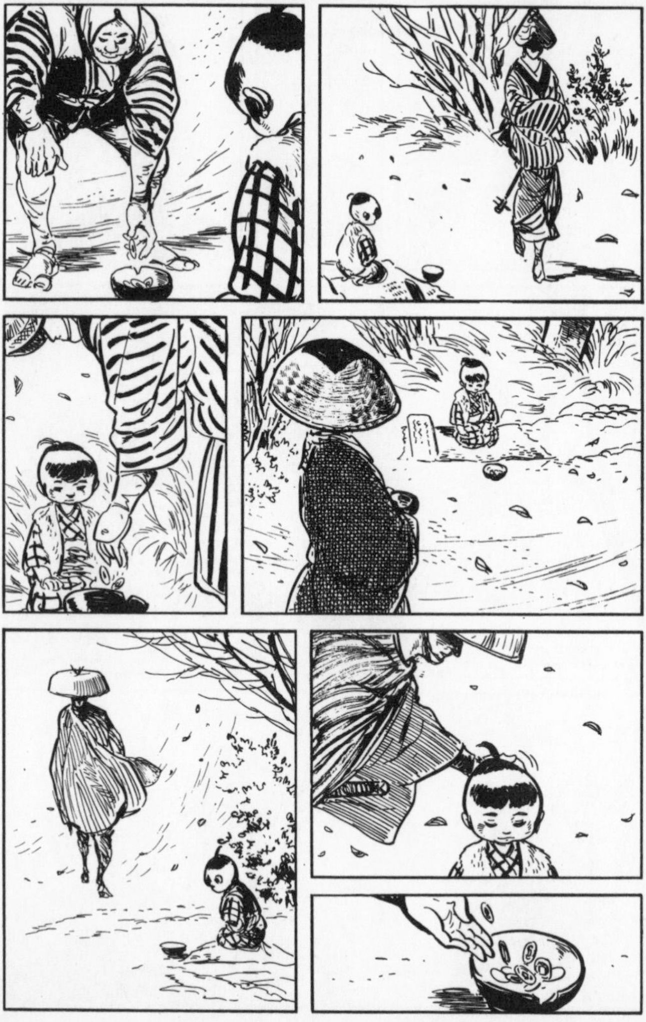

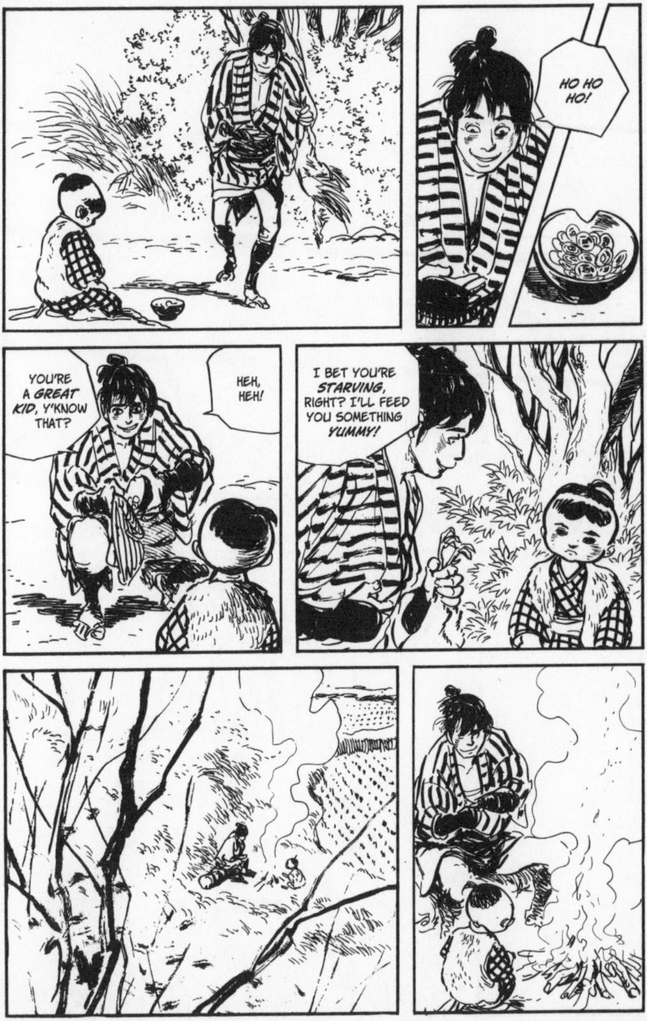
HO HO HO!
YOU'RE A GREAT KID, Y'KNOW THAT?
HEH, HEH!
I BET YOU'RE STARVING, RIGHT? I'LL FEED YOU SOMETHING YUMMY!

HEH, HEH...

FOOD FOR THE TAKING, *DRINKING* MONEY JUST *ROLLING* ON IN—WOO-HOO!

WAY THIS WORLD *WORKS.* IF YOU'VE GOT A GOOD *NOGGIN...*

...AND SOME *QUICK HANDS...*

...YOU CAN KICK RIGHT BACK AND ENJOY *LIFE.*

HEH, HEH, HEH!

SSSSSS

THESE *TATERS* ARE *REALLY* YUMMY.

PO-TA-TERS. WANNA TRY ONE?

BUT LISTEN UP! AFTER YOU EAT, YOU GOTTA SIT AND MAKE MORE *MONEY,* OKAY?

GOTTA *PROMISE!*

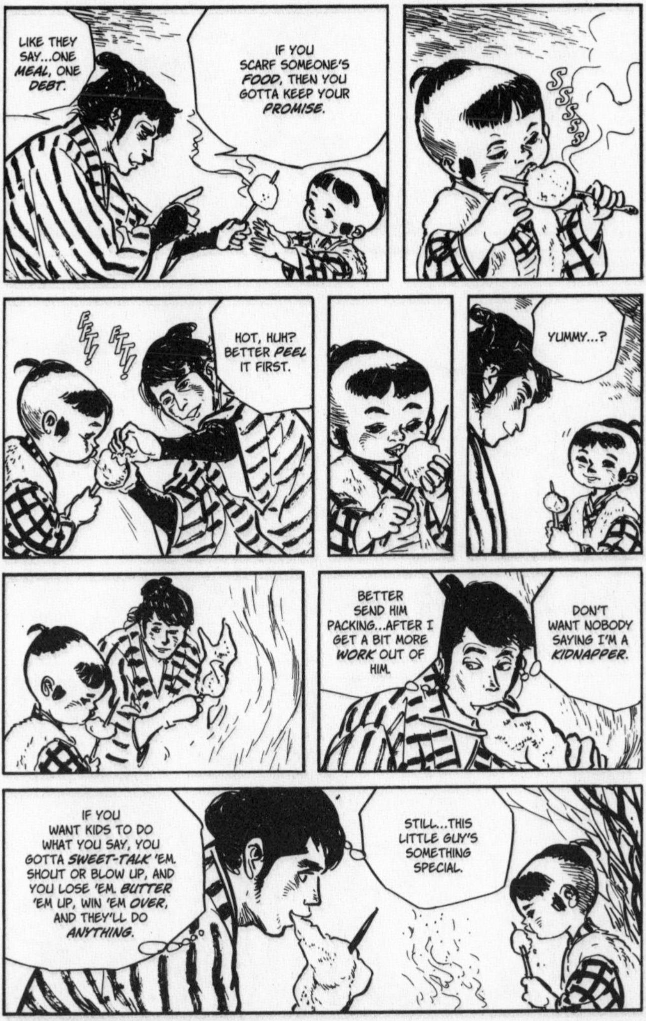

LIKE THEY SAY...ONE MEAL, ONE DEBT.
IF YOU SCARF SOMEONE'S FOOD, THEN YOU GOTTA KEEP YOUR PROMISE.
SSSS
FFT! FFT!
HOT, HUH? BETTER PEEL IT FIRST.
YUMMY...?
BETTER SEND HIM PACKING...AFTER I GET A BIT MORE WORK OUT OF HIM.
DON'T WANT NOBODY SAYING I'M A KIDNAPPER.
IF YOU WANT KIDS TO DO WHAT YOU SAY, YOU GOTTA SWEET-TALK 'EM. SHOUT OR BLOW UP, AND YOU LOSE 'EM. BUTTER 'EM UP, WIN 'EM OVER, AND THEY'LL DO ANYTHING.
STILL...THIS LITTLE GUY'S SOMETHING SPECIAL.

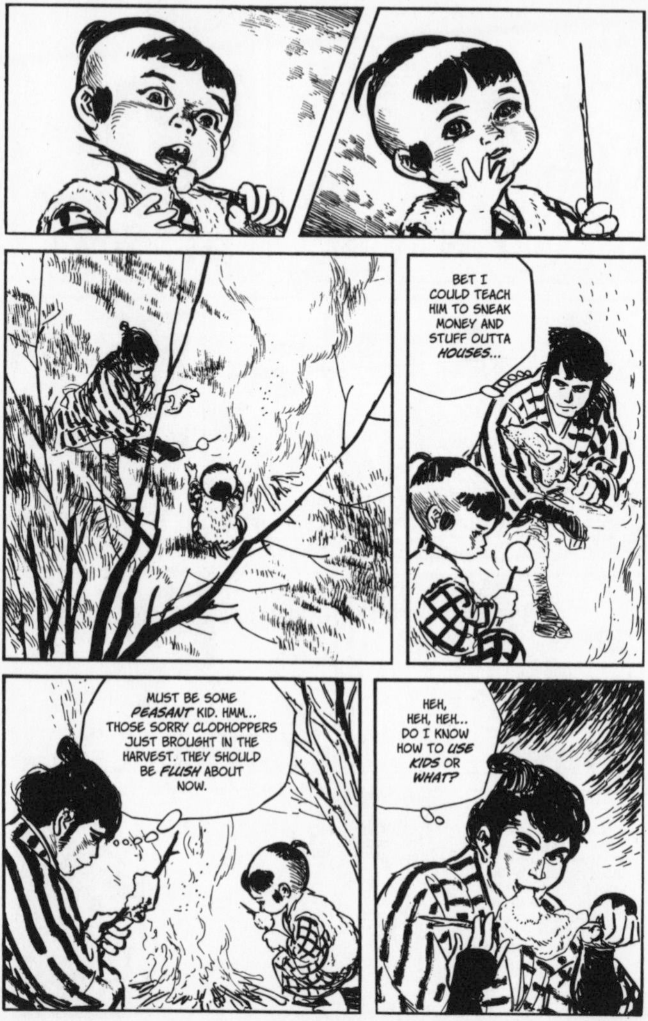
BET I COULD TEACH HIM TO SNEAK MONEY AND STUFF OUTTA *HOUSES*...
MUST BE SOME *PEASANT* KID. HMM... THOSE SORRY CLODHOPPERS JUST BROUGHT IN THE HARVEST. THEY SHOULD BE *FLUSH* ABOUT NOW.
HEH, HEH, HEH... DO I KNOW HOW TO *USE* *KIDS* OR *WHAT?*

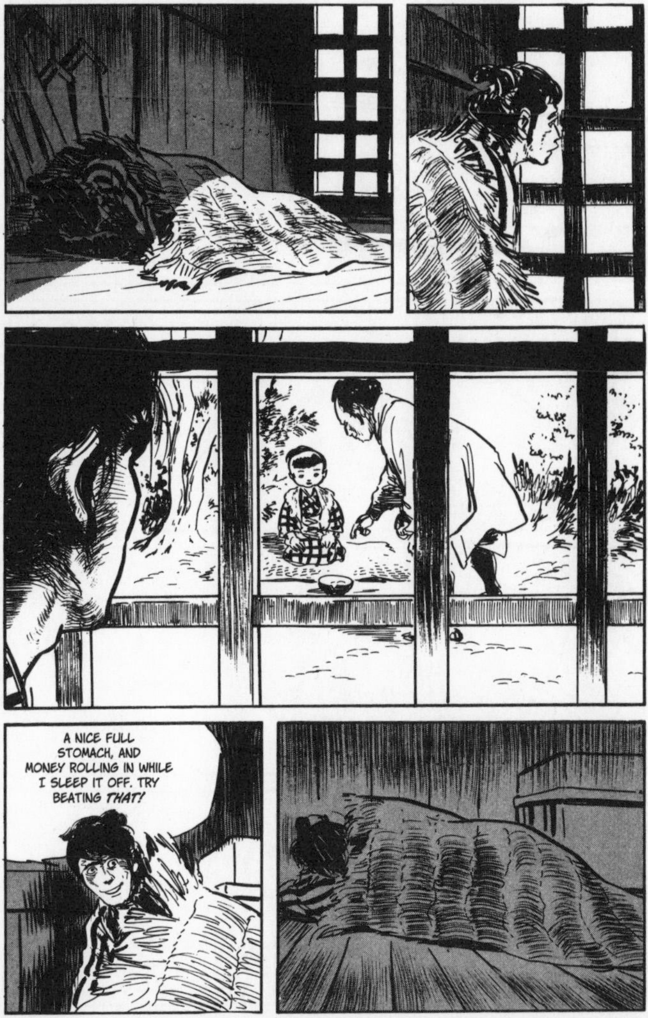
A NICE FULL STOMACH, AND MONEY ROLLING IN WHILE I SLEEP IT OFF. TRY BEATING *THAT!*

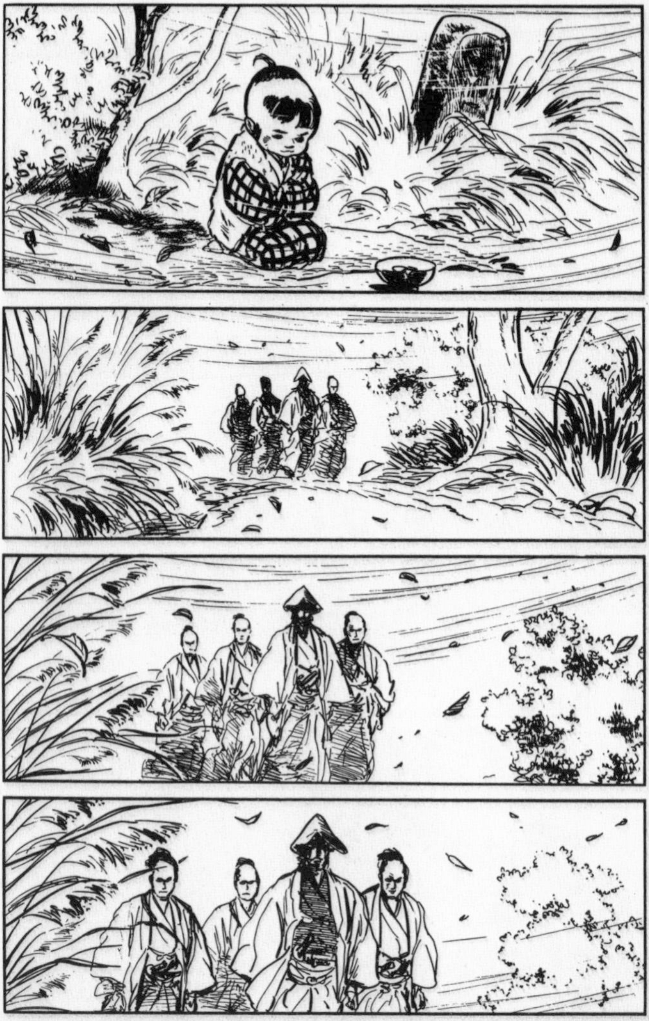

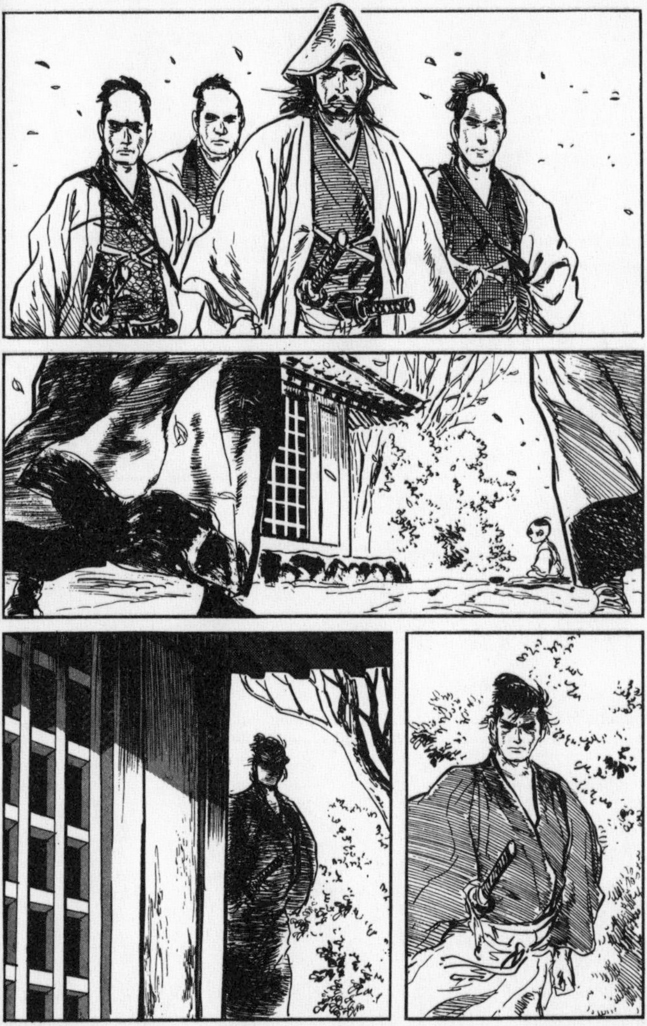

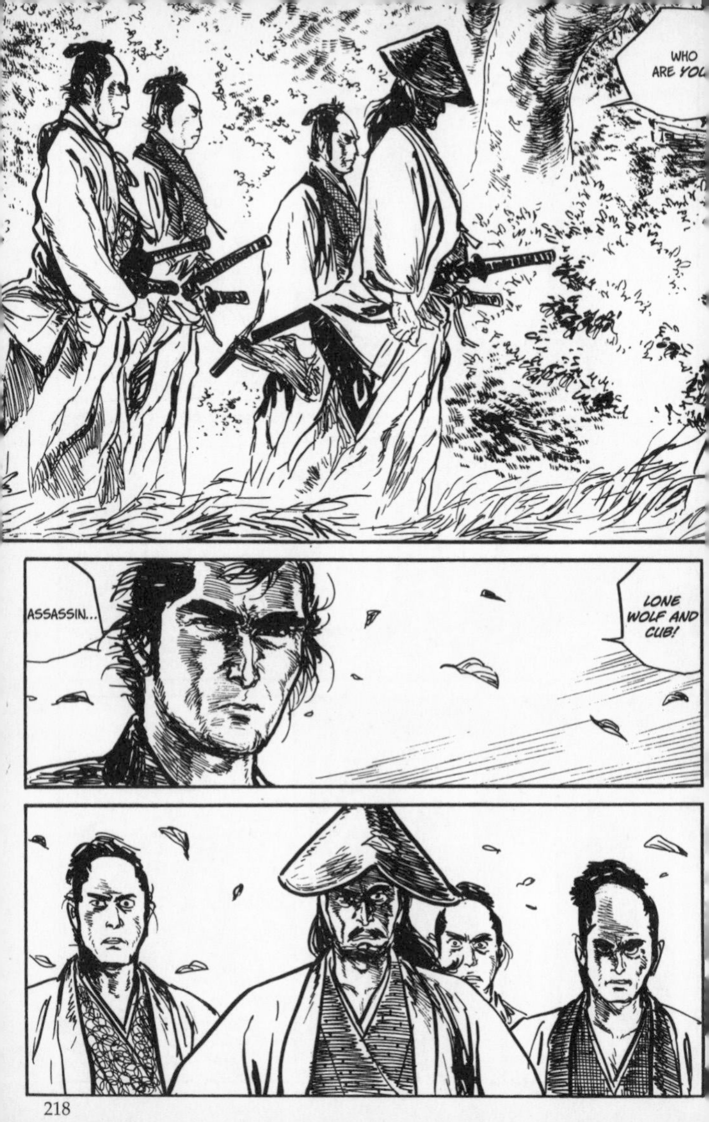
WHO ARE YOU
ASSASSIN...
LONE WOLF AND CUB!

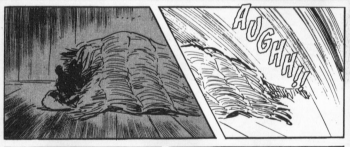

AUGHH!!

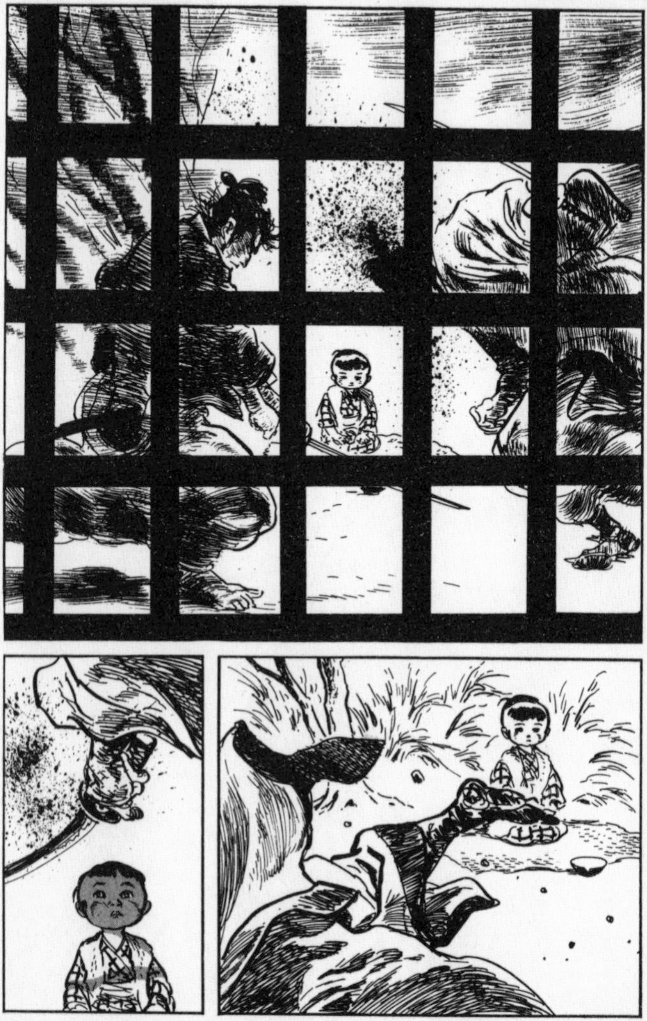

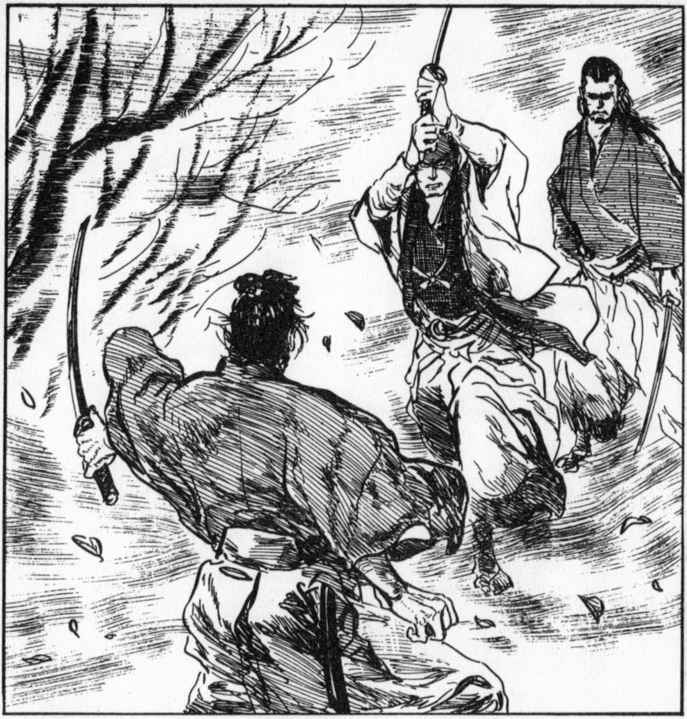

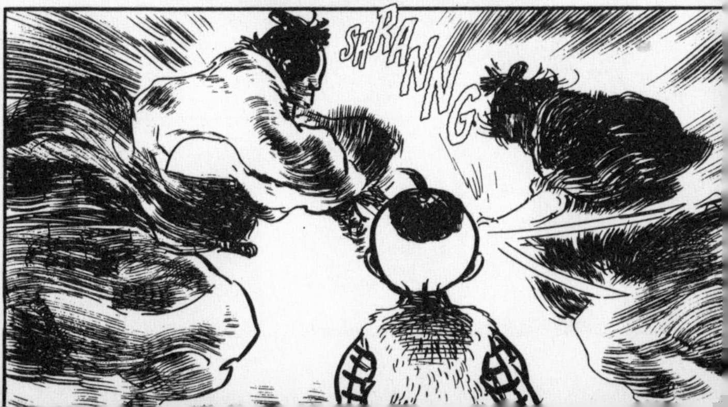
SHRANNG

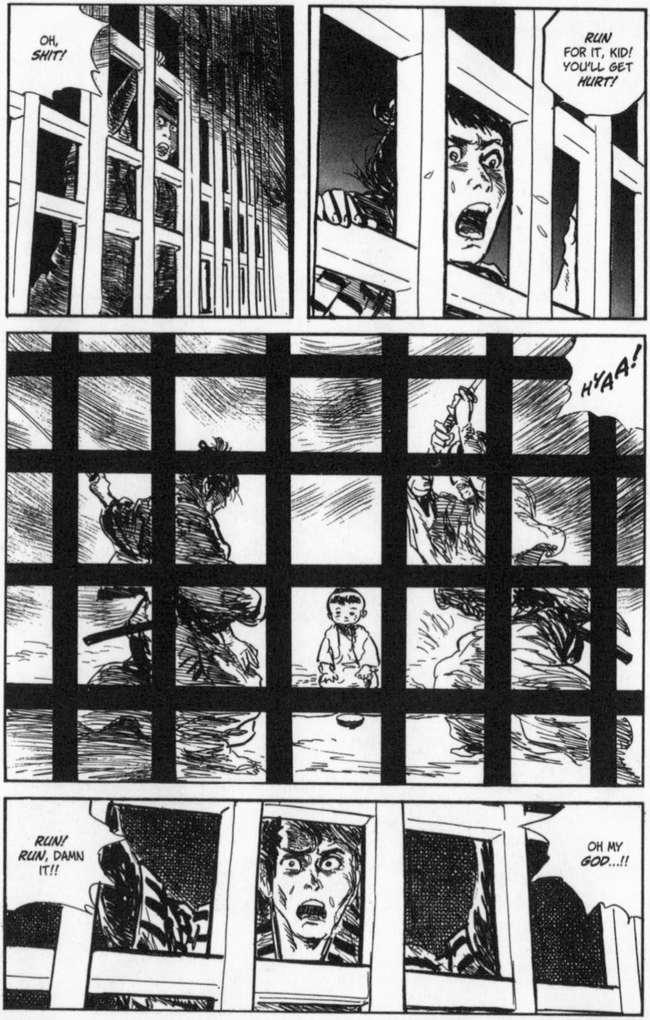
OH, SHIT!
RUN FOR IT, KID! YOU'LL GET HURT!
HYAA!
RUN! RUN, DAMN IT!!
OH MY GOD...!!

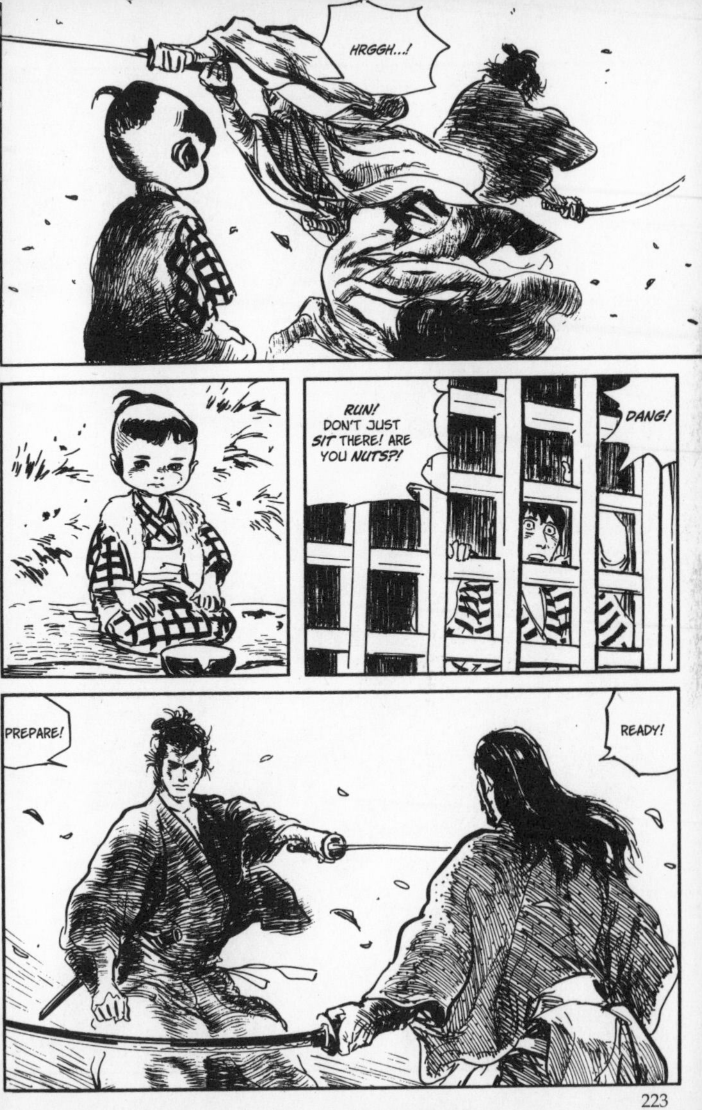
HRGGH...!
RUN!
DON'T JUST
SIT THERE! ARE
YOU NUTS?!
DANG!
PREPARE!
READY!

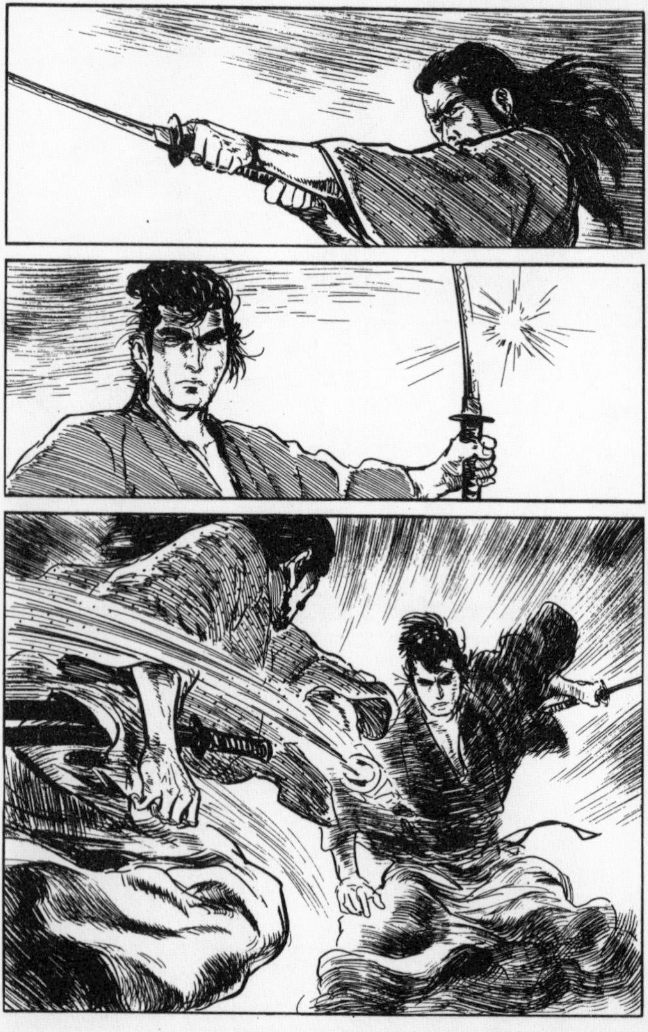

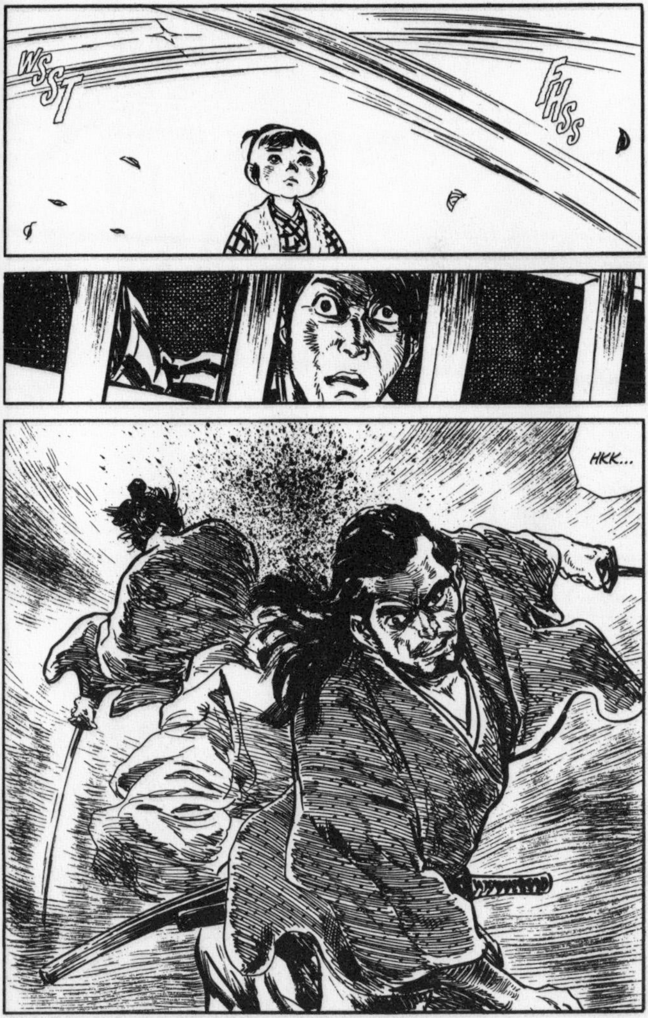
WSST
FHSS
HKK...

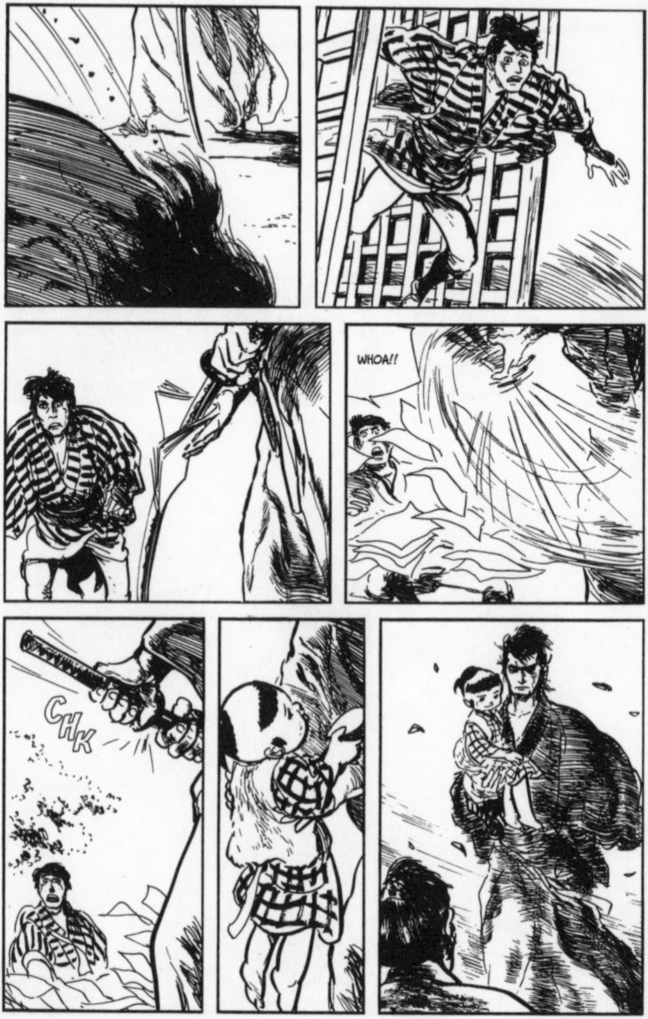
WHOA!!
CHK

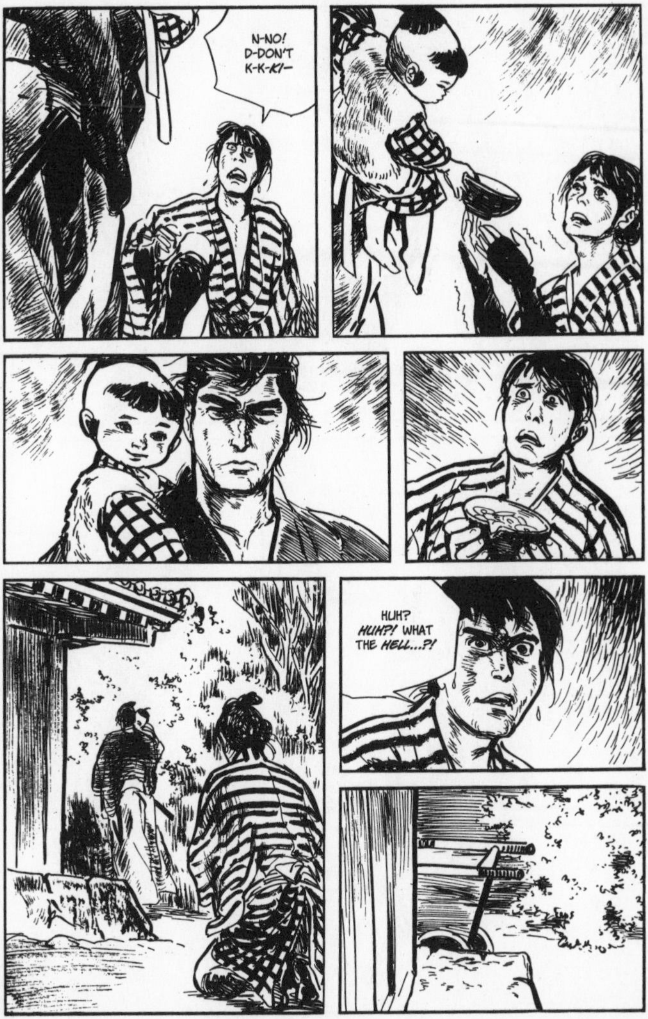
N-NO! D-DON'T K-K-KI—
HUH? HUH?! WHAT THE HELL...?!

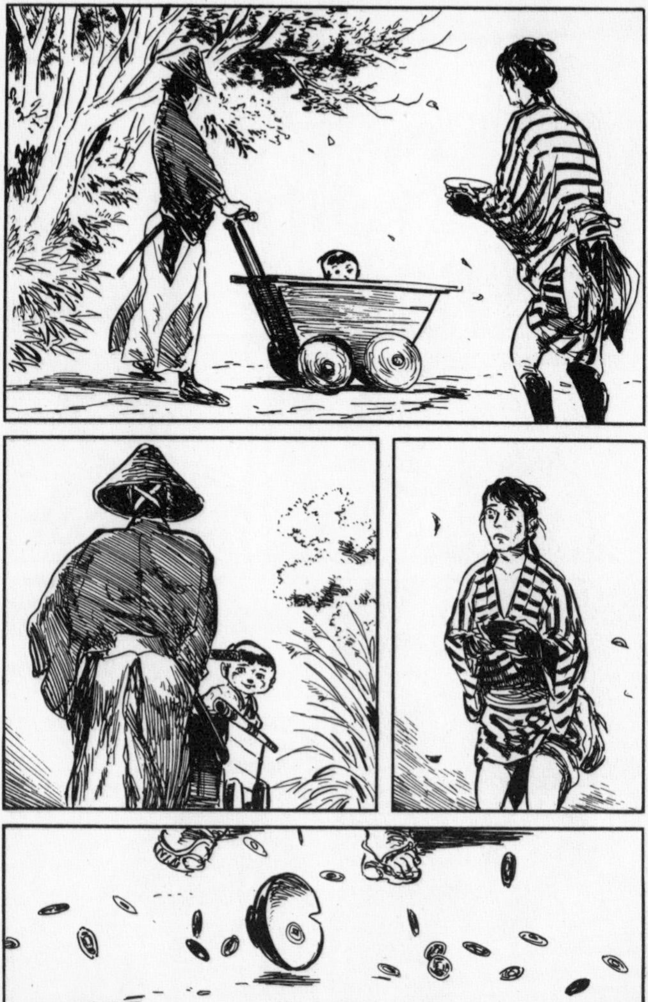

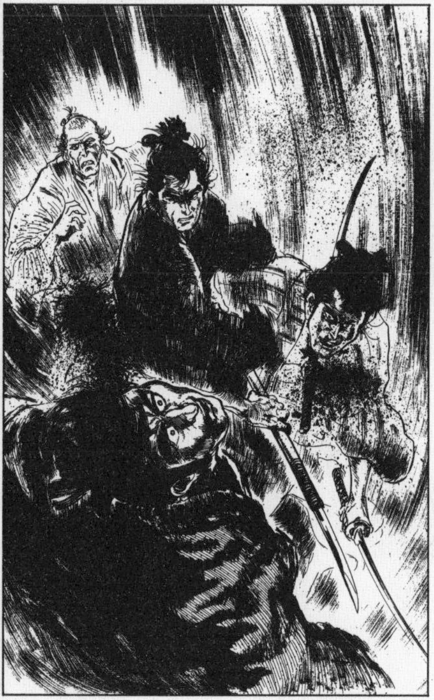

the sixty-third

# Wife Killer

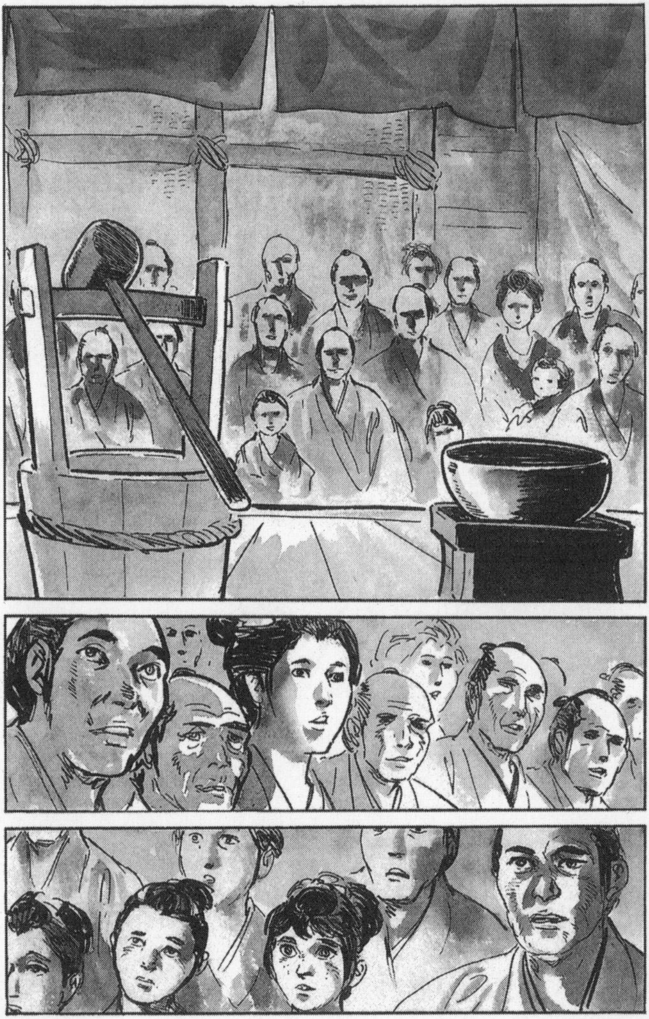

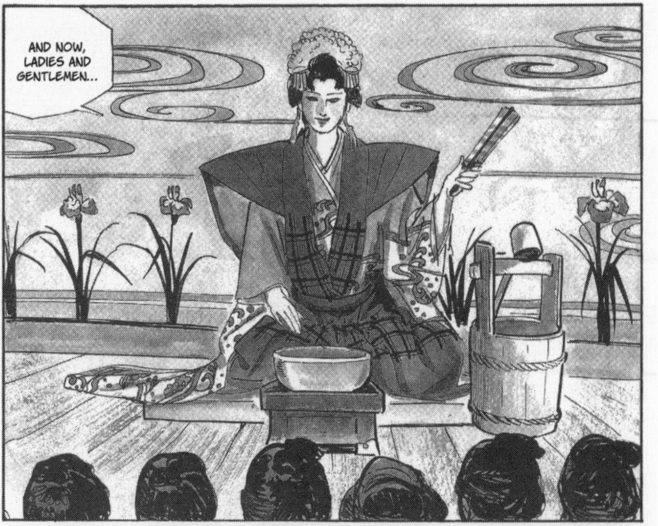
AND NOW, LADIES AND GENTLEMEN...
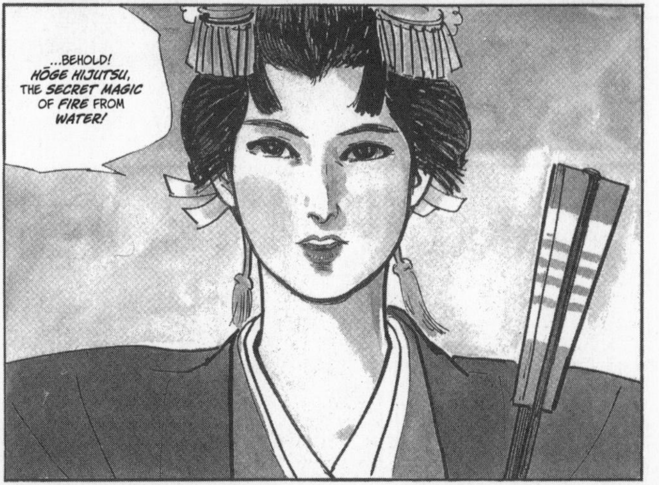
...BEHOLD! *HŌGE HIJUTSU*, THE *SECRET MAGIC* OF *FIRE* FROM *WATER!*

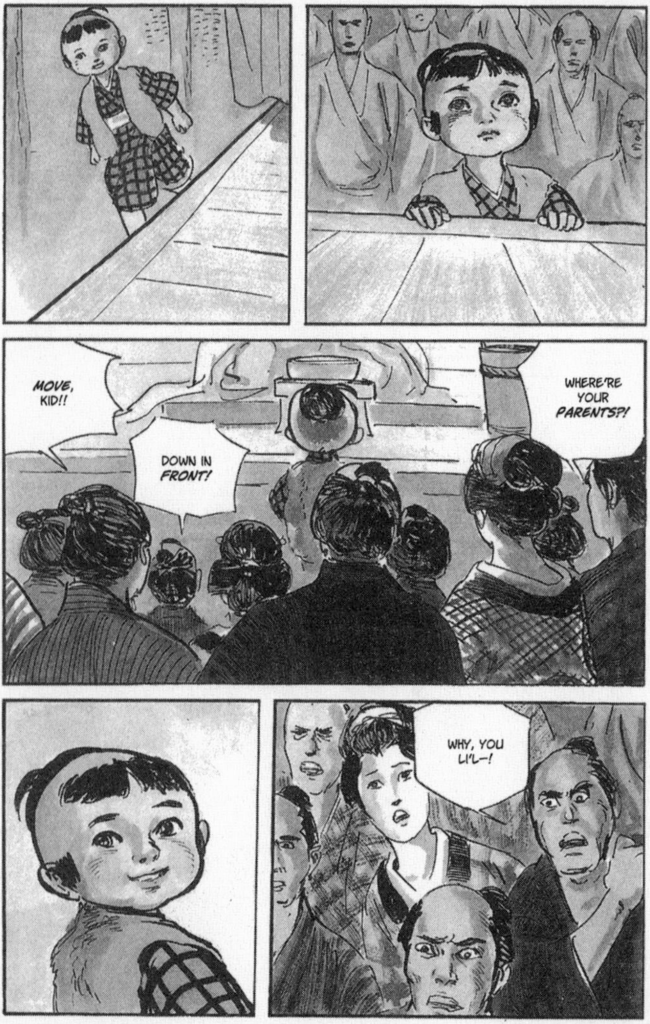
MOVE, KID!!
DOWN IN FRONT!
WHERE'RE YOUR PARENTS?!
WHY, YOU LI'L--!

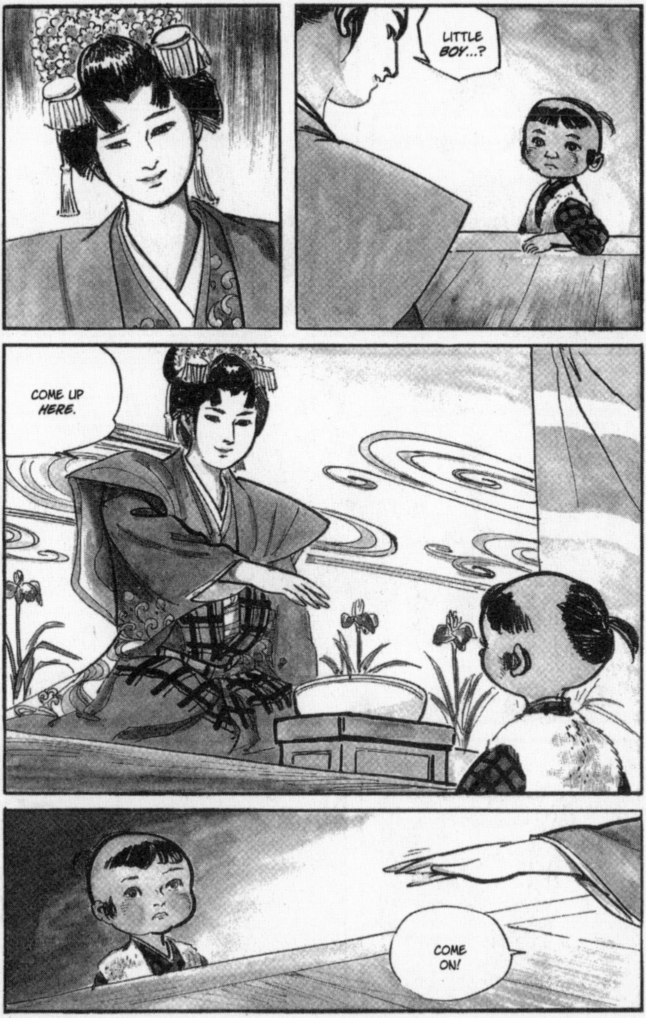
LITTLE BOY...?
COME UP HERE.
COME ON!

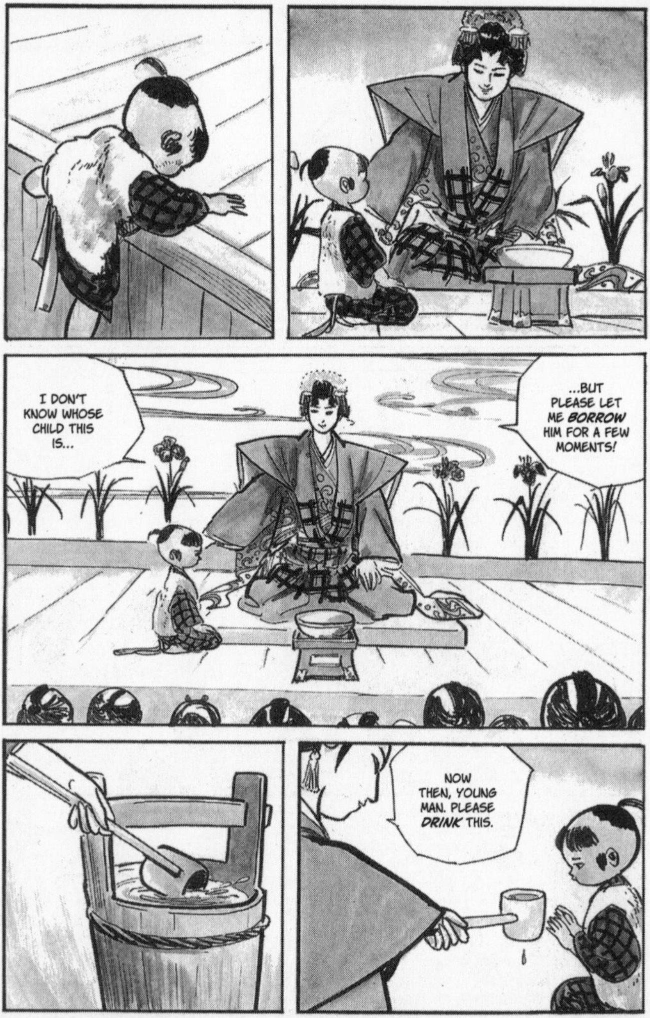
I DON'T KNOW WHOSE CHILD THIS IS...
...BUT PLEASE LET ME *BORROW* HIM FOR A FEW MOMENTS!
NOW THEN, YOUNG MAN. PLEASE *DRINK* THIS.

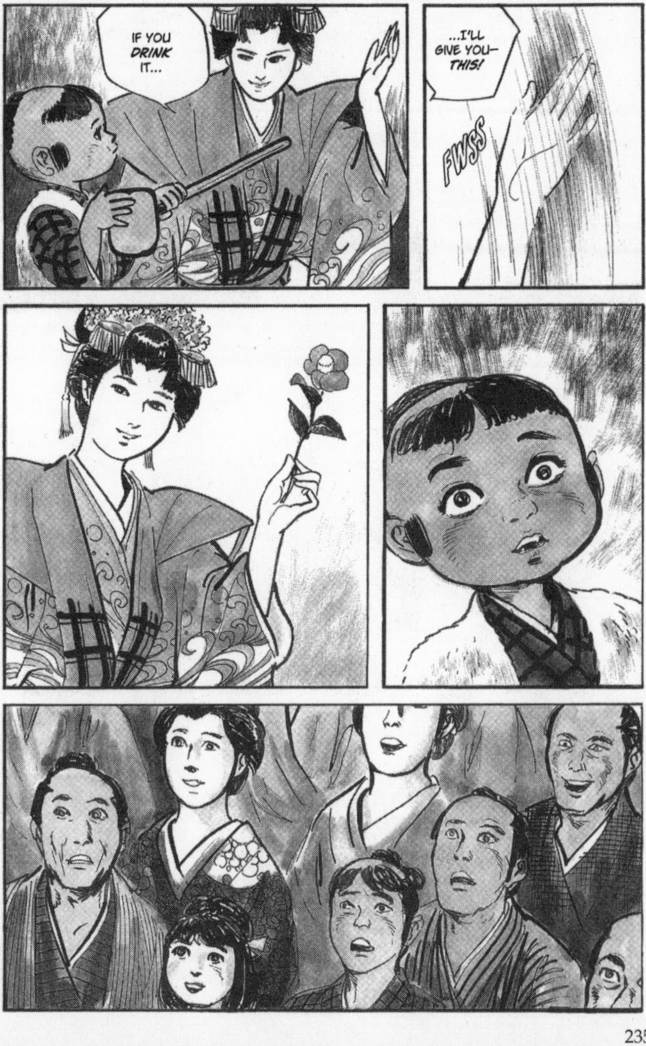
IF YOU DRINK IT...
...I'LL GIVE YOU— THIS!
FWSS

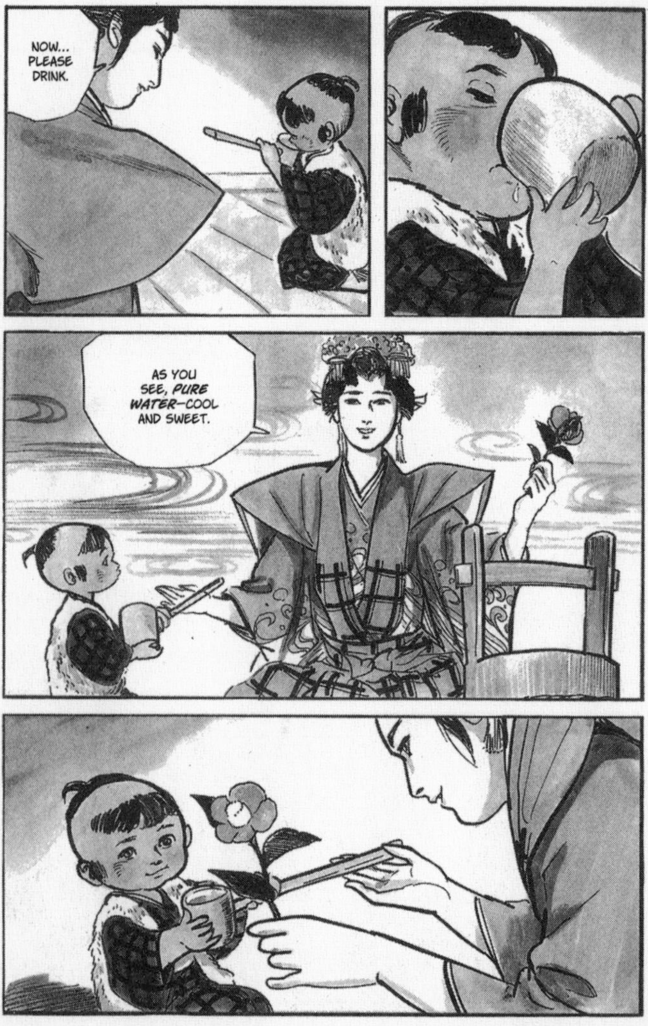
NOW... PLEASE DRINK.
AS YOU SEE, *PURE WATER*—COOL AND SWEET.

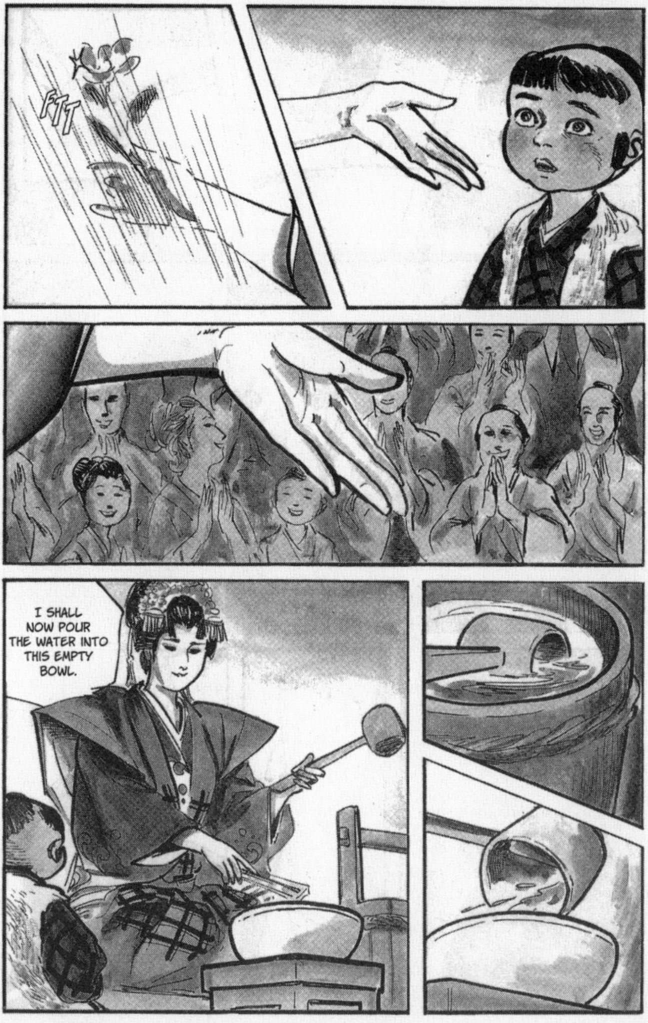
FTT
I SHALL NOW POUR THE WATER INTO THIS EMPTY BOWL.

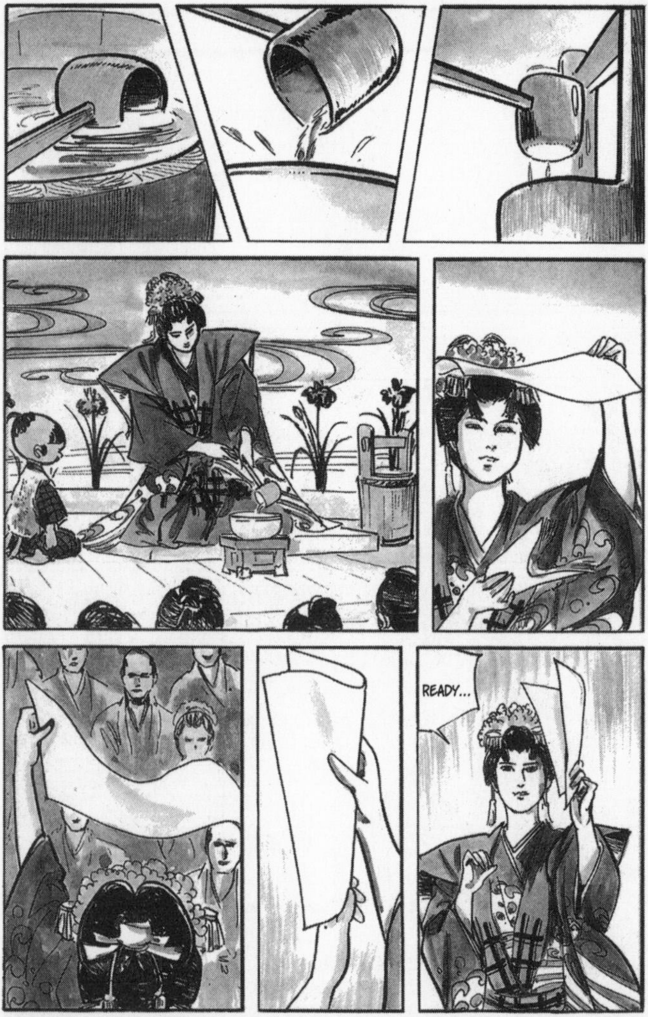
READY...

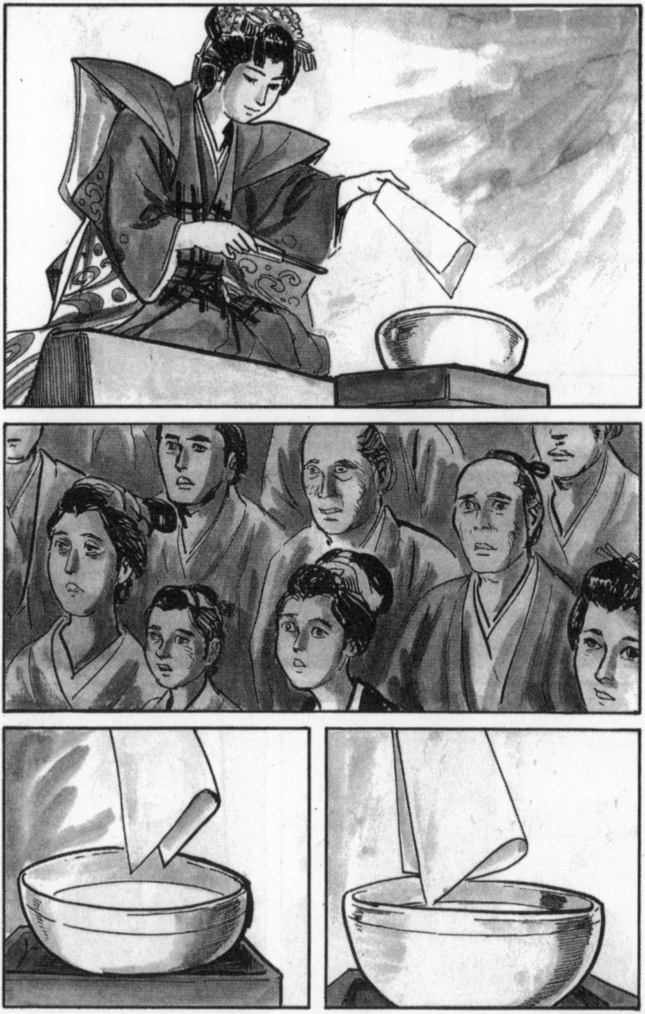

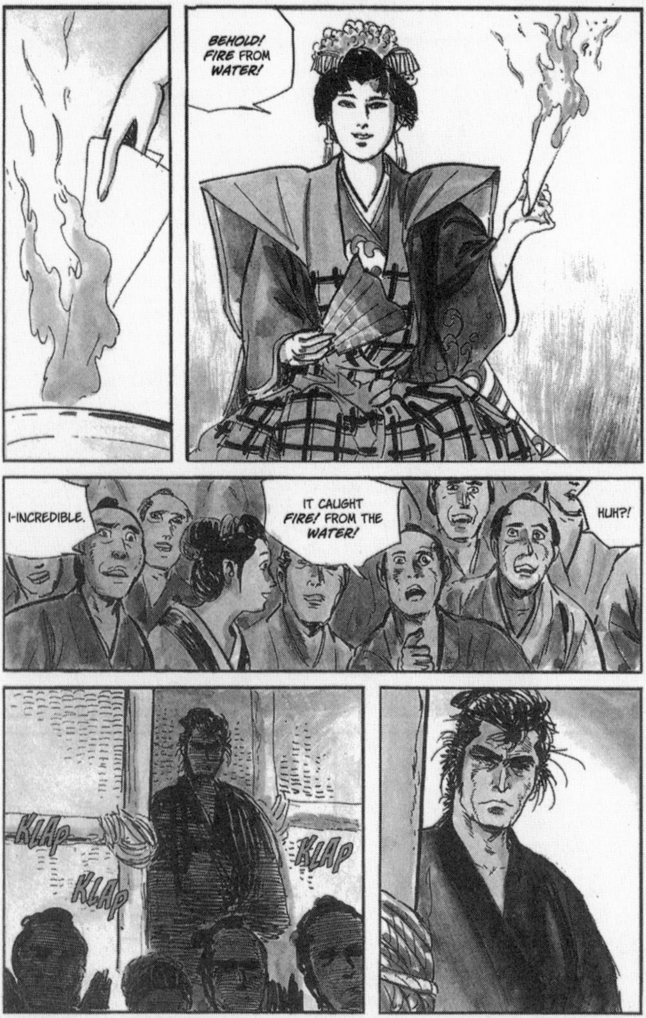
BEHOLD! FIRE FROM WATER!
I-INCREDIBLE.
IT CAUGHT FIRE! FROM THE WATER!
HUH?!
KLAP
KLAP
KLAP

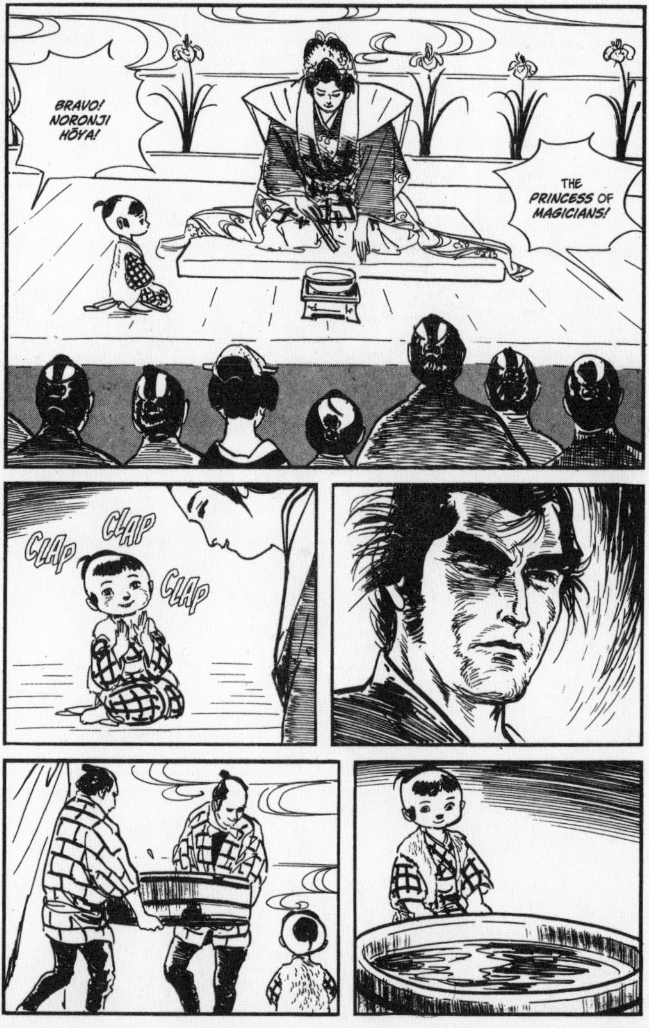
BRAVO! NORONJI HŌYA!
THE PRINCESS OF MAGICIANS!
CLAP
CLAP
CLAP

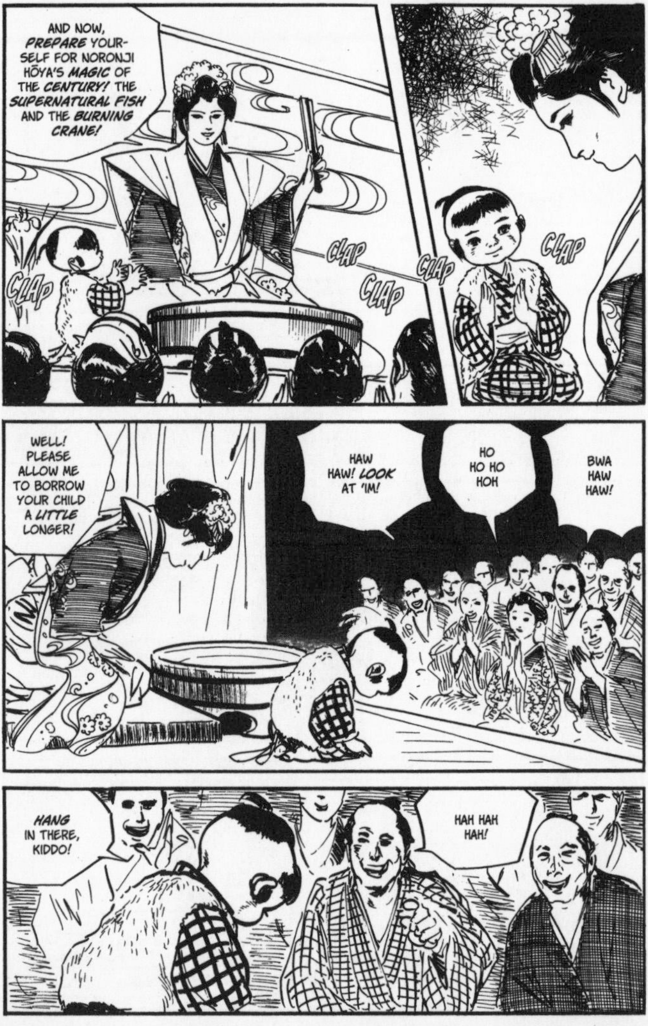
AND NOW, PREPARE YOURSELF FOR NORONJI HŌYA'S MAGIC OF THE CENTURY! THE SUPERNATURAL FISH AND THE BURNING CRANE!
CLAP
CLAP
CLAP
CLAP
CLAP
WELL! PLEASE ALLOW ME TO BORROW YOUR CHILD A LITTLE LONGER!
HAW HAW! LOOK AT 'IM!
HO HO HO HOH
BWA HAW HAW!
HANG IN THERE, KIDDO!
HAH HAH HAH!

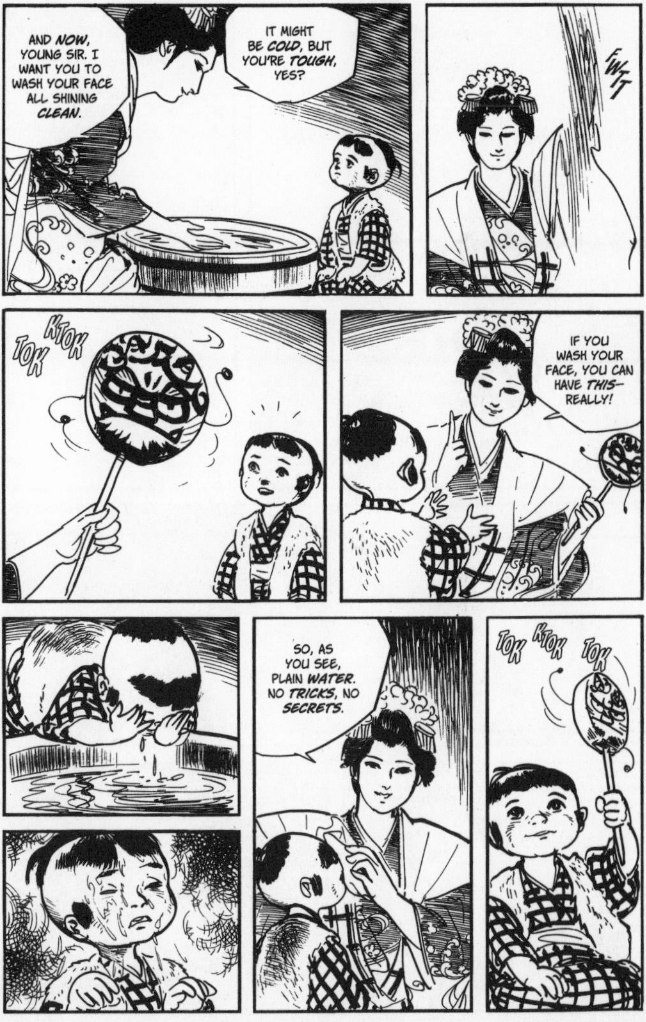
AND NOW, YOUNG SIR. I WANT YOU TO WASH YOUR FACE ALL SHINING CLEAN.
IT MIGHT BE COLD, BUT YOU'RE TOUGH, YES?
FWTT
TOK KTOK
IF YOU WASH YOUR FACE, YOU CAN HAVE THIS– REALLY!
SO, AS YOU SEE, PLAIN WATER. NO TRICKS, NO SECRETS.
TOK KTOK TOK

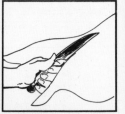

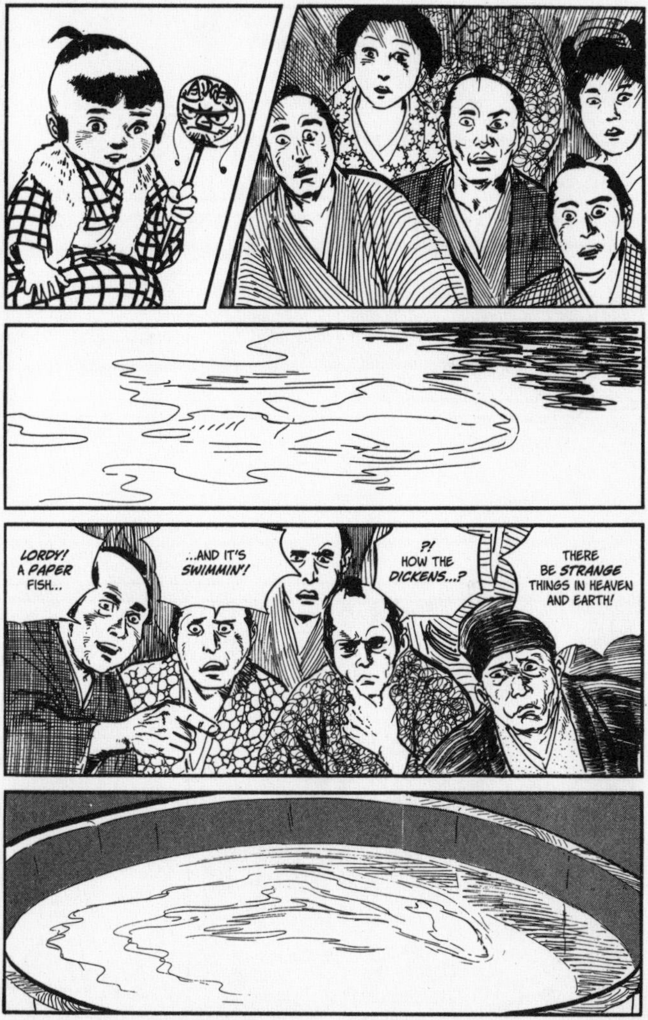
LORDY! A PAPER FISH...
...AND IT'S SWIMMIN'!
?! HOW THE DICKENS...?
THERE BE STRANGE THINGS IN HEAVEN AND EARTH!

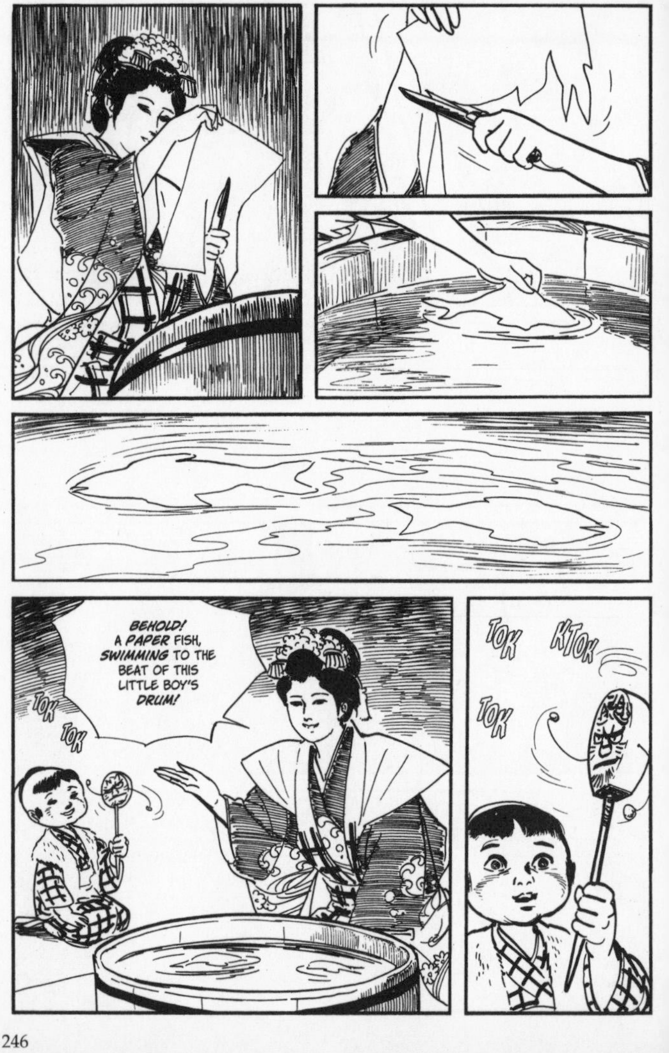
BEHOLD! A PAPER FISH, SWIMMING TO THE BEAT OF THIS LITTLE BOY'S DRUM!
TOK
TOK
TOK
KTOK
TOK

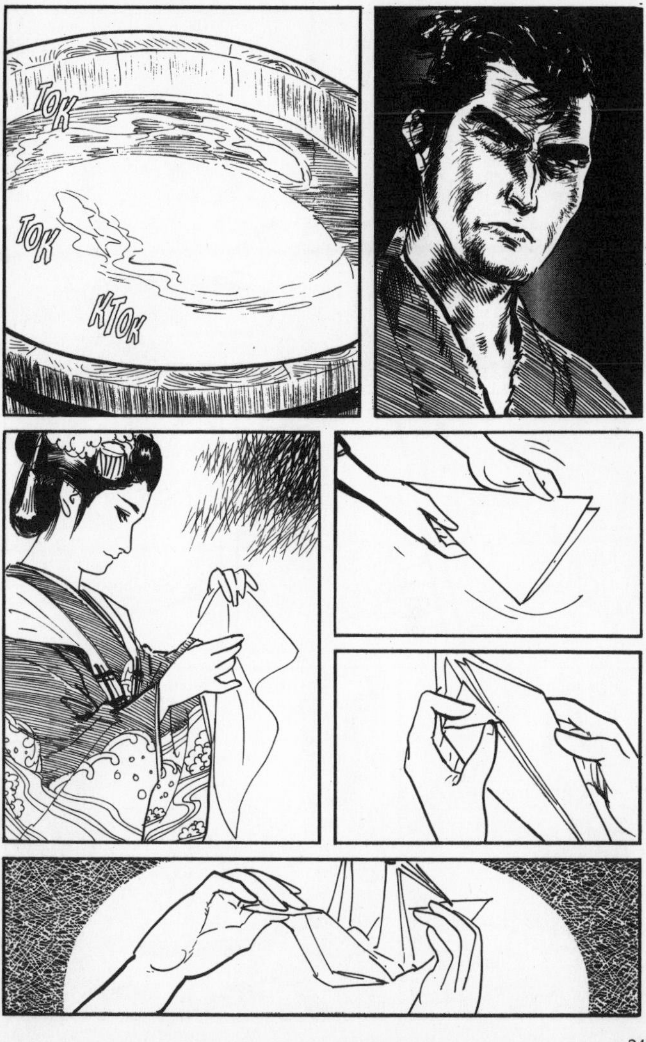
TOK
TOK
KTOK

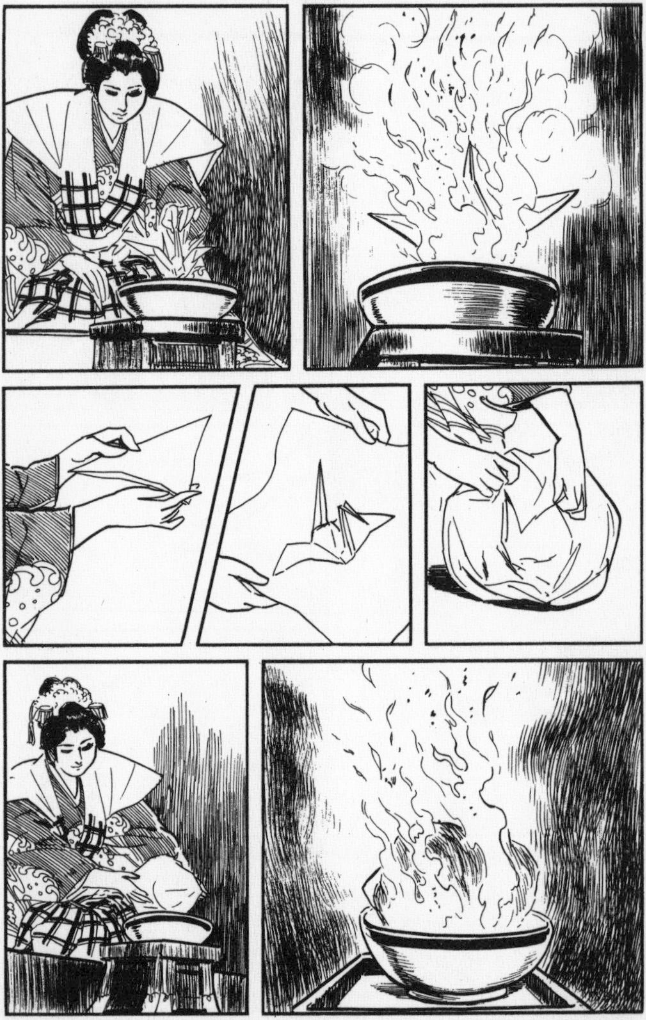

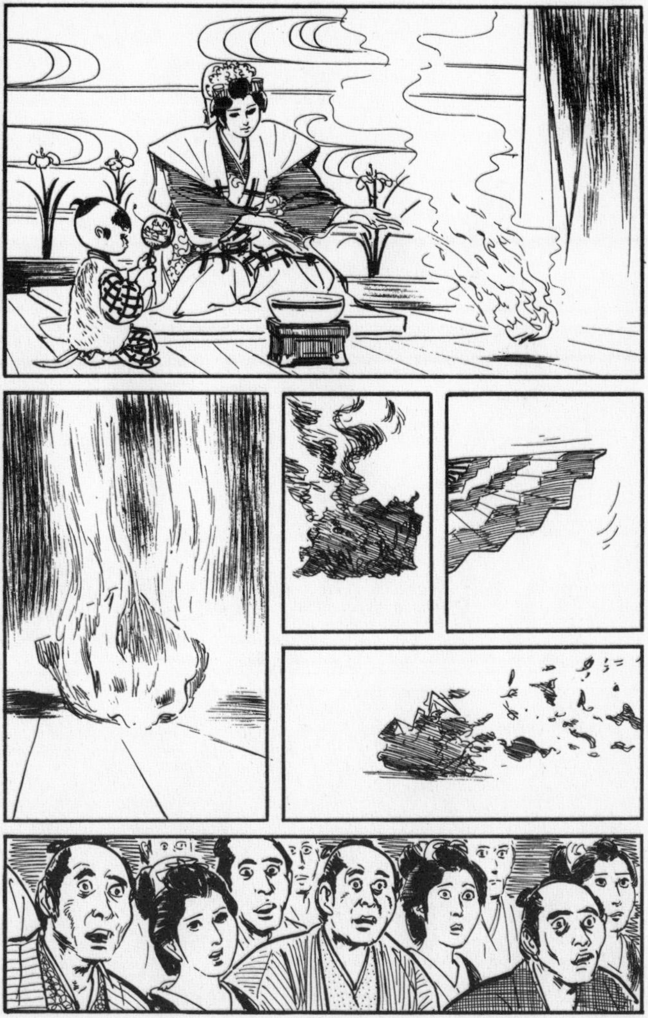

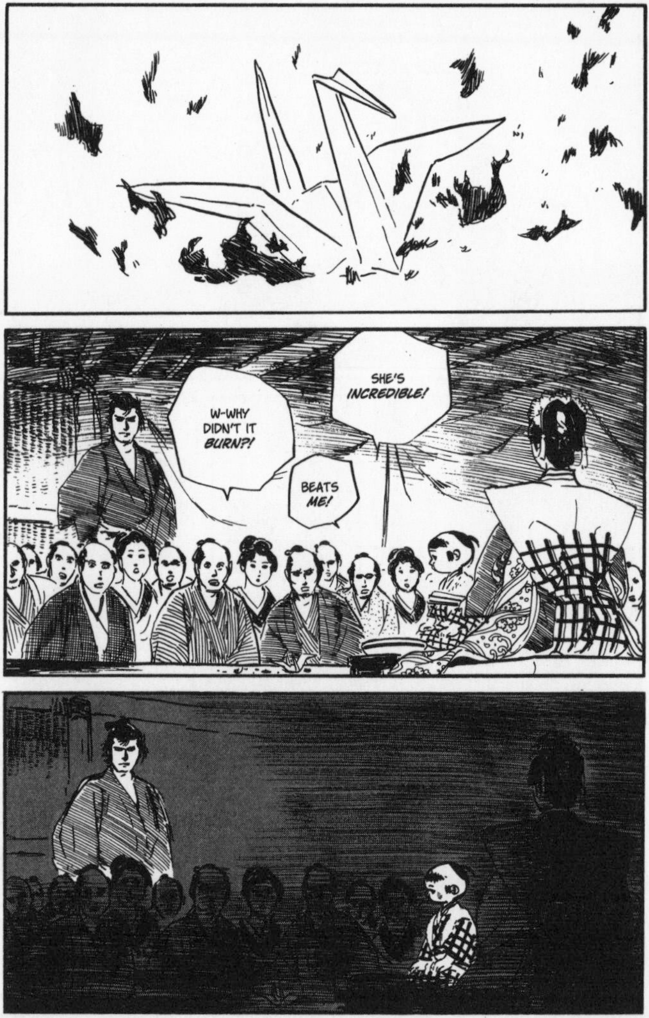
W-WHY DIDN'T IT *BURN?!*
SHE'S *INCREDIBLE!*
BEATS *ME!*

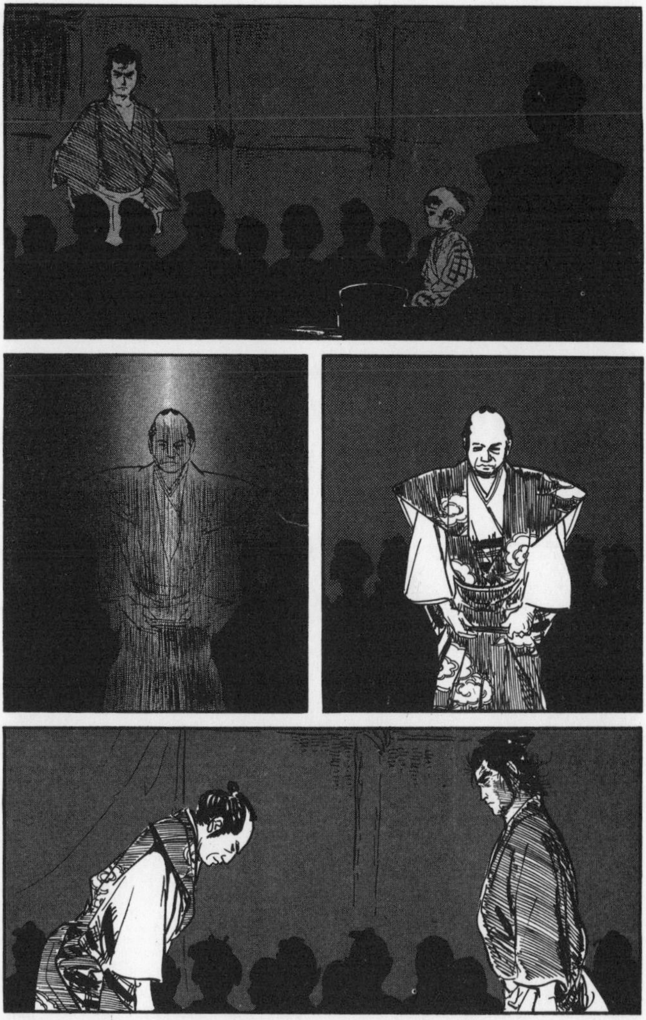

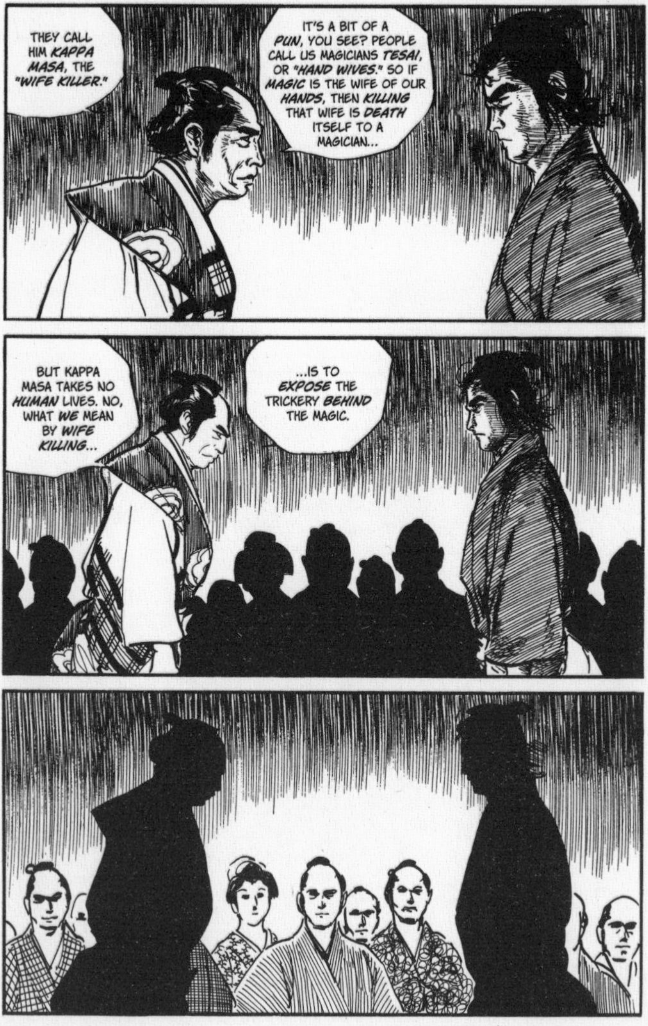
THEY CALL HIM KAPPA MASA, THE "WIFE KILLER."
IT'S A BIT OF A PUN, YOU SEE? PEOPLE CALL US MAGICIANS TESAI, OR "HAND WIVES." SO IF MAGIC IS THE WIFE OF OUR HANDS, THEN KILLING THAT WIFE IS DEATH ITSELF TO A MAGICIAN...
BUT KAPPA MASA TAKES NO HUMAN LIVES. NO, WHAT WE MEAN BY WIFE KILLING...
...IS TO EXPOSE THE TRICKERY BEHIND THE MAGIC.

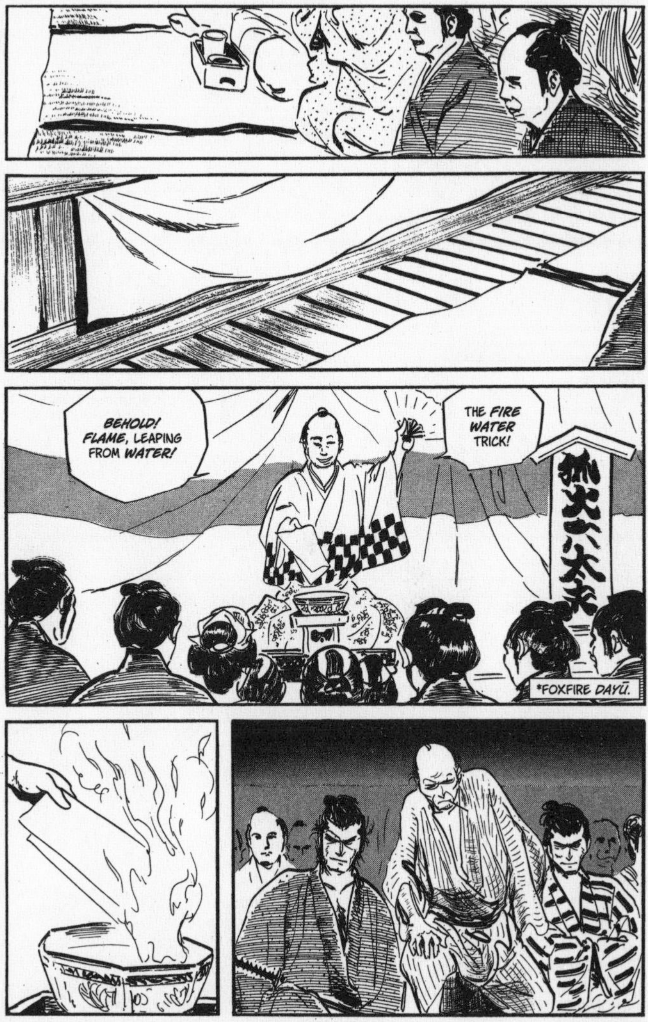
BEHOLD! FLAME, LEAPING FROM WATER!
THE FIRE WATER TRICK!
*FOXFIRE DAYŪ.

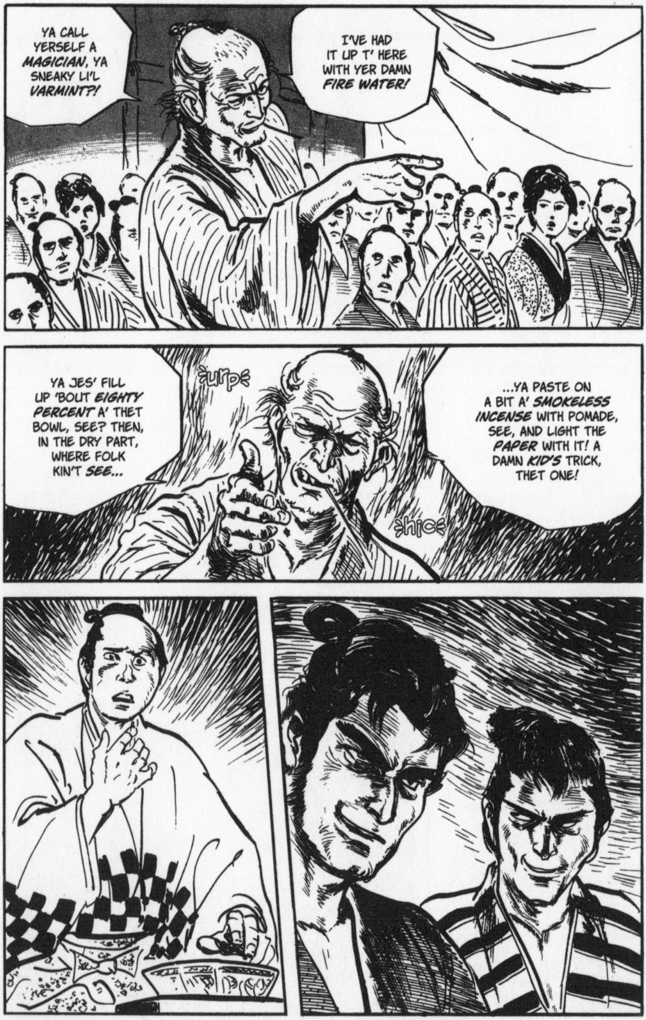

YA CALL YERSELF A MAGICIAN, YA SNEAKY LI'L VARMINT?!
I'VE HAD IT UP T' HERE WITH YER DAMN FIRE WATER!
YA JES' FILL UP 'BOUT EIGHTY PERCENT A' THET BOWL, SEE? THEN, IN THE DRY PART, WHERE FOLK KIN'T SEE...
urp
...YA PASTE ON A BIT A' SMOKELESS INCENSE WITH POMADE, SEE, AND LIGHT THE PAPER WITH IT! A DAMN KID'S TRICK, THET ONE!
hic

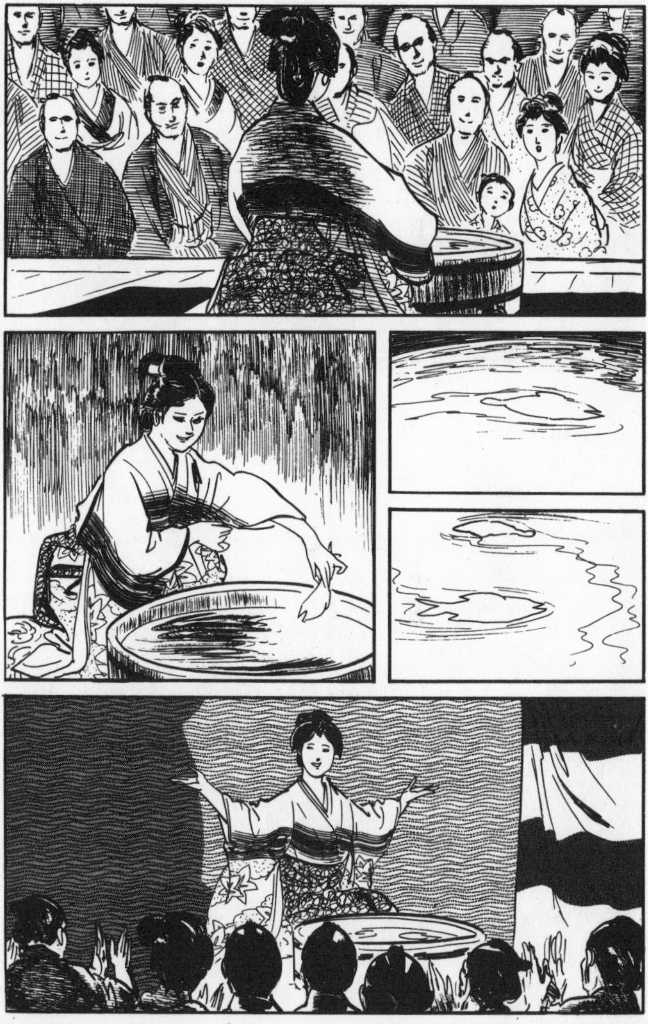

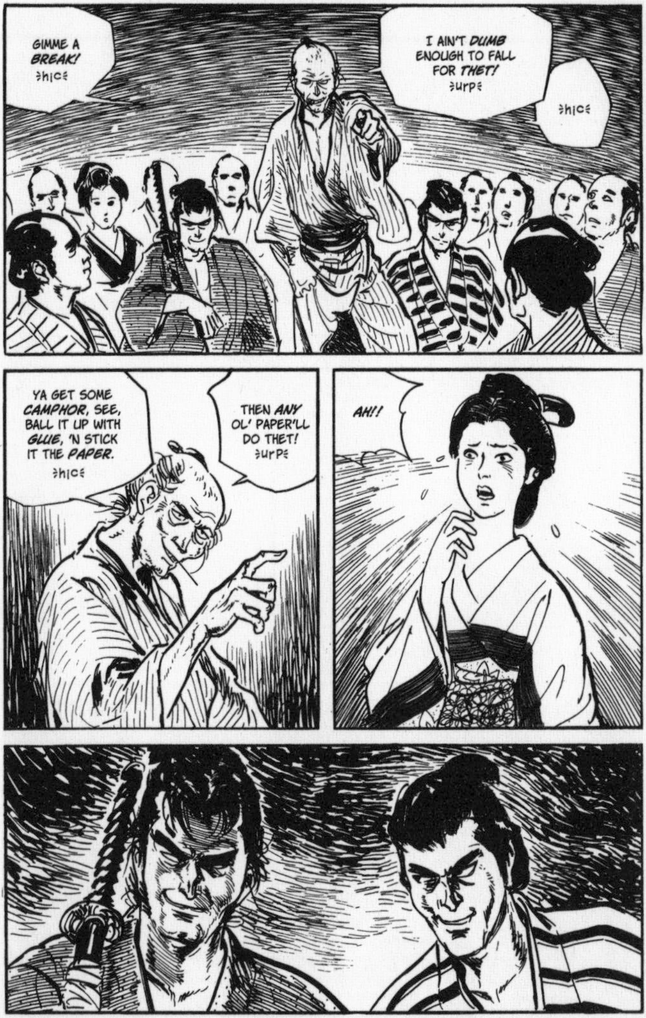
GIMME A BREAK! hic
I AIN'T DUMB ENOUGH TO FALL FOR THET! urp
hic
YA GET SOME CAMPHOR, SEE, BALL IT UP WITH GLUE, 'N STICK IT THE PAPER. hic
THEN ANY OL' PAPER'LL DO THET! urp
AH!!

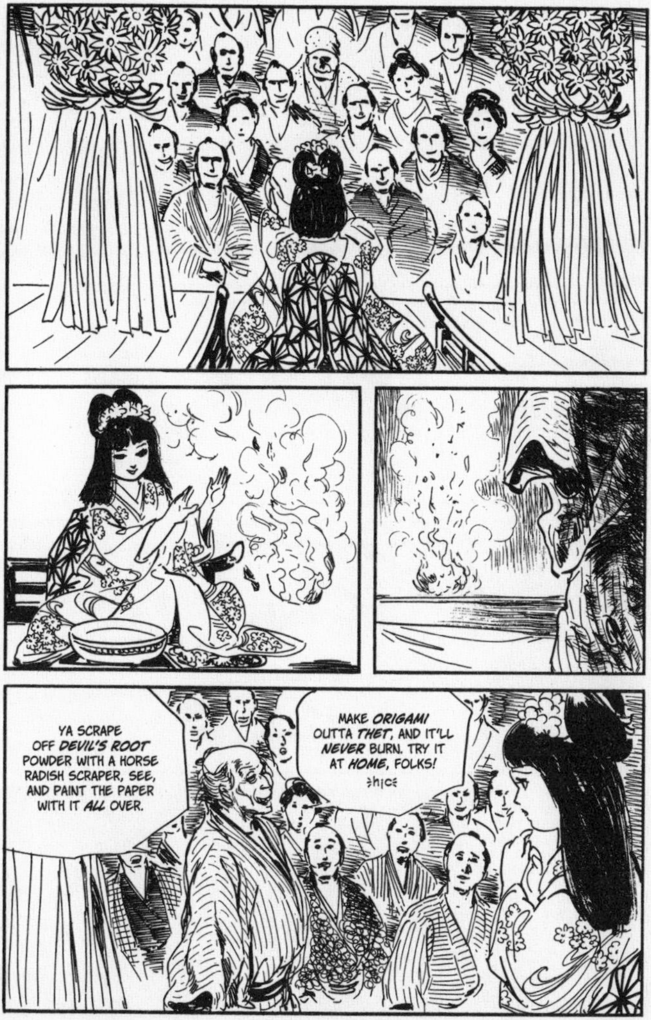
YA SCRAPE OFF DEVIL'S ROOT POWDER WITH A HORSE RADISH SCRAPER, SEE, AND PAINT THE PAPER WITH IT ALL OVER.
MAKE ORIGAMI OUTTA THET, AND IT'LL NEVER BURN. TRY IT AT HOME, FOLKS!
HIC

HEH, HEH, ♪hic♪ *HEH!!*

KAPPA MASA CAN SEE THROUGH *EVERY* NEW MAGIC TRICK WE DEVISE.

AND HE HAS TWO *DEADLY* PARTNERS... KILLERS.

*GREEN ROOM

*THE BUTTERFLY SHOW

*WHEREVER* WE SET UP OUR STAGES, THESE THREE COME OUT OF *NOWHERE* AND DEMAND A *PAYOFF.*

IF YOU GIVE THEM WHAT THEY ASK FOR, THEY GO OFF AND AREN'T SEEN AGAIN. BUT REFUSE, AND THEY START THEIR *WIFE KILLING...EXPOSING* ALL OUR TRICKS.

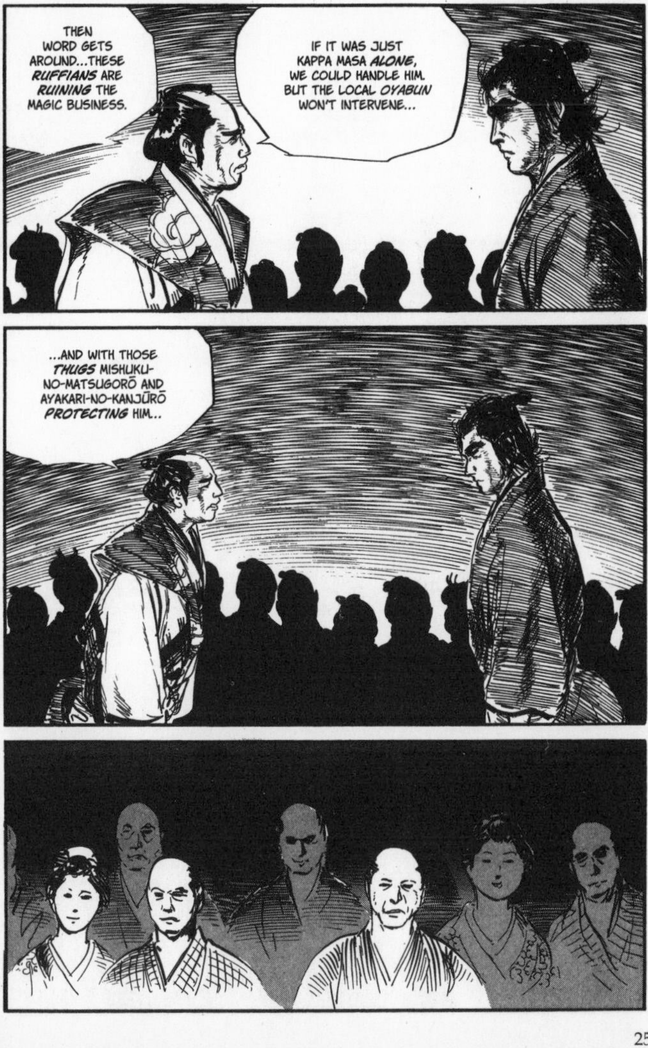
THEN WORD GETS AROUND...THESE *RUFFIANS* ARE *RUINING* THE MAGIC BUSINESS.
IF IT WAS JUST KAPPA MASA *ALONE*, WE COULD HANDLE HIM. BUT THE LOCAL *OYABUN* WON'T INTERVENE...
...AND WITH THOSE *THUGS* MISHUKU-NO-MATSUGORŌ AND AYAKARI-NO-KANJŪRŌ *PROTECTING* HIM...

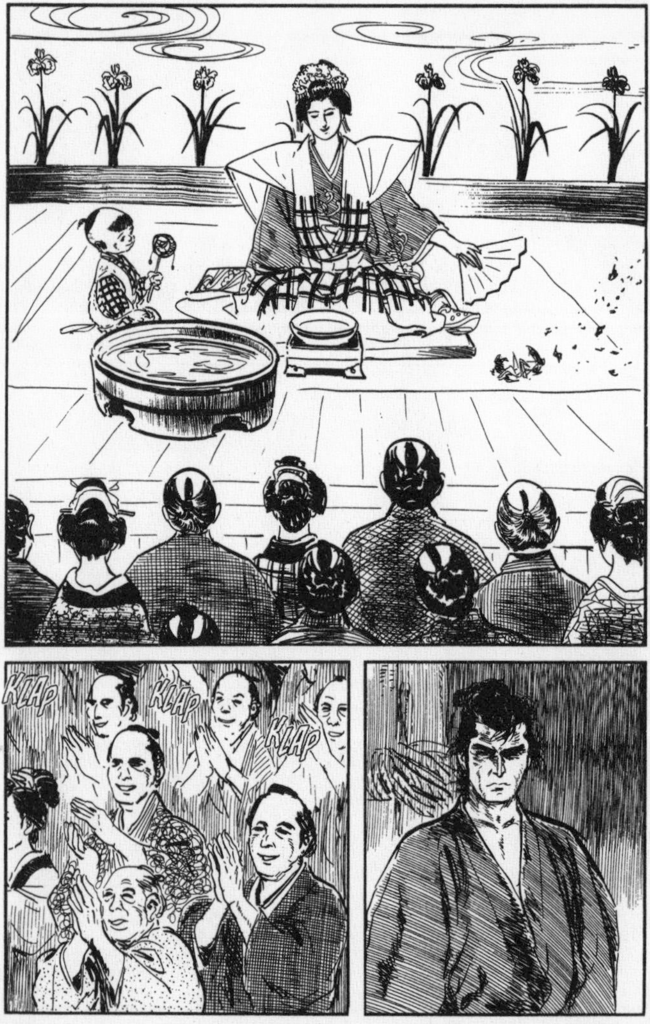
KLAP
KLAP
KLAP

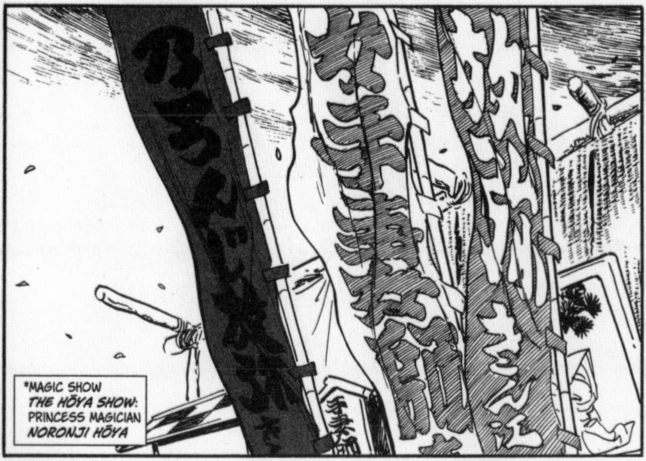
*MAGIC SHOW
THE HŌYA SHOW:
PRINCESS MAGICIAN
NORONJI HŌYA

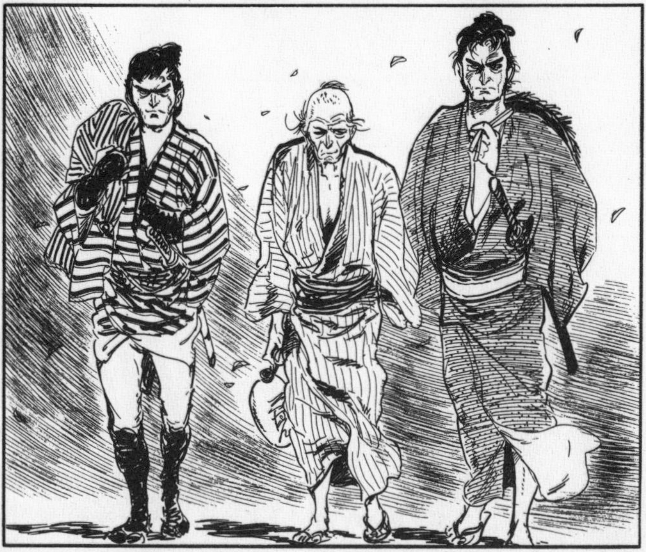

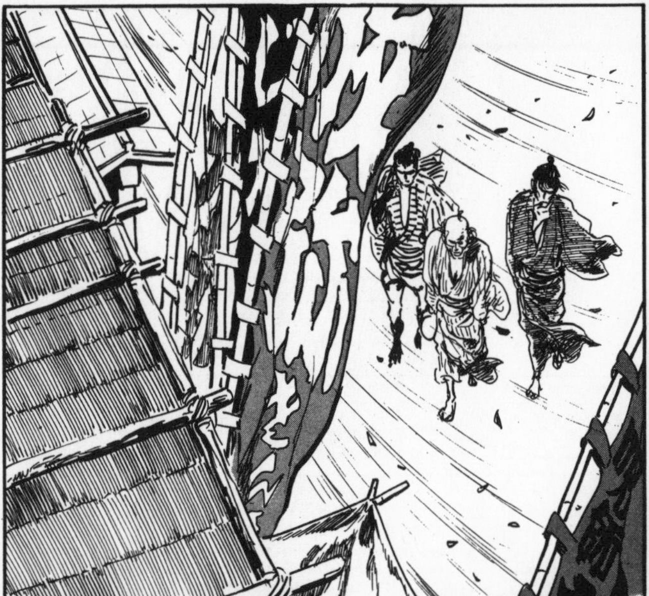

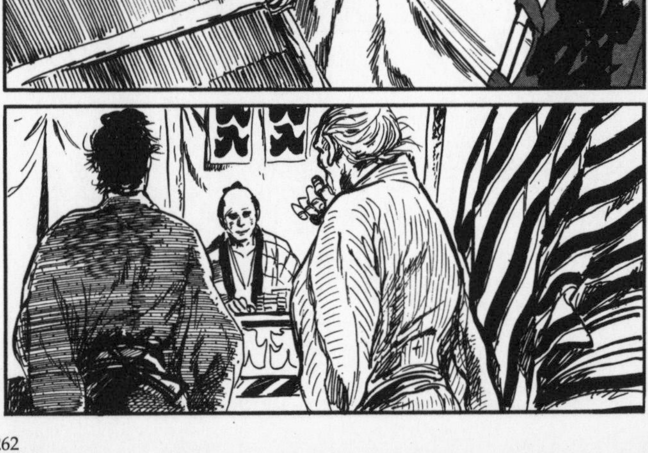

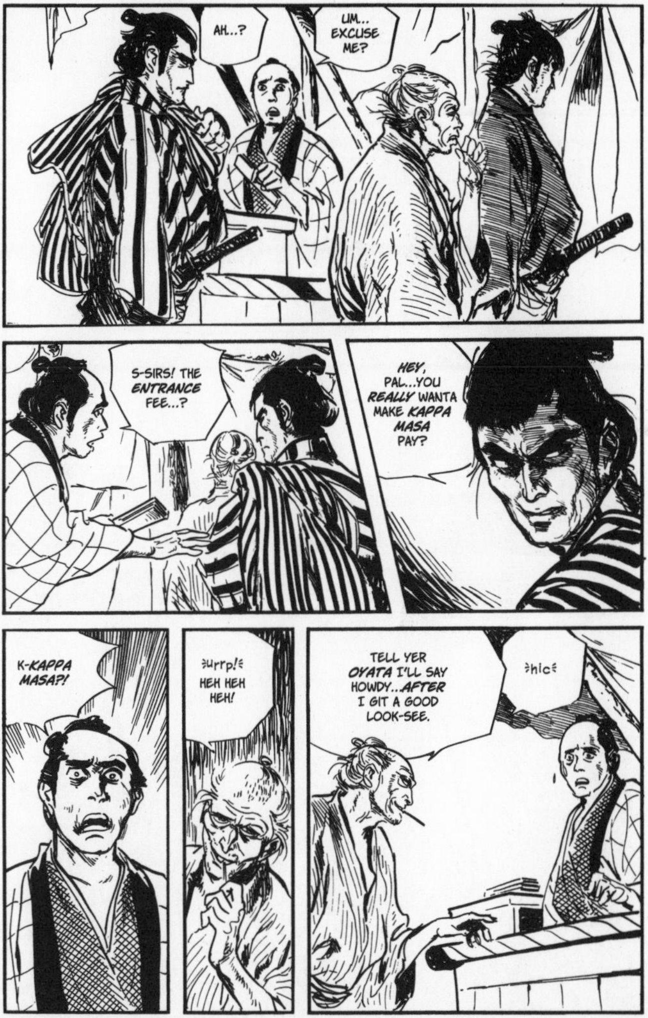
AH...?
UM... EXCUSE ME?
S-SIRS! THE ENTRANCE FEE...?
HEY, PAL...YOU REALLY WANTA MAKE KAPPA MASA PAY?
K-KAPPA MASA?!
urrp!
HEH HEH HEH!
TELL YER OYATA I'LL SAY HOWDY...AFTER I GIT A GOOD LOOK-SEE.
hic

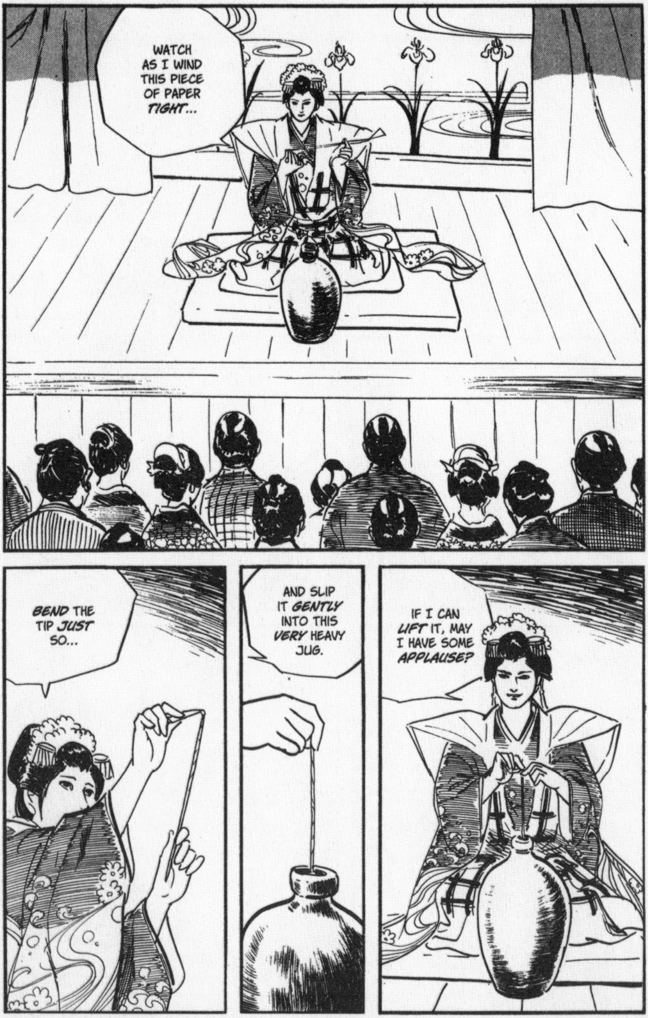
WATCH AS I WIND THIS PIECE OF PAPER *TIGHT*...
*BEND* THE TIP *JUST* SO...
AND SLIP IT *GENTLY* INTO THIS *VERY* HEAVY JUG.
IF I CAN *LIFT* IT, MAY I HAVE SOME *APPLAUSE?*

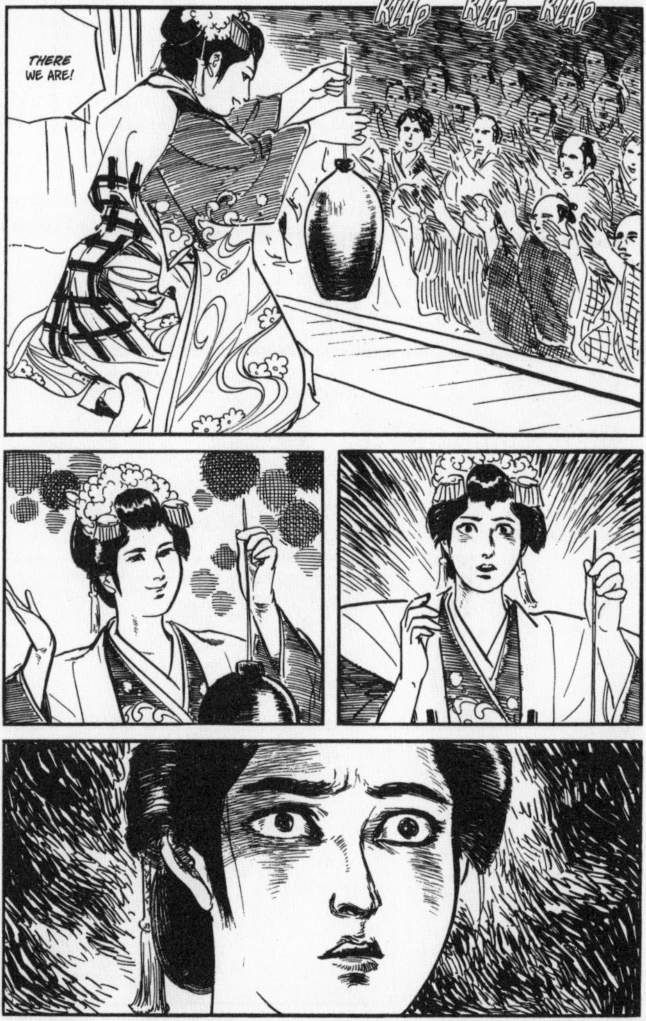
KLAP KLAP KLAP
THERE WE ARE!

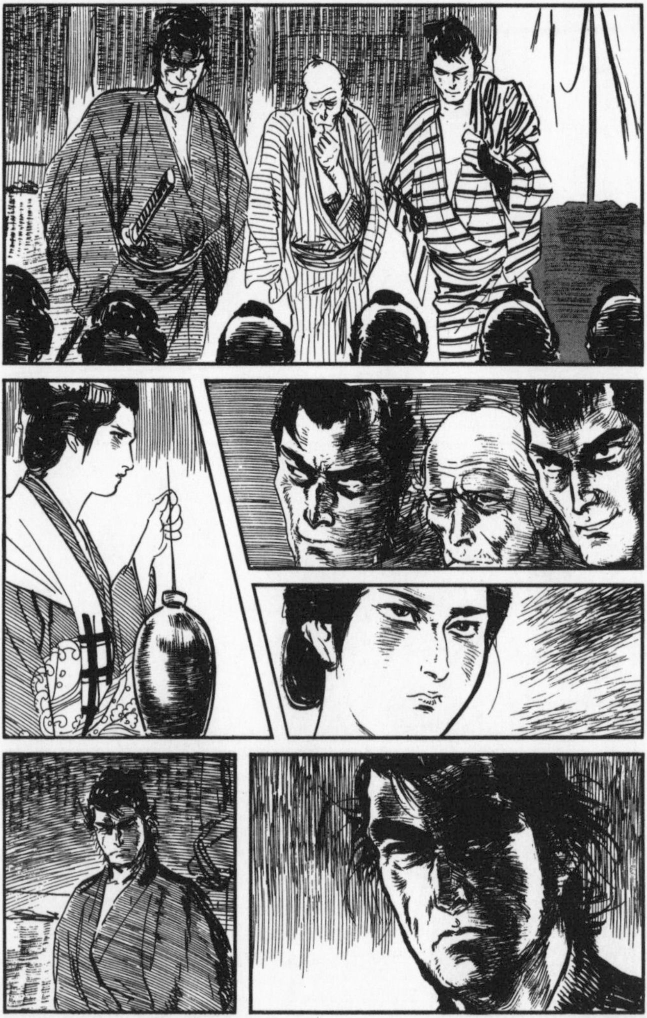

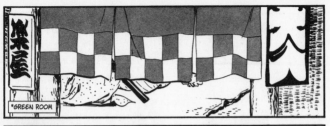

*GREEN ROOM

PTEH!!

267

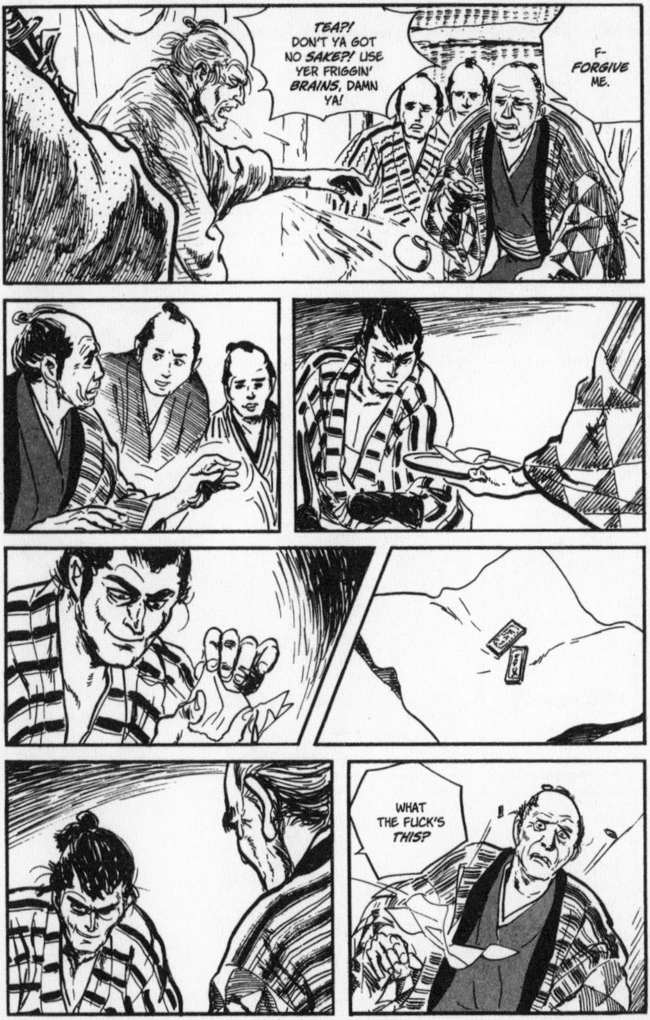
TEA?! DON'T YA GOT NO SAKE?! USE YER FRIGGIN' BRAINS, DAMN YA!
F-FORGIVE ME.
WHAT THE FUCK'S THIS?

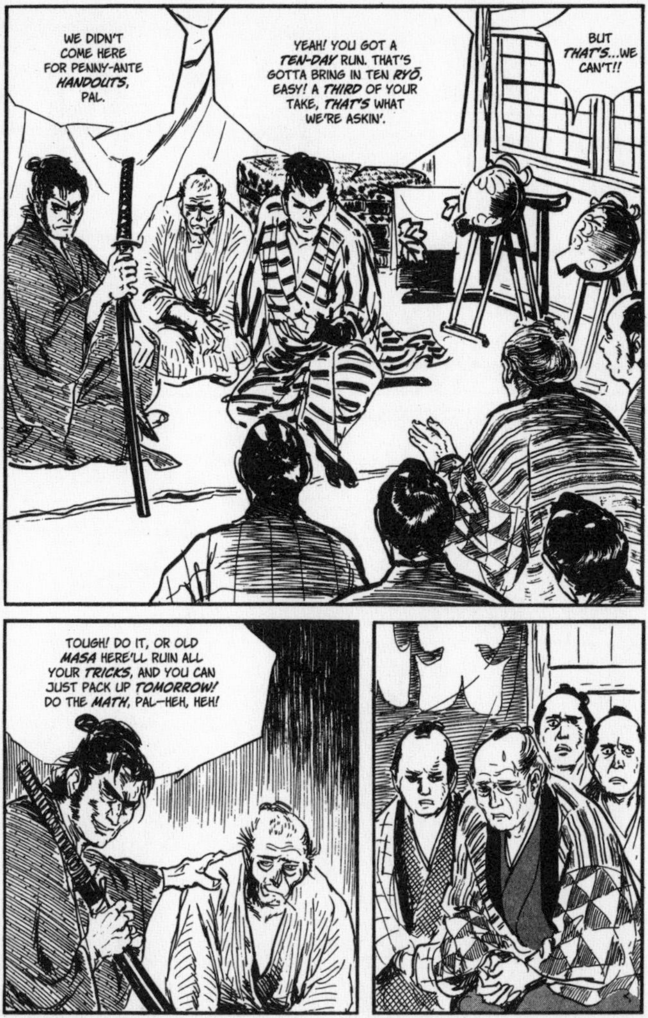
WE DIDN'T COME HERE FOR PENNY-ANTE HANDOUTS, PAL.
YEAH! YOU GOT A TEN-DAY RUN. THAT'S GOTTA BRING IN TEN RYŌ, EASY! A THIRD OF YOUR TAKE, THAT'S WHAT WE'RE ASKIN'.
BUT THAT'S...WE CAN'T!!
TOUGH! DO IT, OR OLD MASA HERE'LL RUIN ALL YOUR TRICKS, AND YOU CAN JUST PACK UP TOMORROW! DO THE MATH, PAL—HEH, HEH!

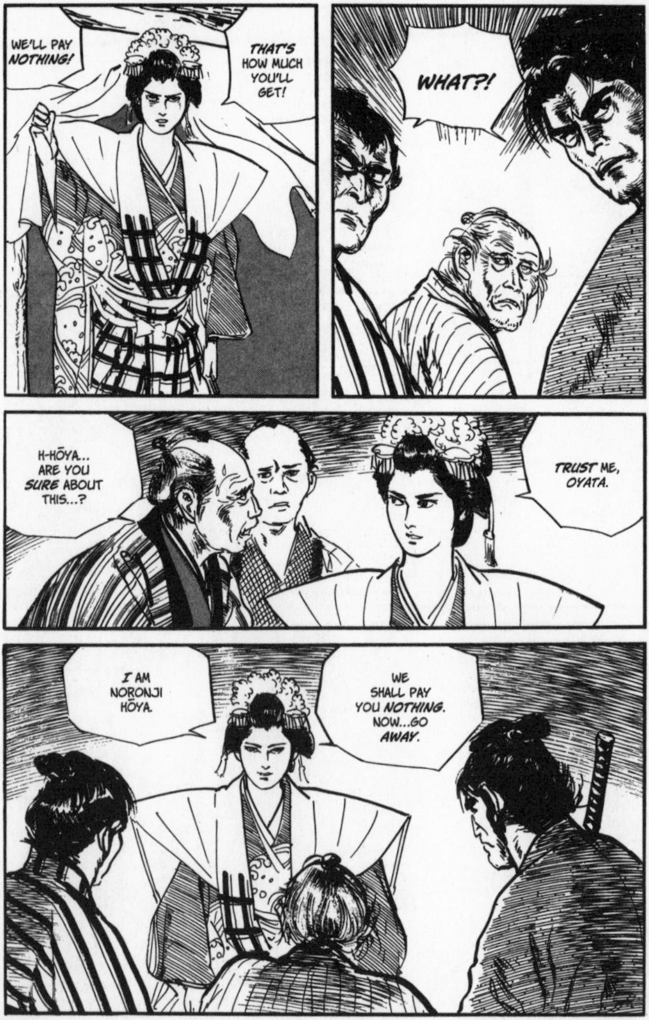
WE'LL PAY NOTHING!
THAT'S HOW MUCH YOU'LL GET!
WHAT?!
H-HŌYA... ARE YOU SURE ABOUT THIS...?
TRUST ME, OYATA.
I AM NORONJI HŌYA.
WE SHALL PAY YOU NOTHING. NOW...GO AWAY.

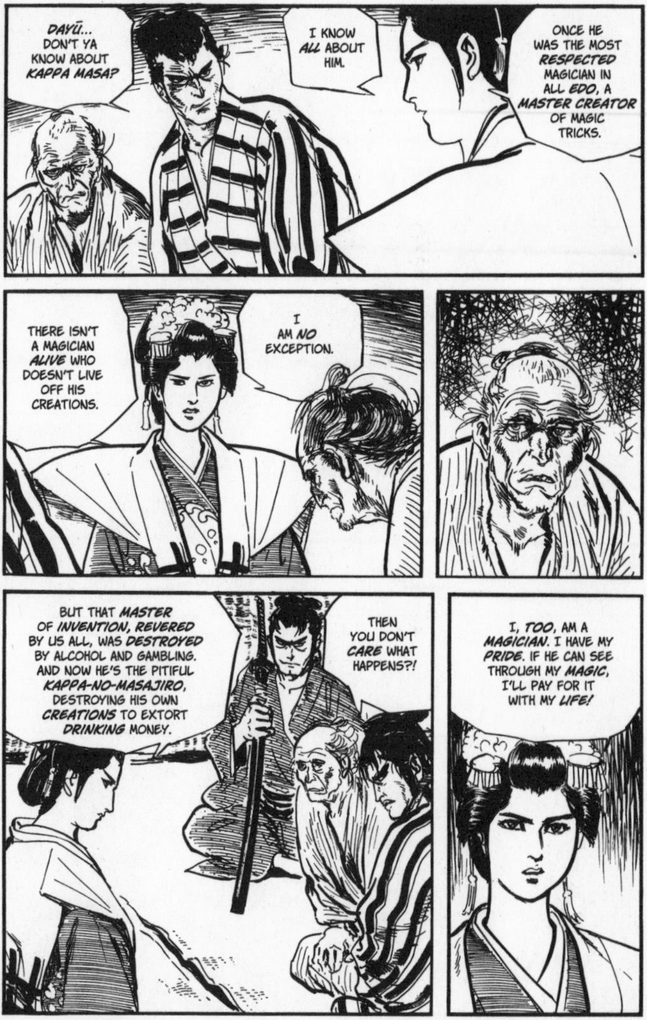
DAYŪ... DON'T YA KNOW ABOUT KAPPA MASA?
I KNOW ALL ABOUT HIM.
ONCE HE WAS THE MOST RESPECTED MAGICIAN IN ALL EDO, A MASTER CREATOR OF MAGIC TRICKS.
THERE ISN'T A MAGICIAN ALIVE WHO DOESN'T LIVE OFF HIS CREATIONS.
I AM NO EXCEPTION.
BUT THAT MASTER OF INVENTION, REVERED BY US ALL, WAS DESTROYED BY ALCOHOL AND GAMBLING. AND NOW HE'S THE PITIFUL KAPPA-NO-MASAJIRO, DESTROYING HIS OWN CREATIONS TO EXTORT DRINKING MONEY.
THEN YOU DON'T CARE WHAT HAPPENS?!
I, TOO, AM A MAGICIAN. I HAVE MY PRIDE. IF HE CAN SEE THROUGH MY MAGIC, I'LL PAY FOR IT WITH MY LIFE!

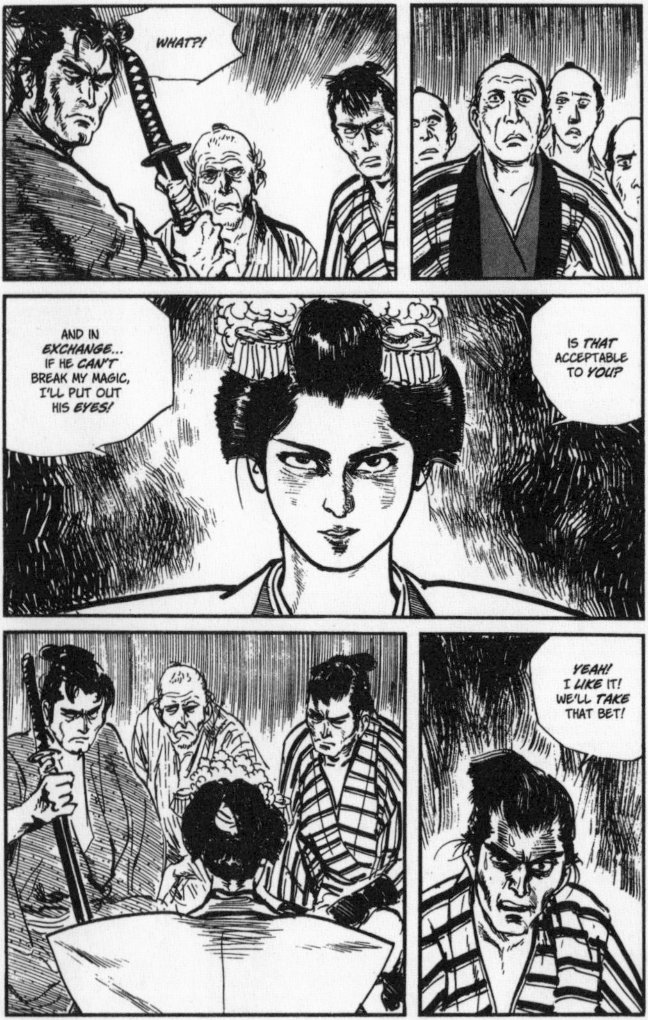
WHAT?!
AND IN EXCHANGE... IF HE CAN'T BREAK MY MAGIC, I'LL PUT OUT HIS EYES!
IS THAT ACCEPTABLE TO YOU?
YEAH! I LIKE IT! WE'LL TAKE THAT BET!

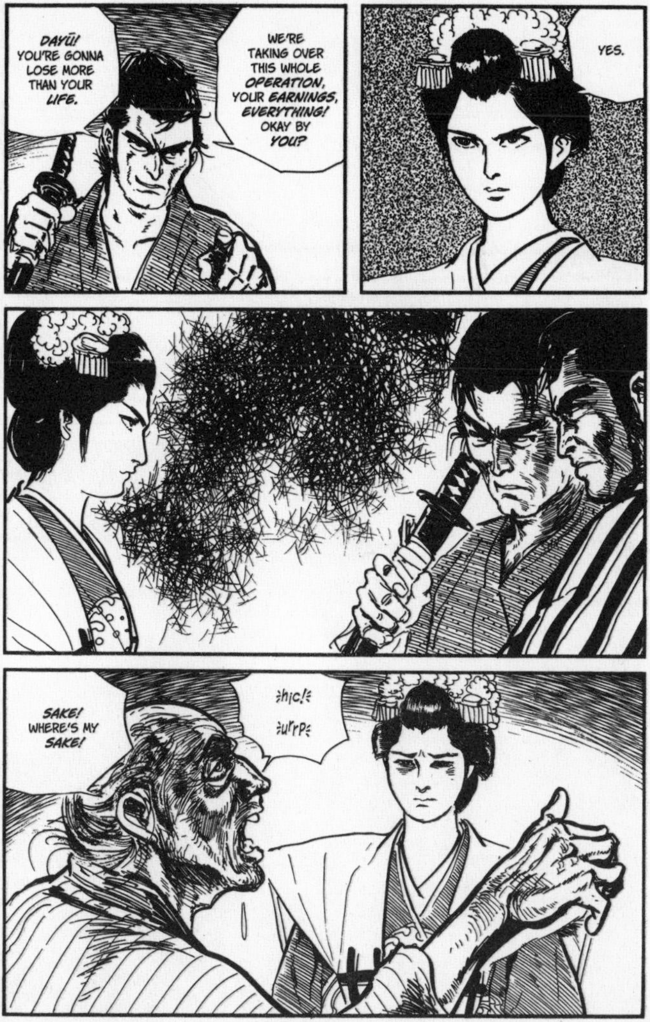
DAYŪ! YOU'RE GONNA LOSE MORE THAN YOUR LIFE.
WE'RE TAKING OVER THIS WHOLE OPERATION, YOUR EARNINGS, EVERYTHING! OKAY BY YOU?
YES.
SAKE! WHERE'S MY SAKE!
hic!
urrp

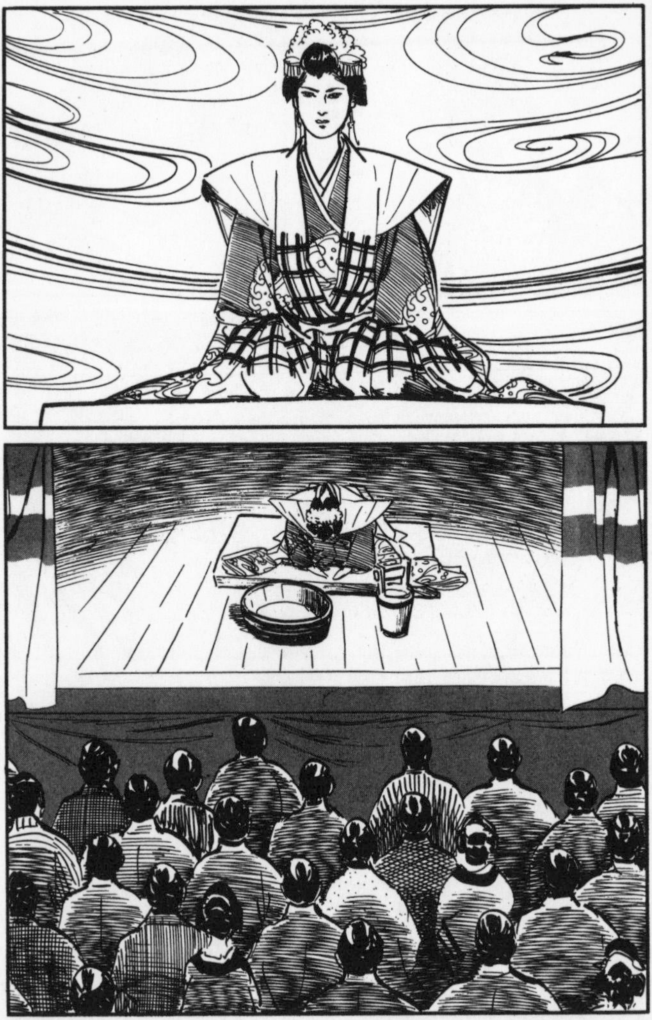

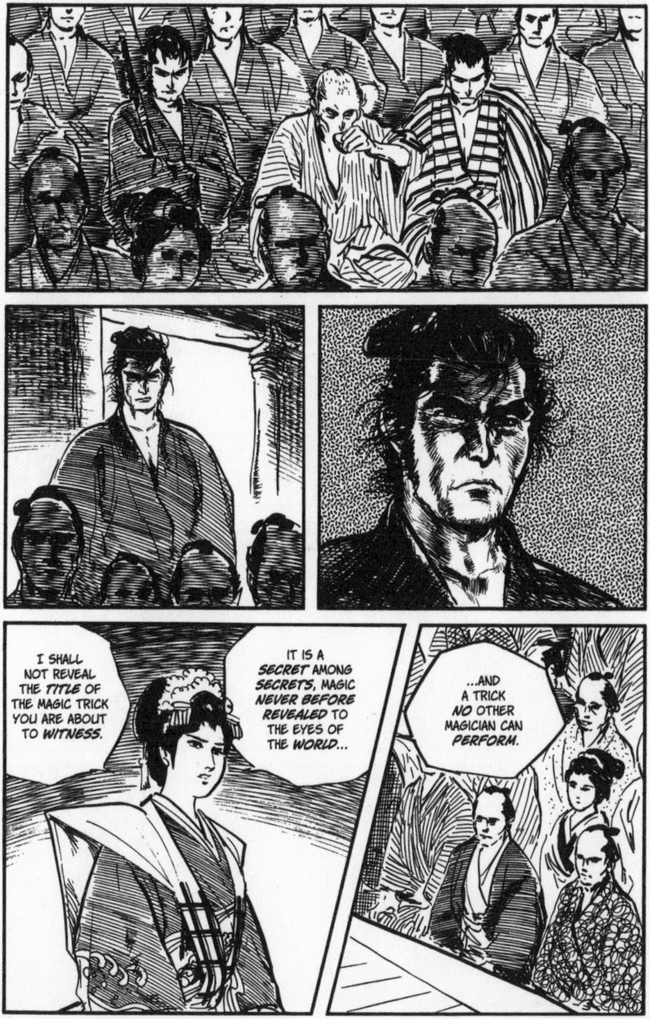
I SHALL NOT REVEAL THE *TITLE* OF THE MAGIC TRICK YOU ARE ABOUT TO *WITNESS.*
IT IS A *SECRET* AMONG *SECRETS*, MAGIC *NEVER BEFORE REVEALED* TO THE EYES OF THE *WORLD...*
...AND A TRICK *NO* OTHER MAGICIAN CAN *PERFORM.*

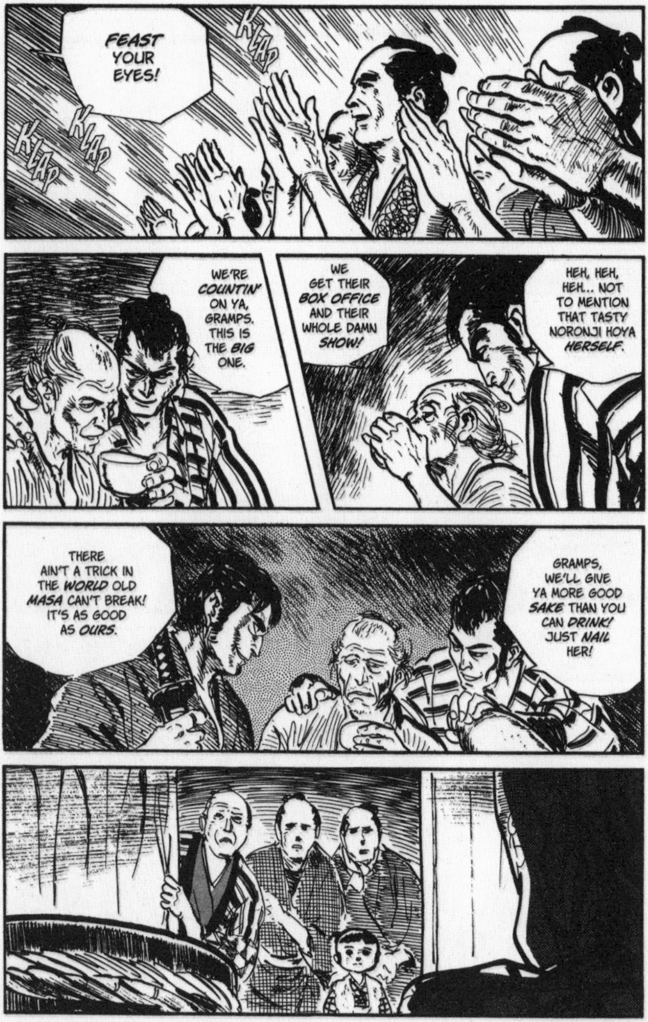
FEAST YOUR EYES!
KLAP
KLAP
KLAP
WE'RE COUNTIN' ON YA, GRAMPS. THIS IS THE BIG ONE.
WE GET THEIR BOX OFFICE AND THEIR WHOLE DAMN SHOW!
HEH, HEH, HEH... NOT TO MENTION THAT TASTY NORONJI HOYA HERSELF.
THERE AIN'T A TRICK IN THE WORLD OLD MASA CAN'T BREAK! IT'S AS GOOD AS OURS.
GRAMPS, WE'LL GIVE YA MORE GOOD SAKE THAN YOU CAN DRINK! JUST NAIL HER!

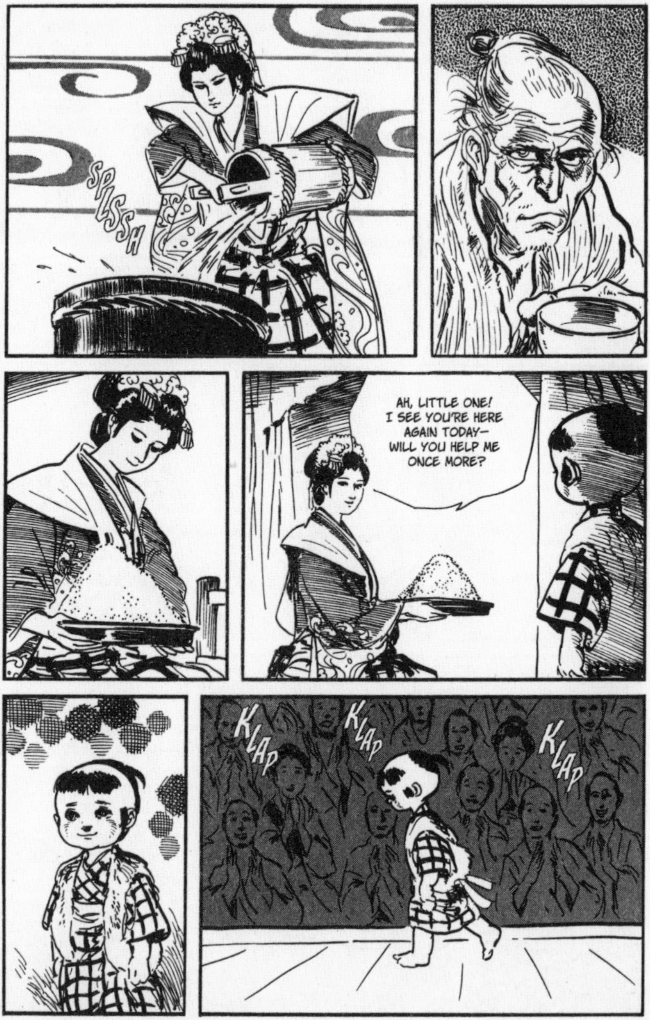
SPLSSH
AH, LITTLE ONE! I SEE YOU'RE HERE AGAIN TODAY— WILL YOU HELP ME ONCE MORE?
KLAP
KLAP
KLAP

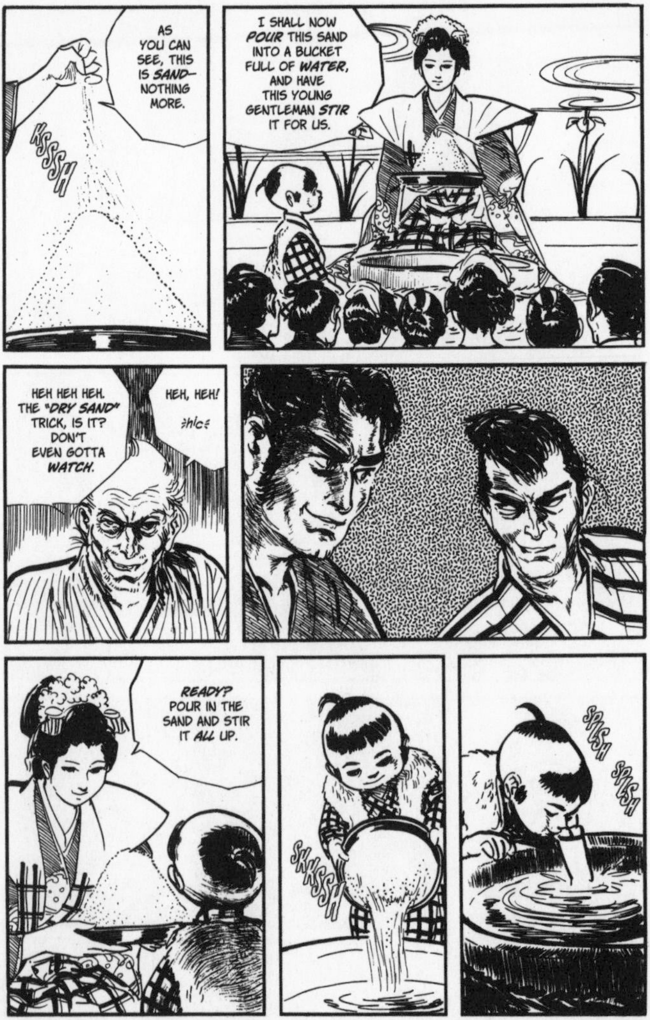
AS YOU CAN SEE, THIS IS SAND— NOTHING MORE.
KSSSH
I SHALL NOW POUR THIS SAND INTO A BUCKET FULL OF WATER, AND HAVE THIS YOUNG GENTLEMAN STIR IT FOR US.
HEH HEH HEH. THE "DRY SAND" TRICK, IS IT? DON'T EVEN GOTTA WATCH.
HEH, HEH!
hic
READY? POUR IN THE SAND AND STIR IT ALL UP.
SKKSSH
SPLSH
SPLSH

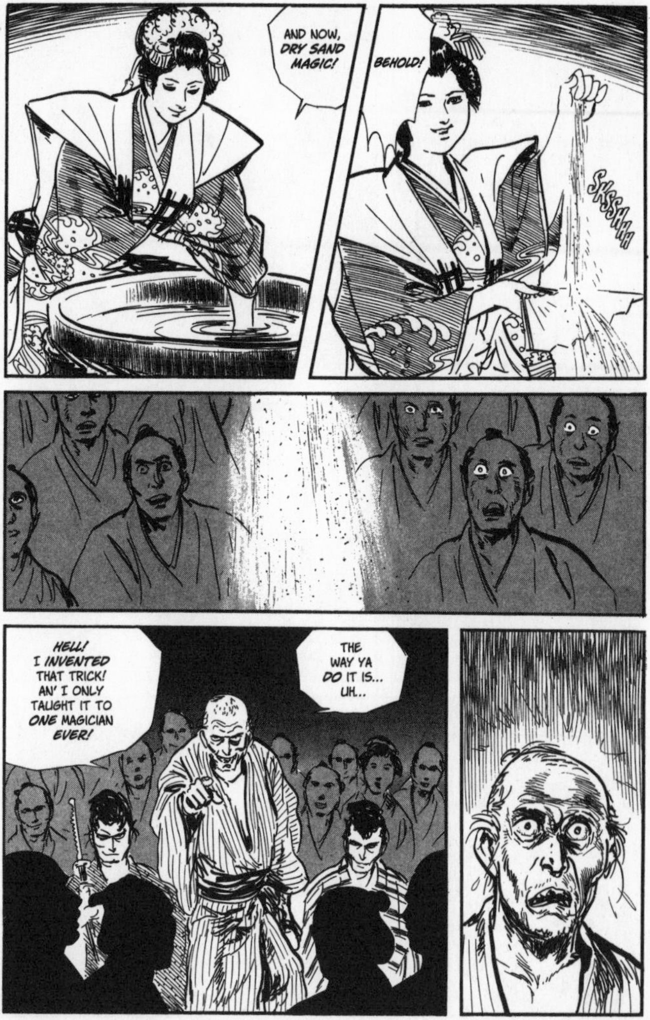
AND NOW, DRY SAND MAGIC!
BEHOLD!
SKSSHHA
HELL! I INVENTED THAT TRICK! AN' I ONLY TAUGHT IT TO ONE MAGICIAN EVER!
THE WAY YA DO IT IS... UH...

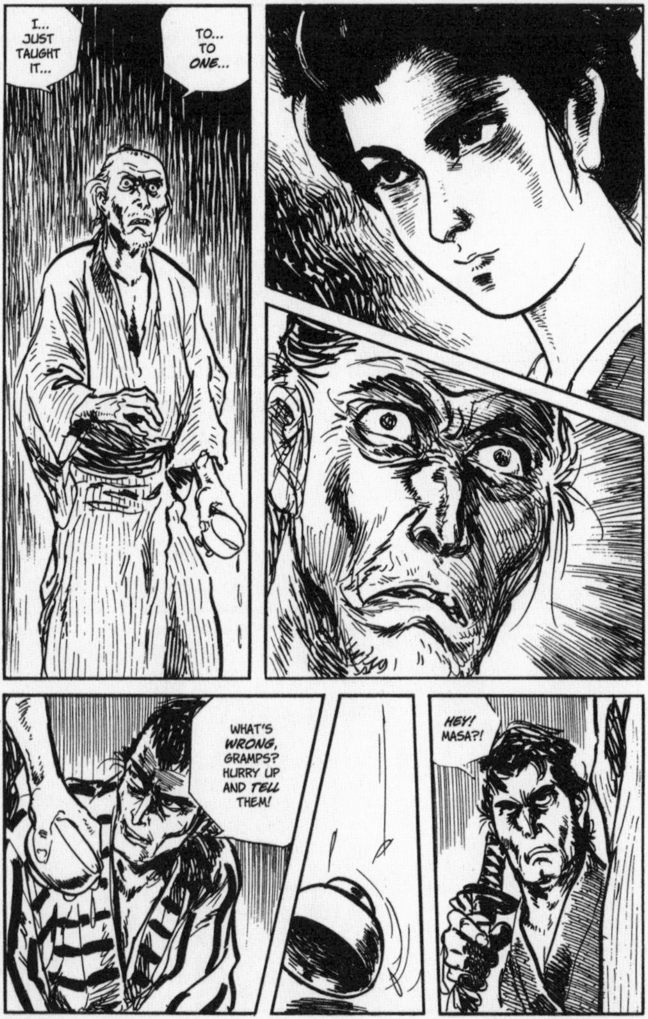
I... JUST TAUGHT IT...
TO... TO *ONE*...
WHAT'S *WRONG*, GRAMPS? HURRY UP AND *TELL* THEM!
*HEY!* MASA?!

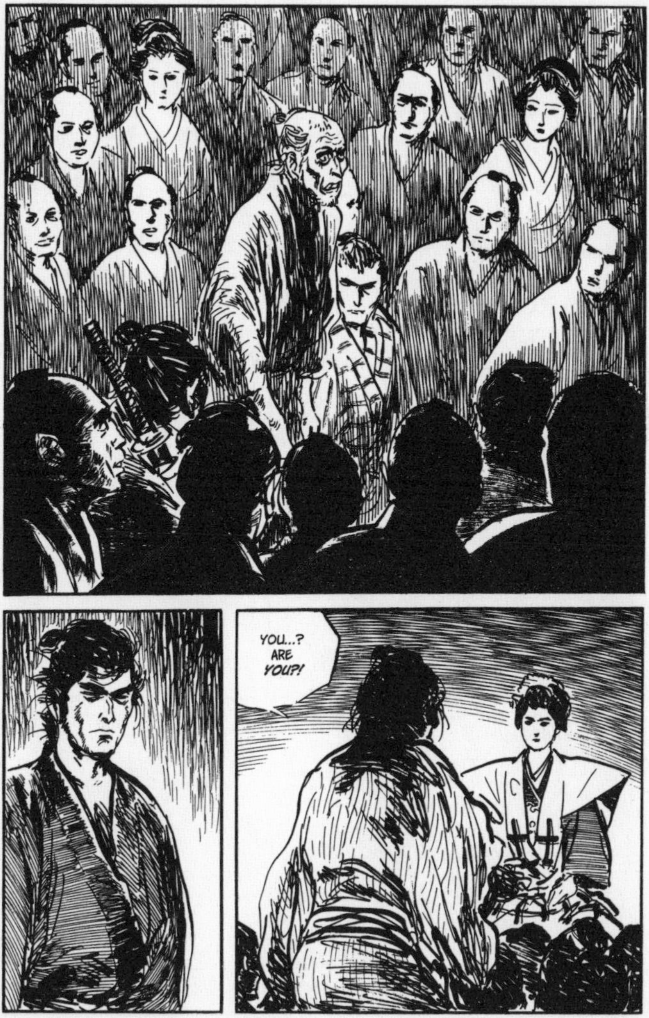
YOU...? ARE YOU?!

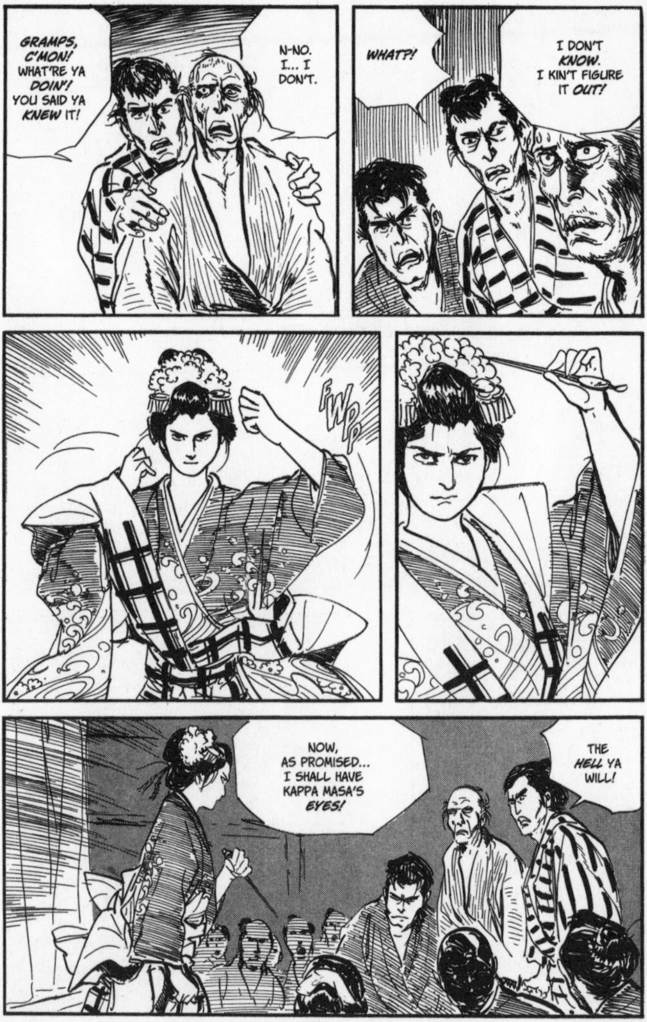
GRAMPS, C'MON! WHAT'RE YA DOIN'! YOU SAID YA KNEW IT!
N-NO. I... I DON'T.
WHAT?!
I DON'T KNOW. I KIN'T FIGURE IT OUT!
FWPP
NOW, AS PROMISED... I SHALL HAVE KAPPA MASA'S EYES!
THE HELL YA WILL!

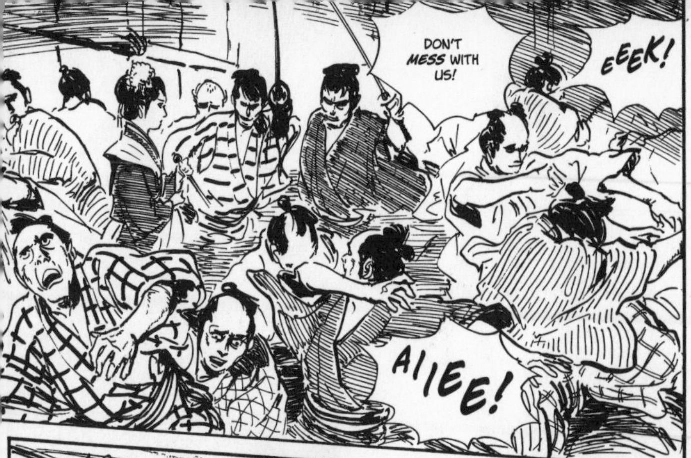
DON'T MESS WITH US!
EEEK!
AIIEEE!
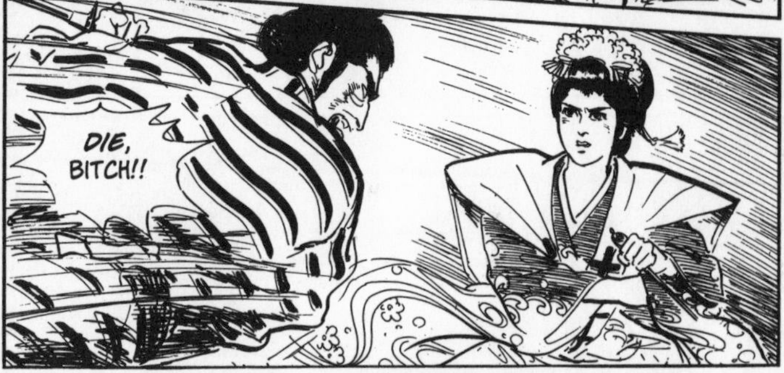
DIE, BITCH!!
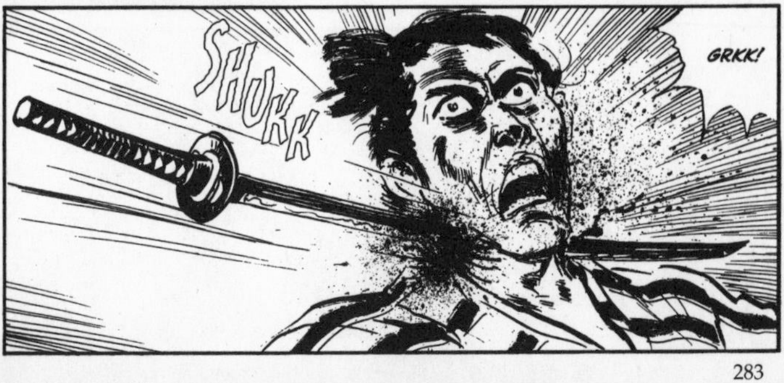
SHUKK
GRKK!

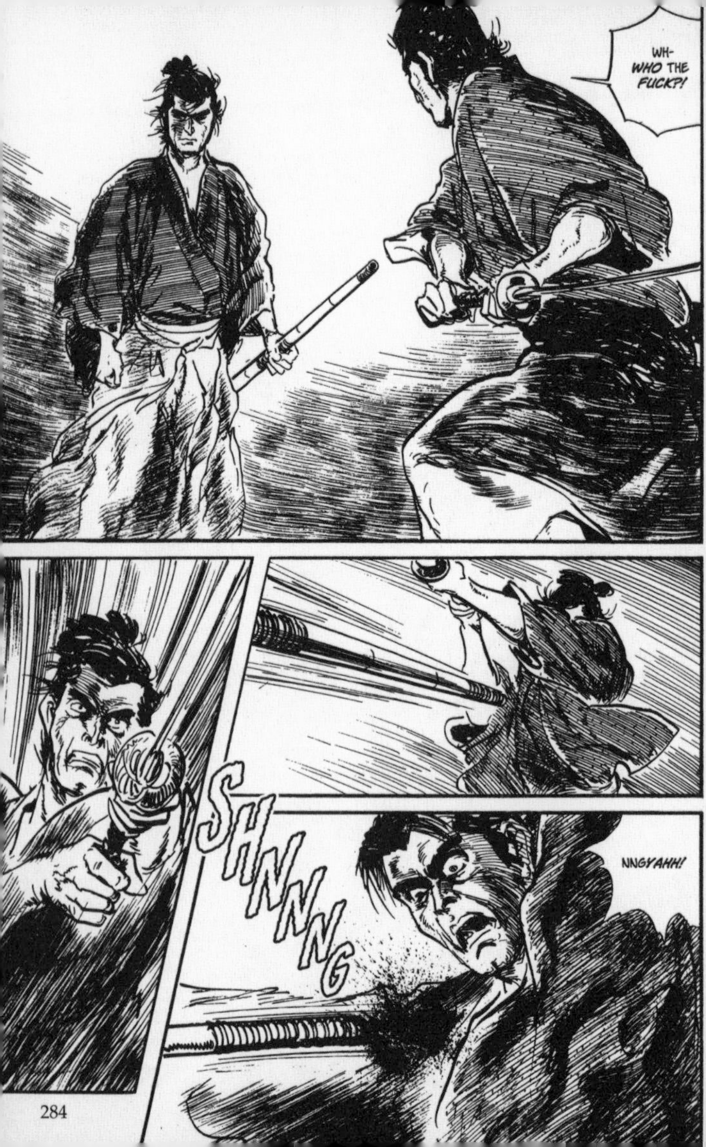
WH-
WHO THE
FUCK?!
SHNNNG
NNGYAHH!

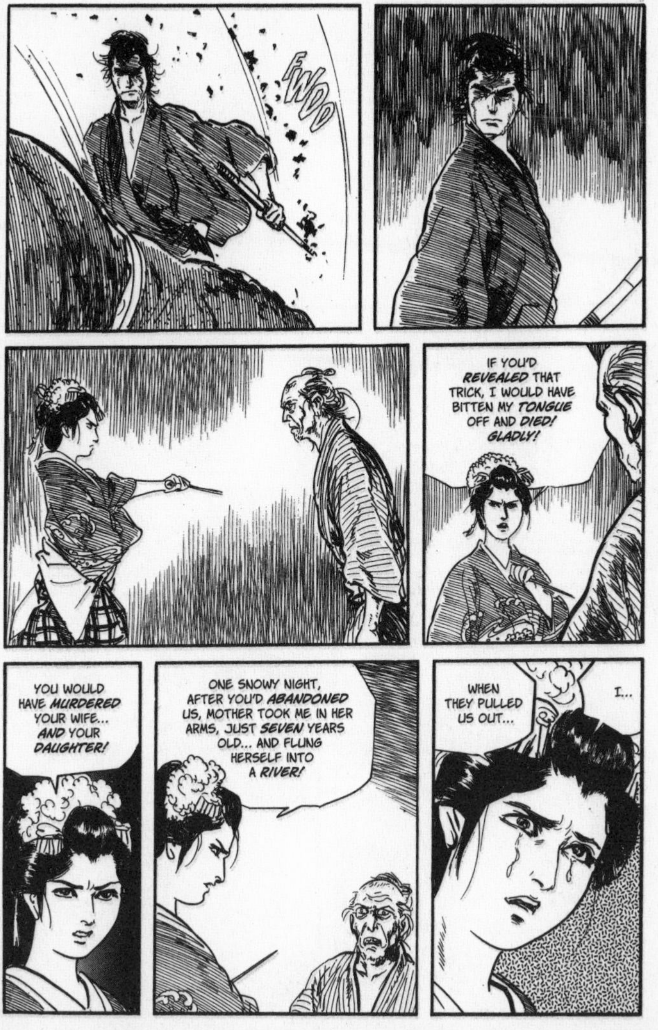
FWOO
IF YOU'D REVEALED THAT TRICK, I WOULD HAVE BITTEN MY TONGUE OFF AND DIED! GLADLY!
YOU WOULD HAVE MURDERED YOUR WIFE... AND YOUR DAUGHTER!
ONE SNOWY NIGHT, AFTER YOU'D ABANDONED US, MOTHER TOOK ME IN HER ARMS, JUST SEVEN YEARS OLD... AND FLUNG HERSELF INTO A RIVER!
WHEN THEY PULLED US OUT...
I...

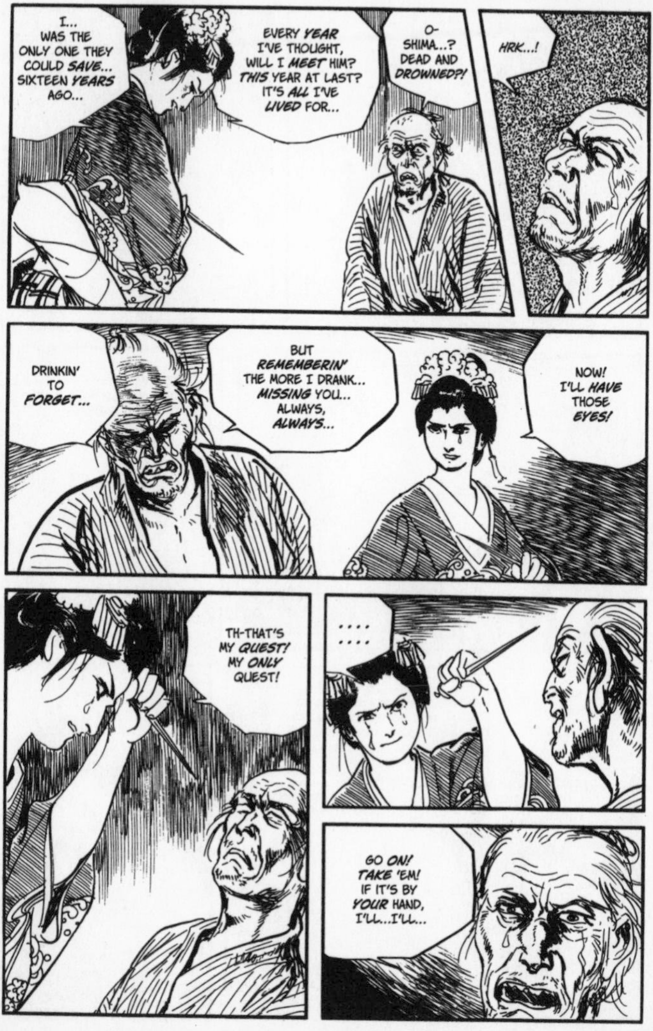
I... WAS THE ONLY ONE THEY COULD SAVE... SIXTEEN YEARS AGO...
EVERY YEAR I'VE THOUGHT, WILL I MEET HIM? THIS YEAR AT LAST? IT'S ALL I'VE LIVED FOR...
O-SHIMA...? DEAD AND DROWNED?!
HRK...!
DRINKIN' TO FORGET...
BUT REMEMBERIN' THE MORE I DRANK... MISSING YOU... ALWAYS, ALWAYS...
NOW! I'LL HAVE THOSE EYES!
TH-THAT'S MY QUEST! MY ONLY QUEST!
.... ....
GO ON! TAKE 'EM! IF IT'S BY YOUR HAND, I'LL...I'LL...

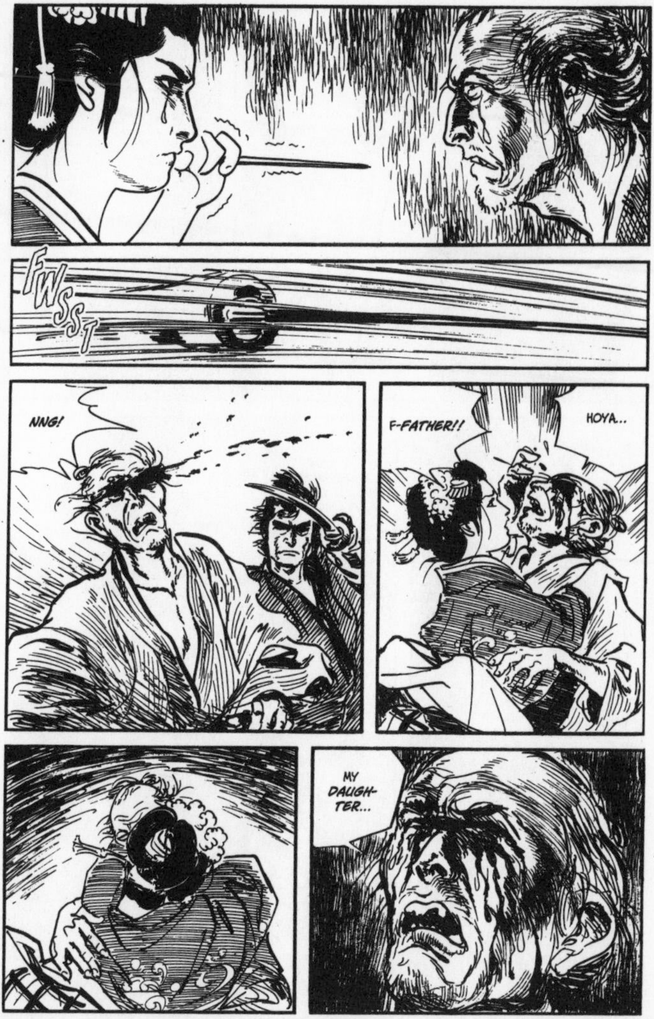
FWSST
NNG!
F-FATHER!!
HOYA...
MY DAUGHTER...

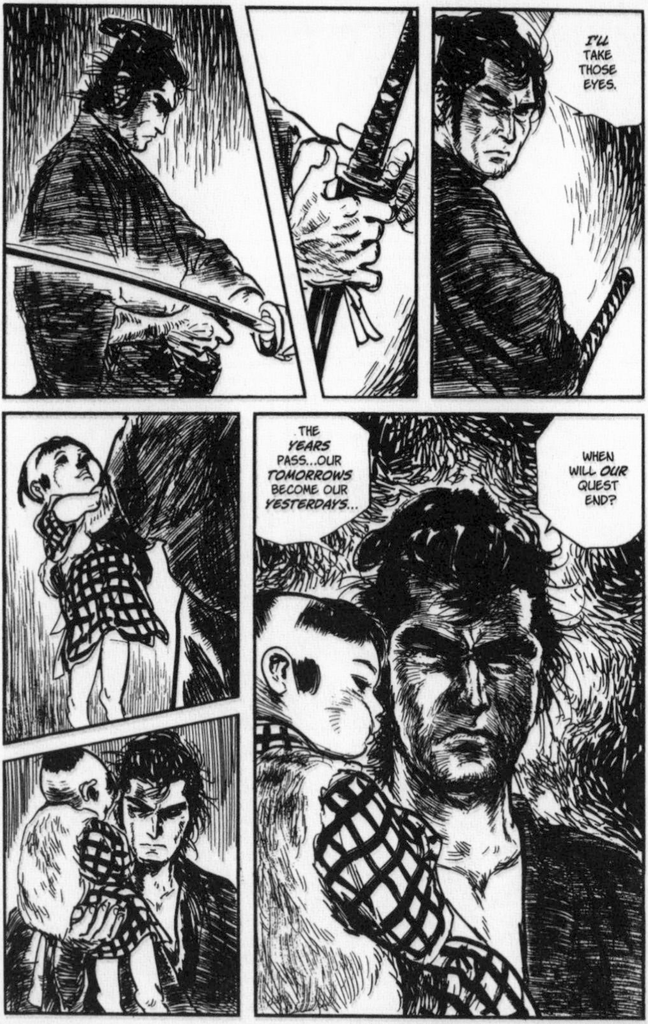
I'LL TAKE THOSE EYES.
THE YEARS PASS...OUR TOMORROWS BECOME OUR YESTERDAYS...
WHEN WILL OUR QUEST END?

LONE WOLF AND CUB BOOK TWELVE: THE END
TO BE CONTINUED

# GLOSSARY

**bangashira**
Commander of the guard.

**bushi**
A samurai. A member of the warrior class.

**bushidō**
The way of the warrior. Also known as *shidō*.

**cho**
1. Approximately 300 meters.
2. Even numbers.

**daimyō**
A feudal lord.

**dayū**
"Maestro." A term applied to musicians and other stage performers. Many performers in Japan take stage names, and name inversions were also common in the entertainment industry.

**Edo**
The capital of medieval Japan and the seat of the shōgunate. The site of modern-day Tokyo.

**fukumi-yari**
A telescoping spear, the segments collapsing into one another.

**haiku**
Traditional short verse, with a 5-7-5 syllable pattern.

**han**
1. A feudal domain.
2. Odd numbers.

**hanshi**
Samurai in the service of a *han*.

**honorifics**
Japan is a class and status society, and proper forms of address are critical. Common markers of respect are the prefixes *o* and *go*, and a wide range of suffixes. Some of the suffixes you will encounter in *Lone Wolf and Cub*:
*chan* – for children, young women, and close friends
*dono* – archaic; used for higher-ranked or highly respected figures
*san* – the most common, used among equals or near-equals
*sama* – used for superiors
*sensei* – used for teachers, masters, respected entertainers, and politicians.

**jōdai**
Castle warden. The ranking *han* official in charge of a *daimyō*'s castle and *han* when the *daimyō* was in residence in Edo. Often the *jōdai* was also the senior elder, or *karō*, of the *han*.

**kaminaga**
A mature woman. Literally, "long hair."

**kuge**
Aristocracy. Members of the imperial court in Kyoto.

**kurokote**
Gauntlets bound with iron plates.

**meifumadō**
The Buddhist Hell. The way of demons and damnation.

**meishu**
A village chieftain. In Edo Japan, a select handful of *meishu* were assigned official duties by the *machi-bugyō* (Edo city commissioner) and local *daikan* (magistrate). Peasants were forbidden to bear arms and had no family names, but these select few were given special dispensation to wear a sword and pass down their family name.

**metsuke**
Inspector. A post combining the duties of chief of police and chief intelligence officer.

**mon**
A copper coin.

**origami**
Literally, "folded paper." The art of making figures from single sheets of folded paper.

**oyabun**
The boss of a *yakuza* gang. Literally, "father status." His underlings were known as *kobun*, or children.

**oyata**
The head of a troupe of performers.

**rōnin**
A masterless samurai. Literally, "one adrift on the waves." Members of the samurai caste who have lost their masters through the dissolution of *han*, expulsion for misbehavior, or other reasons. Prohibited from working as farmers or merchants under the strict Confucian caste system imposed by the Tokugawa shōgunate, many impoverished *rōnin* became "hired guns" for whom the code of the samurai was nothing but empty words.

**ryō**
A gold piece, worth 60 *monme* or 4 *kan*.

**ryū**
Often translated as "school." The many variations of swordsmanship and other martial arts were passed down from generation to generation to the offspring of the originator of the technique or set of techniques, and to any *deishi* students that sought to learn from the master. The largest schools had their own *dōjō* training centers and scores of students. An effective swordsman had to study the different techniques of the various schools to know how to block them in combat. Many *ryū* also had a set of special, secret techniques that were only taught to school initiates.

**sankin kōtai**
The Tokugawa required that all *daimyō*

spend every other year in Edo, with family members remaining behind when they returned to their *han*. This practice increased Edo's control over the *daimyō*, both political and fiscal, since the cost of maintaining two separate households and traveling to and from the capital placed a huge strain on *han* finances.

**Sanzu River**
The Japanese equivalent of the River Styx. On their way to the afterlife, the dead must take boats across the River Sanzu.

**sekisho**
Checkpoint regulating travel from Edo to other parts of the country. All travelers had to submit papers at official checkpoints along the main highways in and out of Edo.

**seppuku**
The right to kill oneself with honor to atone for failure, or to follow one's master into death. Only the samurai class was allowed this glorious but excruciating death. The abdomen was cut horizontally, followed by an upward cut to spill out the intestines. When possible, a *kaishakunin* performed a beheading after the cut was made to shorten the agony.

**shinan**
Chief instructor.

**shiraha-dori**
The Yagyū technique of "naked blade capture."

**shōgi**
A Japanese board game, with rules similar to chess.

**sun**
Approximately 3 centimeters.

**tegata**
Official travel pass for transiting *sekisho*.

**tsubo**
The traditional cry at the start of a dice game. The dice man shows the customers that the cup is empty.

# KAZUO KOIKE

Though widely respected as a powerful writer of graphic fiction, Kazuo Koike has spent a lifetime reaching beyond the bounds of the comics medium. Aside from co-creating and writing the successful *Lone Wolf and Cub* and *Crying Freeman* manga, Koike has hosted television programs; founded a golf magazine; produced movies; written popular fiction, poetry, and screenplays; and mentored some of Japan's best manga talent.

*Lone Wolf and Cub* was first serialized in Japan in 1970 (under the title *Kozure Okami*) in *Manga Action* magazine and continued its hugely popular run for many years, being collected as the stories were published, and reprinted worldwide. Koike collected numerous awards for his work on the series throughout the next decade. Starting in 1972, Koike adapted the popular manga into a series of six films, the *Baby Cart Assassin* saga, garnering widespread commercial success and critical acclaim for his screenwriting.

This wasn't Koike's only foray into film and video. In 1996, *Crying Freeman*, the manga Koike created with artist Ryoichi Ikegami, was produced in Hollywood and released to commercial success in Europe and is currently awaiting release in America.

And to give something back to the medium that gave him so much, Koike started the *Gekiga Sonjuku*, a college course aimed at helping talented writers and artists — such as *Ranma 1/2* creator Rumiko Takahashi — break into the comics field.

The driving focus of Koike's narrative is character development, and his commitment to character is clear: "Comics are carried by characters. If a character is well created, the comic becomes a hit." Kazuo Koike's continued success in comics and literature has proven this philosophy true.

# GOSEKI KOJIMA

Goseki Kojima was born on November 3, 1928, the very same day as the godfather of Japanese comics, Osamu Tezuka. While just out of junior high school, the self-taught Kojima began painting advertising posters for movie theaters to pay his bills.

In 1950, Kojima moved to Tokyo, where the postwar devastation had given rise to special manga forms for audiences too poor to buy the new manga magazines. Kojima created art for *kami-shibai*, or "paper-play" narrators, who would use manga story sheets to present narrated street plays. Kojima moved on to creating works for the *kashi-bon* market, bookstores that rented out books, magazines, and manga to mostly low-income readers. He soon became highly popular among *kashi-bon* readers.

In 1967, Kojima broke into the magazine market with his series *Dojinki*. As the manga magazine market grew and diversified, he turned out a steady stream of popular series.

In 1970, in collaboration with Kazuo Koike, Kojima began the work that would seal his reputation, *Kozure Okami* (*Lone Wolf and Cub*). Before long the story had become a gigantic hit, eventually spinning off a television series, six motion pictures, and even theme-song records. Koike and Kojima were soon dubbed the "golden duo" and produced success after success on their way to the pinnacle of the manga world.

When *Manga Japan* magazine was launched in 1994, Kojima was asked to serve as consultant, and he helped train the next generation of manga artists.

In his final years, Kojima turned to creating original graphic novels based on the movies of his favorite director, Akira Kurosawa. Kojima passed away on January 5, 2000 at the age of 71.

# THE RONIN REPORT

*By David S. Hofhine*

## The Dotanuki Sword of *Lone Wolf and Cub*

I have been working full time as a professional *togishi* (Japanese sword polisher) in the United States for nine years, and I have been a fan of *Lone Wolf and Cub* since the first English translations were published by First Comics back in the late 1980s. I would like to offer some general information regarding the Dotanuki sword depicted in the series.

Throughout the various English publications of *Lone Wolf and Cub*, Dotanuki has been referred to as a type of sword, the name of a specific sword, and perhaps a sword smith. I would like to put to rest the confusion if possible. The type of sword used by Itto Ogami is called a *katana*. This is a curved sword over 60 cm in length. It is worn through the belt, cutting edge up. This type of blade came into widespread use during the middle of the *Muromachi* period (1392-1572) and is the Japanese "samurai" sword best known to this day. The *katana* has a shorter, straighter, and heavier blade than the older style *tachi* sword of the *Kamakura* period. These changes were made to make the blade faster to draw by an unmounted samurai. The shorter, heavier blade was also more effective against the heavier armor of the day.

There have been many famous "named" blades throughout Japanese history: *Kogarasu-maru* ("The Little Crow") and *Hocho Masamune* ("Masamune's Kitchen Knife"), for example. The Dotanuki blade of Itto Ogami does not appear to be one of these "named" blades. Rather, it seems to refer to the historical Dotanuki school of sword smiths. Koike and Kojima, being excellent students of Japanese history, must have been aware of this reasonably well-known and respected group of sword smiths.

The Dotanuki school of sword-making was based in Higo province on the island of Kyushu. It was most active during the late 1500s and early 1600s. Dotanuki school work draws heavily on the Yamato tradition of sword-making. The school featured many smiths who signed the name Dotanuki to their swords along with other information about where and when the blade was made. A typical *mei* (*tang* signatures) would include island, province, school, and personal names, such as: Kyushu Higo Dotanuki Hyobu. The Dotanuki school blades were very sturdy and designed to stand up to heavy use. Their early *katana* are described as rustic, inelegant, and massive, with their greatest asset being their cutting ability.

After the unification of Japan under the Tokugawa shogunate, a period of relative peace came into being. This is known as the Edo period (1600-1867). During this time, the arts flourished and swords became more elaborate and decorative. There was a trend in some sword-making schools toward aesthetic appeal over functionality as their samurai clientele became more affluent. This was the case with many of the swords being produced in Hizen province, a neighbor of Higo province. The Hizen blades of the Edo period were very graceful and refined, but they were also known for their thin skin steel. In time, the skin steel would polish through, revealing the rough iron core and weakening the blade. To this day, Hizen blades are prized by collectors for their beauty and dreaded by polishers for their thin skin steel. The early Dotanuki school blades, in contrast, remained dedicated to material application above all.

In the pages of *Lone Wolf and Cub*, Koike and Kojima do provide us with an interesting bit of evidence as to the origin of Itto's Dotanuki. In Volume 5, page 158, we find an *oshigata* (paper drawing of a

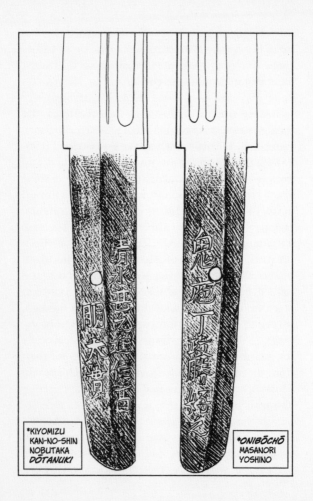

*KIYOMIZU
KAN-NO-SHIN
NOBUTAKA
*DŌTANUKI*

*ONIBŌCHŌ*
MASANORI
YOSHINO

blade or a portion of a blade) representing two swords. The blade on the left, presumably Itto's sword, is signed Kiyomizu Kan-no-shin Nobutaka, Dotanuki. The first two *kanji* (old-style Japanese calligraphy characters) used to spell out DO TAN UKI, however, are different than the *kanji* used by the actual Dotanuki school of sword smiths. Furthermore, there is no record of a smith by the name of Nobutaka ever working with the Dotanuki group.

There was a famous line of smiths named Nobutaka that ran for ten generations from 1573 to 1865, but they were based in Owari province halfway across Japan and never signed Dotanuki. Of this Nobutaka line, one smith did indeed sign with the same *kanji* as shown in the right-hand column of this panel. This signature was used by the tenth and final generation of the Nobutaka, but this smith worked almost 150 years after the events of *Lone Wolf and Cub*, so this could not be the smith who forged the Lone Wolf's Dotanuki. Out of more than 30,000 recorded sword smiths, the tenth-generation Nobutaka is the only one ever to use these exact *kanji*.

Koike and Kojima obviously took some artistic license in their rendition of the tang inscription of Itto's Dotanuki sword. They must be forgiven for this, as these blades are incredibly rare nowadays. Even a reference to this group of smiths that includes pictures of what a typical *tang* signature should look like is extremely hard to find.

It is my conclusion that the Dotanuki sword used by Itto Ogami in the *Lone Wolf and Cub* series must have been based on the reputation of the historical Higo Dotanuki sword-smith group. When it is referred to as "Dotanuki" or "a Dotanuki," the authors are referring to the smiths that made it and the qualities typified in their work. The dates and description of a stout, heavy blade, made for serious cutting, match perfectly. The concept of sword-makers remaining loyal to the tradition of making strong, functional blades during a period of extended peace is a perfect metaphor for Itto's dedication to the code of *bushido* in what is illustrated as an increasingly lawless and corrupt world.

Referring to Itto's Dotanuki is like referring to someone's Colt in a western novel. The gun's "name" is not "Colt," nor does it indicate one specific type

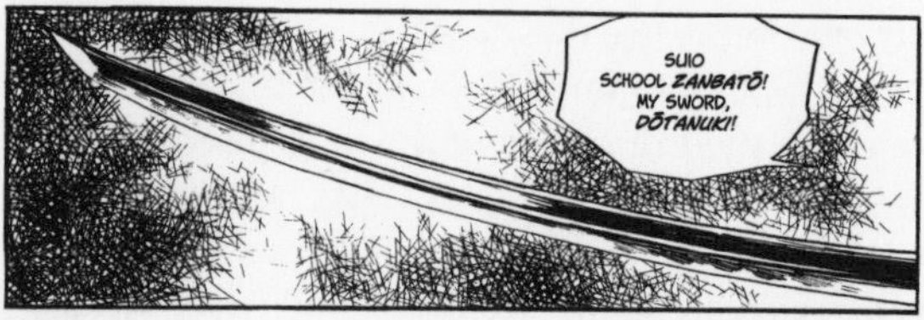
SUIO SCHOOL *ZANBATŌ*! MY SWORD, *DŌTANUKI*!

of gun such as a pistol, rifle, or shotgun. It would, however, be understood by the reader that the gun in question would be the type associated with cowboys and gunslingers, the type used in the "quick-draw" and "showdown." Similarly, Dotanuki is neither a specific blade's name nor a particular type of sword blade such as a *tachi* or *katana*. It is, rather, a reference to a sword made by a specific historical group of sword smiths who were dedicated to producing serious battle swords with a primary concern for cutting ability.

These are conclusions I've reached based on my own research. I hope this information has been somewhat interesting or helpful. If you would like more information on Japanese swords or sword polishing, please feel free to visit my website at *www.swordpolish.com*.

## BIBLIOGRAPHY

Haku, Kozu and Sato Kan'ichio. Harry Weston, translator. *Nihon To Koza*. Vol. IV, Shinto 1596-1771. Rio Ranco, NM: AFU Research Enterprises, Inc. 1992, 374p.

Hawley, W. M. *Japanese Swordsmiths Revised*. Hollywood, CA: W. M. Hawley, 1981, 1,046 p.

Honnami, Konson. *Teiryo Yoji*. Tokyo, Japan. Showa Miznoe Saru (1932), 428 p.

Yoshikawa, Kentaro. "The Characteristics of Kyushu Shinto." *Art and the Sword*. Vol. 4, Breckenridge, TX: The Japanese Sword Society of the United States, 1992, 120 p.

# LONE WOLF AND CUB

**VOLUME 1:
THE ASSASSIN'S ROAD
1-56971-502-5
$9.95 U.S., $14.95 Canada**

**VOLUME 2: THE GATELESS
BARRIER
1-56971-503-3
$9.95 U.S., $14.95 Canada**

**VOLUME 3: THE FLUTE OF
THE FALLEN TIGER
1-56971-504-1
$9.95 U.S., $14.95 Canada**

**VOLUME 4:**
**THE BELL WARDEN**
1-56971-505-X
$9.95 U.S., $14.95 Canada

**VOLUME 5:**
**BLACK WIND**
1-56971-506-8
$9.95 U.S., $14.95 Canada

**VOLUME 6: LANTERNS FOR**
**THE DEAD**
1-56971-507-6
$9.95 U.S., $14.95 Canada

**VOLUME 7: CLOUD**
**DRAGON, WIND TIGER**
1-56971-508-4
$9.95 U.S., $14.95 Canada

**VOLUME 8: CHAINS
OF DEATH**
1-56971-509-2
$9.95 U.S., $14.95 Canada

**VOLUME 9: ECHO OF
THE ASSASSIN**
1-56971-510-6
$9.95 U.S., $14.95 Canada

**VOLUME 10: DRIFTING
SHADOWS**
1-56971-511-4
$9.95 U.S., $14.95 Canada

**VOLUME 11:
TALISMAN OF HADES**
1-56971-512-2
$9.95 U.S., $14.95 Canada

*Dark Horse Comics:* **Mike Richardson** *publisher* • **Neil Hankerson** *executive vice president* • **Andy Karabatsos** *vice president of finance* • **Randy Stradley** *vice president of publishing* • **Chris Warner** *senior editor* • **Michael Martens** *vice president of marketing* • **Anita Nelson** *vice president of sales & licensing* • **David Scroggy** *vice president of product development* • **Cindy Marks** *director of production & design* • **Mark Cox** *art director* • **Dale LaFountain** *vice president of information technology* • **Kim Haines** *director of human resources* • **Darlene Vogel** *director of purchasing* • **Ken Lizzi** • *general counsel*

子連れ狼

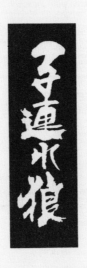